CW00369632

CRUEL TO BE KIND

Also by Tim Wilson

Purgatory
Close to You
Freezing Point
I Spy . . .

CRUEL TO BE KIND

Tim Wilson

HEADLINE

First published in 1997 by
HEADLINE BOOK PUBLISHING

10 9 8 7 6 5 4 3 2 1

British Library Cataloguing in Publication Data

Wilson, Timothy, 1962–
Cruel to be kind
1. Thrillers
I. Title
823.9'14 [F]

ISBN 0-7472-1935 4

Typeset by
CBS, Felixstowe, Suffolk

Printed and bound in Great Britain by
Mackays of Chatham PLC, Chatham, Kent

HEADLINE BOOK PUBLISHING
A division of Hodder Headline PLC
338 Euston Road
London NW1 3BH

For Roy and Maria

ONE

The day Laura Ritchie's life turned upside down was the sort of day when nothing, really, ought to happen.

It was in that grey, harsh, lifeless passage of winter – January going on February – with Christmas long gone and no other landmarks in the bare plain of the season. It was a time that had no sound but the clanking of radiators and the cough of car engines laboriously started in cold mornings along the frosted drives of Duncan Road. It was a time that had no scent but the stuffiness of closed rooms, and the rubbery smell of wellingtons standing in damp pools in the hall; a time of short dim days and ice-green twilights, of numbly waiting until the year, like some endlessly stalled train, began to move again.

And it was a time of year that Laura, in a curious way, had begun to like.

David didn't. He did not so much hate winter as sharply resent it. He took the dark and cold personally: it was out to get him. It was a stalker. David was a summer person. At least, he was now. When Laura had first met him he had been cheerfully indifferent to such things as the seasons. He would wear stifling black in a heatwave and a light jacket in a blizzard.

Then at some point in their married life he had become terribly appropriate in his responses. At the first glimpse of sun he broke out in shorts and sunglasses. There was something fierce and obedient about this. Like Barbie's boyfriend, Ken, he had to have an outfit. Briefly taking up cycling, he dressed as if for the Tour de France. An equally brief flirtation with fishing saw him clad from head to toe in waterproof green – as if, Laura secretly thought, the fish had to be ambushed. And he responded to the personal persecution of the English winter with the same thoroughness.

'I hate this time of year,' he would grumble, ceremoniously putting on scarf, gloves and overcoat as if he were buckling on armour. 'It's all right for you.'

He meant that it was all right for her because she didn't feel the cold, though he managed to put a lot more into the phrase. Or she detected a lot more in it. Whatever.

Whether he said those particular words that particular morning, on leaving the house, she couldn't remember. Nothing stood out, when she looked back. It was all ordinary. The morning, breakfast, David setting out for work, Laura walking Simon to school, Laura coming back and washing the dishes – it was all nebulous as a dream, winter-wrapped, unheeding. Because it was part of a time when nothing was supposed to happen. A time she had begun to like, perhaps, for that very reason. Because it got her off the hook. It postponed decision.

The time did coincide with something, though – one of David's phases. Periodically David decided there was something he had always believed. Last year he had always believed they should eat no red meat; so they had lived on chicken and fish until at last David had signalled, by throwing a plate of tuna pasta at the wall, that he had always believed you needed red meat in a balanced diet. The current phase was to do with cars. They were a nuisance; a plague. All the ills of the world were attributable to them. Some day they would learn, as a family, to do without one altogether. In the meantime he no longer drove to the station every morning to catch the train to London. He walked. It wasn't far. It was ridiculous getting the car out and negotiating the heavy traffic into town every morning, and then having to pay through the nose to leave it in the station car park. He walked – proudly, even dogmatically. He walked as if he were campaigning for it. He walked as if he were the founder of the Walkers' Liberation Front.

And so that morning in January he left the house on foot, at ten past eight. And at just past nine o'clock, when Laura was washing the breakfast dishes, the police came.

TWO

When the knock sounded at the front door Laura had just set the last plate, shining with rainbow suds, on the draining board.

She hesitated. There was one pan left: it had contained scrambled eggs, would need some scrubbing. She put it in the washing-up bowl, then dried her hands: it could be soaking while she answered the door. These little time-management calculations were habitual with her. David hated delay; so she was a miser with time, thriftily storing up seconds and minutes like someone saving the pennies.

The milkman came for his money on Fridays: today was Tuesday. The newspaper boy, Saturday mornings. Jan always came to the side door, where the kitchen was, as did David's friends – not that they would ever call at this time: five past nine on a Tuesday was work time, out of bounds, white on the map.

A parcel, then, or someone to read the meter. Something mildly official.

She ticked off the possibilities, in her time-saving way, as she walked up the hall.

The top half of the front door was inset with frosted and coloured panes. Through them she could see two distorted heads.

Jehovah's Witnesses, then, she thought, the possibilities narrowing.

She opened the door.

'Mrs Ritchie?'

Laura stared upward – they seemed implausibly tall – at the two uniformed policemen standing just outside the porch, at a respectful distance.

'Yes,' she said after a moment – a moment in which it seemed more reasonable to say no. She was Mrs Ritchie, yes, but she wasn't a Mrs Ritchie who should be called on by two police officers early on a Tuesday morning.

Mrs Ritchie, yes. The situation, no.

'May we come in, please? We need to talk to you.'

And again, in theory, yes. And again, when it came to it, no.

The list of possibilities had narrowed to two. And the valves of her heart also seemed to have narrowed, so there was no heartbeat, no motion of blood. Nothing going on there.

'It's all right, Mrs Ritchie. If we could just step in for a moment . . .'

Somehow she couldn't tell which of the two had spoken. But all at once her brain grasped at the fact that one of them was a Sikh, and that his turban had been adapted so that it bore the checkerboard band of the standard policeman's cap all round it. And for a moment all she could do was wonder at the sheer ingenuity of this.

Then, she didn't know how, they were in the house, and making her sit down in the lounge. A feeling of subtle wrongness informed her that she was sitting in David's chair. She never did that.

'Mrs Ritchie, your husband's name is David Ritchie, is that correct?'

That was the other one. Young, with bad skin. The two of them were sitting, perching, on the settee. So weird to see them in here, in those uniforms, those undeniable and yet somehow theatrical-looking uniforms.

'Yes,' she said. No.

'I'm afraid there's been an accident. Mr Ritchie's been taken to Langstead District Hospital. He was knocked down by a car on Bourges Way this morning.'

The words hit Laura: hurtled at her, struck her.

'Oh my God, what . . . Is he . . . ?'

'I believe he's in rather a bad way, Mrs Ritchie. But an ambulance was on the scene very promptly and he was taken straight into Accident and Emergency. That's all I can tell you just now. Our car's outside and we'll take you to the hospital now if you're ready.'

'Are you on your own here, Mrs Ritchie?' the turbaned officer said. 'Is there anyone you'd like to come with you, any family or friends?'

She couldn't think. Her brain was off line, gone. The only thought that came to her was of that pan soaking in the sink. Perhaps she should just wash that before—

A gasp, a moan, some sound, must have escaped her, because the young policeman was on his feet and touching her shoulder.

'Mrs Ritchie. This is a bad shock, I know. Take your time. Is there anyone . . . ?'

'No. There's – there's Simon. My little boy, he's at school.'

'How old is he?'

She couldn't remember. She stared painfully at the policeman's pale blue eyes.

'What school's he at, Mrs Ritchie?'

'Parkhill Primary. He's . . . seven.'

'Does he stay for school dinners?'

Another effort of memory. 'Yes.'

'I think it would be best to leave him at school for now, then. You come along to the hospital with us now, and we'll sort that out later. If you can think of anyone you'd like to contact, we can do that from the hospital. Do you feel OK to get up?'

She nodded, and stood. Her legs felt surprisingly steady. She just wasn't sure she could move them.

'It's cold outside, have you got a coat?' the turbaned policeman said. 'And your door keys, don't forget those.'

They fussed over her like kindly nursery teachers. She let them guide her, whilst something nagged at her numb brain but would not be defined.

Then as they were shepherding her down the front path to the gate it came to her and she stopped.

'How . . .' She struggled to find a voice that sounded like her own. 'How did he come to get knocked down by a car?'

'Crossing Bourges Way, Mrs Ritchie,' the young policeman said patiently. 'The traffic's very busy there in the mornings.'

But she didn't quite mean that. She meant that David was an adult and usually . . . usually one thought of children being knocked down by cars.

And in the fact that it wasn't her child but her husband in this case she found, God forgive her, a tiny element of relief.

Then she had an image of the traffic on Bourges Way – busy, as the policeman had said, very busy, zooming, ring-road, rush-hour busy – and she felt sick and hysterical.

'Oh my God, I can't—What happened, is he – is he going to be all right?' She stammered and shook, there on the pavement of Duncan Road with its bay-windowed façades and little well-behaved trees, looking helplessly up into the faces of two policemen who were strangers to her – though of course policemen always were, that was what they were all about, they brought bad news and transformed your life and they were always these uniformed anonymities whom you would never see again . . .

'You get in, Mrs Ritchie,' the turbaned policeman said. 'The doctors will tell you what's going on. Come on. We'll be there in two minutes.'

A police car in Duncan Road: unusual sight. A net curtain twitched. *They've found me out at last* . . . The flippancy surfaced in her mind with mad incongruity as Laura climbed into the back seat of the cruiser. Even now she could not grasp that this was for real.

The traffic wasn't heavy now. With the passing of nine o'clock everything had changed: they were in the time zone of the workless, the housewife, the skiving schoolkid. Everyone else had gone to their appointed destination.

Except David. He hadn't made it. Random thoughts: they would be wondering at his office; she ought to let his mother know; she had no money on her; what the hell was he doing crossing Bourges Way?

Maybe she could answer that one – to save time. You had to cross Bourges Way to get to the rail station, and there was a footbridge for the purpose. But if you were coming from some parts of the town centre you had to walk along Bourges Way some distance to get to the footbridge. Tempting, if you were in a hurry, to hop over the railing and dart straight across the road.

Except that it was a three-lane ring road that carried most of the arterial traffic of Langstead and fed into the M11 to London.

Laura felt sick again. She looked for a handle to wind the window down but couldn't find one. Perhaps they didn't have them in police cars, in case felons should try to make a squirming exit . . .

'It'll be all right, love.' The young policeman, in the passenger seat. The back of his neck looked raw and vulnerable. 'We'll be there soon. Don't worry.'

David had set out in good time. He hated being late. Why the dash across Bourges Way?

And Bourges Way, what a place for it to happen – named after Langstead's twin town in France, something of a local joke, liable to endless mispronunciations . . . Life never prepared you for these things. You had no way of knowing that something entirely innocent, laughable even, would one day be fraught with horrible association.

A memory: dinner at Jan and Ross's house, and a long pointless discussion about the pronunciation of the local river – Nar or Nare? And Ross at last putting an end to it with a quiet downright 'It's Nare', and Laura, at least, realizing with a shudder that the river they had been trivially discussing was the place where Ross's brother had drowned in a fishing accident. She had mentioned it to David afterwards and David's face had *fallen*, the old phrase for once utterly apt.

David . . .

Oh God, would this journey never end?

'You may not be able to see your husband straight away, Mrs Ritchie. I'm sure you understand that,' the young policeman was saying.

'Yes, I understand.' She found she was speaking quite calmly, as if this were something she was used to doing, like going to the dentist. But she didn't understand, not really. Things like this happened in fiction, on TV: they didn't happen to real people, and she had no idea what to expect.

The hospital was postwar redbrick, big, unloved, necessary. She saw a sign, 'Accident and Emergency Department', written in bland 1960s lower case. Ancillary staff on a break lurked by some bushes, smoking and gossiping. One of them met Laura's eyes as she rode past.

The car had stopped. The young policeman was holding the door open for her.

She felt paralysed. Just let her stay here – just let her stay in the back of the police car for a while because once she got out and went into that hospital it became real, it became *really* real and perhaps if she stayed here then in some way it wouldn't have happened, and later, at six o'clock, David would come home from work as normal . . .

'Come on, love. You'll be all right.'

The young policeman held out a courtly hand. Inviting her to face her destiny.

Accident and Emergency seemed as quiet as a school corridor during classes. She saw an unattended reception desk, a wheelchair that for some reason was covered in Cellophane, a nurse who paused balletically, one hand against the wall, to pluck something from the sole of her shoe before entering a room by a door that made a cavernous bang behind her. No sense of emergency at all: but of course, this was a time when nothing was supposed to happen.

The young policeman's shoes squeaked loudly on the parquet floor. The other officer had stayed with the car and Laura felt vaguely distressed at this, the loss of a landmark in the new world that had begun with that knock on her front door.

But she found she was expected. Another nurse came silently from nowhere and looked in her face.

'Is it Mrs Ritchie?'

Laura must have nodded, because the nurse took her arm – gently, almost tenderly gathering it to her.

'Would you come this way, please?'

And now the young policeman too was left behind, after exchanging some secret signal with the nurse, and Laura was taken into a little warm room with grey carpet tiles and some institutional chairs and a mosaic coffee table and, strangely, a curtained window that looked not outside but on to the corridor.

'My husband,' Laura said, and the words seemed to come out painfully, like retching, 'what's happening, can I see him, what—'

'I'm Nurse Cash. I'm a staff nurse here at the Accident and Emergency Department,' the nurse said, as if she hadn't heard Laura. 'Would you like to sit down, Mrs Ritchie? This is the relatives' room where we can keep you informed of what's happening. Your husband is currently in the resuscitation room down the corridor. As you know he's been involved in a road accident. He was knocked down by a car this morning. Someone rang for a ambulance at once from the scene and he was brought here straight away. I'm afraid he suffered serious injuries, including injuries to the head and—'

'No . . .' An uninhibited wail, issuing from some primitive Laura that she had never known existed before.

The nurse bent down and took her hand. She was plump, fortyish, rough-handed, with a kind wrinkled face. 'A team of doctors is with him now. They're doing their very best for him. There may be neurosurgery. I'll go to the resuscitation room in a moment and find out what's happening. Is there anything you want to ask me?'

'Is he going to die?'
Nurse Cash didn't miss a beat. 'He's in a bad way but the doctors are doing their very best for him. Now is there anyone you wish to contact? Are there any family or friends you want to have here with you?'
'I haven't got any family,' she said – half-apologetically, as if this were an interview. 'David . . . there's his mother. She's old, she doesn't get about really, I . . .'
'Where does she live?'
'King's Ripley, it's about – oh, fifty miles . . .'
'All right. It might be as well to contact her when we've more news. Is there anyone else, anyone who could be with you now?'
'Jan.' The word came simply, the one correct answer to a fiendish question.
'A friend?'
'Yes, she . . . she might be at work, I don't know. What's today?'
'Tuesday.'
'No, she should be at home, if I could . . .' Somehow it seemed an imposition, asking Jan to come here: as if she were a nuisance. But the nurse asked her for Jan's telephone number, and said she would ring her herself, as if it were quite natural. And when Laura looked up, after hearing and not hearing the nurse say something further, she was alone in the little warm room.
Alone.
Where was David? Down the corridor? What did he look like, what were they doing to him . . . ? She got up, wrapping her arms around herself, and walked up and down the room. Her eyes roamed, looking for something, something to fasten on to.
There was nothing. Chairs, table, bare walls, and a window with no view but a corridor wall. The room was designed for waiting, and nothing else.
Terrible things happened to real people every day. Simply the existence of this room proved it. She had known this, of course; but never truly known it till now.
She stood before the window that wasn't a window, gazing out, in. Shock had made her numb and half-childish, thus far. But as she looked out, in, she knew very well, with bleak maturity, that nothing wonderful and redeeming was going to appear before her eyes. David was not going to hobble down the corridor in plaster and reduce catastrophe to manageable proportions with a rueful look and a joke about time off work. She might keep telling herself that this wasn't happening, but it was happening; and the list of possibilities had narrowed and subdivided again. Now there were only two, and one she couldn't contemplate. Just that: she couldn't. It was like looking into the ends of the universe – beyond her.

The nurse was back, carrying a plastic cup of tea.

'I haven't got any news to give you,' she said, putting the cup down on the table. 'The doctors are inserting an intercranial pressure device. That's standard procedure with the assessment of head injuries. I've rung your friend and she's on her way over here now. I've told her to ask for me as soon as she gets to the hospital.'

How good at this she is, Laura thought absently. Used to it, no doubt. But there was no rancour in the thought. She felt, indeed, that she should say thank you, but by the time she had unlocked her throat the nurse was gone again.

The past. Images of it bombarded her all at once, as if some signal had been given for their assault. None of them was of the recent past, though. She still could not, for example, summon up any picture of that morning – the last time she had seen David – other than a generic image of breakfast, newspapers, steam from the shower, the lethargic bustle of a weekday morning.

Just a slice of nowadays. It was odd how *nowadays* always seemed to have a doleful connotation. 'Oh, we don't go there nowadays.' 'I don't read much nowadays.' 'Nowadays we hardly get out of the house.'

And Laura's nowadays, the nowadays she shared with David, hardly occurred to her at all as she sat, stood, lurked about the little warm room. There was David as she had first met him, with his edgy smile and his post-university haircut and the paperbacks jammed, somehow, inextricably, into the back pockets of his jeans; there was David at their wedding, suddenly solemn and full of concentration as if he were taking an exam; there was David in the lovely dingy Enfield flat that was their first home, bringing in a battered table football game that he had bought second-hand to help pass their impoverished evenings, and not only laboriously repairing the little footballers but painting faces on them with an eyeliner brush; there was David when Simon was a baby, coping with the surprisingly awful smell of nappies by biting on a piece of lemon peel as he changed them.

There was more, and more. It was as if the nurse had told her to recall something from David's past, something crucial that might help him, and she were desperately scrolling through her memories to find it. But omitting some files – the recent ones.

Laura found herself at the window again, staring out, in. And then a man appeared. He came rapidly into view, stopped, flung a wild sort of glance around the corridor. Turning, he met Laura's eyes for several seconds.

He was plainly agitated, and it might have been that; he might not even have been seeing her. But she thought he looked frightened of her.

He was a big man, fair and moustached, dressed in a check workshirt, and he gave an impression of tremendous weight and solidity –

something to do with the thickness of the neck, like a bull or a bear. It made that look of fear, vulnerable and almost delicate, all the more surprising.

A nurse – not Nurse Cash – bore down on him, spoke to him with a frown. Laura couldn't hear what they were saying. Then the nurse, quite firmly, ushered him away; and again it was surprising how meekly and unresistingly the big man went, like a lost child amenable to anything.

Now the view from the window was blank again. Laura felt curiously bereft, as at the withdrawal of some hope. Perhaps this was what the psychologists called magical thinking. As long as other things kept happening, then nothing would happen in that room down the corridor.

Laura picked up the plastic cup of tea, but couldn't drink it. She wondered if you were allowed to smoke in here. She wasn't a smoker, but of course plenty of people still were. Did they allow such people to smoke while they waited in here, or did a nurse march in and tick them off?

Again she thought about this room: here all the time, unsuspected. She supposed every town and city that had a hospital had a room like this. The waiting room: the room, waiting. You might be lucky and never be summoned to it, but it was here all the same. Like the cell of your body that started a cancer – it was there all the time, awaiting its moment, the enemy within the gates.

So quiet here, though not silent. Continually there was the muffled bang of institutional doors, more of a vibration than a sound, along with some airborne vibrations that might have been bells or buzzers. Something like, she thought, what sound must represent to the profoundly deaf.

David, how old? Thirty-seven . . . though he would be thirty-eight in a month's time. Did that make him, really, thirty-seven or thirty-eight? Quite young, whichever. He kept himself reasonably fit. Hadn't she read somewhere that this was the optimum age of resilience for a man, the time when he was physically at his sturdiest, best able to overcome illness and injury?

She was sure of it. But then it didn't seem to make any more sense than these things usually did – men reaching their sexual peak at fifteen and geniuses being left-handed and all the rest of it. It was meaningless.

Were they telling her everything? Her experience of hospitals was limited. Her grandmother had been taken to one shortly before she died, but that had been different somehow – a stage in an inevitable sinking out of sight. The only time Laura had been in hospital herself was when Simon was born, and there the atmosphere had been businesslike, almost brusque. What would happen, she wondered, if she left this room and went in search of the place where David was?

She couldn't just wait here. It was simply intolerable. Doing nothing ought to be easy – but in these circumstances it was like undergoing the most strenuous torture.

It was an impossibility.

Laura went and flung open the door, and Jan was standing there.

'Laura. I came as quickly as I could. God, how are you?'

Jan hugged her. She was Laura's dearest, closest friend, the friend to whom she could say anything and everything. But they were not touchy-feely together as a rule, and it felt strange.

Nurse Cash was there.

'No news, Mrs Ritchie,' she said. 'I'll leave you with your friend.'

'Wait!'

The nurse looked at her patiently.

'Isn't there . . . this is so terrible, I mean can't I see him?' Laura said, feeling abashed, a child pleading undeserved indulgence.

'Not now, I'm afraid.' Nurse Cash hurried away.

Not now, not yet, not ever?

Laura turned helplessly to Jan. And here at last was something she could do – say thank you to Jan. She did it, and added, 'I'm sorry.'

'My God, you've nothing to be sorry for,' Jan said. She smelt of outdoors. It was apt, because she also looked subtly different – an outsider, who had chosen to enter the little warm room but did not belong to it.

'Well, I mean – this isn't very nice for you,' Laura said, sitting down at Jan's insistence.

Crazy thing to say, but she meant it. This was a bad deal for a friend. You were supposed to buy friends thoughtful little gifts on their birthday, go for gossipy drinks with them, give them a ring because you cared. Not call upon them to share something like this.

'What's the news? How is he? They just told me he'd been in an accident.' Jan shrugged off her coat, eyes fixed on Laura's – with love and concern, also diagnosis.

'A car. He got knocked down on Bourges Way this morning.'

'Oh Jesus.' This came out, plainly, before Jan could stop it. 'But he's going to be all right,' she said, pitching the phrase between a statement and a question. 'Are they – treating him, operating . . . ?'

'He's in the resuscitation room,' Laura said. 'I suppose that's – where they resuscitate people.' She shrugged, and all at once the shrug became a trembling that started at her shoulders and then took over her whole body.

'Lean forward,' Jan said, a hand on her back. 'That's it – put your head down. You poor thing – oh, Laura, what a terrible shock, my God . . .'

'I'm all right,' Laura gasped, 'I'm all right, really.' She sat up, gripping her own arms. 'I wasn't sure whether you'd be home. They asked me if there was anyone I could have here with me and I just thought . . .'

'I'm glad you did,' Jan said. Then she grimaced. That wasn't the right thing to say: but then, what was? 'How did it happen? You weren't . . . there?'

'No, no. David went off to work and – and then the police came. The nurse has been really kind . . . Apparently he's got serious head injuries.'

Her tone was all over the place, uncontrollable. That last bit had come out urbane, conversational. *Apparently*. Dear God.

Jan was a composed person whose handsome, serious face gave little away. But there was no mistaking her flinch at Laura's words.

'Simon's at school?' she said after a moment.

'Yes. The police thought it best that I leave him there for now. Oh God, Jan, what am I going to do?'

She immediately regretted this outburst – the selfishness, the appeal for an answer Jan could not give. But how *were* you supposed to behave in this situation? What was the etiquette?

'It'll be all right. It'll be all right, Laura.' Jan seemed fastidiously aware of the feebleness of this even as she said it. But Laura tended to regard Jan as authoritative in everything. Jan knew what was what: Jan got things right. Quite without rancour or envy, she had grown used to seeing Jan over the past few years as a model – all that she should have been and was not. The comparison had, indeed, been forcibly made to her several times.

So when Jan said it, it carried weight. Laura even began to back it up herself.

'I suppose,' she said, 'doctors now, they have tremendous things . . . you know, in cases like this.' She hadn't the faintest idea what things she meant.

'The hospital's got a very good reputation,' Jan said.

'Oh yes.' And again Laura didn't know what this meant. Were there hospitals with bad reputations, where you went in with an ingrowing toenail and never came out?

She could feel something like a hysterical giggle rising in her throat. She was afraid she could not keep it in. They were going to take her away, snorting and howling . . .

She clapped her hand to her mouth as her throat broke into a small, abject sob.

Jan held her arm. 'It's terrible,' she said. 'But all we can do is wait. He's getting the very best of care . . . I know it must seem bloody impossible but we've just got to wait.'

'How long though?' Laura groaned, hearing in her own voice the whining note of a child in the back seat of a car, wanting to know when they would get to the seaside. She remembered that at one point during her long period of labour when Simon was born she had found herself sucking her thumb, a habit she had abandoned at five. Perhaps all the most testing events of your life brought out the child in you: perhaps your infant self was the real 'you', and adulthood just the veneer. Perhaps she would go mad with this waiting. Perhaps she should pray.

Hard though. One of the things she had hated about her parents' religion, the religion in which she had been confirmed, was that it never let you go. Even if you abandoned it, they just called you 'lapsed', as if it were a temporary matter. She had always resisted that 'lapsed': she had finished with it and that was that. So she had set herself firmly against any temptation to pray, to wish, to acknowledge even the possibility of belief. It had been that way for years.

And now she found she could not change it. She couldn't pray: not even with David like this. She didn't know how. Prayer was a bargain, she thought, and she had nothing to offer on her side, nothing that was not tainted, qualified. Bad coin.

'Here.' Jan handed her a box of tissues. She had brought them in her bag. It was so typical of thoughtful, practical, birthday-remembering, rocklike Jan that Laura nearly sobbed again.

Instead she thanked her and blew her nose and then said, 'I don't understand why.'

Jan shook her head. 'Accidents,' she said helplessly. 'What about the driver – did he stop?'

'I don't know. I suppose so, the police didn't say they were looking for anyone . . . No – what I mean is, I don't understand why he had to cross Bourges Way. Why he didn't use the footbridge.'

'I've seen people do it. In a hurry, they will do it.'

'But he set off in plenty of time. He always does.'

'Perhaps he had something to do in town. And that made him late for his train.'

'Maybe. I don't remember him saying he had to do anything, but . . .' But that was just it: she didn't remember anything of this morning. It was just another day in her married life. And that in itself . . .

Suddenly Jan's fingers tightened, almost painfully, on her arm.

Laura looked up. Nurse Cash had silently entered the room and with her was a slight sandy man in a white coat. A doctor, plainly; yet so young and small.

A bantamweight, unequal to the fight.

'Mrs Ritchie?' he said, casting an equal glance at Laura and Jan. Of course, how was he to know?

'Me,' Laura said.

'I'm Dr Marshall. Your husband is David Ritchie?'

'Yes.' *Ah, then this is all a mistake, Mrs Ritchie, it isn't your husband at all, it's someone else entirely we've got in that room down the corridor and you can go home and tell this as a quirky anecdote . . .*

'Will you sit down, please?' the doctor said.

All at once Laura began shaking her head like a mutinous child.

'Laura.' Jan urged her into a seat. 'Come on.'

The young doctor pulled up a chair opposite them and perched on the edge of it, as if about to nip off.

'Mrs Ritchie, I'm sorry to tell you your husband has died,' he said. 'We did everything we could. But there were severe injuries to the brain, of a sort beyond medical help. We just couldn't save him. I'm very sorry.'

Laura's hand, pressed to her mouth, began to shake and shake. She dug the fingers between her lips until the nails hurt the soft flesh.

'Is there anything you want to ask me?' Dr Marshall said.

So final. He was perching there, ready to answer a question or two, and then be off and do something else. This was it. David, everything that he was or would be, had come to an end here. But it wasn't possible, it couldn't happen, a person could not just *run out* in this way so that there was no more of them, ever . . .

Jan's hand was between Laura's shoulder blades, gently massaging. 'Oh, Laura, I'm so sorry . . .'

And still Laura couldn't stop shaking. Perhaps if she could stop shaking, she would be able to ask the doctor something, and she felt she ought – he was sitting there so expectantly and something in her felt guilty and abashed that she couldn't think of anything, just like when they asked you that question at the end of a job interview . . .

She tasted her own blood in her mouth, from her digging, jabbing fingers.

'Mrs Ritchie?' Nurse Cash spoke firmly to her. 'Do you feel faint?'

Faint? No . . . just the centre of a great spinning. Like a drain, with the whole world swirling and pouring round, down, into her and through her.

That reminded her: there was a dirty pan still in the sink. David had died and there was a dirty pan in the sink and Simon was at school and David's mother was watching morning TV miles away and David had died and she had forgotten to buy butter and there was blood in her mouth tasting like salty pennies and David had died . . .

'What . . . ?' The shaking, the fingers in her mouth, the whirlpool of the world pouring into her made nonsense of speech. She tried again. 'What . . . ?'

No good.

Nurse Cash made some private gesture to the doctor, who nodded. Then squeezing Laura's hand she said, 'Would you like to see him?'

Laura felt Jan's eyes on her. The sympathy in them was so great it had reached the point of anguish.

But Laura said, 'Yes,' taking her hand from her mouth and sitting up. Not because she felt strong enough to do this but because for a moment she was saved. Saved from having to answer the doctor's question.

Was there anything she had to ask him? Yes. *Answer me this. The other day I was wishing David was dead. I wished he was dead, and now he is.*

So doesn't that mean, really, that I killed him?

THREE

David lay on a bare gurney that seemed abnormally high, like an altar.

Somehow one expected a bed, covers neatly turned down.

How little one knew.

It was David. There were no unrecognizable horrors. He was covered to the chin and his whole head down to the eyebrows was swathed in a way that horribly, grotesquely suggested a mobcap. But the face was David's, and quite normal. Unmarked, not even noticeably pale. And he really did look as if he were simply asleep. It was true. The old chestnut was an eternal verity.

There was a kind of relief in that: there was a kind of relief, though Laura would never have believed it, in simply seeing him. Nurse Cash, that kindly expert, must have known this.

There was a chair, and Laura sat by him for a while. Jan stood behind her. The room was silent, though she could hear faint voices from an adjoining room, and there seemed little more sense of urgency in it than in a dentist's surgery. But then, the banks of machines, with their industrial-looking grey cladding and cords and jacks and crystal displays, were not doing anything. Some of them, she saw, had Dymotaped labels stuck on their panels where the lettering had worn off. They still didn't appear real, though: if anything, that seemed like the last touch of authenticity on a carefully prepared prop.

'If you want to hold your husband's hand, or anything like that, it's all right – it's wholly up to you,' Nurse Cash had whispered to her as they went in.

Laura didn't feel the need to, though this was not from fear of the cold touch. She had often been afraid of David when he was alive, but she felt no fear now.

He looked handsome. Not in the way he had when young: the handsomeness appeared more as a kind of purified essence of him, the man he had been and the man he might have been.

Laura cried, or rather wept, for it was not noisy and abandoned. Some part of her noticed that the other people in the room – Jan, Nurse Cash, Dr Marshall – seemed somehow put at ease by her crying. Natural, no doubt, and correct.

But it was only the surface area of a great mass of feeling. It scarcely even touched what was inside her.

Again she thought of the past, though thinking was too active a word for the torrent of images and recollections that poured into her mind. Perhaps this was because she could hardly contemplate the future that awaited her – the future hovering at her elbow, ready to begin as soon as she left this room.

Impossible. The future was what happened to you next – it was an escalator that carried you, requiring nothing but quiescence. But this future was different, a new and unguessable presence in her life, strange as another planet.

Nurse Cash asked her if she would mind speaking to the police a moment.

'You don't have to do it now. If you want to keep this time separate, that's all right. It's just that they need you to make a formal identification when it's a trauma case – an accident.'

'All right.'

The young policeman was back. He seemed curiously shy of her now, tiptoeing, cumbrous.

'Sorry to have to disturb you, Mrs Ritchie. We need a formal identification from the next of kin.'

Laura nodded, then had a terrible fear, from the way he hesitated, that this meant they were going to throw back the sheet, remove the dressings, reveal all. And for the first time she comprehended the ghastly violence that David had met with. Smashing, crushing. She gasped and looked around for the doctor.

'Please – did he suffer? Did he – was it painful . . . ?'

'Mr Ritchie never recovered consciousness,' the doctor said promptly, almost eagerly, as if pleased to have something to do. 'He wouldn't have been aware of any pain, I can assure you of that.'

They said that, of course: they always said that. But Dr Marshall's young blue eyes held hers frankly.

She looked up at the young policeman, awkwardly waiting on her. Hardly knowing why, she said, 'Was anyone else hurt?'

'The driver of the vehicle involved was badly shaken.'

'Was he drunk, or . . . ?'

The policeman looked momentarily official, about to decline comment. Then he said in a quiet tone, 'That will all be sorted out, Mrs Ritchie. All I can tell you is, it was a very busy road, the traffic was moving very fast, and it appears that Mr Ritchie tried to – get across.'

Smashing, crunching.

'Just your assent is all I need, Mrs Ritchie,' the policeman said. 'Is this your husband?'

'Yes,' Laura said.

'Thank you.' The young policeman was gone.

Yes, that was her husband. And now she didn't know what to do. She was adrift. She looked at Jan. Jan always knew – what was good for a sore throat, the name of a reliable plumber, how to repair your hair if the hairdresser had sabotaged it. But Jan, looking gaunt and pale, seemed just as lost.

And again, Nurse Cash came to the rescue. 'Just say when you're ready to go. Take all the time you need. Would you like to spend a little while alone?'

Even now, her heart gave an instant no. That was how deep-grained was her resistance to being alone with David. They were better with people around them.

Ready . . . she supposed she was. She would have to leave this room some time, and step out on to the surface of that strange planet.

Laura got up. She thought of Simon, at school now . . . wasn't he? What *was* the time? She couldn't guess, and the interior of the hospital, all artificially lit, gave no clues. She would have to tell Simon. On that planet, where she didn't know if she could even breathe the air, she would have to tell her son that his father had died.

She walked to the door. Jan and the nurse attended discreetly, as if prepared to catch her in an all-out swoon. It was weird, the concern and deference. Queen for a day. It seemed as if she should be large, grand, as she walked. But she felt tiny.

Nurse Cash put her in the little warm room again. This faintly surprised her – as if there should be a separate room for this. Before and after.

'I'm sorry, Jan, I'm keeping you from—'

'Don't be daft. I'll stay with you.'

But how long would this go on? Time, as in dreams, seemed infinitely stretched. Laura recalled Simon's delight when she came to fetch him home from his first day at school. Despite all he had been told beforehand, he had somehow felt that school was for ever. Like this hospital: it felt as if they were just going to keep her here. And she had very much the same powerlessness as a child at school. They could do what they wanted: she just waited helplessly for direction.

'I don't know what the . . . procedure is now,' Jan said. 'But I'll help you with everything. Whatever needs doing, I'll do.'

Laura nodded her thanks. 'I'll have to tell David's mother. God – how?'

'Perhaps the hospital will do it for you.'

'I don't know. It ought to be me. After all, I . . .'

After all, I killed him.

Nurse Cash, returning, seemed to have moved to a new plateau of gentle efficiency. She sat by Laura, said she was very sorry and that all the staff who had tried to save him were very sorry. How was she feeling? It might be as well if she saw her GP as soon as she could – and her son too – Simon was the name, wasn't it?

'And now about the arrangements for the funeral. It is hard to think of, I know. But if you take this, look at it when you can, you'll find it gives you details of all the practical things that need to be done.'

Laura found in her hands a laminated cardboard folder full of leaflets. The information pack had completed its conquest of the world.

'Now,' Nurse Cash said, 'in many cases the doctor in attendance would sign the death certificate and then the deceased would be released so you can have the funeral. But in accident cases there has to be an inquest before anything else can go ahead. That means Dr Marshall doesn't sign the certificate yet. He's contacting the coroner's office, and they arrange the inquest. It doesn't mean there'll be any sort of trial or that the death's suspicious or anything like that. It's just standard procedure with road accidents. You'll be contacted when the coroner holds the inquest, but you don't have to attend. Then after that the funeral arrangements can go ahead, though it's just as well to contact a funeral director now if you can manage it.'

As she spoke, the nurse inclined her face increasingly towards Jan.

'What happens to David in the meantime?' Laura said.

'He'll be kept here.'

Run out. No last words, no messages, no significant parting moment. She couldn't even remember, in the sense of calling up a visual image, the last time she had seen him alive. It was the same as any other day. Except that David had exited from it.

Sudden death: people often used the word 'senseless' in regard to it. And yet there was something sensible about it too, something grown-up and impressive. For a moment Laura found herself experiencing the same respectful feelings she had had when she was first going out with David and he knew how to order in restaurants.

'How will you be getting home?' Nurse Cash said.

'I've got my car,' Jan said.

'And is there someone who can be with you?'

'I'll be there,' Jan said.

Nurse Cash nodded. 'All right. Now we need you to sign for Mr Ritchie's clothes and effects, whenever you're ready. Is there anything you want to ask me?'

Laura wasn't listening. She had seen, at the window, the big bear-like man she had seen earlier. He had both hands pressed flat against the glass, and he was looking in at her; and on his face was written all the pure, uncomplicated, inconsolable anguish that she should have been feeling and was not.

His eyes met Laura's.

'Is there anything you don't understand?' the nurse was saying. She touched Laura's hand.

Laura turned. 'No . . . thank you, you've been really kind . . . Who *is* that man?'

But when she looked again, the man was gone.

FOUR

Laura went home to Number 19 Duncan Road with an information pack about death and two white carrier bags, very like the ones that hot takeaways came in, containing the clothes David had been wearing when the car had hit him.

As Jan turned on the gas fire, boiled the kettle, busied herself, Laura found herself concentrating less on what she was feeling and more on what Jan was feeling. She put herself in Jan's shoes – supposing it was Ross who had died, and she were helping Jan in this situation? What would she feel? Probably, she thought, a sort of strained and desperate determination to help and be strong. But there would be a fearful mystery too: there would be a sheer inability to imagine what that person must be feeling. A suspicion, perhaps, that any apparent calm hid volcanic depths. A consciousness of being a handmaid at something too huge, too imponderable, beyond your resources.

That was what she would be feeling, she guessed, if it was Ross who had died.

Ah, but that was different.

Laura watched Jan. Long coarse hair, gone grey early – she was not yet forty – but handsome hair, unthinkable dyed; thin knowledgeable hands; noble aquiline profile; clothes that were just Jan, stylish and individual the way clothes were supposed to look though none of them was out of the ordinary or expensive. She moved about this house, it seemed, with far more authority than Laura did: she fitted it better.

Pressed by Jan, Laura sat down in the living room and pretended to look through the information pack. But her eyes kept roaming round the room, trying to make sense of it. The thing was, none of it did make any sense now. The TV with David's squash and badminton how-to videos stacked beside it, a heap of Simon's toys and games chosen by the two of them for Christmases and birthdays, even the distance of the coffee table from the settee reflecting the length of David's legs . . . this was all changed. It was as if she were seeing the room at the bottom of the sea, tumbled amongst weed and bubbles, sea horses darting amongst the wrack . . .

Laura was gasping like an asthmatic.

'Laura?' Jan hurried to her. Her voice was sharp with anxiety. 'Are you OK? Shall I ring a doctor?'

And then Laura stepped into Jan's shoes again and realized how terrifying a person like herself must seem, terrifying and unpredictable.

'No, no,' she said, getting a hold of herself, 'it's all right. I'm OK. Really. And look, I ought to do things, I should be—'

'You should just sit tight,' said Jan. 'No one's expecting you to do anything. Would a drink hurt, do you suppose?'

Laura shrugged: she really didn't know what drink would be like on the new planet. As far as her old life went, drink was: on David's side, getting red in the face and ceaselessly hammering on at the same subject while his gesturing hands formed fists in the air; when mutually taken, a stepping stone to their increasingly rare sexual encounters with each other; and on her side, an occasional sneak tipple while she made dinner, because it was sort of allowed when cooking was in progress and because it fortified her against David's coming home, the breathlessness when she heard the key in the door, the quick scanning of his face for indicators of mood.

But drink now? She had no idea: that was all changed too. But she swallowed, anyway, the weak whisky that Jan brought her.

'They were very good at the hospital, weren't they?' she said, biting on the sour aftertaste. 'You hear stories of how uncaring they are in these situations – treating you like a number and all that. I've got to ring David's mother – I must do it. And there's Simon – I don't know whether I should go to the school and bring him home. I don't suppose there's anything in this bloody bumf to tell you how to break it to a child that his dad's dead. Oh, but it's not their fault, I know they try. It reminds me of a jamboree-bag, this thing, do you remember those? Little sweets and novelties inside, I loved them. There was a picture of Boy Scouts on the bag saluting . . . Do they lie to you? Was it true that he didn't feel anything, or— You know, I remember reading that in the First World War they always put "shot in the head" when they wrote to the families of soldiers who got killed, even when they died these terrible lingering deaths from all sorts of wounds. It was to spare people but of course everybody knew . . . Sorry, I'm going on.'

'It's all right,' Jan said. She seemed, indeed, rather relieved, just like when Laura had cried. 'It might be as well to leave Simon at school, I think. It's not long now till hometime. And then . . .'

Jan's brows puckered. And then what, Laura wondered. Meet him at the school gates and walk him home trying to be completely normal . . . ? Break the news once they were in the house, the strange undersea house where nothing was the same . . . ?

'Listen, I could pick him up from school for you,' Jan said. 'You could come, or I could fetch him on my own.'

Suddenly it occurred to Laura, seeing the frown on Jan's face, that

Jan was doing her worrying for her. Jan was taking it on. It wasn't right. Jan had her own family.

On her feet, Laura headed for the kitchen before Jan could stop her. 'I should do things. I'm going to have to, so I shall start now. With those bags.'

'Oh – Laura, I should leave that for now—'

Laura already had them, and was emptying them out on the kitchen table.

She knew this would be bloody awful. She was thankful to find it just about as bloody awful as she had expected, and not worse.

Someone at the hospital had folded David's suit carefully, even a little eccentrically. After a moment she saw that it had been done to hide the dark marks.

Blood? Or dirt from the road? Mercifully she couldn't tell.

His shoes, the black lace-ups he wore to work, still as shiny as when he had polished them this morning. Socks, but no shirt or underwear. Too bloodied maybe? Or did they have to be cut off? Her mind skidded away from the thought. Wallet and keys, and something else, in a small burgundy polythene bag. It bore the logo of Rosewood's – a ritzy gift shop full of painted thimbles and wildly expensive models of mice doing anthropomorphic things in bonnets.

Laura held it up, puzzled.

'It's too awful, Laura,' said Jan, pained and anxious at her side. 'Let's just – leave it, deal with it another time . . .'

Laura opened the polythene bag and took out a greetings card. It was a little bent. On the front was an apologetic cuddly hedgehog holding out a bunch of flowers: inside were printed the words 'SORRY I WAS PRICKLY!' There was no handwriting: it seemed David had bought the card in town that morning. Laura looked in the bottom of the bag, drew out a till receipt, examined it. The card had cost one pound sixty. David had tendered a five-pound note. The transaction had taken place at eight thirty-three.

David's train to work left the station at eight thirty-four.

Jan, touching the card gently, murmured, 'Oh God.'

Laura stared at the cutesy hedgehog. Of course, nothing made sense now – but this didn't especially. 'Sorry' cards weren't David's style; and anyway, nothing had happened between them lately that he needed to say sorry for – had it?

She tried to think, her efforts hampered by the whisky which, on top of no food, had set her very veins trembling. Think – when was it he had pushed her in the kitchen and her hip had struck the corner of the fridge, with that quite remarkable pain that was like a small controlled explosion in her loins? A week, ten days . . . ? Perhaps. But then that was just ordinary. That could have been any slice taken out of the last few years.

Try to think of the last few days – the weekend. Shopping on Saturday afternoon, Saturday evening some film on TV she couldn't even remember, Sunday one of David's long pub sessions – again, just another slice from the plain loaf. But no, there was one thing that came to mind. In the supermarket their trolley had had an erratic wheel that screeched like a cat with its tail trapped. The days when this would have sent him into fits of laughter long passed or dead, David had grown more and more irate as they shopped, been rude to the cashier when they paid, and in the car park had shouted at Simon who had wanted to take a packet of crisps from the shopping bags. And as they'd driven home this had led on, in the usual way, to the aria of grievances. Beginning with a comparatively muted passage on the poor quality of Langstead's shopping facilities, their out-of-town situation, their expensive prices, their limited choice, David had soared into an extempore flight of vituperation in which he demanded of the gods whether there were not more to life than shopping every Saturday, and why everyone else looked happy and fulfilled and never seemed to go shopping at all, and whether he could not have had a life like theirs if he had not become tied down by dreary responsibilities . . . The evening that had followed had been, for Laura, one of tiptoeing around him, inducing that peculiar strained feeling in her lower back which she had worried for some time might be kidney problems until she had recognized that it came on whenever she was tensely waiting on one of David's moods. He had stared at the TV, making morose bitter comments on just about everything that came on, and giving a hollow, head-shaking laugh at anything bright or amusing. He didn't touch the tea she cooked, at every noise Simon made he clenched his jaws and cast his eyes heavenwards, and whenever she asked him if he wanted anything – tea, coffee, a drink or, as she did not say, unlimited and self-abasing solicitousness every moment of his life – he merely sighed. It was only after ten that the clouds had broken. He had had a drink, begun telling Laura a work anecdote in tones of venomous sarcasm that made her fear where it would lead, and then with imperceptible moderations and gradations had become relaxed, resigned to his wrongs, cheerfully cynical. By about ten minutes before bedtime he was in a tolerable mood.

So – could it have been that?

And yet that too was not untypical. If you had visited Number 19 Duncan Road at, say, fortnightly intervals, you would have had a fair chance of happening on a similar scenario.

But perhaps he had undergone a change of heart. Perhaps some road-to-Damascus moment had occurred, and he had resolved on a new start, and thought to begin with the sort of cuddly-chops greetings card he had always sneered at.

'This,' Laura said with an effort, feeling she had been silent too long, 'this must have been why he was late. He made a stop in town to buy this and then had to – take a short cut to the station.'

Sorry I was prickly. Could that mean, then, in essence, sorry about the times I clouted you; the time I tore up that book you were reading and stuffed it down the toilet; the time I chatted up Wendy Hobbs at that party and kept putting peanuts down her cleavage; the time I took the money we'd saved for a holiday and wasted it on that phoney timeshare; the time you went to stay with your cousin in Bournemouth and came back and found I'd been drinking all weekend and had turned the bedroom into a sort of art gallery of dirty magazines . . . ?

'Yes,' Jan said, 'it looks that way. But it's one of those things that . . . I mean, it's no good thinking *if only*, because . . . Oh, Laura,' she burst out helplessly, 'I'm not going to say I know how you feel. Because I can't even begin to guess how you feel, I just can't.'

Poor Jan: she was more right than she knew.

FIVE

In the week following her husband's death Laura Ritchie did what was required of her.

This was something she was good at. It had been drilled into her, at more than one stage of her life, as a desirable quality: she had made it a personal virtue, in what she believed to be the absence of others.

You could call her behaviour that week being strong, strong especially for the child's sake, as some people no doubt did. Or, as others no doubt did, you could call it a state of denial, a trance of shock from which there would be a terrible awakening to realization. And there was an element of both, though not in the way people thought. The strength for Simon's sake had been tested before now; and if she was in denial, what she was denying was far from simple.

The hardest thing, undoubtedly, was Simon. It was with Simon that she saw how impossible it was to be prepared for anything like this. Nothing helped. Certainly not the example of that other world of fiction, of TV and films, which Laura was susceptible to in spite of herself. When people argued in soap operas, she could not help noticing the ways they got to 'Sorry' and 'What's wrong?', analysing the stages that at last opened channels to communication. She knew it was bunk: she knew that that looking-glass world through the screen, whilst it might seem to resemble ordinary experience, was as fantastic as Narnia; but it was at least some sort of comparison. But breaking news like this to a seven-year-old child, and helping him cope with its consequences – there was no guidance worth a damn.

Simon was very truthful – the most truthful person, Laura thought, in the family. She and David had always been adept at evading, denying, twisting the truth (at times it seemed they would do anything rather than face it). Somehow Simon had been born without this.

'No – Dad broke it.'

Laura sweeping up shards of glass from the broken conservatory window and saying she had accidentally put the vacuum cleaner pipe through it. Simon, watching with a pained look as if the lie hurt him, not having any. 'Dad broke it when he kicked it.'

There was a promised outing to McDonald's that did not materialize – David started in on some cans of beer, mulishly moved on to Scotch when she protested, ended up too drunk to drive. Simon ignored the promise that they would go later: he took off his shoes and jumper, set out a floor puzzle, settled down. 'We won't go later,' he said. He used the truth, not to salve his disappointment, but to cauterize it.

In the looking-glass world, TV children blinked solemnly as they were told that Daddy or Mummy had gone to heaven and was with the angels: often the comforters threw in a rendezvous with Granny as well. Sometimes they went in for eco-consolation – we all die like the flowers and trees but we never really die because all life is, you know, interconnected. And Mummy or Daddy would always live on in our thoughts and hearts and so we never really die that way either. And even if Mummy or Daddy had died, which they hadn't really, it didn't mean they didn't love us any more. And we who are left must look after each other. And while the TV kids were tearful, mutinous even, they swallowed it and hugged the platitudinizing adults and so began, smoothly, to Grieve and Heal.

Truthful Simon wasn't such a soft touch. That first afternoon, when Laura ushered him into the fatherless house where Jan was desperately making gingerbread men in the kitchen, Simon wanted above all to get his facts straight.

'Dad isn't coming back any more?'

'No, love. A person can't when they die.'

'Not ever?'

'No. But . . .'

He was alert to the qualification.

'It doesn't mean they're gone. They're just in another place.'

'Heaven?'

Laura nodded. 'That's right.'

Simon's thin chest rose and fell resentfully. 'There's only planets and stars up there.'

Perhaps it was her fault. She hadn't tried to teach him either way – memories of her own infant brainwashing had put her off imposing either belief or unbelief – but maybe he had imbibed scepticism with her maternal milk. It was difficult anyway for Laura to convey any coherent idea of heaven. Even during her own childhood, when religion had been inflicted on her like experiments on a laboratory rat, she had never been able to picture it – except perhaps negatively, as a place where the Technicolor torments of hell didn't happen.

'Well,' she struggled, 'people go to another place, where nothing nasty happens. Just nice and peaceful. And where we all see each other again one day, eventually.'

Simon gave this some thought. Was he thinking of meeting his father again in that nice wonderful place? And – oh God, Laura thought – was he already wondering what mood his father would be in when he did see him?

Simon loved his father, all right, but he had also been afraid of him.

He was too truthful to pluck any easy emotion out of this conundrum. Through the first few days he cried, clung and sought hugs, was by turns fractious and demanding and then spectrally quiet; but all the time he kept battering himself at understanding like a moth at a porch light.

'Why did Dad die?'

'It was just an accident. He got knocked down by a car. It was so bad the doctors couldn't do anything.'

'I don't know anybody whose dad died.'

His eyes sought hers. It was the first evening. She had let him stay up late, and he was cramming the gingerbread men that Jan had made in such desperate quantities. A unique atmosphere of wretchedness and indulgence: a horrible treat. Absently gorging, Simon dug and dug at the question Laura could see was, in a way, the crucial one: was this something special visited on them for a particular reason? Why them?

'Was it because he hit you?'

'He didn't mean that,' she said automatically, the reply a habit that would take more than this to break.

'And when he smashed my Game Boy,' Simon said, sobbing again at the complexity of things, cramming another gingerbread man in his mouth.

Ah, yes, she remembered that well. The incident had brought her right to the brink of decision. But not over it. God forgive her.

(And perhaps that was precisely what God had done. Perhaps he was up there after all, watching over her, and had looked at her life and decided to . . .

Evil. Evil thought.)

'Dad loved you very much,' she said. 'He still does. But sometimes these things . . . just happen, and there's no reason you can find. What happened was very quick, and sometimes it's not like that – sometimes people are really ill and in pain for a long time before they die and that's horrible. But with Dad it was just like . . . like he went to sleep.'

Soon Simon was sick. In the bathroom she held his head over the toilet bowl, stroked his hair – her hair, dark and thick, hair that formed masses instead of strands.

'I keep thinking about Dad.'

'I know, love. It's horrible. It'll get better, I promise you.'

Simon shook his head. About two feet away was a hole in the plaster of the bathroom wall, kicked by David and then hastily bodged with filler.

'Everybody dies, don't they?'

'Yes. But remember, it was an accident – it was a piece of terrible bad luck. Nothing's going to happen to you or me.'

Sickness had made Simon look worn and adult. He might have

been her contemporary as he sat up on his haunches and said, 'What are we going to do?'

'Stay close together. Look after each other.'

Simon hugged her and for a little while he was like those TV kids. He couldn't swallow heaven or Dad coming back as a rosebush or Dad living transcendentally amongst them as a cluster of golden memories. But that it was just the two of them and they would have to stick together – that was true.

'Did Nan cry?' Simon asked when she put him to bed. 'Will she be all right?'

She had cried, but she would be all right. Here at least Laura felt she was not fending off nastiness with a Pollyanna bromide. David's mother was as all right as anyone could be on learning of the death of their only child; and she had certain things on her side. One was that she had had to make a choice several years ago, when she had remarried. David's father had died when he was young: between David and his vastly fat, gravel-voiced, delightfully indolent mother there had been an exclusive, almost matey affection that had charmed Laura when she had first seen it. Back then she was fresh from a household where parenthood meant discipline plus emotional blackmail written in the blood of Jesus. Visiting his mother with David during their first flush of romance, Laura had been enchanted at the way be brought her gifts of Guinness, chaffed her, shared private jokes, and was treated with none of the hectoring concern she associated with mothers. He was what he was, and Mrs Ritchie jovially accepted it. Then three years ago his mother met a retired engineer named Reg Winstanley and at the age of sixty-four married him, settling to an overheated, Guinnessy, budgie-keeping companionship in a sheltered housing flat in the Hertfordshire town of King's Ripley. It seemed a good arrangement. She was too fat and breathless to stir much beyond the kitchen, where she had the expertise of the confirmed glutton. Reg was a man's man, a wiry whippet who liked mending things and combing the market at sunup for bargain cauliflowers and eating fry-ups in a din of TV and budgie shrieks.

And David never forgave his mother. Once in a while he spoke to her on the phone in the resentful monosyllables of a teenager, and at Christmas he appended his name to the present Laura had chosen and wrapped and then transported it to the flat at King's Ripley, where he would glower stiffly for half an hour, refusing three and even four times his mother's timid offers of a nip of whisky. It was a measure of his hatred that he refused even to take a drink from her.

By that time, Laura had learnt a lot about David. So learning that that enviable relationship with his mother was something of a sham was not a great shock. The sham was perhaps partly on old Mrs Winstanley's side too. He wanted her as a character, not a human being: she didn't bother him so she wouldn't have to bother about him. And now she had Reg, and Reg, a widower, had grown-up children who lived locally and could bring Guinness and fill the flat to bursting point.

All of which made some difference, perhaps, but it was hard to say how much difference anything could make to losing your only son.

Breathing distressfully down the phone, Laura's mother-in-law took the news as a series of incomprehensibles.

'But how could it be? Oh no, how could he? Oh – oh, Laura, he was so young . . . I just don't understand it. Do you? Can you understand it, love?' This was later that first day, when she called Laura back – it was Reg who had answered the phone on Laura's initial attempt, and Laura had been chicken enough to ask him to break the news. Through the long, stertorous, tearful phone-vigil the same questions had kept coming up. How could it happen? Why him? Why when he was only thirty-seven? Why didn't he take more care? And when Laura, feeling like some battered clockwork mechanism endlessly responding, mentioned the inquest, Mrs Winstanley's voice grew shrill with bewilderment.

'Inquest? What's that about? Do they mean he was murdered?'

'They told me it's what they always do when there's an accident. It's just standard procedure.' How quickly you could become a comparative expert. Just yesterday she knew nothing of this. 'They investigate what happened so they can record a cause of death.'

'But if it was an accident, why do they have to investigate it? Was it the driver – was he drunk? Was he speeding? Oh, he ought to be locked up if—'

'I don't know. I don't think so. But I suppose that's what they sort out at the inquest.' Suddenly she thought about the bear-like man who had appeared at the window of the little warm room. They hadn't told her anything about him at the hospital; but now she had a strong presentiment that he must be the one. The man who had been driving the car that had killed David. Or the man who had killed David. Where did you draw the line?

'Will they want us there? Will we have to go to court? I don't think I can face that, Laura, really I don't—'

'Nobody has to go if they don't want. It's just a . . . a legal thing.'

'But why?' Peggy Winstanley's voice whined so high it seemed to cause feedback in the receiver.

'It's so they can establish cause of death. For the certificate, I suppose.'

'We know what it was. It was a car. I've always hated cars. Reg gave his up because of the price of petrol and the insurance and everything and I'm glad because, you know, it could have been some other mother's son . . .' Peggy gave a fluttery sob. 'Will they open him up?

Will they have to cut him up, you know, you see it on telly . . .'

'I don't know, Peggy. I doubt it.' A post-mortem: yes, if there was an inquest – she was sure she had read it somewhere in the bereavement jamboree-bag. 'But anyway, the thing is we can't have a funeral until after the inquest.'

'Why? Isn't it bad enough without stopping us having a decent funeral for him?'

So the questions went on. And Laura answered as best she could; she did what was required of her. The first night, after she had put Simon to bed, Jan came round again together with her husband, Ross, prepared to stay. They didn't want Laura to be alone. But she wouldn't allow them. She was going to have to be strong and had better start now. It was the right thing.

'We'll be there for you – anything you need,' Ross said. 'There are a lot of – you know, practical matters to be sorted out. I can get time off work. We'll do everything we can. This isn't one of those things people say hoping you won't take them up on it. We want to do it.'

Pressed, unbearably, by their kindness, Laura looked at the two of them and saw the sincere and wholly mutual discussion that had been behind this offer. They had volunteered themselves, unequivocally, as a team: a partnership. Of course one never knew. Perhaps earlier, in Jan and Ross's book-strewn and plant-smothered kitchen there had been sighs and winces and mutterings at the prospect, reluctance on Ross's side, weariness on Jan's, resentments and recriminations salted away. She doubted it, though – she doubted it very much. And was touched by the old wistful envy even now.

They stayed, valiantly, until she pretended she was tired and ready to sleep. They accepted an impossible situation – having to be around someone whose husband had been killed, and whose responses were all out of kilter; offering consolation they knew to be useless, trying to talk of other things when they knew this was futile and could even appear insensitive, making cups of tea that weren't touched, turning on the TV and turning it off when a sitcom made some hideously appropriate and inappropriate jokes about funerals, making her face what had happened and at the same time playing it down in case it was unbearable for her. The whole task was about as feasible as juggling with sandbags, and they undertook it.

They even accepted that at last she was crying inside to be left alone, understood it, and left her.

'You've got the phone by the bed, haven't you?' Jan said on parting. 'Keep it by the bed. And pick it up. Doesn't matter when.'

Laura looked at the two of them standing under the porch light. An exhausting day for Jan, tiredness throwing the noble bones of her face into relief: Ross, a foxy-coloured man with a Beatle fringe who dressed always in shades of woodsy brown, looked tireless as always, a plucky hero out of a boyish English mould. She noticed the way their bodies lightly touched: they were weary and saddened beyond the possibility of desire, but still their bodies fitted together. And again Laura heard the fairy sigh of envy.

'Just pick the phone up,' Jan said again. 'Any time. Four in the morning. Do it, won't you?'

Laura didn't, though she was awake at four. She had been regularly taking a proprietary brand of sleeping tablets for some time, and they were unequal to the extra demands of that night. Yet to be alone, sleepless, in darkness, was not so bad. It ought to have been a distillation of all the awfulness of this thing that had happened – yet it wasn't so bad. Getting some sleep was one of the things that was probably required of her – her first failure, as far as that went; but it was surely also required of her that she shouldn't completely crack up when her hand accidentally touched David's pyjamas folded on the pillow, and she managed that, just.

Thinking about the 'sorry' card helped. It was a tangent: a curiosity; it didn't fit. As long as her mind kept straying down that particular byway, it was off the unthinkable high road.

At some time around dawn, when light had crept into the bedroom and showed her some more details of that undersea world that no longer made any sense – their wedding photograph on the dressing table, David's squash trainers standing jauntily akimbo – Laura put the thought of the 'sorry' card away, and hit the high road once more.

She kept Simon home from school. He had slept, but was grey-faced and subdued. They pretended to have breakfast, and then, because the jamboree-bag suggested it, she telephoned and made an appointment for them both to see their GP. It was part of her habit of obedience. Actually to talk of 'their GP', as these things so confidently did, was nonsense. There was a doctor at the local medical centre whom she had seen more often than the others in the practice, and who whenever she entered the surgery made vague noises of recognition while he peered into his computer terminal. She didn't expect much out of seeing him now: he was only dimly aware that she had a husband to lose. How unlike the looking-glass world, where doctors leaned their leather-patched elbows on the desk and discussed your life with intimate knowledge and concern, and everyone lived in flavourful places like Yorkshire or Liverpool, and drew comfort from the distinctive fact.

She also rang her mother-in-law, tried to answer a new batch of mournful gasping questions, and then spoke a while to Reg. 'This has really cut her up, you know,' Reg said, manly and also faintly accusing. 'She's in a terrible state. I honestly can't remember her quite this bad.' He spoke as if mentally reviewing a whole series of next-of-kin bereavements. Then Laura rang a funeral director and made an appointment. Then the phone rang in turn: it was the coroner's office, and a mumsy lady with a head cold informed her that the inquest was set for Friday, that she and all other interested parties would be notified in writing, and that she was under no obligation to attend either personally or through a proxy legal representative. Finally the mumsy lady offered catarrhal and quite sincere-sounding condolences.

The kindness of strangers. All sorts of people Laura would never see again were taking an interest in her. It was bizarre.

The mention of a legal representative set her thinking. Presumably a whole raft of legal business would need to be sorted out. She was sure David had made a will, because the necessity of making wills had figured in one of his phases, but she couldn't remember him ever saying where it was. In the Yellow Pages she found the name of a solicitor ringed – a familiar name now that she thought about it. Once again the voice on the other end of the phone was kind and obliging. Another appointment.

Simon's school too, she must remember that; and David's office. It had been a long time since she had been confident speaking on the telephone – sometimes lately she would have to take deep breaths first, rehearse what she was going to say, even write it down. But this was different. She felt busy, urgent, and yes, important.

Something else was happening too. Laura had once seen a TV documentary about sufferers of a rare illness that destroyed short-term memory. A man could not remember his wife's coming into the room half an hour ago: he greeted her as if after a long absence. The affection, so genuine and yet so skewed, was heartbreaking. The whole thing was baffling too – you couldn't begin to imagine the feeling of continually not knowing what you'd done so short a time ago.

But now Laura began to know. The feeling was really no feeling. It was a succession of facers, sudden plunges into bewilderment. She went to ring the doctor's surgery, and saw she had already written the appointment down on the pad by the phone. She went to bring in the milk and found she had already done it though she had no memory of doing so and would have sworn in the witness box that she had not done so.

It went on that way. Yet she could handle it. She got things done even though she couldn't remember doing them. If Jan noticed anything strange about her when she called round, she didn't let on. She nodded seriously, listening, while Laura told her of all the things she had done and had yet to do.

'I was thinking I ought to go over and see David's mother too. It's only about an hour's drive. I really think I ought.' David's car stood in the garage, and she was quite able to drive it, though she seldom did.

'I don't know, Laura.' Jan might have been judicious, or dubious.

'That's a bit of a task when you've got a lot on your plate. And an hour's driving . . .'

'Oh, I'm quite up to it.' Laura was cleaning the oven – though she could not recall beginning the job – and she paused in her scrubbing, looking up at Jan, feeling a little impatient.

'Well, look, I could drive you. If you're set on it.'

'No, no, you don't have to do that. I mean, I could even get a train.'

'Where is it she lives – King's Ripley? There's no station, is there?'

This was all very picky, Laura thought, scrubbing, all very negative. Just when she was really getting on. Doing what was required of her, thoroughly, calmly.

'Leave it till tomorrow,' Jan said, 'or the day after.'

Laura frowned, then didn't know what the frown was for. Her mind moved on. 'Oh yes,' she said, tugging off her rubber gloves, 'I was going to ring David's work. I knew there was something.'

She felt Jan's eyes on her as she telephoned. What – she wasn't even up to using the phone, was that it?

John Whiteley was head of department at the advertising agency where David's dream of creativity had apparently ended with his producing copy for travel brochures. David had habitually referred to him as a class A bastard, though when Laura had met him at the odd company bun fight he had seemed a pussycat; and now when she told him the news he sounded as if someone had clubbed him.

'Yes,' Laura found herself saying, very precisely, 'yes, you see, he died. Yes. It was a road accident. So I thought I'd better ring. Let you know.'

John Whiteley stammered, hardly coherent. He started to say how unbelievable, oh God, what a shock, then swallowed audibly, wanted to know what he could do. Meanwhile Laura felt impatient again: this was all very well, but it was taking time.

'My God, he was – I mean, I was set to play badminton with him tomorrow, we arranged it and . . . I'm sorry, Jesus, I'm sorry, Laura, the stupid things you say when . . . But I just can't believe it, it was on my mind this morning, badminton with David tomorrow, and – oh Christ, I just can't take it in . . .'

'Yes,' Laura said, 'but he died, you see.' John's apparent inability to grasp this fact baffled her. He died. David died. How many times had she said it? Well, it didn't matter. 'You see, he died, and so – if you could tell the others in the office and so on. I don't know about the funeral yet, but if you would want to come—'

'Of course, of course. Whenever. Just – just let us know, we'll all . . . I'm sorry, it's such a shock, I mean I know he had all these problems, but when you hear something like this . . . Laura, are you all right? I mean, not on your own or anything?'

'No, no. That's fine.' It was true, she had lots of support, staunch

Jan and Ross and, all in all, she was standing up to it pretty well, wasn't she?

Well, that was another thing done that needed to be done. Laura put down the phone, and just before memory faded again, wondered what John Whiteley had meant. *All these problems . . .?*

SIX

Steps on the new planet.

Laura kept pressing ahead with them, and the fact that it all passed by her in that strange perpetual present was no bad thing at all. It meant she couldn't look back and she couldn't look forward, at least no further than the next step.

The solicitor's office was situated in one of Langstead's handful of old buildings, a miraculous pre-Victorian survival thrusting a leaded bow window out over a tiny street behind the town hall. Like most old buildings, it smelt like a church. In a cold stone-flagged reception two Paisley-squared ladies swivelled at a switchboard desk like a giant pew, speaking into delicate high-tech headset microphones. The combination was dreamlike, as everything was. Laura waited in a sunken room hung with old caricature prints of men in legal wigs and gowns, briefly joined by a haunted-looking youth dressed in the sort of suit that is exclusively tailored for petty court appearances. 'You seeing Mr Clutterbuck?' he asked her, Dickensianly.

She was not: she was seeing a Mr Bussapoon, who came to fetch her, taking her up a stone staircase to a little office that creaked like a ship's cabin. Mr Bussapoon knew her husband was dead, and that they were going to concern themselves entirely with the fact, but it did not seem to discomfit him. Policemen, doctors, lawyers: the people at the sharp end, moving amongst us. How protected we are, she thought.

Mr Bussapoon – she remembered now David, who when she first met him had a Rock Against Racism poster above his bed, making one of his doubtful jokes about the name – was small, youngish, handsome and dark: Mauritian, perhaps. He was curiously soft-skinned and delicate-looking, as if he had been kept in this place like some legal Kaspar Hauser and never been out. He expressed his condolences succinctly and asked how she was coping – this without the usual flinch, as when people feared your answer. This, his manner suggested, was very much his business. Laura answered him, not knowing afterwards what she had said. It didn't matter: if she had been speaking Martian, he gave no sign.

'Well, as you've ascertained, your late husband drew up a will under our direction and deposited it with us. This doesn't mean you're obligated to dealings with this firm in executing it, but obviously we'd be very pleased to help and we can give you a free quotation for whatever fees are likely to be incurred.'

'Yes – I want you to. I mean – I don't know what to do but I want to get it done.'

'OK. What I need to know first is the circumstances of Mr Ritchie's death. I understand from our telephone conversation that it was the result of a road accident.'

Telephone conversation . . . Well, they must have had one, though she couldn't remember it.

'I appreciate it's hard for you at this time,' Mr Bussapoon said. He was wearing a thick golf club sweater; this place felt as if it would never be warm. 'Just the basic facts are all I need.'

She told. It was quite easy. As long as obedience was involved, as long as she had to give answers, fill in forms, fulfil functions, and take steps, she was all right.

'OK. The position is, everything basically waits on the inquest and the coroner's report that comes from it. It's after that that the death is registered and the death certificate is issued. Usually registration is the next of kin's responsibility, but where there's an inquest the coroner signs a Certificate After Inquisition and then the process goes straight through to the Registrar. He'll supply the certificate, and also copies which you may need for insurance companies, credit agreements and so on. Small charge for that. Once the inquest is over the disposal of the body is authorized, which means you can go ahead with the funeral, though it's as well to begin arrangements with a funeral director now. The only complication with regard to the inquest is if there's a question of criminal proceedings. That wouldn't *seem* to be the case here but there's always the possibility in road accidents of compensation. Dangerous driving, drunk driving and so on. This is what will be established at the inquest – basically whether the driver of the car was to blame or whether it couldn't be helped. They'll question witnesses, listen to the doctors' reports and so on. By the sound of it, there'll probably be a straight verdict of accident, or possibly misadventure.'

'What's the difference?'

'It's tricky. Accident is pure chance, misadventure is where the victim voluntarily puts him- or herself in the position where the mishap occurs. If someone falls in the sea it's accident, if they try to swim at high tide it's misadventure. As I say, I don't think it likely that anything will come out of the inquest, but I can attend it as your legal representative if you wish. Obviously I'll give you a quote for that too.'

'Would you advise it?'

'It will establish the facts of your husband's death. People often find that this – helps peace of mind. You can attend yourself, of course, instead. You won't be called on to say or do anything.'

Ah, that was no good then: not if she had no function to fulfil.

'I'd prefer it if you did it,' she said. And suddenly thought: how was she going to pay for all this? She and David had a joint current account, but she knew there was very little in it. There never did seem to be nowadays.

Supersubtle Mr Bussapoon read her thoughts. 'All solicitor's fees are met when the will is proved – that is, once probate is granted, which allows the executors to distribute the estate. Meaning your late husband's property and money, including any life insurance policies. It's a good idea to get together all papers relating to your late husband's finances – policy documents, bank books and so on. And in the meantime I'd advise contacting the DSS about your entitlements – widow's benefits aren't affected by other income.' Mr Bussapoon seemed suddenly to feel that he had become rather inhumanly carried away. 'I appreciate this is all rather difficult to think of just now, and maybe seems rather cold and hard-headed. But anything that can be done now will save more trouble later.'

But it wasn't difficult to think of now. It was the best thing, the only thing to think of: she wished there were a hundred offices she had to visit. She almost didn't want to leave the solicitor's, with its comfortable dry formalities, and go out into the world where she was a person whose husband was not the deceased but dead.

She had to, though. With yet another information pack under her arm, she left the Christmas-card street at last and emerged into the centre of Langstead. It jangled to the eye. Not knowing what it was, Langstead decided to be everything. A dyed-in-the-wool Londoner would call it a dormitory town, a Northerner would see it as practically a suburb of London, but it was too big for the first and too far outside the ring of the M25 for the second. It had had several incarnations – table-mat market town, then Betjeman Metroland, then 1960s mushroom: and it was still growing, throwing out executive estates and business parks into the shrinking Home Counties greenery. It was continuously, self-renewingly modern. Thirty years ago the town centre had been all split levels, slabs and angular statues: now it had been reborn as contemporary phoney-urban, with black wrought-iron lamp standards and mock-Georgian shop windows and neo-Victorian arcades (which real Victorian Langstead had never had).

And it was pedestrianized. No traffic touched the centre of Langstead: all was channelled to the efficient ring road system, which enclosed most of the central amenities. Only the railway station was outside that thrumming perimeter. And for the safety of its citizens Langstead Borough Council had provided a glassed-in footbridge which crossed Bourges Way, the northern section of the ring road, and took foot passengers right to the station forecourt. Sometimes there was a busker in there, or a vendor selling the *Big Issue*; and every weekday morning and evening Langstead's numerous commuters thronged it, keeping left. Amongst them, David.

Without volition Laura found herself walking up the High Street, then bearing right at Woolworths into Sheep Street, then left into a long narrow slit called Rayner's Walk. Home of little specialist shops, shops that sold nothing but chess sets, gents' outfitters for gents who still dressed like Alastair Sim playing a headmaster, teashops where you could pretend that you were in a Lyons Corner House and that the glum youth-trainee waitress was a loyal aitch-dropping Nippy who thought Ecstasy was what Greer Garson felt when Walter Pidgeon planted a frowning kiss on her tightly closed lips.

And home, right at the end, of Rosewood's Cards and Gifts.

Here Laura stopped, but she did not go in, or look in the shop window. She looked straight ahead, to where Rayner's Walk ended like a docked tail: where there was a railing, and beyond it Bourges Way, roaring, thundering, pounding.

Laura stood with her hands on the railing. To her left, perhaps two hundred yards along, the footbridge arched across the road. Directly in front of her, on the other side of the maelstrom of traffic, was the flat roof and dimpled fascia of the railway station. A hundred yards, perhaps.

The hundred-yards dash.

It was midday, and Bourges Way was alive with tons of hurtling metal. The vibrations went through her hands, and slices of slammed air, exhaust-tainted, cuffed her face and tangled her hair.

A memory: holiday in Greece, a few years ago. Very much the backpacker when young, David had grown conservative in the matter of holidays. He wanted sun and sangria and lots of British people in shorts and a concrete hotel in front of a flat beach with behind it a town that existed only to sell hand-tooled leather belts and Taiwanese dolls in what might have been local costume if the locals had thought of it. Beyond these enclaves he seldom wanted to venture, but on this occasion they had, in search of some semi-authentic tourist trap – a working vineyard, she seemed to remember. Walking back from it to the pretend town, David had insisted they take a short cut. They knew where they were going, they weren't tired or late; there was even a road sign pointing straight ahead to their destination. But David got this bee in his bonnet and led them on a short cut he thought he had spotted. Why? For the hell of it. It was one of his abrupt decisions. They wandered amongst a wilderness of trailer homes and abandoned quarries while the stars came out and Simon cried on her shoulder. David didn't laugh about it, nor say he was sorry: when they finally got back to the hotel all he wanted to do was get hold of a route map and find out where they had gone wrong. The failure of the short cut had not ended it as an idea. The idea was everything. This was, indeed, one of the things she had loved and admired about him when they first met. He picked up a notion like a surfboard and ran out to the waves with it.

(So was it possible, she wondered, that the things you loved a person for could be the very things you ended up hating them for?)

Gripping the railing, Laura stared out. He must have climbed over this – easy enough, for it was not high and he was tall.

But wouldn't he have been seen? It had been daylight, or at least the dingy daylight of a winter's morning. If he had spotted a momentary gap in the traffic that seemed feasible for a dash, wouldn't the driver have seen him in time?

She looked to her right, and saw the fat lamppost.

That was how she thought of it from that moment on. You could call it a large street lighting installation but to Laura it was the fat lamppost because that was what it looked like. At the top it was an ordinary lamppost, but from the pavement up to about ten feet it was fat, probably twice the girth of a pillar box. It was clad in featureless grey-green steel: she couldn't see any doors or panels in it but she could only presume that it housed something, some sort of main electrical terminal – probably, for all she knew, if you opened it up and fiddled around inside the whole street lighting of Langstead would go out. What she did know was that if a person with a bee in his bonnet about taking a short cut tried to cross Bourges Way from this spot, the fat lamppost would shield him from a driver's view until the last, too late moment.

She swivelled her eyes again to the busy road. Nothing to show there had been an accident here . . .

smashing crushing

. . . and in fact it seemed impossible that this speeding, drumming onslaught of traffic could ever be stilled or interrupted by anything.

She ought to go home, she thought. Jan was looking after Simon, who was still off school, but obviously Jan would like to see her own family some time. But then again, she ought to stay here because – well, it was a confrontation of sorts, a visit to a shrine of sorts, and an opportunity to straighten out her feelings, of sorts.

But feelings – they just drained away like water in a net. You could dig and scoop all you liked but nothing remained long enough to get hold of. It was as if, from the moment of that knock on the front door, feelings had changed their nature along with everything else, had become elusive and unrecognizable. If she darted out into the road now, were hit, smashed, would she feel anything, or would pain and terror just trickle out of the net too?

SEVEN

'It's all right,' Jan said. 'I don't have to go yet.'

It was late evening, and Simon was already in bed. Laura, working on a heap of ironing – she had washed everything in sight, including David's clothes, for reasons she did not bother analysing – glanced over at Jan with perplexity, a little impatience. Why stay? She was quite all right, and Jan must be tired of being here.

'Well, I'll go straight up to bed as soon as this is finished,' Laura said. 'Need to be up in the morning – I've got an early appointment at the funeral director's, and then there's the doctors.' It was not her habit to iron socks, but she did it anyway.

Frowning, setting down her coffee mug, Jan said, 'How do you think Simon's coping?'

Laura thought. It was difficult: one thing being a parent taught you was the inaccuracy of the formula equating adulthood with reserve and childhood with transparency. If anything stood out from Simon's behaviour, it was a more than usually intense attention to his books. He had returned especially to the Rupert books that were his old and supposedly outgrown favourites. She had admired the imaginative way he expanded this world, speaking as familiarly of its characters as if they were friends, speculating on what went on beyond the frame of the illustration, when the adventure was over. Now he just kept his head down, as if willing himself into that world rather than drawing its charming fantasies out. When she cuddled him she found him tight, hard and hot, like a caught animal.

'I don't know,' she said honestly, then shrugged and attacked the ironing. 'We'll just have to get through it together. I'm trying to keep him near me as much as possible. In case he thinks I might disappear too.'

'And you? How are you feeling?' Jan grimaced. 'Stupid question.'

'No, it's not . . . But that doesn't mean I can answer it.'

Tentatively Jan said, 'Actually I was reading up on it. Bereavement and so on.' Besides being a librarian, Jan had books on every conceivable subject in her house. Reading up was natural to her, whatever the situation. 'Just to see if it could give me any pointers – you know, to help.'

'Oh, but you've been an enormous help, I mean – you've done

everything, you've been there for me. I don't see what more you could do. I think maybe David's mother needs help more than me. She was still in a terrible state when I rang her today.'

'Mm. But she has got her husband, hasn't she? And you're – alone.' Jan seemed at once to regret this phrase.

'Yes, I suppose so,' Laura said, ironing with fierce care.

'Maybe this is something the doctor should sort out. But I was just wondering, there's bereavement counselling and—'

'I don't see the point of that. Really. This isn't some – complicated mystery that's all going to unravel with hypnosis or whatever. You're just . . . cut off. You're bereaved and that's it.' Laura had long had a half-joking animus against the counselling culture: it seemed to her to spell the end of private life. Under it, Hamlet would have got in touch with his feelings about his mother's remarriage and recognized his father's ghost as an externalization of his anger, with the Danish Princes Support Group bucking him up when things got tough. But in dismissing Jan's suggestion she meant something more, or different. All at once she could not hold the iron steady.

'Yes,' Jan said, 'I do see . . . But just maybe it could help, just by – sorting things out in your mind a bit. From what I've read, there seem to be so many emotions you have to go through, that people don't recognize. There's an anger stage, there's a denial stage, a guilt stage . . .'

'How about all of them at once?' Laura said softly. She leant her shaking hands against the ironing board. 'It's because they're all there at once that I . . . All right, anger, yes, I'm angry with David because he's died and suddenly we're left alone with no idea of what's going to happen and everything's just completely – thrown over, flung about, God knows what . . . And what was the next thing? Denial – yes, that too, I'm doing the ironing and bustling about hither and yon and, yes, I'm denying that my husband's dead, I'm carrying on as if he's going to walk through that door in a minute but I don't know how else to . . . And guilt, OK, I've got that too, he's dead and immediately you think there are a million things you'd go back and change and yes, I feel that in some way it's all my fault. It's textbook stuff all right, and I dare say a counsellor could sort it out but I don't see, I just don't see how they can sort out the fact that . . .' She took a deep sobbing breath, and out it came, painfully and gladly and desperately. 'Jan, how do you explain to a bereavement counsellor that you're not feeling what you're supposed to be feeling in the first place? That you didn't like or respect or trust your husband any more and half the time you were frightened of him and only stupid bloody indecision and cowardice was stopping you from leaving him and sometimes, yes, sometimes, you even wished that this would happen – you wished that something would just rub him out, take him away – even death. Is that grief? I don't know what it is – it bloody hurts but whether it's the right hurt or the wrong hurt I don't know . . .'

Laura howled the house down, and when Jan's comforting arm went round her shoulder she howled harder because she could not find in herself a single atom of longing for that arm to be David's.

EIGHT

The inquest into the death of Mr David Ritchie, the thirty-seven-year-old husband, and father of one, of 19 Duncan Road, Langstead, was held on 2 February. After hearing evidence from lay eyewitnesses of the accident, including the driver of the car involved, and police and medical witnesses, the Coroner recorded a verdict of accidental death. A Certificate After Inquisition was issued, and the deceased's family was empowered to proceed with the funeral.

Thus Mr Bussapoon, who attended the inquest as representative of the deceased's married partner and executor, informed Laura by telephone.

'You'll receive written notification, of course,' he said, 'but basically that's about it. The police raised the matter of safety on Bourges Way and how there's been some demand for either a second footbridge or an underpass, but that's a matter for the council to take note of, or not as the case may be. The driver wasn't found to blame. He wasn't speeding or drunk or careless. He was very upset when he gave evidence. Apparently he suffered a minor whiplash injury trying to brake in time. His solicitor made a point of passing on his deepest regrets.'

No one was to blame.

Poor David: how he would have hated that.

Three days later they had the funeral. Held the funeral – conducted the funeral – where were the words? You celebrated a marriage, but there seemed no equivalent term for its sibling event. For they were, after all, similar. The boards outside churches always used to bear the words 'MARRIAGES AND FUNERALS', Laura thought. They were occasions that people were invited to and had to dress up for. And often they were the only occasions on which people entered a church.

No church this time, though. David had spoken scathingly of the archaism of burial, and whilst Laura's family had had an old-fashioned Catholic aversion to cremation, Laura's family weren't around any more. The funeral director seemed quietly to approve her choice, like a tailor commending a tasteful commission.

Snapshots.

The photographs made a salient difference between marriages and funerals, of course. No one took snaps at a funeral – though Laura remembered that her grandmother had had photographs of her husband's grave. (And had taken them out and looked at them, too. They really were a very strange lot.) But then, strictly speaking there were no photographs of a marriage either. People kept big white cushiony albums inscribed *Our Wedding*; but, for whatever reason, a book of snapshots entitled *Our Marriage* was not something you ever saw.

Laura had one, though, in her head; and throughout the day of the funeral she found herself leafing through it.

David's mother and her husband came up for the day in a car driven by a friend whom Laura knew only as Marj, a little silent woman with a fierce dewlapped face like a boxer dog. Chauffeur-like, she stayed with the car the whole time: it was an ancient Consul with a back seat roomy enough to contain Peggy Winstanley's huge black-clad form. Appropriately, the only modern vehicle that could do this easily was a funeral car, and Peggy settled into it beside Laura and Simon with sighs that had something of contented expectation about them, as if she were on a day trip in a charabanc.

'It's not a bad day,' she said as they drove to the crematorium, a curious building on the outskirts of town that looked like an Art Deco cinema set down on a bowling green. 'Not a bad day for the time of year.'

'You keeping all right?' Reg demanded of Laura in his abrupt way.

'Yes,' Laura said, 'thanks, we're OK.'

'I wish I could be more help to you,' her mother-in-law grunted, folding and refolding her handkerchief between red hands that, like inflated rubber gloves, were delicately unaltered as far as the fingers went and monstrously swollen above the knuckle. 'You must have had a struggle. A lot to do. I wish I could have helped. Looking after little 'un, things like that. I'm useless, though. Just getting out of the house – that's enough for me.' Breathlessness made her concise. 'Nan can't move a lot, pet,' she added to Simon, who was sitting very quietly, almost unbearably adult in his little black blazer.

'Don't worry about that,' Laura said. 'You just concentrate on taking care of yourself.'

'Oh, I take care of Peggy. I do that. That's my department.' Appearing to think his caveman credentials impugned, Reg became dogmatic. 'She never has to worry while I'm around.' He set his jaw and nudged a little closer to his wife, who could have worn him on a charm bracelet.

'Not a bad day anyway,' Peggy said, looking distractedly out at Langstead's golfing suburbs. 'Not bad. He left you all right, though, didn't he, duck? You'll be managing all right?'

'Oh, yes,' Laura said: not that she knew. Since giving up work, since the Duncan Road life, she had become dissociated from money. Lately there never seemed to be enough, but it was hard to assess the truth of this between David's complaints that he was underpaid and that she didn't manage the housekeeping properly.

A snapshot from the prologue to *Our Marriage* – for that was how Laura saw her life before David, no more than a prelude to the real matter – showed her own father, checking his football pools on a Saturday afternoon and putting the coupon aside after the first few results. 'No,' he would say, when she asked him why he didn't check the rest, 'it's statistically not possible now.' And he would try to explain it; and Laura, half-comprehending, would still think it must be nicer to cling on to that infinitesimal chance and check them all. But he was never disappointed: seemed rather to take pleasure in his capacity for rising above it. He watched every TV weather bulletin, local and regional. Nowadays, though not then, they sometimes had round-ups of world weather too and she had no doubt he would have studied them with the same thoroughness, just in case Hurricane Cindy hung a right at Miami and headed across the Atlantic to flatten Cheadle. 'Forewarned is forearmed,' he would say. As a girl Laura thought it was probably better not to know, but had seldom said so with conviction under her parents' roof, simply because they were such authoritative personalities. Not that this meant they knew what they were talking about; just that they said it as if they did.

A wizard mathematician, her father was in insurance, which eminently suited his temperament. Her mother's too, even though she was a more emotional individual, for the emphasis on being continually prepared for any eventuality tallied well with her fervently held religion. For Laura's mother the fires of hell were always just around the corner and only the most dutiful observance would keep you from them. Not to be prepared was actually to invite catastrophe: a missed Mass, Laura gathered, increased the likelihood that you would keel over. In hindsight Laura could see that her mother was priest-ridden in a way that was positively medieval, but at the time she had felt only a cringing inferiority. Her mother paid her heavenly dues on the dot whilst young Laura, forgetful, erratic, careless, was a bad debtor. Thus she had guilt the way some children had asthma. It probably didn't help having her schooling conducted by musty-smelling nuns, at least until they got so decrepit that they admitted they couldn't teach instead of just continuing to do it badly. After that Laura went to an ordinary denominational school. It was strict but there were no weirdos in cloaks, and things were a little better then.

And they got a little better still, strange though it was to think it, when her father left. Strange, because she had always found him the less intimidating parent; and she did miss him. The party line was that he had left because he had gone crazy, and prayers were to be offered accordingly for his distracted soul. In fact he ran off with another woman. How long it had been going on no one knew, but prudent to the last he had made sure the house was paid for and there were some savings in the bank before he hooked it, never to be heard of again. In her shame and mortification, Laura's mother cleaved ever more firmly, even fanatically, to the Church; and she didn't shrink from the odd suggestion that the whole thing was Laura's fault. So all in all, it was perhaps surprising that Laura should date from this time the beginning of her emergence from a cocoon of guilt and gloom and her birth as a person who had at least the potential for happiness and fulfilment.

It was because, she realized now, the heavenly insurance policies hadn't paid off, and the young Laura had been sharp enough to see the results. Her mother had been discredited. She might try to shift her authority to the ground of martyred and betrayed womanhood, but it didn't work: she had been perfect too long. Her own mother, Laura's grandmother, came to live with them a while later – for companionship, because she was old, because she would swell the coffers, Laura never knew which or which combination of motives was behind it – and she was like Laura's mother only more so. Spending her teens in a house full of crucifixes and muttering women, Laura avoided growing up a psychotic because that scepticism had arrived luckily just in time. The pair tried to present an image of righteousness in retreat from a sinful world that had injured them, but they just looked like witches.

Meanwhile Laura did well at school and showed talent at art. Probably it was in reaction to all those Technicolor Marys and gaudy saviours: you either developed your aesthetic sense or let it atrophy. She had a facility for languages too and when it came to college applications she was indecisive. Backed by an optimistic art teacher, she applied to a high-grade art college and prepared to shake the dust of suburban Cheadle from her feet. She didn't get in. The art teacher admitted his optimism had been misplaced, and plans were made to apply to polytechnic the next year to study languages. The plans had more grounds for optimism. Aspiring artists were ten a penny but people who could understand German and Spanish were in demand. The prospect had less glamour but it still had plenty.

And yet, and yet . . . Too young to know that success means having options in reserve, Laura felt like a failure. And unfortunately there was nothing her mother liked better than someone feeling this. It was meat and drink to her. Hugging the knife of her own bitterness to her, Laura's mother made sure that her now declaredly Godless daughter knew that pride came before a fall. It was grisly and it was made worse by Laura's mother deciding that having an idle daughter on her hands for a year was too much of a cross even for her saintliness to bear. Laura caved in and began taking a bread-and-butter typing course at a Manchester tech. It was a sort of caving-in, at any rate. She was eighteen, and not one of those eighteen-year-olds who know what they are going to do with their life right down to the pension plan. She was disappointed and uncertain and impatient and her home life stank and a year was a very long time. She didn't know what the hell she was doing.

Probably, hindsight said, she was waiting.

And then one evening she met David in a Manchester pub.

. . . As they got out of the car at the crematorium Simon clung tightly to Laura's hand, his shoulder tensely digging into her side. He didn't much like new places at the best of times, and this place with its spooky rosebeds and sunburst glazing and the black-clad undertakers wiping their patent shoes fastidiously on the step must seem the ultimate in disorientation.

This was Simon's day. She had decided that. She was grown-up and could wrestle with her own demons, and Peggy had Reg. But Simon was seven and having to attend his father's funeral. He was the one who must, somehow, be made to feel all right, or better, or not quite so awful, or whatever love and reassurance could manage.

She spoke with him before they went in, kneeling down, holding his hands.

'You know what we're going here for, don't you, lovey? It's so we can say goodbye to Dad properly – you and me and Nan and everybody who knew him. It's sad but it's a time to remember nice things about Dad too, and think about how we still love him although he's not here now. You've been ever so good and helped me a lot. I know it feels like you're going to have to be good and quiet because you're all dressed up. But it doesn't matter how you feel, if you make a noise or cry or anything, or if you don't feel like crying and you see other people do it. Just remember it doesn't matter. I'll be with you, and it won't be long, and after we've said goodbye we'll go home. So don't worry about anything, will you?'

She kissed him. Love didn't well or sweep over her or any of those things. With Simon her love was just there, with her and of her, invulnerable. It held her together.

People spoke of funerals being simple and dignified. She didn't think they could ever be the latter. Even in a modern crematorium, where the Gothic elements were kept to a minimum, there was still something grotesque and horrific about the whole business: a coffin was a coffin. Also human nature kept breaking through. In the chapel, where the other mourners were already seated, there was the constrained atmosphere of a waiting room. The simple fact was there were people here to whom this didn't mean a great deal. It meant something, certainly, but not the weight of solemnity that the occasion demanded. Following the coffin in, Laura saw Jan and Ross, John Whiteley, a couple of David's other colleagues, friends, neighbours, dressed in the sort of clothes they would be glad to take off. Her feelings were so tortuously complex it was hard to trace any of them out, but she recognized within herself a definite gratitude. They didn't have to do this, and they did it out of decency and kindness.

David, who felt so unappreciated, would have been pleased. Or would he have called them hypocrites?

A minister who had elicited from her a potted biography of David took the service. Snuffling with a heavy cold, he spoke of David as a family man, hard-working, full of life. And, without being specific, as a man of creativity.

Snapshot: David and his play. When she first met him he had recently graduated from university and was still living in Manchester, where he had studied, sharing an impeccably shambolic flat and working on a play. He had left university with an indifferent second but that, he explained to her, was the result of the intellectual timidity of the examiners. David was an artist, not an academic. The play was the thing, or plays. It kept mutating: stage play, radio play, TV play, film script. Each mutation allowed David to map out a new career. Someone older or less ready to be dazzled might have seen even then that David had the creative temperament without the talent, but that was really beside the point: just the temperament would do for Laura then, because it had glamour. Also David was good-looking in a pale, high-strung, Tom Courtenay, grim-up-north manner; and in him were concentrated all the things she had expected and hoped from the college world and which seemed postponed beyond endurance just then. He was bohemian to the extent of not washing his clothes much and he knew about jazz and weird plays and he was a voluble talker, which at the time she thought to mean the same as a great talker. He introduced her to cannabis, which she found she liked too much for comfort and soon learnt to avoid, and he was full of poverty-chic wheezes and gimmicks of studentdom – hand-rolling cigarettes and reusing teabags and taking a dose of Night Nurse before you went to the pub because it maximized the effects of the alcohol. He bought her tricksy gifts like Tove Jansson's 'Moomin' books and a hip flask and old 45s of Bobby Vee songs. When she gave herself to him he had, she believed even now, genuinely fallen in love with her, but even if he hadn't it would still have been like shooting fish in a barrel.

The play never was finished, and Laura never did go to college. David got a job in London, and she went with him. Cohabitation was the original plan, but instead they found themselves getting married. Perhaps Laura thought of this as a sop to her mother, who had been alternately vinegary and inquisitive through this gadabout phase; but in fact her mother was noncommittal, even mildly approving of Laura's settling down with David Ritchie. It was possible that she had the measure of him then, and was not averse to her daughter finding out the hard way.

. . . The minister finished his potted biography with some references to David's memory living on. It was all quite wishy-washy and non-denominational, as she had wanted it to be: David had begun as a fiery atheist and ended up pronouncing that you had to believe in something, though he didn't say what. Accompanying the service was some gentle piped New Age music, which was the best she could think of; David hadn't liked any music in recent years. Thinking of this she felt a true resounding sadness like a note on a gong. He had an expensive hi-fi, but he never played it and all music irritated him. If they had lost each other in the past few years, then David had also lost himself.

Sniffing, the minister assured himself and the mourners that their thoughts were with David's family – his wife, Laura, and son, Simon, and his mother, Peggy. Simon seemed acutely embarrassed at this mention of his name and Laura, who kept her arm around him all the time, gave him a squeeze. Was that it? She supposed so. One of the funeral director's myrmidons creaked forward, took the wreath from the coffin and added it to the floral display at the side of the chapel. As for that coffin, Laura had set herself from the first moment not to think of it, not even to see it, except as one would see a bubble in the fluid of the eye – not part of the real world even though it bulked so large to the sight. And of course, David wasn't part of the real world now. He had left it. The person she had slept beside for so many years, whose characteristic scent she knew as well as the smell of roses or of almonds and which she could imagine, now, as well as she could imagine the feel of his hair with its wiry crispness at the sides where the grey had started – that person was simply gone and he certainly wasn't in that box.

The only way. She hoped that Simon, with his pale concentrating look, was employing some similar tactic in his mind.

She had dreaded this part. As far as she knew the coffin was spirited away by some sort of conveyor belt and the whole idea was so ghoulish and horror-movie ludicrous that she wasn't sure she could bear it. But all that happened, as the minister spoke the words of committal, was that a curtain moved in front of the coffin with a faint hissing noise.

That was it. There was a silence broken only by some breathless pinings from Peggy Winstanley. People began shuffling, and looking over at Laura: what now? She knew, but had forgotten, and it was one of the undertakers who steered her and Simon over to the floral display.

Holding Simon's hand, she looked at the wreaths and bouquets, read the cards, encouraged him to read some. There was a large bouquet from David's office, the card signed at various angles by his colleagues: it reminded her of the Christmas cards they sent. A wreath in the shape of a prayer book from Reg's family – thoughtful of them.

'Who's that?' Simon said, pointing.

'Which, love? Oh . . .' She bent to read the card. The bouquet was at the base of the display, and the biggest of them all. It read 'With deepest regret, Mike Mackman.'

She thought she had heard the name somewhere, but she couldn't remember where. It was an extravagant tribute, whosever it was.

'I'm not sure,' she said. 'Someone who knew Dad.'

'Can we go home now?'

Snapshot: their first home. A first-floor flat in Enfield. It was full of inconveniences. An electricity meter about the size of a car engine stuck out across the staircase, and if you were in a hurry you had to scuttle up at a crouch like Quasimodo. The draining board sloped, so you had to dry everything up pronto before it slid back into the suds. The heating made up with noise for what it lacked in warmth. Here they ate tinned tomatoes on toast and peered mystified at incomprehensible thrillers on a black and white portable TV. The equation of poverty with happiness was usually made by rich people who wanted to stay rich, but in this case it was true. They were crazy about each other and as happy as kids playing house. It might have been a blinkered dream and little to do with reality, but that didn't much matter as long as the dream stayed the same.

Inevitably, things changed. David's first job, with a small company that made training films and videos, came to an end when the company did. He landed another, better paid and with very good prospects – the same advertising agency in fact that he was working for when he died – but the step up seemed like a step away from what he really wanted to do, and that was probably when the bad taste first set in. At about the same time Laura, who had been helping out with various dogsbody jobs, unexpectedly began making money from her neglected artistic skill. A friend proudly showed her a composite pencil portrait of her children she had had drawn from photographs. The kids looked like Venusians. The perpetrator had walked off with a fat fee. Laura had always been stronger on likeness than imagination, and gave it a whirl. The results were surprising and gratifying, but not to David. He didn't like her having to do it; there shouldn't be any more scrimping and scraping: his new job would give them a proper standard of living without her having to prostitute her talents like this. Pregnancy gave him the opportunity to convert his disapproval into insistence that she lay off. She was disappointed because she enjoyed the work, but realization that what David didn't like was the combination of enjoyment and success only came later – several years later, when he responded to her attempts to take it up again by tearing the drawings across and jamming them into the bin like fish-and-chip papers.

. . . At the house, where Jan had laid on buffet food, and bottles of spirits and cartons of orange juice, fetched by Ross from the local supermarket, lined the kitchen worktops, everyone strove valiantly to ignore the after-funeral paradox. How could you eat and drink and not be merry? Peggy, sipping whisky while taking up the whole sofa, told anecdotes about David's childhood, laughing tearfully. Talking out grief, as Laura's doctor had told her the other day, was an effective way of dealing with it and it seemed to be doing Peggy good. Not everyone came back, but Laura's neighbours, perhaps because of geographical convenience, were there, and though she didn't know them well she found herself rather monopolized by them, perhaps because she in turn was the only person there that they knew. Strange situation, bringing to mind her wedding: as the only children in either family were some distant cousins she hardly knew, these were the sprogs who acted as bridesmaids and pageboys and who appeared in practically every photograph, playing a leading role in a script that was really nothing to do with them.

Laura's neighbours from the left-hand side were an elderly couple called Stimson. She was a deaf and mumsy poppet, he a South African curmudgeon with hair growing out of his ears who often talked of 'back home'. 'Back home,' he said, a lot of his old friends were looking to get out of the country. 'What with the new situation there,' he said, hardly moving his lips, tiny eyes boring into Laura's. 'You understand.'

'You must call on us if you need anything at all,' Mrs Stimson said. 'We're old but there's life in us yet.'

'Anything,' Mr Stimson hissed. 'You name it.' Especially, he seemed to suggest, if it involved the use of a sjambok.

Laura's right-hand neighbour was something of a bane to her. She knew her only as Eileen, though she sometimes mentally referred to her as Wonder Woman. Eileen was getting on for sixty – a thing she often drew bashful attention to, usually when she was performing miracles of selfless energy – and a widow. Her husband had died of a satisfyingly long and complex and agonizing disease – satisfyingly, because this had allowed Eileen to exercise her gifts of indomitable resilience and cheerfulness. Spectacles gleaming, home perm a-wobble, dentures fixed in a permanent grin of aggressive optimism, Eileen now spent her days bustling on sensible flatties hither and yon, being indispensable to her grown-up children and anyone else who couldn't get out of her way quick enough. 'It's a good life if you don't weaken,' she would say, with absolutely no sense of irony. When she was not pushing a pram she was pulling a shopping trolley: Laura speculated that without one or the other she would fall over. The pram, and the succession of babies that occupied it, belonged to her daughter, who seemed simply to give birth and then withdraw from the scene. Maybe she was marketing her milk.

'I haven't seen you at Mass lately, Laura,' Eileen said now, slightly modifying her tone of upbeat belligerence in deference to the occasion.

The thing was, she never had, for the simple reason that Laura didn't go. But on first meeting Eileen, years ago, she had unwisely let slip that she had been raised in the faith, and since then Eileen, who was from Derry and a gung ho churchgoer, had never let it drop.

'No,' Laura said. 'It's not for me.'

'Well, now might be the time. The Church was a great comfort to me when I lost my Jimmy.'

'I don't know,' Laura said, glancing around for Simon, who seemed to have made himself scarce, 'I think I'd feel a bit of a hypocrite.'

'You might be surprised,' Eileen said, her face a few inches from Laura's. 'We all need something to lean on. Even the strongest of us. I remember talking to your David about that just before he died as a matter of fact. And he agreed with me.' Eileen, one of those people who refuse alcohol because they claim to feel just as good without it, took a sip of orange juice. 'He was a good man.'

Laura nodded vaguely. 'I'd better see where Simon's got to,' she said. (David had thought highly of Eileen. 'An amazing woman,' he'd said. 'Never seems to get tired.' Eileen had baking days, and would bring round cakes and pastries when she had made too many, which was often. 'How come,' David had said to Laura in what she thought of as his Only Joking voice, 'you never have a baking day?')

'There's a reason behind everything,' Eileen asserted after her. 'There's a Providence behind it all.'

Laura went through to the kitchen, where John Whiteley was nursing a whisky and talking to Ross. She was surprised that John had come back to the house, and she was more surprised when he touched her arm as she passed and said, 'Laura. Don't let me forget before I go. I've got some things of David's to give you.'

Things from the office, she presumed, nodding, though she couldn't think what. The only time she had been there, David's workstation had been notably bare. No gonks or comical signs, and no family photographs. Again she felt that profound, empty sadness as she thought of the man David had become. He didn't like things: he was the opposite of a magpie. Guilt ground at her. Had she made him that way? Had marrying her finished him, as he had raged at her not so long ago?

Snapshot: moving to Langstead, six years ago. Good reasons: it was close to London and David could commute very easily, and the property prices were reasonable – they could never have afforded a house like 19 Duncan Road in London itself. Then there was the quality-of-life argument, which was a little more dubious. Langstead had plenty of green spaces and a leisure centre and you could drive home from the retail park with your rose bush and your tin of wood-stain in the reasonable certainty that you wouldn't be stuck in an hour-long traffic jam or fired at by street gangs poking semiautomatics out of the windows of speeding hot rods. But there were still high-rises and housing estates which no one in their right mind would want to live in, and where the people who had to live in them drew some appropriately negative conclusions about the suburban dream. There were drugs and crime just like in London, but no vast urban size to put them in perspective. The lowlife was high-profile. Meanwhile no one on the lucky side of the fence bothered much with culture: like Christmas shopping, they could get it in London.

But Laura and David didn't know this back then. Langstead looked a good place to settle, and Duncan Road was a big step up from the Enfield flat. Here was solid pre-war brick, roomy drives, flowering cherries, long mature back gardens backing on to other long mature back gardens. Here were two large receptions and a quarry-tiled hall and a conservatory. Here was coving and a heated towel rail. Here was richness.

But how forlorn their furniture had looked, plonked down in the middle of it all. The general effect was as if they had just been burgled, the burglars having taken all the good stuff. So they began to decorate and accumulate. David was earning a decent salary, and they could manage it. But there was something dutiful about it – as if they were doing it to please the house rather than themselves. Somehow the pleasure that had attached, in the old flat, to buying a second-hand bowl and filling it with potpourri didn't materialize when purchasing a pine dining table and six ladder-back chairs.

A trap was closing round them, maybe, but it was one that plenty of couples survived with love intact. Probably it was futile looking for blame. David hadn't had to look far, once the bad times set in. Laura had alternated between accepting it – the guilt habit wasn't so easy to break – and, increasingly, rejecting it on the grounds that wage slavery and frustration weren't a sufficient excuse for clobbering someone when you came in drunk.

But there was one ineradicable guilt, now. There was no pretending that David had been any less unhappy with the situation than Laura, in his way; but the terrible difference was, his unhappiness had carried on right to the end of his life. For him it could never get any better. Meanwhile Laura was still alive, and young, and going through experiences such as looking at the clock with a thump of the heart at six because that was when David came home and she had to be prepared for anything from niggling criticism to full-scale combat, and then feeling a different thump of the heart as she realized he wasn't coming any more and trying, so hard, not to recognize that side by side with the bewilderment and grief there was relief.

She found Simon in his bedroom. He was sitting on the floor, chin resting on one upraised knee, a Rupert book open before him.

Laura ached for him. Her arms went out, but she reminded herself that sometimes, without meaning to, you acted on the assumption that children were like pet animals: a cuddle and a caress and there, all better.

'I was wondering where you were,' she said, kneeling down beside him.

'I got fed up,' he said. He kept his eyes on the book.

Laura looked at the page, her eye falling on an illustration of Mr and Mrs Bear on holiday. You could tell they were on holiday because they were wearing slightly more clothes than usual and Mr Bear was carrying a deckchair.

'Is this a good story?'

'It's the one where he finds this shell and you blow it and all the fish come . . . When does everybody go?'

'Soon, I think.'

'I wish they'd hurry up,' he said, and added after a long burning moment, 'Then I could cry.'

'Oh, love, you can cry now. You do whatever you feel.'

Simon pushed back his fringe. 'I want to cry but I can't.'

'I know.'

'Do you want to cry, Mum?'

'Yes,' she said; and she could feel her throat tightening.

'Mum. You know when I lost that money for the school trip,' Simon began to sniff. 'Dad said I was a little – he said little shit and he said he wished he'd never had me.'

'Oh,' she said holding him, 'oh, love.'

'Did he mean it?'

'He . . . I think he'd been drinking beer probably. And sometimes when you do that, when you drink too much, you say things you don't mean – things you really don't mean one tiny bit.'

Snapshot: David raging at her, a couple of years ago, shortly after her mother's death. 'Some women treat their men like heroes. Bloody plug-ugly slobs, bone idle, never bring in any money – and they adore them. And look at you. I don't think you know how to love a man at all. You should have stuck with bloody Jesus like your mother.'

'But you know,' she said now to Simon, her lips in his hair as she hugged him, 'you don't have to cry, either. You don't have to do anything.'

'You're crying.'

'I know. That's because you are.'

They both were, and she wondered if they both knew that it was for the wrong reasons.

'Shall I read a bit?' she said after a while.

'OK.' Simon wiped his face.

Laura read out the galloping verses beneath the pictures, her voice shaky with tears. The verses might be awful but, she noticed, they scanned perfectly. The rhythm was comforting: she understood why Simon had sought out these old genteel volumes.

'When I go back to school,' Simon said, 'will I have to tell everybody about Dad?'

'Well, I told your teacher, and she's told the class about it. But if you need to talk about anything, when you're at school, just tell Miss Robertson.'

'All right. I don't think I'll need to.'

Snapshot: David, just before last Christmas, responding to her final, insistent suggestion that they should go to Relate and try to sort their marriage out. Having begun by denying that anything needed sorting out beyond her feminine propensity to complaining, he had got to the nub of the matter on his fourth whisky. 'I'm not going to sit there with a bunch of freaks and trendies and people who've read too many bloody self-help books. I'm not going to spill my private business to some half-assed social worker in dangly earrings. That's you women's answer to everything, isn't it? Fucking jabber jabber.' And he had given an illustration of his own answer by kicking the Christmas tree over.

And that was when she had told herself she would have to leave him. She had told herself that before, of course; but this time she had listened, had taken it in, had even begun seriously to plan how she would do it. And then in the dull dead nothingy winter of the new year she had let the plans slip. She had decided on one more try for their marriage – if you could call decision what was really a kind of unconscious shifting of ground. If David refused Relate again, if he got violent one more time, if he showed any nastiness to Simon, if, if, if, then . . .

In other words, she had hidden.

'Laura?'

It was Reg. He had pushed open the door, and was looking at her as if he had caught her in the midst of a riotous knees-up. That was just Reg, though. She had seen him give that same rigid glare just before throwing his arms around his daughter and blessing her cotton socks.

'Peggy's getting ready to go,' he said. 'Marj don't want to drive in the dark.'

'Do you want to say goodbye to Nan?' she asked Simon.

He nodded, polite and stoic, and they went downstairs, where Marj the spectral chauffeur was helping Peggy on with her coat.

'Bless you, love,' Peggy said, kind and a little sozzled, pulling Laura into a blundering embrace. 'It went off nice. You saw him off nice. It's all you can do really, isn't it?'

'Take care of yourself, Peggy,' Laura said.

'I shall be all right, gel. It's you I'm worried about. I wish I could be more use to you. It's not right, is it? I should have died first. Not him.' For a moment she sounded faintly aggrieved, as if she had been queue-jumped. 'Give Nan a big kiss, Simon love. Now you be good.' She scattered farewells: she had made friends with everybody. That reminded Laura of David when he was young; and the gong of terrible, insoluble regret sounded again.

The departure of Peggy was the signal for a general move, perhaps because the house looked so empty once she had left it. Mr Stimson, a sausage roll still in his hand, promised Laura a chat on international relations. Eileen beseeched her, threateningly, to give Mass a try. Jan, having done a miraculous high-speed wash-up, squeezed her hand and said she'd call.

Last to leave was John Whiteley. She thought, indeed, that he'd gone along with the others, and she was just about to start tidying up when there was an apologetic tap at the front door.

'Sorry – just been to fetch these from the car,' he said as she opened up. In his arms was a large cardboard box. 'David's things from the office.'

'Oh, of course,' she said stepping aside. 'I'd forgotten. That is kind of you, bringing this.'

'Well, you know,' he said vaguely, setting the box on the kitchen table. 'I mean, you may decide there's nothing here you want, but I thought it was just as well – you know.' He dusted his hands and stood looking at her and then away again. He was a handsome man in his late thirties, whose blue-jawed, high-cheekboned, lamp-eyed looks had been the subject of some of David's most scathing derision. 'So you're all right, Laura? I mean, obviously you're not, how can you be, but you know – managing. Coping.'

'Well, yes, those two,' she said with a faint laugh. She glanced into the box. Papers, mainly.

'I shall miss him at Fairway Denny,' John said. 'It won't be the same. You know, in spite of everything I think we could have sorted the trouble out. David was still a good man at his job. It's not the sort of firm to give a guy the bum's rush when there are a few problems. Still, it's no use thinking of that.'

Trouble? thought Laura. It was the second time John had talked in these terms. But he spoke as if it were something she already knew about, so she could only assume he was referring to increasing spats between himself and David. If David's temper at work was anything like it had been at home towards the end, there were bound to have been problems.

'Listen, I'd better be getting back. By the way, people in the office said to pass on their, you know, condolences. You've got my home number, haven't you? In case you need anything.'

'Yes, it'll be in David's – in the address book. Thanks, John.'

John left. Laura found Simon in the living room, staring at the TV. There wasn't, she saw, much tidying to do: a couple of filled ashtrays, a glass that Jan had missed. The room had a faint, not disagreeable smell of other people in it – hairspray, perfume, aftershave, powder, tweed, leather.

Snapshot: a real one this time, for they had taken a photograph. The last party she and David ever held in this house. His thirty-seventh birthday. He was well-oiled but genial, and the photograph Ross had taken – it was still in a developer's envelope somewhere – had reflected it. Surrounded by people, smiling, glass in hand, David looking somehow like a man who had been rescued – a released prisoner, a hostage returned, triumphant and hopeful. The next day, hung over, mournful about his new age, unsupported by company, David had had one of his blackest moods and hit her. Life had taken him hostage again.

Laura mentally closed the album of *Our Marriage*. She sat down beside Simon and put her arm round him. Curiously, Rupert Bear was on the TV too, in a cartoon version with American voices. The Nutwood chums sounded like hoods. It was strangely insulting, but she watched it through. She was putting off looking in that cardboard box. The box, the cuddly greeting card, John Whiteley's odd demeanour – Laura, numb from facing up to unbearable things, had a feeling that the facing up was not over.

NINE

'Perhaps he didn't want to worry you,' was all Mr Bussapoon could find to say, nervously eyeing the array of papers spread out on his desk, like a Tarot reader finding nothing but doom and disaster in the cards and trying to think of a way to say it.

'Yes, it might have been that,' was all Laura could find to reply. She felt dazed. The cardboard box had not exactly been a box of delights.

'Well, as I said, all these companies and individuals will receive their due from your husband's estate once probate is granted. It does look a lot but I think with the life insurance . . . well, you should be able to keep the house.'

Bills, bills. Some were trifling: some, like the statements from David's credit card company, were not. But it was the sheer number of them that made her head swim. That, and the fact that David had been hiding them. Even everyday ones like gas bills.

Wondering how this could have happened without her noticing, Laura realized that the ones he purloined were the red ones, the reminders and warnings. The initial bill had been left open on the dining table; and she had assumed, as no reminders came after them, that they had been paid by direct debit from their bank account as usual.

But now it turned out that the direct debit facility had been withdrawn some time ago. And when those red reminders dropped through the door David had spirited them away, and put them in his desk at work, and let them get redder and redder.

That was how it had happened. But as she cast her eye over the alarming collage of debt assembled on Mr Bussapoon's desk, Laura saw that it wasn't that simple. It was unfair to say that David had done this on his own, because she had collaborated. She had collaborated by doing nothing, by not noticing, by closing her eyes. With her marriage on the slope, she had let everything else slide too.

Sitting in Mr Bussapoon's office, Laura admitted to herself that she had been hiding from the truth. And having admitted it she did not go straight back into hiding again: she shouldered her portion of the blame for what had been happening. This was one of the strange things about the death of love. The most basic interest went with it – the ordinary decent sympathetic interest that you would show towards a friend's or even a casual acquaintance's affairs. If she had not been so closely tied to David in the meshes of a failing relationship, she would have taken more notice: she would have cared more.

This was a shocking and shameful revelation to her. And it would have been worse if her attention had not been continually distracted by that one particular bill, just to the left of Mr Bussapoon's right sleeve.

It was a telephone bill, but it wasn't theirs. The name on the bill was Ms Vikki Trayford, and the address was in Ealing. It was an itemized bill, and their own telephone number appeared on it a couple of times.

Vikki Trayford.

There was something familiar about that name, but Laura couldn't place it. She kept trying, and then giving it up and going back to the primary question: what was Vikki Trayford's phone bill doing in David's desk?

'I think you should draw a distinction between these various creditors,' Mr Bussapoon was saying. 'The utilities – well, perhaps if you could pay *something* to them, until probate is granted, and notify them to that effect. Have you had a DSS payment yet?'

'Yes, this morning.' The Widow's Payment. How archaic the terminology was – it called up images of Old Mother Hubbard, of Hans Andersen crones gathering sticks in an Arthur Rackham forest.

'Anything you can throw at them, then. To avoid disconnection. There's nothing to be done about the arrears on the mortgage – the lenders will have to wait for probate, which they'll understand anyway. Likewise with the Inland Revenue. These are your basics. Now on the other hand there's this loan from the Beneficial Bank—'

'I never knew about that,' Laura said; and for the first time she articulated the thought: what the hell was he spending it on?

'Ah-hah,' Mr Bussapoon said, neutrally. He was wearing half-moon glasses today, which made him look more subtle and judicious than ever. 'Hire purchase agreements – they're not usually transferable. The only significant ones are on the cars.'

'We've only got one car,' Laura said.

'Oh.' Mr Bussapoon scrutinized inscrutably. 'Well, there are payments here on a Cavalier—'

'That's ours.'

'And payments outstanding also to a London dealership. Harling Motors.' The solicitor raised his eyebrows.

'Search me – we've only got one car,' Laura said, and had to fight off an urge to laugh hysterically. Don't ask me, he was only my husband.

'Well, no doubt all will become clearer when the estate is distributed after probate,' Mr Bussapoon said tactfully. 'This – ' he fingered the inexplicable telephone bill – 'wouldn't seem to be in your husband's name, so that's nothing to worry about.'

Maybe not. But it was certainly something to think about. Add it to the astonished bafflement with which she learnt of the financial hole David had been digging himself into, and she was pretty well ready for her head to explode.

The only thing that was not surprising, she thought as she left the solicitor's, was that David had not been able to tell her about it. Because that was the whole point: this was the sort of miserable mess their marriage had got into. Maybe if they'd got on better he could have told her about the money problems, but then maybe if they'd got on better there wouldn't have been money problems – and so it went on. Every cause was a symptom and every symptom a cause.

She knew he had become difficult about money: sometimes the squander-bug bit him, other times he bemoaned every penny. But he had always had contemptuous words for people who got themselves into financial fixes. He was particularly scornful of the homeless, saying they must have been unpardonably irresponsible to have ended up that way. And if you had to name something more dislikeable than these opinions, it was the expression on his face as he voiced them.

Still marvelling, she dropped into Boots to buy sleeping tablets, which her doctor had refused to prescribe her. It was running away from the problem, he said, and he didn't want her to become dependent. So she just went on buying a proprietary brand, the makers of which were presumably very happy for her to become as dependent as anything. In the perfume department she heard a saleslady of a certain age advising a male customer. 'There's the body spray,' she was saying, 'or there's the Owe DeeToilet.' Confidence, Laura thought, was everything: the lady made that sound like not just the right way to say it but the sophisticated way, the way of inside knowledge.

'Have you used these before?' the pharmacy assistant demanded cutely before handing Laura the sleeping tablets. 'They are only for temporary sleep disturbance and not for long-term use.' Everywhere now were chummy, hectoring robots like this. A simple phone call to the water board elicited the chirpy reply, 'I'm Debbie, how can I help you?' It was enough to make you long for the days of the anonymous jobsworths.

VikkiTrayford.

Laura had a hundred things to worry about. Perhaps it was the sheer volume of worries that made her brain select the most trivial, and gnaw over the question of where she had heard that name before.

She drove home: it was the first time she had used the car since David's death. It had been very much David's domain and there had been some bad moments this morning when she had seen his driving gloves tucked into the pocket on the door and the little heap of change he kept on the dashboard for parking fees. Always a cautious driver, now she found herself handling the car with an almost fearful respect. These were dangerous machines, and it seemed crazy that ordinary human beings were so readily permitted to be in charge of them.

A second car . . . Where the hell did that fit in?

She turned into Oberon Road, home ground. All the streets in this district – the residents would never call it an estate – were named after characters from Shakespeare: she remembered David joking, early on, about there being no Bottom Close or First Messenger Gardens. Later, though, he became very loyal to his patch, in a prickly way. Perhaps some part of him despised it, but it was his.

Vikki Trayford. Laura disliked that double 'k'. It was takki, also yukki. It made her think of mirrors with pictures of Laurel and Hardy on them.

She told herself to forget about it as she turned into Duncan Road, which was still February colourless, its neatly pollarded trees looking no more alive than the lampposts regularly spaced between them. She checked her watch, noting anxiously that it would be another two hours before Simon finished school. Today was his first day back, and it had been a wrench seeing him off this morning. He was bright and had lots of friends, and he seemed to be coping well now – but still school was a pitiless arena to enter carrying a hurt and vulnerability such as Simon must be experiencing. TV kids might gather like tender fawns around a bereaved playmate, but the real thing were more likely to see him as a freakshow.

Going in, she decided she would prepare his favourite tea – make a fuss of him. This would also help keep her mind from churning over the baffling things she had learnt this morning. This turned out to be unnecessary, however; for she had barely begun slicing the cauliflower (Simon had very idiosyncratic tastes) when she was interrupted by a visit from Angie, a person who never claimed less than your undivided attention.

'Laura. You must think I'm the world's biggest bitch and I've got no excuses except that I was *away* on this damn course and then I had to go and see Mum and Dad because he was ill and actually stay for a couple of days, which was too much. My God, how are you? I couldn't believe it when I heard, I mean I *literally* couldn't. Come here.'

Angie, who went in for hugs in a big way, got hold of Laura and did some fierce squeezing and back-patting. 'It's good to *see* you. You've really been in my head a *lot*,' she said, letting go at last. She habitually talked with these thumping emphases, which were very like underlinings in a speech. A small, dark, ringleted woman with huge eyes, she was dressed in a short padded coat and canvas trousers that gave her something of the look of a Chinese peasant. Her little feet were clad in boots rugged enough to climb Ben Nevis in, though she worked in an ultra-modern office in Langstead town centre, as an education co-ordinator for the local health authority. Laura had met her at, or outside, the child welfare clinic when Simon was small;

perennially forgetful, Angie had lost her car keys and Laura had helped her break into her battered Mini. They had been friends since then, though the friendship was not of the constant and everyday sort Laura enjoyed with Jan. Wildly busy, and with a complicated love life, Angie could only descend on her at periodic intervals like a benevolent whirlwind. Perhaps as a result of her career, about which she was passionate, Angie's kindness tended to take an instructional form: she was likely to turn up out of the blue and briskly instruct you how to use a Femidom or urge you to throw away your aluminium saucepans. David had loathed her.

'Let's look at you,' Angie said, shedding her handbag, about the size and weight of an infantryman's pack. 'You look tired. Are you on medication?'

'Nothing prescribed.'

'You're getting grief counselling, of course.'

'No. I don't really see the need—'

'My God, you *must*. I'll give you a number to ring.' Angie knew of a counsellor for everything: you could probably get counselling for being in counselling. 'Listen, you've had people saying how sorry they are and asking how you're coping and all the rest of it. You've got sympathy fatigue. I'm not going to do that. But probably nobody mentions David. People are scared of talking about a dead person. Do you want to talk about him? I've got some time. Let's do it. Memories, feelings. It's your agenda.'

'Well, not really, Angie, I . . . I'm just really pleased to see you. You tell me what you've been doing. Is your father better?'

'Sure. It was flu. I've *told* him to have the jabs every autumn, but no.' Angie was a little dismissive: illness had to be sexually transmitted or the result of industrial conditions to engage her full interest. 'I had to stick around, though. There was the usual emotional blackmail. Plus they're selling the house and it all had to be *clean* for this prospective buyer. As if they were being *judged*, you know, for respectability. I mean, it was like a shrine already. God, my place is a *tip* but I wouldn't care who saw it, you know, because it's me.' Though a generally devoted daughter, Angie could not quite forgive her parents for giving her a nice middle-class upbringing instead of dragging her up in a slum.

'What was your course about?'

'Oh, updates on AIDS treatments and preventives. There's some iffing and butting about the use of non-microwavable cling film as a protection in oral sex, but on balance I shall still advocate it.'

Laura didn't mean to begin laughing. She didn't know why she was doing it, and it must have looked terrible. But she just couldn't help it. She sat down at the kitchen table with her head in her hands and whooped and snorted.

'That's good,' Angie said eagerly. 'That's a good reaction. Now we're getting somewhere.'

'Oh, Angie, I'm sorry,' Laura moaned helplessly.

'Yeah? You're bereaved, your emotions are shot to hell, you've a million things to work out inside yourself, and you feel you should apologize?'

'It must look like I'm raving bonkers. And I haven't even offered you a cup of tea . . .'

'So now you have to be the perfect hostess too. I'll make the tea. Sit there. Let it out.'

'But there really isn't anything to let out. I mean it is out anyway. I mean . . .' Laura sighed. 'I don't know what I'm supposed to be thinking or feeling any more. It's too weird. We – we weren't going through a good time, David and me. Damn it, we were near the end of the road. Then this happened. And it's terrible. And it's terrible in a different way because I half-hated him. And now I've found out this morning that David had got us knee-deep in debt. Plus . . . it looks as if he may have been playing around. But if we were . . . I mean, why should I care about that?'

'Because you're human,' Angie said, filling the kettle, her Betty Boop eyes wide with interest. 'Feelings are what they are. There are no rules. So tell me, did you have any suspicion of this before – David playing around?'

Laura couldn't answer for a moment. She was remembering evenings when he rang to say he was working late: evenings when she refused to admit even to herself her relief that he wasn't coming home yet, that there was a few hours' reprieve before the back-tightening tension began.

'Maybe,' she said. 'But – well, it shouldn't matter.'

'Deception. Betrayal. These are going to give you strong feelings of hurt and negativity, no matter what the circumstances. Listen, it's all right to feel *anger* at a dead person, you know. Being dead doesn't put them on some pedestal.'

'I know – I see what you're saying. But I ought to just let it rest, surely. For Simon's sake. He needs everything I can give him just now. We've got to make a new start. That means practicalities first – and, God knows, it looks as if they're going to be difficult enough.'

'OK. But listen, Laura. Practicalities are all very well.' Angie made heavy-handed tea and banged the two mugs down on the table. 'But you can't put off a confrontation with your feelings.'

Can't you? Laura thought. It seemed to her that she had been doing precisely that for several years. She knew it was axiomatic with Angie, and the world Angie belonged to, that nothing could be really buried: repressions manifested themselves, skeletons came clattering out of cupboards, internal dragons roared until slain. Laura wasn't so sure. Living a lie might be bad, but it wasn't that hard. Probably you could go on with it for ever, if nothing else intervened.

But something had, in her case. Everything had changed, and she was going to have to change with it. The alternative – to go on being the frightened, self-deceiving, self-despising wife of David Ritchie – just wasn't on, because he wasn't around any more. She would have to take her hands away from her eyes and have a good look.

'What about Simon?' Angie said. She held the mug of tea by the rim and sipped hastily: the action suggested years of Styrofoam cups from vending machines in institutional corridors. 'Is he talking? Or is he bottling it up?'

'A bit of both, really,' Laura said, truthfully. She couldn't fit Simon's reaction into any classic pattern. Like her, he was just all over the place.

'I'll give you another number,' Angie said, scribbling. 'Child grief counselling is a different ball game. And just remember, you're not alone. I'm always— Damn.'

Her mobile phone trilled from the pocket of the Madame Mao coat.

'Yep? Oh, heavens above. Oh, buggery. Yep.' She interrupted herself to mouth 'Sorry' to Laura, who was used to this. Angie was always being urgently summoned and having to dash, presumably when somebody needed educating about health very, very quickly. 'OK. Give me ten minutes. Bye.'

'It's all right,' Laura said pre-emptively, as Angie slotted the phone away and grimaced her contrition. 'Don't worry. It was really nice of you to come.'

'Listen, we'll talk, yes?' Angie hefted her bag, staggering a little on the backswing like a weightlifter, and then gave Laura another of her hugs. 'I think you're doing great. I *swear* I'll make time and we'll talk.'

But Laura felt, waving her off, that the talk had been done, and that it was good. And though she headed straight for the phone once Angie had gone, it was not to ring either of the numbers she had scribbled down for her.

John Whiteley, his secretary said, was in a meeting; but he rang her back within a few minutes.

'Laura. How's things?' He sounded weary, also a little wary.

'OK, thanks, John. Hope it's all right to ring you like this—'

'No problem, no problem.'

'Only I wanted to, um, say thank you for bringing over David's things from the office and also to ask you – er, ask you something if that's all right.'

'Fire away.' Now he sounded more wary than weary.

'You said something about all these problems of David's.'

'Yes . . .' the intonation almost made it *No*.

'Well, I just wondered what you meant. Were there problems at work?'

'Ah, some.' John coughed. 'Sure, some. I mean, David wasn't . . . he wasn't entirely at home with his work just lately. Not giving his best. Often he was . . . Damn, it seems bad talking like this, you know, after what's happened. To be honest, I don't like to dig it up for no reason.'

'Could you think of me as the reason?' Laura said. 'I wouldn't ask if I didn't really need to know.'

John sighed. 'Well, this is precisely it. Not knowing how much you knew. I mean, David's absenteeism was getting pretty bad, for one thing.' He left a pause, which Laura did not fill. 'Also I'm afraid his drinking was a bit of a problem. I tried to cover up but the MD's no fool. You know, it was – it was obvious, he would come in in the afternoons just stinking.'

'I see.' She didn't feel the need to say more: the revelations were beginning to have a grim relentlessness of their own.

'Um, the thing is, he was liked here, Laura. Really. When people began to get fed up it was the things he was doing rather than David himself.' John hesitated, seeming to examine this not wholly coherent statement. 'Borrowing money. Not paying it back. I mean, we all have cashflow problems, but it was just getting a bit ridiculous. You know.'

'No,' she said. 'This is it. I don't know. Are there people at the office who are – out of pocket?'

'Oh, don't worry about that. Thing is, people just . . . refused, in the end. Especially when . . . Look, Laura, this is putting me in a difficult position,' John pleaded.

'Yes, I'm sorry.' It was reassuring to know – at least, David would have been reassured to know – that flat-stomached, groovy, heartbreaking John could be as little-boy mournful as any man when pressed. 'But I do need to know.'

'Well, people wouldn't lend him any more when they found out where it was going. One evening someone saw him at this . . . there's a casino not far from here, Euston way.'

'Oh.' She couldn't think what else to say. A casino. The very word was weird, faintly silly, like cocktails and wife-swapping.

'And there's a branch of Ladbrokes across the way who, er, got in touch with me one day. A cheque drawn on the company account. Oh, I had him on the carpet about it, and we talked it through, you know. I'm just glad it came through to me and didn't go higher.'

That bastard Whiteley wouldn't help an old lady across the road, Laura remembered David saying. Her cheeks burnt with transferred shame, as they used to in company when drink turned him deadly and vindictive and he would wait, grinning and watchful like a goaded dog, for someone to commit the error of saying something he disagreed with.

'Look, like I say, we sorted it out,' John said, interpreting her silence. 'I think we were really on our way to a new start, which is what makes it such a terrible pity . . . I'm afraid all this is news to you.'

'Um, it ties in,' Laura said. 'The money thing does – does tie in.'

'So when I said about David's problems – basically I meant what we could see at this end all too clearly. That's all.'

'Yes,' Laura said, 'thanks, John, you've been . . . Do you know the name Vikki Trayford?' she said, blurting it out.

'Sure. That's Tom Trayford's wife – well, ex-wife. Divorced a year or so ago. I think you might have met Tom at an office do, maybe? He's been with us a long while. Well, came to us about the same time David did. Yeah. Tom. Nice bloke. Vikki too, nice woman I mean.' These last spurts were plainly a substitute for what he really wanted to say: *Why do you ask?*

'Oh, that would be it, then,' Laura said blankly, needing to say something, not knowing if the words made any sense.

'By the way, Laura, David's last month's salary should be going through to his account about now. We, er, rounded it up, you know.'

'Oh, right, thanks.'

'Shit, I'm feeling that I should have, you know, said something about all this.'

'No, no.' How could he? she thought, thanking him and ringing off. It wasn't his job to say something.

Maybe it had been her job to know. To guess, to gather, to divine. Yet she hadn't. David had become difficult, untrustworthy, sporadically violent, and a drinker. Yet she had thought of these things as somehow exclusive to her orbit: had perhaps even imagined David away from her as the original David, the nice David she had married.

Now, it seemed, David had not so much had a secret life as the same life multiplied to the extreme.

Gambling. That was the thing that made her feel as if she had walked into an unlikely dream. Not just the bookies but the roulette tables. There was something so cheesy and old-fashioned about the picture it called up – something out of a seventies film. Men in purple ruffled shirts and big bow ties, and women looking like Nyree Dawn Porter.

'My God, David,' she said aloud, 'what the hell were you playing at?'

But as with most such questions, she felt she knew the answer, deep down.

Laura went back to preparing Simon's tea. There was another phone call she had to make, but it could wait, now that she knew why she had to make it.

TEN

Flat 2, 29 Beckford Road, London W5 turned out, the next day, to be hard to find, and even when she rang the bell Laura wasn't sure. The name plates by the four doorbells were all blank or illegible. The place itself was unrevealing to an unnerving degree. It was in a small straight street of terraced Edwardian houses that seemed, uniquely, not to have gone anywhere sociologically interesting – upmarket or downmarket, ethnic or WASP, owner-occupied or rack-rented. It might have been anywhere.

Yet when the woman answered the door, Laura somehow knew at once that this was Vikki Trayford. Bottle-black hair in a grown-out bob, cheekbones, long angora sweater carefully pulled out of shape, leggings. While Laura could faintly remember meeting Tom Trayford at an office do, as John had suggested, she hadn't ever seen this woman before. She just knew.

'You got here, then,' Vikki Trayford said, holding the door only partly open, as to a salesperson.

'Yes.'

'Traffic bad?'

'Not too bad. Can I come in?'

'Well, yes.' Vikki made a half-hearted welcoming motion. 'I mean, I don't really know what this is all about.'

'Like I said on the phone,' Laura said distinctly; beset by misgivings and collywobbles on the drive down here, even to the point of feeling physically sick at one point, she was now clear-headed and almost businesslike. 'I need to talk to you about David.'

'Uh-huh. Your husband.' Vikki moved aside, not much, to let her in. 'Come through. You know, I – didn't really know him all that well.'

This had something perfunctory about it, like an apology for the mess. Which Vikki made, sighingly, as they went into a living room that was decently furnished but had something dismally squirrelly and den-like about it. The curtains were closed, the roaring gas fire intensified the intimate smells, and a portable TV pantomimed, volume down, in lurid off-colours. The magazines and embrowned coffee cups and dirty clothes had not been artfully left about: they had just been left about. Most of all, the room had no suggestion of time of day about it. It was noon, but in here it was anytime.

'Have a seat.' Vikki had been, thus far, restrained and even heroic in not giving Laura the full assessing head-to-foot look, but at last she went ahead and did it, under pretence of shifting the coffee table to make room. 'I'm sorry, by the way. To hear about it. It must have been an awful shock for you.'

'When did you find out? You said you knew, last night when I rang you.'

'Er, it was the day after it happened. I think. Yes. Want a drink? It's cold out.' There were bottles on a corner table – gin, whisky, vodka, a fair stock. 'I'm having one.'

Laura shook her head.

'Yes, I . . .' Pouring vodka, Vikki seemed to decide to cross the bridge. 'I rang his office, and they told me.'

'You'd been expecting him?'

'He'd said he was coming, the night before. That is a different thing entirely. Different from me *expecting* him.' Vikki sat down on a cushion with a swift gathering in of her legs that suggested she had either had some sort of dance training or fancied herself as the sort of person who had. 'Look – I know what you think—'

'You don't,' Laura said. 'Because I don't. All I know is . . . since David was killed, I've found things, in his stuff from work, there was your phone bill for a start—'

'He said he'd paid it,' Vikki said with a displeased look. 'Then last week along comes a reminder. So much for that.'

The businesslike strength suddenly, dismayingly left Laura and she couldn't speak. She ached with miserable hurt and anger.

'Have that drink,' Vikki said. Her shoulders were round her ears and her eyes were peeping up at Laura in a way that, with its coy calculation, its shy sussing, reminded her strikingly of someone. After a moment she had it: the Princess of Wales.

'Did you know David was married?' Laura found her voice, and it came out sharp. Yes, there was anger at this woman, but not her alone: the anger included David and herself, the whole destructive dance they had played out.

'Yes, I knew.'

'No doubt he said I didn't understand him,' Laura said, drawing in a scornful breath.

Vikki got up, poured another vodka, and handed it to Laura. 'He never said much,' she said quite levelly. 'Hardly anything, really, as far as that went. Drink that drink and listen. It was a crush. Him on me.' Again she folded balletically on to the cushion. 'You may know I was married to Tom, at David's office. We split up. Nastily. I moved here. I'd met David, maybe once or twice, through Tom's work, but I never . . . well, he was just someone I vaguely knew. Then I bumped into him once on the Tube. And then he started ringing and coming round. He kept doing it. At first it was, you know, if you need to talk, need a friend, all that.' In Vikki's voice as she spoke of David there was a faint, resigned undertone of contempt that Laura found horribly recognizable. 'I know he must have skipped off work a lot. Don't know if Tom knew. Probably not. He's seeing someone else and *very* wrapped up in her. Anyway, that's how it went on. It was a crush. David was – well, maybe obsessed is a bit strong, but he certainly wouldn't leave it alone.'

'Did you sleep with him?'

Vikki lit a cigarette, puffing painstakingly and then delicately exhaling, just as if it were a cigar.

'Once or twice,' she said.

Once or twice? Laura thought. Once, or twice? How could she not *know*? And then she realized that she couldn't remember the last time she had slept with, in the sense of made love with, David. And the realization stilled her anger. Because that was how it was, when it didn't mean anything.

'I didn't feel right about it,' Vikki said. 'It was a while ago. He knew I didn't . . . I didn't want that any more. If I ever did. But he just kept coming round. He said he wanted to help me, look after me. Wanted to be someone I could lean on. God, I don't know. I was having money troubles. There were the payments on my car, which I really do need. This big phone bill came in. I mean, I just *mentioned* them,' Vikki appealed, princessing again.

Laura, taking this in, felt a great black mass of scathing judgement soar up from her. But, like a barrage balloon, it just hung there: it didn't descend. Because really, morality didn't come into it, certainly not at this late stage. Most people weren't heroes, anyway. You only had to look at the unheroic situations they created.

'I couldn't stop him,' Vikki said. 'I mean, he said he could afford it.'

'He couldn't,' Laura said: simply offering the information.

'Well,' Vikki said, tugging her pullover down over her knees with a curiously prim action, 'I didn't know that.'

Laura found herself thinking about David in this flat, with its clutter that he so disliked, the subdued light that he couldn't bear . . . But the bitterness she felt, though acute, also had something distant about it. It was as if she had already experienced it; as if she had always known, subconsciously, that this flat with its resident helpless look-but-don't-touch siren existed for David and made him, partly, what he was. That it was a crush, a one-way pursuit, fitted exactly. If David had been planning to head off into the sunset with the woman of his dreams, he would have appeared a lot happier than he had.

And now she knew it all, pretty well. Vikki Trayford might have been lying, but Laura doubted it. There was nothing to be gained from lying, and Laura understood, or disliked, the woman enough to detect that as her primary consideration.

But there was, as Columbo would say, just one more thing.

'Did you have a quarrel?' Laura said, tasting the fiercely strong drink Vikki had given her. 'Just before he died?'

'Mmm. We had a bit of a . . . well, he was coming on strong again. He'd been drinking. Said he wanted more than I was giving him, said he deserved better, you know. And then he called me a – well, a tease is nearly the word.'

'Did he hit you?'

'God, no.' The look of surprise on Vikki's face seemed genuine; and it was followed by a certain creeping smugness, as if to say no man would ever lift a hand to *her*.

Well, well. Laura swallowed it down, as she swallowed the vodka down, wincing and just hoping she could take it. She recalled the phrase: *what doesn't kill you makes you strong.* Well, she would see.

'I think,' she said, taking the cuddly hedgehog card from her handbag, 'this was probably meant for you.'

Vikki took it, looked at it. Her expression was unreadable.

'I'm afraid those car payments won't be kept up,' Laura said, getting to her feet.

'Oh, they weren't anyway, not after a while,' Vikki said promptly. 'That was more bullshit. So really, we're both in the same boat.'

Laura's teeth clenched tight. She had tried to be fair, but there was a limit.

'Did he ever mention Simon?' she snapped.

Vikki looked at a loss.

'His son. My son.'

'He said he hadn't got any kids,' Vikki said, with a strange wonder. Then she started to cry, wetly, droopingly. 'Like I told you, it was a crush. I tried to stop it. I should have . . . But he saw himself as this knight in shining armour, you see. And it's flattering when you're on your own . . .'

Tears are a strong trigger signal. Laura found herself making an involuntary movement – to touch, to comfort – instinct momentarily overcoming what was a pretty well-founded aversion.

But what stopped her was a belief, equally instinctive, that Vikki Trayford did a lot of crying, and for precisely that effect.

As if on cue, Vikki peeked up through her tearful hair at Laura heading for the door, and said, 'You're going?'

'Yes. Thanks for seeing me.'

'How old are you?'

The question took Laura by surprise.

'Thirty-three,' she said.

'Same as me . . . You look younger.'

'Thanks.' True enough. It was no big deal: Laura knew she just had one of those faces. Probably it was something to do with her propensity to put on weight, which as yet was a potential rather than an actuality, her nervous or nervy energy staving the fat off and giving her that soft unfledged look. As soon as her body met its buxom destiny, the years would show.

'I never meant any harm,' Vikki said.

'Neither did I,' said Laura. 'And look where it's got me.'

This, though, introduced a note of self-pity that she did not want. She certainly didn't want to be Vikki Trayford's co-victim or sob sister. So she got out of there fast, with a goodbye as breezy as if they were chums adjourning a chinwag.

She was glad, though, as she got in the car: glad she had come, seen, spoken. In the most brutal sense, David was the past, in so far as he could never be anything else. Now that past was mapped, its white spaces filled in. And so it was time, somehow, to put it away.

ELEVEN

She reached Langstead in time to pick Simon up from school. Feeling strong and purposeful, she was pleased to find Simon apparently in similar fettle. He was full of what he had been doing, which included telling an overinquisitive schoolmate where to get off.

'She kept asking where my dad was buried. I said he wasn't, he was cremated and she said what's that and I said it shows you're stupid.' Having satisfyingly vanquished this tormentor, he had gone on to make an exceptional wax resist picture and known how to spell umbrella.

So that was all right. Except it wasn't, as teatime became evening. Simon behaved like a pain – maddening repetitions, determined carelessness, empty giggles, sulks, the whole brat repertoire. Laura did a lot of gentle probing to find out if he had something new and troubling on his mind, and was a long time realizing that she was on the wrong track. Simon was not a TV kid, and there didn't have to be anything at the bottom of it. He was just manifesting a child's chaotic normality – exercising his glorious freedom to be beyond cause and effect. Understanding this made it less bewildering, if no less wearing, and she was glad to pack him off to bed.

And then – sitting down before the TV, preparing to bathe her eyes and mind in anodyne soap – Laura found that she was not feeling strong after all. She felt like old cabbage leaves in a dirty sink.

Unlike Simon, Laura wasn't free from cause and effect. Today she had confronted the woman who would have been her late husband's mistress if she had liked him more, and on whom he had lavished money which, as Laura had also learnt just recently, he simply did not have. And it was all very well to say that the experience had strengthened her, made things clear to her, set her mind at rest, and bracingly freed her for the challenges of the future. It was all very well, and it was probably even true, but still the experience had been bloody awful and, the pain of it welling up inside her, Laura bawled.

For fear of alarming Simon she had to keep down the decibel level of the pagan hooting and crooning by burying her face in cushions and biting till she almost gagged; but at any rate that stage did not last long. After the deluge came a period of lonely and silent lamentation that did not get any better. This wasn't catharsis: this was what happened when you came to the end of your rope.

Laura felt bad about many things, but the thing she felt worst about was her capacity to go on feeling bad in new ways. From David the boozy bully to David the cheating rat shouldn't have been such a great leap: neither was very nice and both, as she was now fully recognizing, had gone for ever. Yet the whole Vikki business had left her staggering again, just as if she had gone to London today expecting to find that David's secret life involved running an orphanage or ferrying meals on wheels.

So at some level she must have still cared. Perhaps this told her something about human nature, but she could have done without the information. She wanted, if anything, uplift. It was a measure of how low she felt that her thoughts turned momentarily to the religion on whose bitter teat she had suckled. Perhaps, after all, she should follow Eileen's unflagging flatties down to Mass: perhaps the call back to the fold had come at last, the call that her mother and her grandmother and their pet priest had always warned her she would hear some day. She remembered a quotation her mother had approved, something about being tied to a piece of string that was long enough to let you go right round the world but pulled you back with one flip of the finger. Waugh quoting Chesterton, or perhaps it was Chesterton quoting Waugh, or perhaps it was Graham Greene quoting both of them: all her mother's fave left-footers seemed to take in each other's washing. A dismal idea, whatever. Faith as an unbreakable leg-iron.

No, no church for her. Perhaps she should turn to drink instead; though the vodka Vikki had given her made her feel nauseated on the stop-start journey back out of London, and she couldn't fancy any more. Maybe, she thought, this was her lot: maybe life, like water, always found its own level, and this was it. Life just wasn't going to get any better. She remembered reading some Sunday newspaper article about the happiest days in people's lives, and dwelling on the proposition that, if such a thing existed, you might already have had it. Suppose there were some way of finding it out? Some kind of office where a functionary consulted a database, and then said, 'No, I'm sorry, madam, you had your happiest day back in 1986 and there really isn't anything to compare with it in your future. There is a patch of modest contentment due in 2009 but basically it's downhill from here . . .'

Now she was laughing. Her head felt light, about to float away. So strange, the emotions: they really didn't form much of a spectrum. The wail of someone crying in mortal loss and the wail of a toddler over a dropped ice cream were exactly the same in tone and timbre and intensity – *exactly* the same. Did that mean they were both equally sincere? Well, sincerity was absolute, not relative, so they must be. You were either sincere or you weren't. Thus emotions weren't such a big deal, when you thought about it. Telling herself this, Laura felt worse than ever. And then there was a knock at the door.

Jumping up, she was conscious of a guilty wish for it to be Jan. Guilty, because she was afraid the sight of her friend's face would set her off on a maudlin confessional, and Jan must surely have had enough of that by now. How often Laura had winced at the advice of agony aunts who counselled the agonizer to talk it out to a sympathetic friend or family member – what about, she thought, the poor sod who had to listen to it all?

No, she wouldn't do it: she darted into the downstairs toilet and flannelled her face to erase the tears, because Jan being Jan would see and ask, and it wasn't fair. But it would be good to see Jan anyway, not lean on her, just see her . . .

Opening the front door, Laura found herself whisked back to the day the police had come.

The figure standing there was tall, as they had been; and stood stiffly and respectfully back from the porch, as they had done. What was more, she had seen this man on that very same day. The image came freshly to her mind, though as far as she knew she hadn't summoned it consciously or unconsciously since then: the little warm hospital room with the window looking out, in, and this man pressing his hands against the glass and gazing in at her. Big and mature and bear-like, and yet with a somehow awful vulnerability about him.

'It's Mrs Ritchie, isn't it?' he said. His voice was at once gruff and curiously light, like that of a youth whose voice has just broken.

'That's right,' she said; and as he was silent, seeming to wrestle with a shyness that again was oddly boyish, she added, 'Can I help you?'

'Ah, not really,' he said, and a spasm crossed his face. 'Well, maybe . . . if you'll let me just have a word. My name's Mike Mackman.'

He paused as if the name should mean something to her. It did, but it was a moment before she remembered, a moment during which he hung his head – actually hung his head before her, not theatrically, but in a way that to Laura's church-sown mind suggested the religious – the *pietas* and Annunciations, martyrs and flagellants, the spooky storyboard of her childhood.

Mike Mackman: the name on the huge floral tribute at the crematorium. She had seen it in print somewhere too – it came to her now; the official inquest report. Of course, of course. It all came together.

The driver. Whiplash and shock. No blame. Accidental death. Mike Mackman.

And here was the odd thing: she hadn't thought about the driver of the car, hadn't wondered or speculated. She had just viewed him as, if anything, an impersonal force of nature like a fire or a flood or a massive myocardial infarction. The idea of a flesh-and-blood person being responsible for David's death, even though unintentionally, simply hadn't been part of her mental furniture since the event, perhaps because there was no room.

And now that she did think of it, she did so with a peculiar hop of viewpoint. She saw it through the driver's eyes, and it looked pretty awful from there too.

'Your husband's accident,' Mike Mackman said, lifting his head, looking with painfully blue eyes into hers. 'That was . . . I was the one who was driving the car.'

'Yes,' Laura said.

'Look, I quite understand if you – you know, if you don't want to see me,' Mike Mackman said. 'I really do understand. Only I thought I should. I would have come before, I kept wanting to, but I didn't want to intrude on you and . . . Same with the funeral, I wanted to pay my respects but the idea of me turning up there just seemed . . . it seemed . . .'

Laura nodded, partly to try to relieve him of what seemed a mounting distress. 'Yes, I see,' she said. 'Well, er, the flowers were there. Thank you for that.'

'I just wanted to say sorry. I don't know how you say sorry for a thing like this, it's crazy, it's terrible, but I just wanted to try and . . .'

Laura hesitated, looking at the big cumbrous man hovering there, pink-cheeked and stricken, arms hanging by his sides. She was feeling down, down enough to hide in the corner and rock. Today had been the pits, and the last thing she wanted was to conclude it by talking all about David's death with the man who felt responsible. Enough was enough.

And yet she had made that hop of viewpoint, and it changed things. She, after all, had everything from a daily batch of Eileen's scones to the phone number of a counsellor who specialized in exorcising the psychological demons of thirty-three-year-old road accident widows with one Irish grandparent and an 'r' in their names. She didn't suppose this man came in for any of that; and he looked burdened.

'Would you like to come in?' she said.

'Thank you.' He didn't just say it: it burst out of him like a long-held breath.

She led him through to the living room. Size was her abiding impression of him, but here in her home where everything was, as it were, a measuring stick, she saw that he wasn't really tall: his hair didn't slightly brush the fringes of the central lampshade as David's used to when he crossed the room. Mike Mackman was just sizeable. Nothing tapered: his neck, his arms, his legs were all massy and trunk-like. Recalling the life-drawing classes of her arty youth, Laura remembered the schematic figure technique that reduced the body to two parallelograms, shoulders and hips, connected by a waspy waist and adorned with pipe-cleaner limbs. That just wouldn't work with this man: he was all blocks. Fortyish, she thought, despite the fairness, which was of the sort that usually faded after thirty. He had on a suit which was neither cheap nor fancy, and which he seemed used to wearing, without looking in the least like a businessman. While he was rather awkward, no smoothie, he wasn't clumsy either. Generally – and it was impossible to say precisely what this impression consisted of – he looked like a person with a stake in the world.

But his eyes sought hers like a boy's, like Simon's when he had done something that he couldn't gauge the adult response to, when he was all at sea in the awfulness of childhood.

'I saw you,' he said. 'That day. At the hospital. Some sort of waiting room. They took me in – after the accident. Outpatients, it wasn't anything. I came trying to find out . . . what had happened. The feller I hit, whether he'd . . . I saw you in there. I knew. They wouldn't tell me anything, not yet. I knew, though. I just knew. After a while, when I kept hanging around, they told me he'd passed away.'

Odd to hear that phrase, usually to be found only on the lips of the old, though he made it sound more respectful than evasive.

'It did me in,' he said, quite matter-of-fact. 'It did me in completely. To think that I . . . I mean, the accident was terrible. Shocking. The way it happened. I mean one minute I was driving along and the next minute there's this man from nowhere really, up on your . . .' He stopped abruptly with a snapping motion of his jaws, as if he were literally biting his tongue. His baleful eyes tugged at Laura's. She shook her head faintly, feeling she should make some response, though she didn't know herself what she was conveying – it's all right, please don't, go on, don't go on. 'But you expect wonders, don't you? Surgery and hospitals and everything, you expect . . .' He hung his head again, shuffling. 'It did me in. When I had to go to the inquest I felt like I . . . I wanted to ask them to lock me up or something, I don't know . . .'

'No,' Laura said. 'It was an accident. They told me about it. It was one of those things – you couldn't help it.'

'I couldn't,' he said, with a sudden grim energy. 'I swear to God I couldn't. But that doesn't make it any better. At the inquest I . . . it was terrible. I thought you might be there. I'd have to look you in the face. Then when you weren't, I felt like I'd got off lightly. I don't know. I was in a daze. Then it was in the paper. Father of one, it said. Little seven-year-old boy. Christ.' He swayed mournfully, his jaws working. 'There was a kiddy without his dad. I know there was nothing I could have done, but . . . that's a hell of a thing. There's a husband and a father gone because of you.'

For a moment Laura, weary and heart-wrung, misunderstood that *you*. Ah, no. He meant him.

'I just keep thinking of that day. Wishing I'd never gone out. I mean, it was business, but I didn't need to be there that early. I'm a builder, you see. Mike Mackman Builders.'

She nodded, accessing a fuzzy visual memory of these words, red and white, on scaffolding and the sides of vans.

'We're doing a site over Goldcrest Park. Starter homes. But I mean, I didn't need to be there at that time. No need at all. I'm just a bit of an early bird by nature . . . I wish to God I wasn't!' he added, with that same anguished gust of energy.

'It couldn't be helped,' Laura said, and thought: I'm comforting him. How weird. Yet fair enough, maybe. He did look in need of it. 'You shouldn't worry about it.'

'Well.' He shook his head vehemently, as if she had just offered him a kindness generous beyond the possibility of accepting. 'I had to come, anyway. Just come and see you, and . . . well, it was only right. I'm sorry – bringing it all back. Only I had to, you see. Couldn't live with myself otherwise. I got rid of the car, by the way. Scrapped it.'

'Oh . . . goodness, you needn't have done that,' she murmured: with what she had learnt of their finances, any mention of extravagance alarmed her.

'Oh, nothing,' he said, and his absence of expression showed he meant it. 'I just wish I could turn back the clock.'

Again she momentarily misunderstood, and thought he meant the milometer on the car. Then, seeing, she said, 'Oh,' and the hysterical giggle bubbled up again and she plonked down into a chair and then, helpless as a heaving drunkard, she was back in her crying fit.

Not so deep in it this time: part of her mind pulled back, disapproved, told her this waterworks stuff was a bad scene. But it also understood why. She had been crying before, and like sneezing or hiccoughs, tears tended to recur. And besides, crazy as it might sound, here finally was someone who sort of understood what she and Simon had been through. The death of David Ritchie had been a shattering event for this man too, if in a different way. She even felt less alone, in a way that she supposed support groups made you feel.

And perhaps she was crying too because here, it seemed, was a man with a conscience. And she had spent the last couple of days walking in the footsteps of a man who, it seemed, had had absolutely none at all.

'Sorry,' she gasped, 'sorry sorry.' Enough: this was a bum deal for the poor man, who was already in a state. 'Not you – I just had a bad day.'

She saw, through the desperate swatchings with the heel of her hand, that Mike Mackman was standing in a kind of wordless, speechless wonder and slowly extending towards her, like some delicate living thing, a neat clean handkerchief.

'Oh – thanks,' she said. The feel of the handkerchief elicited some old, consoling folk memory: these things belonged, like brown earthenware teapots and the wooden toggles on duffle coats, to a different tactile past. It was too nice to dampen. 'I really am sorry about this.'

'My God,' he said. He did not so much sit as drop down and find a seat underneath him. 'My God, this is . . .' He was stranded again in muscular, staring silence.

The strange thing was, Laura was quite together again: the jag was over; like the drunk straightening up shaky and refreshed, she knew she had finished. The one who was at the pitch of misery now, she could see, was Mike Mackman. Her husband's killer – he must see himself as no less.

'I'm sorry,' he said, with a trancelike glance about him and a vague motion towards getting up. 'I've made it worse, coming here. I'm so sorry. I shouldn't have . . .'

'Really, it's OK,' Laura said. She couldn't explain what it was that had set her off – that it was not the pure undiluted grief of loss he supposed but something much more complicated and ignoble, an accumulation of stresses that felt just now like layers of ineradicable grime. And yet she had to explain, somehow. 'It's like I said, it was a bit of a bad day. A lot of things to do, you know, niggling things, ordinary problems. Made me really tired.'

'I'm going to go in a minute,' he said rigidly.

'No, no, I didn't mean that—'

'I will though,' he said. 'I don't want to trespass on your grief.' Again he invested the slightly quaint and old-fashioned language with a sort of ingenuous dignity. 'But I need to know what I can do. That's the other thing. When I came . . . I wanted to know if there was anything I could do.'

She was used to being asked this. *If there's anything I can do . . .* It was what people said when confronted with bereavement (the subject on which she had became a dismal expert). But the way he said it was different. It wasn't a stock response. Big bristling head lowered, he demanded it intensely. He wanted to know.

'That's kind of you,' she said. 'But we're fine, really.' As he did not moderate his look of determined interrogation she went on, 'Everyone's been very good. Friends, neighbours. Family. Solicitors. Simon's teachers. Everyone.' She was getting stuck here. Still his eyes bored into hers. It occurred to her, for some reason, that he would not be an easy man to lie to.

'These niggling things you mentioned,' he said. 'Problems. What about them?

'Oh, you know . . . everyday life.' She shrugged, hoping that would do.

'I realize it may seem none of my business,' he said. 'Only it is, in a way, because I'm responsible.'

'Please, you mustn't think that—'

'Just the way it is,' he said with a wave of his big scrubbed hand. 'What were these problems you mentioned? Practical?'

'Yes,' she said, grabbing at that because it seemed easier, less heavy. 'Just practical things, you know—'

'Money,' he said. 'Are you having difficulties? Again, it's not my business, and you can tell me to clear off. Only it is my business.'

'No, really, we're managing very well,' Laura said, beginning to feel very slightly trapped. 'These things just take time, you know, probate and so on.'

He studied her, like a fair but tough and painstaking copper. 'Your husband was the breadwinner, wasn't he?'

'Well, yes—'

'So you're not going to be managing very well. The family's lost its breadwinner. Husband, father, breadwinner. Gone. Now I want to know what I can do.'

'Honestly,' she said, 'we're fine.' She was touched – both profoundly and purely touched, as one is by the gift of a child, made without the self-considering calculation that lurks behind all adult offerings. Because, shattered and conscience-stricken as this man might be by what happened, he quite plainly wasn't doing this to make himself feel better. (A stratagem she knew: back when quarrels between herself and David were rare traumas instead of daily occurrences, she would repair her side with wine-accompanied dinners and little prezzies by his plate and would know, even then, deep down, that what she wanted was to feel less awful *herself* and that in that respect it was money well spent.)

Touched, then. But rather nonplussed too. She didn't know what else she could say. It was kind of him to offer but there really wasn't anything he could do – which was a convention most people readily accepted.

Suddenly, Mike Mackman was looking raptly over at the TV. For a strange moment she thought his attention had been captured by the silent spectacle of a game show. Then he lifted a slightly unsteady finger.

'Is that your nipper?'

'Oh – yes, that's Simon,' she said, realizing. On top of the TV there was a school photo of Simon, hair glossily combed as no child's hair was ever combed except in school photos, the purpose of which seemed to be to produce an image which looked as little like the real child as possible: they might as well have given them false noses and whiskers.

'He's in bed?' Mike said, at the same moment lowering his voice and moving over to the TV with almost pantomime care.

'Yes. He was full of energy today. Tired himself out at last.'

As Mike picked up the photo and studied it Laura saw on his face something that was unusual nowadays – nowadays when childhood is a minefield, the child an icon of ambiguous vulnerability and the hospital-chart of society's sickness. He looked at the little boy in the picture as if he were not afraid to. He looked with an unabashed, Dickensian sentimentality.

'Nice age,' he said, putting the photo reverently back. 'Full of interests at that age, aren't they?'

'He's very lively.'

'Computer games, is it? That's what they all seem to go for now.'

'Not yet. It'll come, I should think.' Simon had a little hand-held game, a novelty really: the techno bug had yet to bite. She rather dreaded it, because she would be shut out. Raised on the lush anthropomorphism of Disney cartoons and Narnia stories, Laura looked uncomprehending at those fizzing screens with their primitive hard-edged graphics and relentless nonentity protagonists. 'Have you got children?'

'Me, no. I would have loved to. My wife and I separated before . . . you know.' He smoothed his moustache thoughtfully. The moustache too was slightly unusual. On men below pensionable age, Laura knew only two types of moustache, gay and dodgy-geezer. This was neither. It was an unaffected statement of maleness, and, like much about him, old-fashioned in a not dislikeable way.

'So,' he said. 'Tell me what I can do.'

'Really, there's nothing,' she said. An untruth that was a strict truth. She had problems galore, she didn't know whether or how they were going to manage, and it would be very nice indeed if someone could step in and make it all better. But no one could. That was the point. It was up to her to stand on her own two feet, and she meant to do it. She might have let herself down with a crying fit or two – but then it was during the course of those, somehow, that she had decided she had better shape up or else. It was nobody's job to get her out of this, and certainly not the man who happened to be behind the wheel of the fatal car. His concern did him credit, plainly he had already suffered over this thing, and that was enough. 'It was very kind of you to come and see me, and . . . please, don't torture yourself over it because it was an accident, it was a terrible accident and – and they happen.'

'But I must be able to do something,' he said doggedly. Though it was more than dogged, which implies trying, pursuing. He didn't shift ground: just massively, stolidly repeated himself. 'I must be able to do something.'

'Thanks, but we're OK,' she said, getting up – an action that should serve to make him change track if not actually leave.

'I've robbed you and your son,' he said. 'I've got to try and pay something of that back.'

'No, no, you shouldn't think in those terms—'

'Well, who's going to look after you?'

Kindly meant, no doubt: more paternal than patronizing, really; and of course he couldn't know what she knew; but still. Coming on top of what she had recently learnt about David, this was a bit much to take.

'I'll look after myself, and Simon,' she said as temperately as she could.

For a moment, as he stared at her, she thought he was just going to repeat himself again, and in mild despair she wondered what she could say to convince him.

And then he surprised her, breaking for the first time into a smile. It was a tight, frowning, intense sort of smile: it didn't make his hairline go up, as the smiles of serious people usually do. And she saw that he was the sort of manly man who smiles to express admiration and approval, not cheer.

'You're brave,' he said, huskily, almost melodramatically except that he was so patently sincere, 'you're damn brave.'

She had strong doubts about that: where was this courage three months ago? But she couldn't, of course, say anything of that to him; and in fact the whole consciousness of being something of an imposter fretted her. This admiration was the last thing she wanted, or felt she deserved.

'Simon maybe,' she said uncomfortably. 'Not me.' Realizing she was still holding his handkerchief, she held it out to him.

'Keep it.'

'No, no, I couldn't.' As he wouldn't take it she had to press it on him hurriedly. Keeping a handkerchief struck her as unlucky or unwise for some reason. Maybe a memory of A level *Othello*.

'Right,' he said, pocketing it at last, and speaking with sudden decision. 'I've kept you long enough. Just let me give you my card and I'll be off.'

She was relieved. It wasn't that he was horrible or anything like that. His presence was just so insistent – he was so very *there*: she needed to breathe. The card came from a heavy tooled leather wallet. It simply said, in bullish capitals, 'MIKE MACKMAN, BUILDING CONTRACTOR'. There was an office number and a home number. She felt somehow that she shouldn't be taking it; but he was already heading down the hall for the front door, with a speed surprising in so big a man.

'Thank you for coming,' she said, as the cold night air whipped in. 'It was kind of you.'

He didn't seem to be listening to her. He crunched down the path, shoulders square and head lowered, an economical sketch of single-minded motion. And then with his hand on the gate he turned round and said, 'Don't forget.'

She didn't know what she mustn't forget, so she said, 'No,' vaguely and agreeably. Meanwhile he gave her a long arrested look that seemed to include the lit porch and doorway that surrounded her and the black shape of the house around that: it must have looked something like those novelty Christmas cards you held up to the light. Too potent an image, in fact, for someone as troubled and punctilious as this man seemed to be, and all at once she felt she should have said something more, something conclusive and dry and accurate.

'It wasn't your fault.' That was all she could think of, and by the time she had called it out he had got into his car (not *the* car) and the purposeful *whump* of a powerful engine had drowned out her words.

TWELVE

The long mature back garden of 19 Duncan Road led on, via the respectable interposition of a tall creosoted fence, to the long mature back garden of a house in Beatrice Road – what number Laura didn't know. All she knew – apart from the fact, in which all the residents of the Shakespearean enclave were secret sharers, that the backs of the houses were very penny-plain compared to the bay-windowed carriage-lamped fronts – was that a family lived there who had a son in his young teens. You could often see him in his back bedroom window, where he sat at a desk staring away from his homework into wistful teen dreams, and you could often hear him too. Quite unusually for the district, he played loud music. Being a teenager, he liked to have the window open, even in cold weather, so as to broadcast it; an impulse which Laura remembered, and correctly identified not so much as a rebellious wish to annoy as a rather sad hope that people would listen, like it as much as you did, and generally know what you were all about.

Laura's neighbours on right and left often complained about this, to Laura at least. 'Thet led,' Mr Stimson would hiss at her, the syllables as curt as a jail door slamming. 'You hear him? He needs a good *talking* to.' And Eileen too, though mumsy tolerance of youthful high spirits was surely on her saintly CV, had words of disapproval. 'The lad ought to turn it down a little,' she quacked. 'His mommy and daddy should tell him. I don't mind it but it's the bebbies. You've got bebbies around here and bebbies need sleep.'

Laura usually murmured vague agreement through the maltreated vowels, but in fact she had never minded the music that floated across the frigid grid of lawns and clotheslines. There was life in it, and sometimes it had seemed, during her years at Duncan Road, that the place had been designed to exclude life altogether. Often all you could hear from the boy's bedroom was bass and beat, nothing intelligible – a radio transmission from a distant galaxy; but to Laura it was mildly uplifting nevertheless.

And in the weeks following David's death – weeks that ponderously became a month and then, leaner, brighter, put on speed – she kept hearing one song across the gradually defrosting gardens, and willy-nilly it became her mantra.

The lyric cheerfully and repetitively emphasized that it was necessary to roll with it. Laura wasn't sure of the band: in her own youth she had embraced a polite variant of Punk called New Wave, and after the musicless years of marriage it remained the only pop she knew chapter and verse, whilst Simon was still at the indiscriminate stage, liking advertising jingles and dancefloor mixes and Strauss waltzes equally. But whoever and whatever it was, she took the message in. You had to roll with it.

As in: take what came your way, roll with the punches, ride the waves, keep your head above water, take the rough with the smooth, keep on trucking . . . It was as good advice as any she got at that time. Sometimes, on bad days, it seemed almost mocking, almost ironic in its application – but at least it was still relevant. It understood. And this could not be said for Peggy, with her kind and nostalgic gaspings down the phone about the times Laura and David had had together: nor the well-meaning Angie, who in the course of several more comet-like visits prescribed, not counselling any more, but recruitment. Use her experience: contact organizations; donate her learning-and-suffering fourpennorth to this acronym and that helpline . . . But Laura didn't want to share with other women whose partners had died and left them staring at unpaid bills and love letters with someone else's name on. She had enough of that, living it. She wanted it to stop.

And the song understood as even ever-understanding Jan perhaps could not. Even before Laura had made her dilemma of grief clear in that outburst over the ironing board, Jan had surely known that all was not well with their marriage. But empathy could only go so far when you started from where Jan started from, which was a marriage as happy as they came. Of course one never knew. Behind closed doors and all that. And yet one did know. Ross Coombes was a paranormal buff and subscribed to various flaky magazines which proved to their own satisfaction that the Egyptians had built the Great Wall of China and that there was an anthropoid monster living on the Isle of Wight, and Jan, rational to the core, sometimes rolled her eyes . . . But that was it; that was what the bastard quotient in Jan's man amounted to. And so inevitably Jan assumed that David had left behind him more of a residue of decency than was the case.

The case was bad. David had not just got into financial difficulties. He had plunged; he had vastly overstretched; financially speaking, he had invaded Russia without winter clothing or supply lines. Or, the two of them had. Laura might not have contracted the debts or even known about them, but she still couldn't acquit herself of complicity. She had been a lily-livered ally in the whole débâcle, an Italy perhaps, dreamily pretending everything was all right while the snows fell and the troops retreated in starved columns.

And so she could only roll with it; she could only collect together the bills and warning notices that kept turning up crumpled in David's pockets and stuffed into crannies of the car. She could only wait for probate, meet the creditors' demands, and then see what was left. Subtly informed by Mr Bussapoon, and the evidence of her own eyes, that what was left would be sweet damn-all, Laura knew that big decisions impended. She would have to sell the house and she would have to get a job. And fortunately, as the bewildered mists lifted from her mind, she found that she also wanted to do these things.

'Somewhere smaller,' Jan said, nodding. 'Easier to manage and heat.'

Made sense. The house had been sold to them as a four-bedroomer; though when a couple of years ago they had briefly toyed with the idea of selling and moving, the estate agent's draft details had named three bedrooms and a boxroom. The dimensions hadn't changed – it was just that four bedrooms sounded vulgar, eightiesy, carporty. People wanted to pretend their houses were small now. They wanted boxrooms and steep stairs and authentic inconvenience. But whichever way you looked at it, the house was beyond Laura and Simon.

'And then I dare say there's the memories,' Jan said, leaving it at that.

Yes, the memories. A move of home was the traditional remedy for that, though Laura had private doubts about how much even that could do. She had already begun disposing of David's clothes, bit by bit, a bag here and a bag there to various charities. Beyond that it was tricky – the hi-fi had been chiefly David's baby, but Simon liked to listen to it; and what about this umbrella – his or hers . . . ? These, she supposed with sorrowful insight, were the very quiddities and quibbles that separating and divorcing couples had to concern themselves with. And they showed you how little, once two people had committed themselves to one another, each could call their own: really it came down to the clothes, which the other person had no use for. Moving home was sensible, it was a way to begin again, but it could only do so much. To marry and live with and have children with a person was to put them right inside you, in your blood, and a complete transfusion was impossible.

She had discussed the idea of moving with Simon, who was excited, as children generally were by ideas. Move, yes – let's do it now. Later, saying goodnight to him, her hand on the light switch, she heard him clear his throat in the bed and then, after a couple of solemn eye-blinks: 'Mum?'

'What, sweetheart?'

'When we move, will it be a long way away?'

'No, not if you don't want.'

He exhaled, blowing out a child's long-brewed, suffocating, silent anxiety. She knew she should have made herself clearer, and hurried to do so. She hadn't thought of leaving Langstead. For her part, there were friends and familiarity, which she had nowhere else. London, which sometimes on summer nights could be seen faintly glowing like a mass of radioactive matter beyond the parkways and golf links south of the town, offered only fairy prospects; and most importantly, Simon was settled here. There were his friends, and there was his school – she wanted to keep him at the same one if she could manage it. A couple of conferences with his class teacher had established that he was doing well, that after suffering an inevitable dip his work was fine, and that he had a circle of playmates there at least as bonded as Rupert and his plus-foured comrades.

So, they would stay in Langstead. Reassured, Simon wriggled in the bed with new excitement.

'Nearer town?' he said. 'Will we move nearer town?'

That too would make sense, if it could be managed. Shakespeareland, in the way of such places, was rather cut off from amenities. The only shop was a tiny crammed emporium on the corner of Miranda Avenue called Josie's. Josie herself had retired years ago and her place had been taken by a tall lordly Sikh; but he had kept the sign, kept the trade name, and gradually taken on the name itself. 'Any new wool in, Josie?' old ladies would ask as he loomed, bearded and testosterone-soaked.

But even Josie's closed occasionally, and then the estate was a petrified forest of TV aerials, bleakly residential. Nearer to town would be better, especially as Laura wasn't sure whether they would be able to keep the car. Much depended, of course, on the job which she intended to find and about which Jan was rather more hesitant and judicial.

'Full time?'

'If I can square it with looking after Simon. The benefits would keep us, just, but it'd be tight. And apparently your widow's entitlements aren't affected by earnings. So it would make sense.'

Because she wanted more for Simon, more security, more possibilities. Of course. At the root of this, though, was the matter of his heart and mind. She didn't want him to observe the scrimping and draw conclusions such as: Dad went away and we were left with no money. And so resent his dad, which wasn't fair; or resent her, which wasn't fair; or both of them, ditto. Such a tangle inside him mustn't even start.

It was up to her, then. A challenge to be faced. She had been very bad, for a long time, at facing challenges. So bad that she had refused even to face facing them, which at least she was doing now.

'It's tough,' Jan said, 'getting a job. There's so little nowadays.' She was too kind to point out that it would be even tougher for someone who, like Laura, hadn't worked for years and had so little under her belt that employers wanted.

She did have something – the old secretarial qualification that some benign spirit had pressed her to go ahead and get, in the intervals between loafing sexily about David's flat, way back in pre-nuptial Manchester. Apart from that it would be, as Jan said, tough. Langstead was southern-prosperous, but sometimes it looked as if all that meant was half the working population commuted while the other half sold birthday cards to each other. As for Laura, she had lost confidence during the years of motherhood and housewifery: the world outside these things had gone on without her. Yet here too there was progress: Laura now went out more, and did more things, because she had to. Married to a David who became ever more hypercritical and demanding, Laura had stayed in and cultivated homebody accomplishments because it was something she could do well that he approved of her doing. Also to go out was to go away from him, manifest less than total absorption and delight in the fact of his existence. But again, even taking into account all the sulks and bullying and manifold manipulation, to blame him was a cop-out. She had collaborated in her own stunting. Now she had to come out of hiding for Simon's sake, even if she still didn't like herself enough to do it for her own.

'You managing all right, duck?' Peggy huffed down the phone. 'He left you all right, did he?'

'Yes, we're fine, Peggy.' Laura hadn't told her mother-in-law about the debts, seeing no reason why the old lady should lose her son twice over.

'Ah. He was good like that. Looked after his own. Still, it's a job, isn't it? Managing the pennies. I wish I could be more help to you. When we win the lottery, eh? Reg has got it all worked out . . .' She went on to detail the various fortunes Reg was going to bestow on his kith and kin when his numbers came up, sounding as admiring as if he had actually done it. The lottery, Laura noticed, had produced a widespread outbreak of self-esteem. Lots of people could now congratulate themselves on their generosity with phantom sums. Usually they were the same people who would lend you a fiver with as much willingness as a Dobermann surrendering its last pup.

Anyhow, it was up to her, not Reg, not Peggy. And certainly not Mike Mackman.

The first cheque arrived two days after his visit. Her initial thought, when it dropped out of the envelope and she glimpsed the figures and bar codes, was that it was a bill, or an invoice, or a reminder, or one of the computer-generated *non sequiturs* that kept coming her way in response to her straightforward explanations that Mr D. Ritchie was dead ('Dear Mr Ritchie, please forward your customer number so that we may prepare a full statement').

But no, this was not a debit but that rarest of rare birds, that

December rose, that Hadean snowflake, a credit. The cheque was made out to Mrs L. Ritchie, for five hundred pounds, and signed M. J. Mackman.

Laura, who had been impatiently ripping open the post while the milk for Simon's Ready Brek agitated on the stove, sat down at the kitchen table with the traditional flop of the flummoxed.

There was a note on blue writing paper, in handwriting that was literate and schoolboyish and somehow – the image of his earnest face came back to her as she saw it – painfully sincere.

Dear Mrs Ritchie,

Thank you for seeing me the other night. It was kind of you and I'm sorry for disturbing you. Please accept this to help you in your present difficulties. It is the least I can do, and if you are in need of anything else at all, don't hesitate to contact me at the above address and telephone number. Once again I am so sorry for what I have done and want to make amends.

Your sincerely, Mike Mackman.

The address, printed on a gold stick-on label, was Champaign Park – a modern executive development on the outskirts of Langstead which used to make David run a twitchy finger under his collar whenever he saw or heard tell of it. 'Oh yes, all double garages and Georgian windows. Watch it fall down in ten years' time. Just watch it.' It wasn't casual. David really wanted Champaign Park to fall down.

The pan of milk hissed, extinguished its flame. Laura jumped up swearing, just as Simon made his usual freefall descent of the stairs. Most of the milk was lapping around the hob. Enough remained only for a *nouvelle cuisine* portion of Ready Brek, to Simon's wheedling disappointment.

'Isn't there any more?'

'That's all the milk we've got. You could have some toast.'

'Eer.'

'Come here – your jumper's on inside out. Where's this hole come from?'

'Don't know. What's that letter?'

'Nothing much. Do you want some of this juice?'

'It's gone off. Mum, you know that school trip, can I go?'

'What school trip? It hasn't gone off.'

'It smells funny. I gave you the letter. The castle thing of London.'

'Perhaps it has gone off a bit . . . Oh, yes. The Tower of London. I should think so. It's not yet, is it? Where's your lunchbox?'

'You have to pay the money now. I think.'

'All right, I'll find the letter later. Where *is* your lunchbox?'

It would have been a lie to say she wasn't tempted. For perhaps fifteen minutes that morning, the time it took to get Simon to school and to come back to the house and look again at the cheque lying on the kitchen table, Laura lived with the temptation, cohabited with it, got to know it. But by the end of the fifteen minutes, Laura and the temptation were through.

By the standards of temptation it was a very brief affair. She could remember being tempted to poison David's coffee for a whole evening: going further back, she recalled a two-hour temptation to smack the chops of her mother's pet priest who, invited to tea, had only taken his eyes off her seventeen-year-old bosom to examine what he found in his teeth. And this temptation didn't even have that much going for it. It might have been a good thing to have punched out the leching padre, leaving aside the consequences. But cashing that cheque was unthinkable, as she found out as soon as she thought about it instead of just feeling weak and harassed and ready to take any easy way out.

What was remarkable, she thought as she sat down to write a quick reply and return the cheque, was the insistence. Emotional as Mike Mackman had been on his visit to the house, she had supposed that the visit itself had been a catharsis for him – indeed, she had hoped so, because it was plain that he had been feeling pretty awful about the whole thing. Now it seemed that the burden hadn't been lifted after all. In spite of all she had said, he still felt responsible. And so had taken this surprising, drastic step.

She didn't know how she felt about it. It was bizarre. It left an unpleasant taste, although the gesture still had that clumsy chivalry about it and there really wasn't any suggestion of money making up for the loss of a life. Mostly she was conscious of hassle, and she didn't want any more of that just now. She was looking forward to the day when there were no letters on the doormat.

Still, a cheque was different from a confessional. Cheques were suggestive of an urge to have done with things. 'Look, I'll write you a cheque,' people said, meaning, *And that's the end of it.* So, she hoped, it might be with Mike Mackman. And she hoped that his getting the cheque back wouldn't make any difference – would even, perhaps, draw a line under the line. *Well, I did all I could.*

She wrote, 'Thank you, but I can't possibly accept this. It was good of you to come to see me, but as I said we're fine and there's really no need for you to think about this any more. Yours, Laura Ritchie.' She enclosed the cheque and sent the letter off at once.

Four days later she came downstairs to find the usual brown drift of morning mail heaped on the doormat. Right at the bottom there was one pale blue envelope addressed to her in big sincere handwriting.

Right at the bottom. Like hope in Pandora's box. And what, incidentally, was hope doing in a box full of all the evils of the world? An odd bit of packing. Wouldn't have suited David, who at the supermarket checkout was achingly fastidious, and had once become wrathful over her putting long-life pizza bases in the same bag as chilled goods. 'Refrigerate *after* opening. See? Clear enough?'

Laura knew, sort of, before she opened the envelope. Hassle had a feel, a smell, and it was here now.

There was no note. Just another cheque, signed by Mike Mackman. Made out to her, for a thousand pounds.

Laura watched the milk pan this time, served Simon with his full measure of Ready Brek, poured him juice from a freshly opened carton. In control, she took him to school and at the gates handed him an envelope containing the money for his school trip, breaking only moderately into the sweat that all financial transactions occasioned in her now (*where's it coming from? how much this week? how manage?* were the marginal jottings her mind made at such times). Then she went back home to face that cheque and its accompanying freight of hassle.

There was a phrase she had heard amongst children older than Simon, and which for all she knew he used himself when away from her. It was a common enough phrase in adult lingo too, but the young seemed to use it differently. 'You're taking the piss,' they said. And they did not mean, as an adult might, 'You're kidding me!' with an implicit readiness to be amused and convinced. The scepticism in the words was both deep and flat. It was an absolute rejection, with a hint of deprecation at a lapse of taste, and a bit alarming. They would have said it to the Railway Children, running up to tell them that the three fifteen was going to run smack into a landslide unless they did something – 'You're taking the piss.' They would have said it to Elliot, inviting them to take an aerial bike ride with E.T. On the other hand, they would probably have said it to Hitler and all his searchlit theatre too – 'You're taking the piss.'

Now Laura found herself echoing the phrase and its stymied disdain. Perhaps not its pitilessness; because you had to feel sorry for whatever the man was feeling to make him do this. But the cheque was so ridiculous . . . and she didn't like whatever it was that had made him up the ante – a belief that she had turned it down because it wasn't enough? A belief that her defences would be worn down by adding noughts? Or that she just didn't think he was for real?

Well, she didn't, in a way. 'Get real' – that was another of unimpressible youth's deadpan tags. 'Get real.' 'Get a life.' It helped to think in these terms. It kept at bay that slightly trapped, suffocated feeling that she had experienced when he had come to the house and which the sight of the cheque revived in her. The trouble was, youth didn't acknowledge human frailty, whereas she lived and breathed it. In her response to this cheque, this hassle, she had to take into account that something was up with this poor guy.

She could just tear it up and forget about it. But then Mike Mackman might suppose for a while, until his bank statement said otherwise, that she had cashed it. In any case, it would seem that she had reacted to this cheque differently from the first one. Not a signal she wanted to send, because not clear. She wanted the same signal – thanks but no thanks.

How to say it, though? The assertiveness gospel – she had read the books – preached the broken-record technique: you got your way by saying exactly the same thing over and over. Laura tried to remember precisely what she had written in her first note, but she doubted the efficacy of this – because what happened if you came up against another broken record? Assertiveness only worked if the people you were dealing with weren't assertive. Once everybody had read the books, the fun would really start. People would be hitting each other over the head with chairs.

She had Mike Mackman's phone number, of course. But a moment's thought nixed that idea. She wanted to end communication, not open up new avenues. Not because she hated him or anything like that – though he might well see it that way. As far as he was concerned he had destroyed a happy family, and if the bereft widow didn't fly at him all nails and teeth it was because she was exerting the maximum of self-control. Impossible, of course, to convey to him the true, complex, twisted shape of things. But she didn't want to convey anything to him: that was the point. She just wanted him to get on with his life.

'Get a life,' again.

The cheques were visible proof that he wasn't doing that. She hoped they weren't proof that he *couldn't* do it. If so, all she could think of was that contemporary panacea called Getting Help: Angie, for example, would probably know of some counselling service for people in Mike Mackman's situation.

But Laura concluded that that just wasn't her business. Guilt – her allergy, her condition, her perennial distemper – crept familiarly over her as she concluded this, yet it didn't disable her this time. She rolled with it; and after a very few minutes' indecision put the cheque in an envelope without a note, addressed it to Champaign Park, stamped it and took it down to the postbox on the corner.

For a flippant moment, as she dropped the envelope through the slot, Laura tried feeling good about herself. A cheque for a thousand pounds in her name, and she was getting rid of it! Rubbish, though. This situation was no comedy: there wasn't a laugh in it. The business with the cheques was giving her a dentist's appointment feeling, a feeling of discovering a lump under the skin, a wake-in-the-night-and-worry feeling. Just let it stop, and then she could lighten up. Or rather, she could go back to worrying about everything else, which at least had the comfort of familiarity.

The envelope dropped into the postbox, and Laura went home, and for the next three days envelopes dropped through her letterbox, and they were all brown and full of microchip mystifications ('Dear Mrs Bitchie, please forward your account number . . .') and that was it. The boomerang hadn't come back. What did come, on the third day, was a kind letter from Tricia, her cousin in Bournemouth. Tricia, always the lone outpost of sanity in Laura's family. Much occupied with the care of a young son who had spina bifida, Tricia hadn't been able to make it to the funeral, but her letter was warm and considered. Another pulse from the distant galaxy, telling her she was not alone.

That was a Friday morning, and it seemed like a pretty good one. Maybe not in the running for best day of her life, but as days went it looked to have a lot going for it. About eleven o'clock, it turned nasty.

THIRTEEN

Estate agents – that was her first thought when she answered the door to the brisk knock. She had some coming to look at the house, and supposed she had mistaken the day of the appointment. They were old young men in suits with fat necks throttled by tight collars and trademark haircuts and the sort of red slick hands you dreaded shaking.

Then one of them said, 'Mrs Ritchie? Is your husband in, by any chance?'

Laura said, 'No,' and then, perhaps because she had said it so many times in so many ways over the past month, didn't know what to say.

'We're from Meares Finance,' the same man said. He had a leather zip-up document case under his arm. Later, cursing herself, Laura realized that she shouldn't have been cowed by that, that Mormons and other doorstep flakes carried them, but at the time it had conveyed just enough authority, when he added, 'Is it all right if we have a word, Mrs Ritchie?' for her to say yes, or at least not no, or at least not to fling herself at them when they stepped past her into the hall.

'What's this about?' she said, following them. They went into the living room, but not before poking their heads, in solemn peek-a-boo, into the kitchen and the dining room.

'I wonder if you could tell us where Mr Ritchie is,' the man, obviously in charge, said, swivelling about and presenting her with a jaded bouquet of liquorish aftershave. 'He usually communicates directly with our office, and we were wondering why he hadn't been in touch.'

The second man, seeming free of the necessity of saying anything, was making a circuit of the room, hands wedged in his trouser pockets, looking at things.

'My husband's dead,' said Laura.

The first man's eyebrows went up.

'That's unfortunate,' he said

As a response to the news, this was original. It also told her a good deal about where these men's interest in her husband lay.

'Where exactly is your office?' Laura said.

'London.' The first man, the talker, sat down. He gave the little hitch of his trouser knees as he did so – one of those gentry tics that only the dodgy classes have perpetuated. 'Highbury.'

'I've never heard of you,' she said, with a confidence that was nearly total: she certainly couldn't remember the name of Meares Finance amongst the sorry compendium of debt that David had left her to edit. 'I'm sorry, I really don't see that you've got any business—'

The talker opened the leather case with a sudden rasp and held out a Xeroxed form.

'That's your husband's signature, yes?'

Laura looked, with a glum tightening at her chest. She nodded. The form disappeared again.

'When was this, Mrs Ritchie, may I ask? Your husband's death?'

'The end of January. It was a road accident.'

The talker exchanged a glance with the silent one.

'That *is* unfortunate,' he said again. For the first time he looked a little uncertain. 'I wonder if you can give us any proof of that. Mr Ritchie's business with Meares Finance being what it is, we—'

'I don't have to give you anything,' Laura said. 'I don't think you should even be here. Either you tell me what this is about, or I'll call the police.' Unsteadily enough she moved over to the phone and stood by it, in what some part of herself that wasn't thoroughly alarmed recognized was a slightly ludicrous posture. See, I have a phone. It's loaded.

'What you must appreciate,' the talker said, shifting and sniffing a little disdainfully, 'is that your husband—'

'Late husband. Don't – don't touch that,' Laura quavered, as the silent one experimentally clicked the power button of the hi-fi.

'All right, your late husband has an outstanding balance with Meares Finance in respect of an unsecured loan advanced to him in November of last year. As you've seen, we have photocopied documentation. The originals are at our office. This undertaking was—'

'How much?'

'The principal is five thousand pounds. Repayments, monthly at an agreed interest rate of fifteen and a half per cent plus arrangement fees.'

Laura tried to take this in – it wasn't a matter of conquering disbelief any more, just taking it in – whilst at the same time trying to keep an eye on the silent one, who kept roaming, inspecting, fingering.

'I'm afraid Mr Ritchie is in arrears with his payments,' the talker said. 'So you must appreciate our position. Hearing nothing from him—'

'Look here.' The silent one spoke. He had plucked a letter from the cabinet – a solicitor's letter, Laura realized, *in re* the seemingly endless wait for probate. He waved it, grimacing. 'It's right. Late Mr David Ritchie and everything.'

'Put that down,' Laura said, angry and relieved at the anger, at having found an appropriate response. 'That's private correspondence, you've no right to touch that. Get out now or I'll call the police . . .'

The talker gave a little intimate nod to his colleague, got to his feet. 'Well, Mrs Ritchie, we won't take up any more of your time just now. You'll be hearing from us soon. Believe me, I'm very sorry about all this, but you must understand that your husband's financial obligations have to be met. We do have a business to run. I'll leave you our card if I may.' He spoke delicately, but tossed the card on to the coffee table with a flick full of contempt.

'Get out.' She was wild, she was all rage, but she knew that at last the rage was against David, all the rage she had repressed because he was dead and so beyond it. 'Out – out . . .' She pounded down the hall, only dimly aware as she reached for the handle of the front door that someone was knocking at it. 'Out . . .'

She wrenched open the door, looked into the startled face of Mike Mackman, hand raised from knocking.

'We'll be in touch,' the talker said cheerfully, as the pair brushed fatly past her, leaving a cloud of spivvy male fragrance, and crunched down the front garden path.

'Don't bother!' she yelled unimpressively, a child's yah-boo. They were grinning, folding themselves squatly into a car parked fifty yards down the street.

'What on earth's going on?' Mike Mackman said. 'Who are those characters?'

Shaking and speechless, Laura watched the car cruise away. She felt soiled and invaded, everything you'd expect; but also ashamed. David's world – yet hers too. She must have helped to make it.

'Meares Finance,' she said. 'Of Highbury. Whatever happened, by the way, to an Englishman's home being his castle? Or Englishwoman's.'

'It still is. Or should be,' Mike Mackman said, seriously.

The red mists cleared from Laura's eyes, and she saw him, properly, for the first time, with a weary sense of another problem shouldering its inexorable way towards her. She half-knew, but she asked the question anyway.

'What do you want?'

There. How she wished, at such times, to be a man, or at least to have a man's voice. A man could say that and sound all right. He could sound as if he had a lot on his plate just now but was still your basically approachable mixture of toughness and vulnerability, like Humphrey Bogart. Say it in a woman's voice and you immediately felt self-reproachful for being whingey and petulant.

'I need to talk to you,' Mike Mackman said. 'But . . . if this is a bad time . . .'

Laura shrugged. Some doleful gypsy-granny part of her had known something like this was coming, and now was as good a time as any.

'You'd better come in.'

'What was it?' he said, following her into the living room, where the armchair still bore the imprint of wide-boy buttocks. 'Trying to sell you something? These people do that. They look out for widows – move in on them when they're vulnerable, try to sell them some worthless investment. It's shocking.' He saw her shaking her head. 'Or were they dunning you for money?'

'Something like that.'

'What did they do? Did they make threats?' He spoke urgently.

'No, no. It was . . . Oh, they were under the impression that David was still around. God,' she said uncontrollably, 'if only he was . . .' She managed to stop herself.

'Loan sharks,' he said. 'I get the picture. They've no right to come into your home, you know.'

'They've been in.' Laura very nearly said that he had no right either – but that was unfair. 'What was it you needed to talk about?'

'Well, this.'

He took a cheque from his breast pocket. She recognized it.

'Yes. I sent that back because I didn't want it. Same as with the first one. You really must see that.'

He folded his arms. He seemed like a person who is always ready to talk anything out at whatever length.

'I do,' he said. 'But you can't honestly tell me – ' he made a grim backward gesture with his thumb – 'that you're not having difficulties.'

'They're difficulties that I'll sort out,' she said, feeling glassy, shattery with brittle-blown nerves. 'Look, that's what I was trying to say when I sent those cheques back. It was kind of you but it isn't right. It's not your responsibility, Mike.' She found herself using his name because the essential truth of this sentiment, its utter concreteness and sincerity, struck through her for the first time. Hey, David was my husband and Simon's father, and he didn't seem to think it was his responsibility. Hey, I was David's wife and Simon's mother and I didn't seem to think it was my responsibility. I just went on pretending I was locked in an unhappy marriage rather than hiding in it like a den. I was the one who would eventually write to an agony aunt and you'd read it and think, what the hell was the silly cow playing at and why is she so surprised at the way things have turned out? We are the guilty ones. If there's an innocent party, it's you.

'So look,' she said, restive under his bright, aware gaze, 'please believe me. It isn't anything to do with you – any of this. The accident was – an accident. If you're finding it hard to forget then all I can say is – please try, because I want you to, that is what I most of all want you to do. Forget about it. And tear that cheque up. I don't want it. Please.'

Drawing in a deep breath, Mike folded the cheque and put it back in his breast pocket.

'I insulted you,' he said. 'I insulted you with that. I'm sorry.'

'It isn't that at all—'

'My God. I can't believe it. I can't believe I did that. How *bloody* insensitive.' He paused on the 'b' and almost subvocalized the mild curseword, as if it were an uncontrollable obscenity. 'Throwing money at you like that,' he said, beating his palms against his big thighs. 'No wonder you were insulted. I just don't think – that's my trouble. Pig-headed. I'm sorry. It's a bit late, I know, but I am sorry. It's just that when you sent the second one back, I . . . I mean, I've been so worried. Thinking about you and your little lad all on your own—'

'You shouldn't do that,' she said. 'That's precisely what you shouldn't do.' She meant: you shouldn't think in those terms, 'little lad' terms, 'all on your own' terms. It invested them with a pathos they did not have. The trouble was, telling him this only sharpened the pathos, until . . . 'Oh, damn it, look, I wish I could help you,' she burst out. 'You're all in a state about this and I'm sorry, I wish I could make you feel better but I can't. It's done. I know you're upset, I can see why, I'm not going to say you're making a fuss about nothing. But all I can do is ask you, please, to forget about it.'

Hearing herself, she felt subtly annoyed. Somehow when you talked to him the conversation, willy-nilly, moved into personal gear: you couldn't use an unemotional tone.

'You're proud,' he said. 'I know about that. I'm proud myself. It's a good thing to have.'

'I'm not,' she said with a helpless gesture. 'I'm just . . .' she sought an emphasis that would convey this, get it through to him, 'I'm just *normal*.'

'Like I say, I'm proud myself. I understand it.' Not for the first time he seemed to carry on his own one-way conversation. He listened to her, he attended devoutly, but he just steamed on, a juggernaut taking up all the room. 'But you can be too proud as well. I know *that* because I'm the same. Never take a favour from anybody. It's just . . . well, think of your little lad if you can't think of yourself.'

She thought she had thrown all her rage after the designer greaseballs, but no. 'You've no right to say that. You've got a bloody cheek saying that. I am thinking about Simon. I'm thinking about him every minute of the day, not that it's any of your business. He comes first and even if there's not much I can say for myself I can say that and I'll bloody well give a piece of my mind to anyone who says otherwise. I'll make sure Simon's all right and that's not pride, it's— I don't know what it is but it's nobody else's business. All right?'

Oh, again, to have a man's voice: Bogart not fishwife, and never mind if it was cultural conditioning that made you perceive an angry woman as shrill, hysterical, etc. It still sounded that way.

Mike Mackman's lips moved a little. His child-blue eyes did not blink. The juggernaut had pulled over.

'I'm—'

'I'm sorry,' he said, taking the words from her. 'I'm so sorry . . . I'll be off.'

He moved with a sort of hearty bounce, heading for the door. Following him, not knowing what words to add or subtract (how many words were there in the world, and what happened if you just ran out?), she saw him make a hunched hesitation in the hall, feared for a moment the production of another cheque, and then saw that he was crying.

Oh no.

'Mike . . .' Now she was having to use his first name: nothing else for it. She sacrificed her resentment at this to contrition. 'Please – don't . . .'

'Sorry. I'll be off,' he said again, in a strangled voice. But he couldn't – she could see it – move a muscle. It was that stage of tears. Red-faced, noiselessly crooning, he hung his head blindly while the tears oozed.

'Oh Lord, I must have sounded very harsh. I am sorry for that.' Never apologize, the assertiveness books said. But the thing about the assertiveness books was, they didn't know shit. 'I'm a bit touchy today – what with those awful goons swanning in here and everything. I didn't mean to . . . Come and sit down a minute. Have a cup of coffee.'

He shook his head tightly, raised his head with a gasp like a surfacing swimmer. 'OK now,' he said. 'Don't know what came over me.' His big face was quite fierce and grim with the shame of it. Like a disgraced legionnaire having his epaulettes publicly torn off, she thought. She could have told him that men were supposed to cry nowadays: it was encouraged, it was a big thing. (She could also have told him that women didn't much like it. In small doses, and under such emotional stress as this man was plainly feeling, fine. But then they never had minded that. It was when men went in for strategic new-man blubbing that women longed for the old macho dumb-ox.)

But all she said was, 'It does make you feel better. Terrible old cliché, but it's true.'

'I'll be off now,' he repeated, shuddering and swiping at his eyes.

'Wait just a minute. You won't be safe to . . . drive.' She finished the sentence, which had already crashed its significance down between them like a falling roofbeam.

'I'll be all right,' he said, after giving her a tortured look. 'I'll just . . . if I could just . . .'

'Of course,' she said in answer to his gesture. Too punctilious to enter her living room again, he sat himself down for a moment on the telephone seat in the hall. Every house had a place where no one ever sat, and this was theirs. Too draughty for phone calls, it had become a repository for odd gloves and junk mail. But Mike sat here as if it were a place of honour. Half-shy, half-defiant, he sat on the telephone seat and wiped his eyes with his handkerchief and apologized again.

'It's all right. You haven't done anything wrong,' Laura said, sitting on the stairs. A lot of bizarre things had happened to her in the last couple of months, and here was another.

He shook his head, swelled with an enormous sigh. 'You're kind,' he said. 'You're so very kind. I don't deserve this.'

'No, I was out of order. You were just trying to help, I know. But you must understand that you can't keep – trying to give me this money that I don't want.'

'Well. I'd give the world to . . . to undo what I did.'

'I know you would. But that's another thing you shouldn't be thinking. I'm sorry I've been a bit dismissive. I mean the whole thing must have been a nightmare for you too, I see that now. I was wondering, you know, if it's still preying on your mind, whether there was any sort of help you could get . . .'

'Me?'

At first she thought she'd offended him. 'Well, if you wanted, I mean, not that you need it, that's not what I'm saying . . .' Having half dug herself into the hole, she gave up; and then saw the rapt way he was looking at her.

'Me,' he said, whispery, marvelling. 'You're thinking about me. Robbed of your husband. Struggling to make ends meet. And you're thinking of how it's been for me.' He made a cramped, aspiring movement, as if striving against tight bonds. 'I . . . I don't know. You're just . . . I think you're a bloody saint.'

'Oh goodness, I don't know what's happened to my halo, if I am,' she said – quickly, flippantly, *shriekily* in fact, because this was just a bit excruciating. She was meant to be in control, he was meant to be cooling it, they were meant to be reaching a new realistic accord. Not this. 'Seriously,' she said, 'it's terrible if this thing goes on haunting you and messing up your life. If what you need to bury it is to know that the people left behind are all right, then – you've got it. You've got that assurance, now, from the horse's mouth. We're all right. Without the cheques. If it needs something else, then . . . there must be help you can get. You were a victim of that day too and people should see it.'

She felt a certain clammy hypocrisy as she spoke. But he nodded, slowly: taking her in, it seemed, like an oracle.

And suddenly he was on his feet, his hand on the door, with that economical swiftness of which he was surprisingly capable.

'I apologize again,' he said, pausing. 'For what just happened.'

'No, no need.'

'I think so. I think it's just about the worst thing I could have done.'

So serious, she thought with some bewilderment: she had known serious people, people who just couldn't lighten up, but this . . .

'I'm glad I saw you, though. Glad to – get things straight.'

'Oh yes,' she said promptly, because this sounded hopeful. 'That's always best.'

It sounded hopeful; but she couldn't feel quite so hopeful about the look he gave her as he ducked his muscle-bound way out – the look you gave someone who had an unmistakable halo floating a few inches above their head.

FOURTEEN

'They haven't got a leg to stand on,' Mr Bussapoon told Laura, quickly and blessedly, when she finally got through to him on the phone.

Then he proceeded to modify and qualify this until, it seemed to her, the baby had very nearly gone the way of the bathwater.

'If they have a legitimate claim against your husband's estate, they really should have made it by now. They could still apply to the Probate Office. But that's all they can do. When I say they haven't got a leg to stand on, I mean in pestering you. Once the residue of your husband's estate becomes yours, they can't have any of it, simply because it's yours. If it's a genuine claim against the estate then yes, I'm afraid they're entitled to that money. If, as sounds likely by what you've told me, the deal's a bit shady, then they may be a bit chary of laying it under the scrutiny of the Probate Office. I'll tell you what, if you give me the address I'll write to them. Just a simple standard letter requiring them to forward details of the claim to the executor. If they're not kosher, that'll make them back off.'

'Oh, could you? A solicitor's letter – I'm sure that would help . . .' Wow, she thought with an anxious image of tenners flying away like birds, a solicitor's letter.

Mr Bussapoon, who was omniscient even on the phone, chuckled and said, 'Well, we'll see. All fees to this office will be payable *after* probate. So don't worry. It'll be itemized, and you don't have to pay it yet, and it won't be *that* much.' The last clause of this sentence she did not believe, but the rest was reassuring as far as it went.

Which was only so far, because whatever happened those trolls had been in her home and she didn't like it. The urge to spray and disinfect afterwards was conquered, partly because Mike Mackman's presence had followed immediately on from theirs and for all the annoyance of it, the thumping insistence, the emotional hard-sell, the sheer *unwantedness* of it, Laura couldn't compare. She didn't want to wipe him away, or feel that she was doing so. All the same, she didn't want him to come any more. It was just too heavy. He made *you* heavy, in spite of yourself.

Shades of Rod, the only other man there had been in her life. (And not even that – he had been a chaste post-sixth-form interlude before fate had led her to David in that Manchester pub. She was, perforce, a one-man woman. My God, she thought, I am a living country-and-western song.) She and Rod had really got on. They had got on as a male and a female seldom did: they had been able to tell each other anything; they had always mutually understood. They talked and talked – and invariably ended up on a real downer. They were perfectly matched, and they made each other as miserable as sin. (David, on the other hand, made her laugh and took her out of herself. And then they ended up as miserable as sin. Hey-ho.)

It was troubling, anyhow. While quite straightforward gusts of anger and indignation kept whipping through her at the thought of Meares Finance and their fat-lipped envoys, a low note of trouble whistled softly and constantly for the rest of the day, Mike Mackman its theme.

The thing was to ascertain how troubled she should be. Laura was a citizen of the modern world, and so her senses were attuned to catching loopy vibes. Thinking of Mike Mackman and the way he had behaved, she measured the tingle. It was there, but . . . but then it was there to this sort of degree in everybody. Every person you knew manifested some trait which, considered in isolation, could only be ascribed to raving madness. Laura believed that most individuals of the human species were more or less mentally ill for much of the time – just an evolutionary thing, the big trembling overdeveloped brain as vulnerable as a forced fruit. It was something you had to make allowances for. Mr Stimson next door thought that communism was poised to take over the world and had bugged his phone for the purpose, and this was crazy. Every year intelligent actors cheerfully appeared in, and intelligent people went to, an unspeakable exhibition called panto, and this was crazy. Laura could not go to sleep if the open end of the pillowcase was on the left rather than the right, and this was crazy.

So you had to make allowances, and allowances duly made, Laura permitted herself to think that she shouldn't be too worried about Mike Mackman. The guy was all hung up with needless guilt and concern over her plight and he seemed to have conceived a chivalrous admiration for her that was wildly misplaced, and getting her message through to him had been tough . . . But. It had to end, because things did, and the tears – heartbreaking as they had been to see – were a good sign. It was a crying fit, after all, that had dragged her into a realization of what the hell she was doing, or not doing. Perhaps it would do the same for him. She hoped so, and not just for her own sake.

Going out to Josie's that afternoon to buy the local paper, Laura got abruptly tired of thinking about the morning's visitors, raging at the loan sharks, gnawing in disquiet at Mike Mackman. She was in the familiar state of being just fed up with men – a state that had nothing to do with feminist perspectives, of new starts or altered consciousness;

it was just a feeling you had now and then, a feeling to be acknowledged and respected. Men, she suspected, didn't experience this feeling in regard to women, because women simply didn't impinge on their lives in the same way, didn't hedge them about with great blocks of gender. Somehow men always had somewhere else to go.

Whatever the outcome of Meares Finance's irruption into her financial affairs, it had certainly given her an added impetus to hunt down a job. Before she picked up Simon from school she trawled with dusty hope through what the local rag, in shiny nineties-speak, chose to call its recruitment pages. Some of this stuff was terrifying, also mysterious. What *was* a systems analyst? Could you really earn up to five hundred pounds a week in your spare time by ringing Gary, and if you could, why didn't everybody?

Somewhat daunted, she dug out her old typewriter that night after Simon was in bed and set about composing a CV, one eye on the job adverts. It was pretty plain, pretty soon, that her CV was dreck and that what she had thought of as her one undeniable strong point, the old secretarial qualification, was no damn good at all. It wasn't just old, it was ancient, it was a vocational Dead Sea scroll. Nowadays they wanted Windows, they wanted Excel and Lotus and other things that sounded like contraceptives and that simply hadn't been around fifteen years ago when Laura had sat in headphones typing 'Dan had some hash' and thinking of the next time she would see David. Her skills were as obsolete as this machine with its flailing levers and power-loom racket.

At last she wrote off, shrugging, to a couple of outfits which sounded low-rent enough to employ her dim office talents, but at heart she knew she would have to set her sights on something else.

A trip out that she and Simon made with Jan and Ross on Sunday offered a chance of guidance, of a sort. A vast businessman's hotel on the outskirts of Langstead was staging a Psychic Fair, or Fayre as it was inappropriately medievalized on the posters. Very much Ross's thing, not at all Jan's: Laura was somewhere in the middle, didn't know what to think. The Fayre was held in a not very large conference hall. There were a few stands selling Tarot decks and crystals and the usual jiggery-pokery, and many more selling books, which one glance showed to be literally beyond a joke, in as much as you couldn't invent a mockingly exaggerated title without finding reality had beaten you to it. *Astral Healing for Cats.* It was there.

The various psychics were seated at various dramatically clothed tables around the room, offering to read your palm and your cards and your handwriting for a not noticeably small consideration. Laura, with no money to waste, was prepared to sit out. The last thing she expected was to find herself seated at one of those starry-moony tablecloths. But Ross was enthusiastic and wanted to share his feeling, and as it was a given premise of their marriage that Jan always firmly nixed the hocus-pocus, he insisted on treating Laura.

The woman who did her reading was, her flyer stated, called Binkie, was Hungarian by birth and had inherited her gift from a gypsy grandfather. The combination of Noel Coward monicker and Transylvanian flimflam was extremely rum, but the woman surprised Laura by seeming rather ordinary. She was fat and spectacled and middle-aged and spoke in a chesty voice with a faint accent, complaining about how cold it was in here. Again Laura was surprised, perhaps expecting a fakir-like indifference to such things. Only in the profusion of rings, like crusted knuckle-dusters, was there a touch of the old fairground Petulengro.

There was a trick to such things. Of course there was. And Ross had been up to have his bumps read just before her and had, for all Laura knew, let something slip about her or had had it wormed out of him by the deceptively prosaic Binkie. And yet when the woman laid out those inexpressibly corny-looking cards and immediately pronounced, in the matter-of-fact tones of a bank teller giving you your statement, 'You have recently suffered a terrible loss,' Laura's heart stopped beating for several seconds and there wasn't a thing she could do about it.

But then Binkie seemed to veer off on to some very well-travelled roads. 'I see a child,' she said. Which of course she could – Simon was in full view a few yards away, peering into a lava lamp. 'Motherhood means a lot to you. You've had some tough times money-wise, but they'll get better. You sometimes suffer from low self-esteem.' But everybody in the world did these days. Modern man had low self-esteem the way medieval man had original sin. Laura, overcoming her shock at that first, spookily prescient announcement, allowed herself to slip into comfortable scepticism.

'The changes you're going through are huge,' Binkie said abruptly, after staring into the middle distance for some moments. Her eyes, almost black and swimmingly magnified, caught Laura's and held them. 'But they're good, mainly. You should just let them go on. You should just . . . roll with them.'

Laura stared back at her. Two lucky hits, then. But really, this was pretty weird. All at once an enormous self-consciousness came over her. As the saying went, she didn't know where to put her face: certainly didn't know what expression to wear, how to compose herself. Here she was having her life frankly talked about in an echoing roomful of strangers, and yet the funny thing was, all she seemed to hear was her own and Binkie's voices, as if they were sealed in a bubble.

'This thing that just happened to you,' Binkie said, 'was utterly unexpected, wasn't it?'

'Yes, it was,' Laura found herself saying. No, don't give anything back, that's how they do it, they call it cold reading. 'Yes, it was – out of the blue.'

Binkie nodded, her pudgy hands fluttering over the cards. 'It was like someone stripping every inch of skin from your body.'

Laura almost flinched, the language was so unexpected – language that felt like a flaying in itself. A long way from tall dark strangers. Unable to meet Binkie's eyes any longer, she let her gaze stray over the cards. Death was there, the old bag of bones. But it always was, wasn't it? And it didn't necessarily mean death, she remembered Ross saying. In fact the whole shebang could mean just what you wanted it to mean, that was the point of it . . .

'I keep seeing wood,' Binkie said, flicking her hand in front of her eyes as if brushing away a fly. 'Wood, woods – just a flash and then it's gone. Does that mean anything to you?'

'The back garden fence is falling down,' Laura said. It was nerves. She didn't mean it quite as flippantly as it came out. But her face flamed as Binkie's unreadable eyes bored into hers.

'You've been hurt quite badly,' Binkie said. 'You've got a lot of questions inside yourself. I can't give you all the answers. It wasn't your fault, though – I can tell you that. That's what you've got to get over. You'll need to remember it in the times that are coming.'

'What sort of times are they?'

Binkie snorted through her nose, scanning the cards. Laura couldn't decide whether Binkie disliked her or was struggling for the right words.

'You're going to be doing something very different. I don't think you've ever done it before. It's profitable. Maybe quite hard, but there are definitely rewards. It's not something you need to worry about because it's going to come.' Binkie's fingernails drummed on the table top. 'Someone's watching over you.'

'What – like a guardian angel?'

Binkie half-smiled, half-shrugged, eyes squirrelling into Laura's soul. 'Is that what you believe in?'

'Well, no. I mean, I was brought up with that, but . . .' It had been her grandmother who used to speak, almost casually, of Laura's guardian angel: never her mother, presumably because she didn't suppose Laura worthy of one. Anyhow, she had always thought the idea creepy beyond words.

'Someone's looking out for you. It's good. You're going to need help.'

'I need it now, I think,' said Laura, a laugh a minute, gags galore.

'No.' Binkie was solemn. 'You're all right now. I just want to ask you to be very careful. Because, you see, it isn't over. The bad things. You're not out of the wood yet.' She gave a sudden and wholly surprising giggle. 'The wood – perhaps that's the wood. But no. Listen to me.' All at once she had hold of Laura's hand. Her own was very dry, very soft. 'You will be very careful, won't you? Because it isn't over yet. I'm afraid it isn't over.'

FIFTEEN

Not having known what to think when she entered the Psychic Fayre, Laura found herself still not knowing what to think afterwards. You couldn't call Binkie impressive – and yet somehow she was impressive. You could very easily label her a jabbering old fake with a knack for lucky guesses, but that wasn't right either.

And when the week began she still didn't know what to think. Because it presented her with two developments which seemed to show that, if she wasn't out of the wood yet, she was surely on the right path.

Mr Bussapoon called her with the wonderful, perplexing news that she had nothing more to fear from Meares Finance. The late Mr Ritchie's account with them was closed and they had no claim to make against the estate.

'What does it mean?'

'It means there's one less debt to worry about,' said Mr Bussapoon, who for once sounded a little rushed and a little less than cool. 'We have it in writing, so you're in the clear. Basically, forget about it.'

'They couldn't have written it off, could they? They didn't exactly seem the charitable sort.'

'I'm sure they're not. As I said, the terms of the agreement may well have been of the sort that won't stand up to scrutiny. From what I can gather they're a pretty lowlife operation. With respect, Mr Ritchie should never have got involved with them.'

No indeed. But then they were part of David's other life, his shadow life. Bookies and casinos and Vikki Trayford in her lurking flat. Laura found herself feeling miserably sorry for David: a castle in the air built out of rubbish. Never mind the banality of evil – this was the evil of banality.

A weight lifted, at any rate. Mr Bussapoon of course knew his business, and the plain message coming from him was that she should not look into it any further, advice she was happy to take: the knowledge that she was free of those barbered gorillas was like a heart-warming gift. If a puzzled part of her still insisted that there was something not quite right about this, Laura put it down to the lingering influence of Binkie and her Starkadder wisdom. Many a slip and never count your chickens, etc. It was an easy habit of mind to slip into. But the alternative, Laura told herself, was just as viable – good things could happen, just like that, without a catch. Surely.

The second development followed swiftly on from the first. The Probate Office, after deliberations that seemed more appropriate to a Victorian novel (real will purloined by wicked nephew and hidden in boot of saintly cripple), at last 'proved' David's will and authorized her to distribute the estate, or start throwing bones to the circling hyenas. This was good because it ended uncertainty. She already knew there would hardly be anything left, but it would be nice to know the exact amount, in pennies.

And there was a third development – or negative development, at least. Mike Mackman sent no more cheques. He didn't come to the house, or communicate with her at all. Mike Mackman, apparently, understood now: he had, she genuinely hoped, exorcised his demons. Negative, but positive. For him too, she thought.

Good things. And Simon was coping, and there were daffodils in the front gardens of Duncan Road. Laura had to keep these good things fixed in her mind as the daffodils stiffened in the suburban spring and the weeks melted by and she set about, seriously, dead seriously, trying to get a job. Because this involved things that by no stretch of the imagination could be called good. Frustrating, yes. Disappointing, certainly. Infuriating and chastening and humiliating, without a doubt. Maybe even character-building. But not good.

Much of the job hunt was a curious phantom activity, like high-level espionage. She wrote off as requested enclosing a CV as requested. Sometimes that was the end of it: ghostly silence reigned. But sometimes, in return, an application form arrived to be filled in with all the things she had put on the CV. So she did that, and sent it off. Cue, mostly, the ghostly silence. Once or twice in her innocence she rang to see what was happening. Oh, the vacancy had been filled: the job centre should have taken the notice down. The vacancy had been filled ages ago, it seemed. The person who filled it was practically ready for retirement. Weirder, more cryptic and spy-like, were the times when there didn't seem to have been a vacancy at all. No one had heard of it. Her application had gone somewhere – who knew where?

But just occasionally she penetrated these strange thickets and got an interview. There was the job as receptionist at a doctors' surgery, for which she was cross-examined not just by one of the doctors but by the chief receptionist, an acid-faced queen bee of a certain age who writhed and deliquesced and yearned whenever the doctor spoke, her eyes narrowing with hate when she turned them back to Laura – spaniel to cat in one movement. The menopausal hag sniffed about experience, fiddling with Laura's CV, perhaps unsure whether she was holding it the right way up. Of course one couldn't discriminate on grounds of age, but they had tended to find that mature candidates responded better to this particular working environment . . . Not enough of a boiler to pose no threat to the orthopaedically shod witch's dreams of Dr Kildare gropings, Laura exited in the full knowledge that she hadn't got the job.

In contrast, she was looked at in the next place to grant her an audience with barely concealed astonishment at her advanced age. It was a hamburger joint, and they carried on as if she had creaked in there with a Zimmer frame. In an oniony office she talked to a young boy while waiting for the manager, then realized he was the manager. They were really looking, he said, seeming to refrain from shouting in her ancient ear, for a school-leaver. Why hadn't the advert specified that? Rules. They were only allowed to do it, not say they were doing it.

But these were, at least, the jobs they pretended to be. There was a full-time job packing fresh foods in some unspecified silo in the middle of nowhere that turned out to be not a job at all, though she only found this out after performing the unlovely task of submitting a sample of her stool in a plastic bottle for health tests. 'Basically it's as and when,' the striped-shirted gangmaster told her. Meaning, they hauled you in when they wanted you, which might be next week or next year or never. Tough banana.

She had hopes of the old people's residential home. They wanted a day care assistant, they wanted one urgently, no experience was required and hours were negotiable. The proprietress showed Laura desultorily round on the way up to her office. Old ladies sat and sat, hands shielding their eyes as if from a bright light, though the place was plushly dim. One had been sick down herself, and kept glancing down at the results as if it were a necklace not hanging right. Meanwhile, a TV blared, tuned off-beam to a satellite sports channel. In her office the proprietress, a mean-mouthed woman in underpowered power-dress, did a lot of the sort of sighing and paper-shuffling that is meant to show how overworked you are. Then it came out that negotiable meant all over the place. The woman wasn't sure when she would want her, except that it would be some nights, some mornings, all Bank Holidays, and whenever anyone was ill. That was, if she decided to create a post at all. She might be able to swing it by reshuffling the rota and increasing the hours of some of the part-timers . . . When at last Laura decided it wasn't worth their wasting each other's time any more and said so, the proprietress grew hurt and huffy. She seemed to expect Laura to understand and sympathize with the manifold problems of owning a large house and charging helpless old things six hundred quid a week to rot in it.

This one had alarmed her, though, because the woman's proddings about how flexible she was had made Laura realize that she wasn't.

Her assumptions about being a single parent and going out to work, she realized, had been too blithe, as assumptions tended to be. (In fact she couldn't think of anything else that was blithe. That was what the word was for.) She would have to address this question a lot more carefully. To start with, only a standard nine-to-five was at all viable. That left a gap between half-past three, when Simon finished school, and five: there was an after-school club expressly designed for such contingencies which Simon was keen to attend because his best friend did, and what was more Jan, who only worked mornings, had offered her help. Jan's eleven-year-old daughter was at the same primary school and could take Simon back to their place, if Jan was ever unable to pick them up. Workable stratagems abounded, but Laura ticked herself off for having thought about them so vaguely. The habit of hiding was hard to break. Whatever happened, whatever job she got (or failed to get), Simon must be safe. Lately he had dropped hints about the privilege of walking home from school on his own – three or four streets, only one to be crossed and that one with a lollipop man – but Laura wasn't having any. She remembered going home from school alone herself when she was about his age, but that was different, and never mind the memory-and-enchantment stuff. Back then, in Cheadle, all you got was the solitary flasher in a traditional gaberdine mac who might as well have had a numberplate and a police escort. The true, creative, insatiable barbarism hadn't set in then. No, and no.

But as yet the question was academic and she couldn't help a despairing feeling that it was going to stay that way as she opened yet another thin second-class letter ('Dear Mrs Mitchie. We regret to inform you that after careful consideration . . .'). And yet what Laura felt, most of all, was shame. Not at her own cringing, obedient, effusive need, her dismal willingness to fit the square peg of herself into round holes, but at the fact that she hadn't known about this, not at first hand. She had been sheltered. She had been off the hook.

It was when the daffodils were drooping and dying (they were at 19 Duncan Road, anyway – Laura was no gardener) that she finally received a job-related phone call which seemed promising. The lady who spoke to her sounded recognizably human rather than like an alien intelligence imperfectly grafted on to a dead body: she wanted Laura to come to an interview tomorrow morning first thing; and Laura had applied for this particular job so long ago she had forgotten all about it, which somehow seemed the most hopeful sign of all.

Sprignall's, Langstead's snootiest and largest department store. The job was full-time catering assistant in Sprignall's restaurant, a top-floor café with pretensions – it called itself 'the restaurant', in lower case, and ladies put on hats and furs to meet each other there. Laura wondered why the long delay in summoning her. The likeliest explanation was that they had employed someone who had either left or been given the boot. Neither alternative said much for the job – but she didn't care, she had a feeling about this one, a Binkie-ish feeling perhaps.

The interview was at a quarter to ten. Laura put on her employ-me gear – blue suit, blouse, sensible shoes – first thing. She could drive Simon to school, then head straight on into town, which would leave her plenty of time for nervous tummy attacks and mental rehearsals. That was the plan, anyway.

The car wouldn't start. It made noises of chugging willingness when she keyed the ignition, but that was it.

'Why won't it go, Mum?' said Simon, on a note of cheery enquiry.

'I don't know.' She knew nothing about cars except the sound a flat battery made, and this wasn't it. David had been the same. If something went wrong, he let the local garage handle it. The local garage, as she recalled, seemed to charge by the second like showbiz lawyers. She supposed she could look under the bonnet, but really that was as fantastical as if she had proposed to shoe a horse.

'What shall we do?'

Laura cursed her helplessness. 'I'll walk you to school. Come on.'

Simon moved obligingly fast, but the journey still took fifteen minutes; and then at the school gates she was unlucky enough to run into Miss Robertson, his teacher, who wanted to take the opportunity for a friendly chat . . . Laura made her excuses as soon as she could, but the teacher looked put out. So now she was a bad mother as well. Making the sort of poor decision that stress invariably produces, Laura elected to run back home and try the car again. It chugged and wheezed efficiently, even complacently, as if it were a machine designed only to make noises and nothing else. On TV this was the moment when people slammed an open hand against the steering wheel. Laura thought about it, but the way things were going she'd probably break her wrist.

She got out, looked with a faint beseeching *Why?* look at the car standing there in the drive as if it had been cemented into it, then addressed herself to another decision. She had twenty-five minutes. That would give her time to walk to town, briskly, and get to her interview with about a minute to spare. She would probably arrive breathless and red-faced and uncollected, leaving aside the distinct possibility of those black clouds turning into rain, but barring a fall down an open manhole, she would certainly get there. The alternative was to get a bus from the stop on Beatrice Road, which would get her there in plenty of time and normal-looking – but she had to gamble on the bus not being late, and indeed coming at all, which sometimes it didn't. If she waited at the stop ten minutes, then her chance of getting there on foot in time had gone, and then . . .

Twenty-four minutes later, Laura arrived at Sprignall's, slightly more red-faced and breathless and uncollected than she had expected. The shop was a big self-contained building of the pure 1930 style that made you think of picture palaces and Art Deco vacuum cleaners and *Miracle on 34th Street*. It was actually rather a good shop that sold a large range of goods quite cheaply, but people who weren't well off tended to be a bit frightened of it, its library smell, its polite, neck-scarved assistants: they went and got fleeced at chain stores instead. Laura rode the lift to the top floor. The lift had a mirror but she turned away from it after an appalled glance. She looked like a district nurse who had been in a punch-up. Instead she concentrated on quelling the flush of panic as she realized that she'd forgotten to lock the car door. Relax. It wasn't as if that car was going anywhere.

'Excuse me. I've got a job interview. They said to ask for Shirley.'

The woman serving at the glass counter smiled. 'That's me. Hello, it's Laura, isn't it?'

'Oh! Oh, yes, that's right.'

The first 'Oh', which must have sounded pretty stupid, was one of surprise. In spite of the pleasant phone call, Laura had not expected Shirley to be serving at the counter, or to be a small pretty fortyish woman with hastily tied-back hair and laughter lines round her gemlike eyes. She had expected some sort of grisly eminence in a panelled office, planning a copperplate menu. Perhaps Shirley was some sort of catering NCO and not the manageress . . . But then Shirley said, 'I'm the manageress,' and took her behind the counter and into a sort of broom cupboard-cum-storeroom where they sat knee to knee on tiny stools whilst tremendous kitchen clankings went on next door.

'Thanks for coming. It was a bit of a cheek ringing you so long after you applied. There is an explanation. As you know we're a franchise. The franchise company got taken over by another franchise company and everything was up in the air for a while. All on an even keel now, anyway, as much as it ever is. Anyway. Sorry about that.'

'Oh, no, not at all,' said Laura. She looked on with the usual pained apprehension as Shirley examined her CV. The damn thing seemed such a pathetic, almost lunatic imposture. Like handing someone a cuddly toy and saying it was your purebred Siamese.

'About the hours. I think the ad specified nine till four. I should say that in the month leading up to Christmas there are some evenings, say till seven. They've had some pressure on them to open late on Thursdays all during the year as well, though I don't think they will. Sprignall's is a bit old-fashioned like that. I thought I'd mention it because sometimes husbands and partners and so on can cut up a bit rough when they find there's the odd evening involved.'

'Well, that shouldn't be any problem.'

'No? Oh – sorry, you've put single on the CV, I should have noticed.'

She had, as she had on all of them. It seemed easiest. Shirley was the first one to bring it up. Laura felt she ought to be saying something.

'I've got a seven-year-old. I've been, you know, being mother and housewife and superstar. That's why I've been out of the, er, workplace for a while.'

'I know, terrible word, isn't it? Like when they talk about "the marketplace" on the news. So now you're looking to go back into full-time work?'

'Yes. My husband died, and—' Oh no. That sounded as if she were using her widowhood as a lever to get the job. 'And anyway, I really want to get working again. My last catering experience was – well, as you can see, it was a while ago, before my son was born.' Four months in an office canteen back in the days of the Enfield flat, which she had inflated to a year on the CV. 'But I really enjoyed it. I like being on the go in somewhere busy.'

'Well, we're certainly that,' Shirley said, as there was a great sheet-metal crash from the kitchen. Laura smiled, thinking: it sounds a bit chaotic in here and I like it. She remembered her application to a china-and-glass shop a couple of weeks ago, the tailor-made manageress intoning, 'We get quite busy here, you know,' with a sweeping gesture at a shop that looked like an unvisited museum. This was more like it. Frightening, but nevertheless . . . Give me the job, her eyes begged.

'This is one of the quieter times of the year,' Shirley said. 'From October to January it's madness. But you've always got people in. We try to be a bit upmarket because there aren't that many places in Langstead which are and basically Sprignall's don't want a naff caff on the premises. The idea is to have something like the London stores have. But people can still come in just for a pot of tea.' Shirley put the CV aside, adding casually, 'Yes, my husband died a couple of years ago. It's a bugger, isn't it?'

'Shirley, is there . . . Oh, sorry.' A man in a white smock put his head round the door, saw Laura, withdrew with pantomimed apology.

'I'll be there in a moment, Liam,' Shirley called after him. 'That's our chef. I was just going to mention that actually. Your duties wouldn't include cooking as such. We serve cooked breakfasts and set lunches and various posh sweets each day, and obviously that's Liam's department. As a catering assistant you'd only be preparing the snack meals, baked potatoes and so on. Then you've got serving, clearing tables, washing up and cleaning. In theory the cashier's job is separate but you're bound to end up on the till at some point.'

Laura nodded, split three ways between hope, fear, and that crucial portion of empathy.

'It's monthly pay. Uniform's provided, so you don't actually have to pay for this sailor suit,' Shirley said, with a gesture at the clunky blue and white outfit she wore. Her sparky eyes, Laura thought, suggested that she could be a bit of a devil over a drink and a chat. 'Hair has to be tied back. Do you have any holidays booked? Because basically you can't have any in the first three months.'

'There goes that fortnight in the Bahamas,' Laura said. There was another crash from the kitchen.

'It is quite hectic,' Shirley said. 'We have had people who obviously thought it was a cushy little tea-shop number and got a shock.' She studied Laura candidly.

'Well, as you know I haven't been out to work for a while. But I do want to go in at the deep end.'

'You feel you'll be OK, you know, looking after your little boy and working?'

'Well, I can arrange for him to be picked up from school and looked after till I get home. For the school holidays I was going to suss out a childminder – I've got a friend who used to have one for her children. I'm pretty sure it'll be tiring, but – well, life is, I suppose, but you keep going. I can say that for myself, anyhow, I keep plugging away. I'm determined not to let anybody down, Simon or the job.' Selling yourself. It sounded like gush, and mush, but she did mean it.

Another industrial-size crash from the kitchen almost drowned out Shirley's next words: 'When can you start?'

SIXTEEN

Floating, Laura stopped off at Sprignall's toy department and bought a remote-controlled car for Simon. Handing over the money, she felt the old reflex of alarm and joyfully recognized it for what it was – a reflex. She could do this now. She had a job.

Everyone seemed nice, as they usually do when something good has happened. The shop assistants were charming. The bus driver was cheery. Even the woman who sat next to Laura on the bus, and steadily devoured a packet of fruity boiled sweets with as much crunching, candid relish as if the two of them were sharing a delicious meal, seemed merely comical instead of irritating.

She was to start on Monday. Shirley had given her a quick tour of the kitchen, where the chef had said an absent-minded hello out of the back of his head and a muscular West Indian woman, toiling over the washing up, had looked her gratitude at the prospect of reinforcements. It was real: it wasn't a dream. Any retrospective glance Laura gave at the dreams of her youth, when she was going to be either a ground-breaking artist or an interpreter for the United Nations, was without regret. She had done a lot of living since then – more especially in the last few months – and she knew that good fortune was a limited commodity. You took what you could get of it.

Must ring Jan later, she thought as she turned into Duncan Road, and ask if she could take her up on that offer to pick Simon up after school once she was working. The sight of the car in the drive caused her feet to touch the floor at last. There was always something . . . But given that inevitability, then at least this was a something she already knew about, which was reassuring in a way. She wouldn't have to wait for the fly to hit the ointment.

Besides, now she had a job the prospect of getting it fixed wasn't such a headache. Maybe she could try somewhere other than the local garage. Of course, there was the question of getting it to a garage in the first place. She seemed to remember that Mr Stimson had a towbar on his car, presumably for post-lynch-mob draggings, and maybe . . .

Laura stopped, doorkey raised. There was a piece of paper tucked under one of the windscreen wipers of the car.

A parking ticket in her own driveway?

She took the piece of paper out. It was a note, written on a sheet that looked to have been torn from an organizer.

Mrs Ritchie. I happened to be passing and saw you having trouble with the car. So I took a look, hope you don't mind. It was your transmission. I'm pretty handy with cars. It's fine now. Lucky this time you left the door unlocked, though it's not advisable generally, there's so much crime nowadays. Hope you are well. Best regards, Mike Mackman.

Laura stared in bemusement from the note to the car and back again. Then she got in and tried the engine.

It was, as he said, fine.

How had *he* tried the engine? Must have jump-started it, she supposed. It was an explanation, though somehow not one that she found very comfortable.

She went indoors, thinking.

Thinking: what, precisely, is going on here?

Well, a man who felt that he had done her a great injury was trying, as he said he wanted to, to offer her practical help. Which he certainly had: the mending of the car was real elves-and-shoemaker stuff, and had lifted a considerable burden. That was one way to see it.

Ah, but what was *really* going on here? Because there was something not right. His happening to be passing, for one thing. That was a pretty stiff coincidence. Duncan Road really wasn't on the way to anywhere. But even if you could swallow that, there was still something invasive about the whole business. She couldn't like the idea that someone had been watching her this morning when she was trying to start the car. (She hadn't noticed anyone driving by, slowing, looking . . . but then she hadn't been expecting it.) Of course it was kind, but it was also funny, as in peculiar.

So what *was* going on? There was one simple conclusion that she supposed anyone hearing about this would jump to – Mike Mackman had a straightforward thing about her, fancy romancey – but she was a lot slower to make that leap. Partly this was the result of life with David, who when he suspected any man of taking a shine to her would speak of it as if the poor wretch suffered from some ugly and slightly discreditable disease. 'Oh, yes – the one who starts drooling when you walk into the room. He's really got it bad, hasn't he? Really thinks you're *it*.' But mainly it was because of what she knew of Mike Mackman. Prurient interest was the very last thing she would have ascribed to him: he seemed to view her as a combination of Mrs Miniver and Saint Joan. And besides, what sort of man would try to move in on the widow of the man he had killed, even accidentally? Actually, she thought, there were plenty of men who *would* do that, testosterone and conscience not tending to go together, but she was almost sure Mike Mackman wasn't one of them.

So, if she was definite about him not being a pervy creep, why worry? The guy had mended her car gratis. Great stuff. Laura knew that just as there were many men who would throw morality out of the window for any sexual chance, there were women who would say this – whose frank motto was Take, Use, Who Cares? But Laura wasn't one of those either. And she couldn't rest easy with this.

She found the card he had left, and rang his home number. She wasn't sure what she was going to say – that was what was so tricky about this. You couldn't not say thank you to someone who had just saved you a lot of trouble and expense. But thank you implied an approval of the deed that she couldn't quite feel. When people said, 'You shouldn't have,' they didn't mean you shouldn't have – it was just another expression of appreciation. But Laura did mean he shouldn't have.

There was no answer at his home number, and she didn't want to speak to the answerphone if she could get him at work. Luckily with that number she got him on the second ring.

'Mike Mackman.'

The name was so him, she thought – a fistful of consonants . . . 'Hello, it's Laura Ritchie.'

'Mrs Ritchie, hello!' His voice was suddenly uplifted: very much how she must have sounded when Shirley told her she'd got the job, Laura thought. She tried to fend off a curious feeling of oppression.

'Um, I hope you don't mind me ringing you at work—'

'Not at all, not at all. I'm glad you did. So how are you?'

'Fine, fine, I . . . The reason I'm ringing is I just got home and found you'd done this repair job on my car, which was, er, quite a surprise.'

He gave a boyish, satisfied chuckle. 'Thought it would be.'

'Yes, well – that was very kind of you to do it, and . . . helpful, but—'

'Oh, it wasn't much of a job. As I say, it was your transmission. I promise you it was really very little trouble. For me – I mean I'm a bit of a car man, there was no reason why you should have known what to do. I'm just glad I could be of service, you know.'

'Yes . . . and thank you for it . . .' He sounded, Laura thought, like a man whose day has been made. This was hard. 'The thing is, I don't like to think of you going out of your way like that, I mean it must have made you late for work and—'

'It doesn't matter if I'm late for work, I own the place,' he said, bullish and cheerful. 'Like I say, it was nothing. You will lock your car in future, though, won't you? You can't be too careful these days. There are a lot of dodgy people about.'

Well, from the first she had had him down as a person entirely impervious to irony . . . 'Look, it's kind of you to be concerned like this, but I did think we'd agreed that, you know, there's no need for you to go on – troubling yourself like this. You really should get on with your own life, because – because it isn't fair on you.'

'But I want to help,' he said. 'I *want* to help you.' Not tentative: just massively puzzled.

Well, I don't want you to. How on earth could she say that?

'Mrs Ritchie? Laura? Are you all right?' Pouncing on her hesitation.

'Yes, sure. I – I do think we ought to get this sorted out, though. You putting yourself out like this, it isn't right, and after what we said I really thought—'

'I'll come round. I'll come over there now.'

'I—' What? She always seemed to be too slow for him. 'No, don't do that, there's no need—'

'Are you busy?'

'Well no, but—'

'We can't talk on the phone. Obviously we need to talk. I'm not quite getting the picture here. I'll come over.'

The line purred. He was gone.

For God's sake, this was . . .

Well, it was too heavy. That was the word that suggested itself above all to Laura as she stood frowning in bewilderment at the phone and with the exultation of that morning wearing perceptibly away, like the freshness of a shower being eroded by the grime of the streets. And heavy, she realized, was the word and the concept that came to mind when you thought of Mike Mackman. Weight, solidity, ponderous assurance, unsubtle sincerity. In that alone – even if she had not come to view romantic love between the sexes as a lethal curiosity, like white-water canoeing or keeping tarantulas, with which she had nothing to do – Laura would have found a limit to her response to the man, one of those marks by which everyone sorts out their own sheep and goats. She liked lightness. She trusted it more (perhaps unwisely in view of her recent past, but there it was). She would rather have been a sceptical Georgian than an earnest Victorian. You were supposed to respect people who had an unshakeable, fervent, unchanging belief, but she didn't: how could anyone be sure what they believed? Teutonic men were not her cup of tea: one of the things that had first attracted her to David was an element in him – a kind of reverse of pomposity – that could only be called camp, though he would probably have been perturbed to know it then and horrified later.

But this shouldn't be an issue, anyhow, when it came to Mike Mackman. Because he had nothing to do with her. That was what was so subtly frustrating. Here was another set of sheep and goats: the people who had something to do with you and the people who hadn't. He just didn't seem to see that he was one of the latter. Tragic chance had brought them into contact, but that was it: the contact simply shouldn't lead on to anything else. This – this intensity out of nowhere – was all skewed, out of focus, wrong.

But she couldn't feel any relief that he was coming over so that she could put this to him face to face. Because she had done that already. The very fact that he was tearing over here showed that he hadn't listened. Laura just didn't know what she could do to cool him off that she hadn't done already. The only remaining option, it seemed, was to turn nasty – which was hardly an appropriate response. The man felt guilty and responsible – he shouldn't, but he did – and was trying by his slightly strange lights to make amends. How could she bawl him out for that? This was hardly a stalker she was dealing with. (Mrs Ritchie, what is your complaint against this man? Well, your honour, he kept trying to help me out with money, fixed my knackered car, and generally treated me like a trembling rose.)

No, it would be cruel to get shirty. And she didn't want to. The only attraction the idea held was that it just might, ultimately, be the thing to cool him off. He was idealizing her, the suffering grieving widow with child on hip, too proud to accept help: a heroine. Perhaps what he needed was to see her as a cow. The trouble was, though she knew there was plenty of cow in her, she didn't much want to show it, or rather put it on. You behaved quite badly enough for one lifetime without forcing it.

Hearing a car pull up outside the house, Laura felt a craven impulse to escape by the back door or hide in the attic. But she obeyed a contrary one and went straight to the front door and opened it before he had a chance to knock.

Walking up the path, Mike Mackman paused and gave her that arrested, deep-breathed look; then came ploughing on.

'It's not running right, is it?' he said.

'Eh?'

'The car. I'm sorry. It was a bit of a rush job and she's probably not turning over as well as you'd like. I meant to say, I'll do a proper job on her when I get some time. Proper tools and—'

'No, no. Look, that isn't why I—The car's fine. And that was really kind of you to do it. I mean . . . it was too kind.'

'Not at all,' he beamed.

Too kind. He took it as conventional compliment. When what she meant was . . .

'Morning, Laura.' It was Eileen, marching past with her usual props – double pushchair, bags of shopping, sack of flour for making her own bread, eight-foot crucifix, etc. – and she slowed to a military-funeral pace when Laura and her visitor caught her voracious eye. 'Keeping all right, are we?'

'Fine, thanks.'

'Morning,' Mike said with a nod. 'Nice bit of warmth in the air today.'

'It's not before time,' Eileen said, half-closing her eyes to evoke a lifetime of hard winters cheerily borne.

'Ah, it seemed like we'd never see the sun.'

'You'd better come in,' Laura said, trapped.

'Nice to meet you,' Mike called after Eileen, who moved glacially on with her head facing backwards. 'Neighbour?' he said to Laura, following her in.

'Yes.'

'Well, that's good to know,' he said seriously, nodding. 'Listen, I know – I know it's a bit of a cheek. I know it's a bit much.'

This was precisely what she wanted to say, and couldn't say, and so she said, 'Well, no . . .'

'It did occur to me afterwards. I mean, I do know cars, always try to fix up mine if the problem's not major, but of course I'm still an amateur. There's really no reason why you should trust me with a motor. So it was a bit of a cheek, I must admit. But believe me, I wouldn't tinker with it unless I was absolutely sure of the problem. Now you give her a run when you get the chance, see what you think, and if there's any more problems ring me at—'

'Mike.'

He was silenced, stockily at attention.

'What I want to know is, how come you knew about the car?'

'Like I said, I happened to be passing. I saw you having a bit of trouble. I thought while you were out it would be like a nice surprise if I could get it mended.'

'Just passing,' she said.

In fact all she was really doing was repeating the words, and mentally giving it up in weariness (this peculiar feeling of fatigue, of being unequal to things, always seemed to come over her in his presence). But as she said it, his entire face and neck turned brazenly red. His hand went nervously up to his moustache and he dropped his eyes, which against the throttled blush looked as pale and glintingly colourless as the scales of a fish.

It was as painful to see, in its way, as the tears; but Laura knew that she had to follow up her advantage.

'Nobody really passes down this road, you know,' she said. 'I mean, where were you going?'

Mike leant his big hands on the back of the sofa. The blush did not fade. It was such an intense effect that it seemed there must surely be a further development – the skin bubbling and blistering, the nose bleeding.

'Well, you've got me. I wasn't just passing. I mean, I was, but only passing like I normally do. I always drive this way, when I go to work, when I come back. Odd other times, lunch and that. It's just a way of keeping an eye on you – you know, reassuring myself that you're all right.'

'You drive past?'

'Yes. Sometimes park up the road a little while and keep a look out. Just to make sure everything's all right.'

Laura swallowed. She felt about as comfortable as most adults, children and animals generally feel when they find they are being secretly watched.

'What did you expect to see?' she said, and at last her insubstantial resentment had a shape. 'Burglars climbing up the front drainpipe? A bomb on the roof?'

'It's just a little habit I've got into, that's all.' Her anger didn't faze him: he didn't seem even to acknowledge it.

'Oh, but that . . . that isn't right. Don't you see? You can't go around spying on people like that. Even if it's well meant, it still makes you really uncomfortable to think . . .'

'Not you. I'm not spying on you. I'm looking out for you. Listen, the last time I was here there were some very unsavoury characters hassling you. I know their faces and that car of theirs – I want to be damn sure they're not around. Obviously I can't be here all the time but I can keep checking up. Just in case.'

In those last three words there was the faintest smack of satisfaction, of interior knowledge, and it did something to Laura. It prodded into sudden, rearing life a suspicion that had been sleeping deep within her since Mr Bussapoon had given her the good news about Meares Finance – so deep that she hadn't really been conscious of its existence down there.

But now, up it sprang; and it quickened her into an instant, necessary cunning.

'Well, as it happens those two came round here yesterday. About five—'

'What?' he barked – though it was the deep bark of a slow tireless hound. 'They had no right to do that, that's out of order, they . . . they shouldn't . . .' He trailed into silence, evaded her eyes, shut his mouth with a snap.

'Oh, my God,' she said, sitting blindly down.

'It was out of order,' he repeated softly. 'Well out of order.'

'Oh God, Mike, you paid them, didn't you? You paid off Meares Finance.'

'I wanted to help you. When I came round that day, and you'd had them on your backs, I thought – well, I thought maybe here's something I can do.' He spoke without arrogance, with a labouring honesty, like a plucky schoolboy owning up. 'So I got in touch with this Meares Finance, said it was about the late Mr Ritchie's account. And then –

well, sure, I paid it. Christ, that wasn't much to do considering what I'd done to you and your little lad. I mean, it just seemed right. You wouldn't take any money from me – which I don't blame you for at all, by the way, I admire you for it – so I tried to help out this way. It's really no big deal. It's – well, it's paying a debt. That's what it is. Not half of what I owe you, but—'

'You don't owe me anything, Mike, that's what I've been trying to tell you . . . My God, that's such a lot of money, you just – you just shouldn't have done that . . .' Impossible knot of feelings. Grateful, yes, but really *no.* Disappointment because what had seemed good fortune – Meares Finance backing off – was really no such thing. Desperation because he hadn't got the message and now she was under an intolerable obligation to him . . .

'I made it a strict condition that you shouldn't know about it,' Mike said with renewed confidence. 'That was the deal. You should never have found out. Well, I've got a few choice words for them, let me tell you. They had no right to come round here again and—'

'They didn't, it . . . I made that up.'

He stared at her, though without hostility.

'I was trying to get to the truth, and . . .' And now she had. So what could she do with it? 'You shouldn't have done it,' she said, shaking her head. 'It was so generous, but . . .' *Generous to a fault*: the phrase had never been more apt.

'I didn't want you to know about it. But, well, now you do it doesn't really matter. Just forget about it.'

'That's what I can't do. I've told you, Mike, told you till I'm blue in the face that you shouldn't feel this – responsibility, it just isn't right . . .'

'It's what I want to do,' he said, with a terrible obtuse freshness, as if this explained everything.

She couldn't answer that one.

'I'll pay you back,' she said, 'I'll pay you it all back. It'll have to be bit by bit but I'll do it.' She began making mental calculations. If she could put aside maybe fifteen pounds a week from her wage . . . 'What was the exact figure you had to pay those sharks?'

He shrugged. 'It doesn't matter. I don't want it back. That was the whole point. To free you.'

Cornered by obligation, short-breathed, helpless, she said, 'But you must realize I can't – I can't just accept this. I have to pay it back, all of it – you must realize that.'

Again he shrugged. He looked airy and pleased with himself. 'I suppose I can't stop you.'

'I'll send cheques.' And so a link would be forged. There was no getting out of it.

'And you can't stop me not cashing them.'

'Why are you doing this?'

The question seemed to catch him a little off guard – it had come suddenly and surprisingly to her too.

'Because – I want to make it up to you.'

'I've told you about that. There's no question of—'

'I want to watch out for you. I want you always to feel that you've got something to depend on. So you're safe. Protected. I know what you're going to say – you don't need it, you can stand on your own two feet. That's because you're brave and I bloody admire you for it. But I want to be brave for you. That's all.'

Her guardian angel. Laura remembered Binkie with her owlish disconcerting gaze. Had *this* been on the cards? If it had, then no wonder Binkie had found no words for it. She dealt in good luck and bad luck, whereas this . . . this was neither and both.

'Well.' The search for words felt like a physical groping – hands fumbling amongst Scrabble letters. 'It's not a question of me accepting it because you've done it. So all I can do is ask you to – to give me your promise that that's the end of it. No more. And when I've paid you the money back, which I'll do as soon as I can, then we're quits. Please. You get on with your life and let me get on with mine.'

That last bit felt soiled – because after all the things he had done were *enabling* her to get on with her life, though she hadn't wanted it that way. A cleft stick or horns of a dilemma or no-win situation. The phrases existed, so people must have found themselves in such a fix before. But it didn't feel that way: its awkwardness felt unique.

But Mike said, rubbing his hands together, 'Fair enough. If that's what you want, of course I respect it. It doesn't alter my feelings, though. I'm no great brainbox but I stick to my guns. You just have to do what you feel is right in this life, don't you?'

'Yes, I suppose you do. But please don't do that – that driving by the house any more. It's . . .' *It's creepy.* But how could she say that to someone so transparent, who only wanted to help, who had just swatted away two good-sized problems for her? 'It's not necessary.'

He nodded his great head, whole-hearted, obedient. But the look he gave her was all twinkling, wistful, indulgent admiration – like a father observing his small child resolving to carry a big suitcase all by itself.

'Whatever you say,' he said. 'All right, I won't take up any more of your time. I'm glad we got this all sorted out. And listen, don't hesitate to ring me again, any time you need anything.'

He left with the jaunty step of someone who has won a victory. Meanwhile Laura had to struggle to remember that she had a job and that there was accordingly no need for her to feel this oppressive sense of defeat. Which stole over her, none the less, like a waft of unhealthy air from a closed-up room.

SEVENTEEN

The job.

Thank God for the job.

It wasn't just the prospect of – eventually – getting enough money together to pay back this new and bizarre debt. It was the occupation too. Work was a crucible. It melted down the energy that would otherwise, she knew, have gone into worrying about Mike Mackman and his stifling generosity and what form it would take next, with nerve-grinding results.

So her job at Sprignall's was a double boon. And even if that prospect of paying the debt was only a distant one – they certainly did not pay her in shovelfuls – she had another iron in the fire, one that might enable her to do it quite quickly. The estate agents (she had chosen the town's oldest and most reputable firm, established five whole years and with only a dozen swindled and gibbering ex-clients in their wake) came, valued, and hoisted their sign. If she could sell, and buy somewhere very much more modest as was her intention, then there ought to be enough left over to clear that debt at a stroke. Good thought. And there must be some legal way of making Mike Mackman take the money, if it came to it: there were enough legal ways of making people cough it up.

She did wonder about him, sometimes. In spite of her own internal assertions that he was nothing to do with her and therefore not to be wondered about, she couldn't help trying to get a fix on him, understand what he was about. A builder – she kept seeing the name around, with little plunges of the spirit – and obviously a successful one in the sense that it wasn't he who mixed the cement, though she had a strong feeling that he had once: he had the look of a self-made man about him. Lived at Champaign Park, that place of artfully curving roads, balled gateposts and Lego-brick finish that David had so despised because it housed executives who earned more than he did. Mike lived there alone, presumably – he had mentioned splitting up with his wife, and there being no children. He had money to spare. He was rather old-fashioned in his morality; and there was a terrible sensitivity alongside the bullish robustness.

And one day in January he had accidentally knocked down and killed a man in his car; and he simply could not put this aside.

Laura added it all up, seeing what she got. But the sum, though plain enough, couldn't account for the sheen of unease that covered all her thoughts of Mike Mackman.

All she could do was try to keep those thoughts to a minimum. So thank God for the job and thank God too for her work colleagues, who excused her initial nervous ham-fistedness and refrained from pointing out that for the first week she was more of a hindrance than a help.

Some of this was oddly familiar, from her marriage. Indeed that was part of the problem. She needed to remind herself, when she toted trays or pushed laden trolleys back to the kitchen, that it didn't matter if cups toppled, if crockery clashed together: noise was part of the deal and there was no David wincing fastidiously at the dining table and rolling his eyes if she showed less than a conjurer's dexterity with physical objects. When she called out a table number, there was no need to be hesitant: the people in the restaurant had ordered that food and it was part of the deal that they be alerted – as opposed to the days when she would tell David dinner was ready and find him sighingly relinquishing a task that could not really be interrupted for such a trivial matter.

So the chief thing she had to conquer was herself. For the rest, it was a matter of staying upright. The working day was a shape that rose steeply to a peak at lunchtime and then tailed gently down to four. This suited Laura: she had always functioned best in the mornings, and that was when the bulk of preparation needed to be done, the peeling and scraping and slicing and buttering. For most of this time she was in the kitchen, which was big though not quite big enough, and where the catering-size packages bearing familiar logos – giant drums of salt, huge firkins of cooking oil, outsize tubs of margarine – gave her a strange childlike feeling as she grasped at them with hands that seemed too small. Later she usually took a turn out front, serving or clearing tables, sometimes concluding the day with cleaning out the temperamental dishwasher, though this machine tended to be the preserve of muscular Becky, who had a love-hate relationship with it. Sometimes she could be seen lying on the floor with her head in it: she was servicing it, car-mechanic style, but at first glance it looked as if she had been driven to a quirkily apt suicide.

Working brought back to Laura the consciousness of being an individual. 'Laura,' they called, 'could you go on tables?' – and that was her, a single self-contained person out in the world. She saw her name on the rotas pinned up in the kitchen – Wednesday – Colette, Becky, Laura – and thought with a wondering recognition: that's me. Not David's Laura, not Laura and David, not David's wife, not Simon's mum, not Mrs Ritchie – the only representations of herself she was used to seeing as valid. 'So what are you doing this weekend, Laura?'

Shirley or one of the others would ask when they crammed into the storeroom for a break (they were entitled to use Sprignall's staff room, but peculiar in-house rivalries made it uncomfortable) and Laura would think: wait a minute, she means *me*. For so long, 'you' had been a plural. Work highlighted the transformation in her as nothing else had.

And maybe some day a loneliness would set in with this. When someone spoke of their husband's birthday or their feller's parents coming over for dinner, perhaps it would begin to pain this solitary, single-case Laura she had become. For all she knew, that was an inevitable stage. After the agonizing surgical dislocation of the first months (an unhappy marriage, sure, but it was still a severing, a ghastly amputation) there came the stage of bemused revelation and adaptation – and at last, the wistful sadness as you came to perceive that this was a world of couples, a Noah's Ark world that went two by two.

Maybe. Laura couldn't see it happening to her. But then she couldn't see herself old either, white-haired and stiffened: that was surely going to happen to some different self from the one she inhabited now. And look what a fallacy that was, because she could remember feeling exactly the same about marriage and motherhood. So who knew? All she could say was there were no signs, and if the sap ever did rise again, she would be very surprised.

Shirley, likewise a widow, certainly didn't seem to have got to that stage yet. Not that there were any confidences. That revelatory glimpse at the interview did not open out into wide prospects. Shirley was friendly but businesslike. She did not go in for casual soul-baring (as you sometimes saw the girls who worked at Sprignall's, head to head like chess players, solemnly spilling the beans, I told him I finally told him) and gave the impression that she would have found it tasteless. Only once did Laura get another glimpse. A multiple sclerosis charity asked permission to leave a collecting tin by the restaurant's till. There were objections from the catering manager – an on-off presence who formed part of a Byzantine chain of command that included the Sprignall's head office and the franchise head office and then disappeared into the sky somewhere – who didn't like the look of it. Blue plastic would lower the tone (the restaurant was natural wood, earthenware cruet, Little House on the Prairie curtains). Shirley stood up to him with unusual tenacity – unusual in that he was just too repulsive to argue with for long.

'That's how I lost Bob,' Shirley remarked to Laura when she was wiping down the counter, tapping the collecting tin. 'Not a nice way to go.'

It was all she said or needed to say. A thing had happened that was not going to fade. Laura's experience wasn't comparable, but she recognized the impress, the mark that lasted.

So when Shirley was scabrously saucy Laura knew it was something quite separate. Shirley often was, but it always made you gasp and laugh because she never prepared and paraded it. (Laura remembered that now from her previous jobs – the ponderousness of workplace ribaldry: the women had a special wiggle that announced they were about to be uninhibited.) Shirley was deadpan. 'Tell which side he dresses,' she would murmur as a tight-jeaned teen angled past the till. 'Oh look, truth and fiction,' she remarked on seeing a gherkin and a cucumber side by side on the chopping board. Sometimes she used it to defuse a situation. Colette, Laura's fellow full-timer, contracted a hacking cough that had Liam, the chef, flapping and wailing about germs on the food. 'Yes, Colette,' Shirley said, 'you should know it all comes out when you cough.'

The testy chef tyrannizing his kitchen was such a piece of modern folklore, like merciless traffic wardens and philosophizing taxi drivers, that Liam could have been forgiven for playing up to it. But mostly he resisted the temptation – in fact laid-back was the term that suggested itself, though Laura didn't suppose it a contradiction when she characterized Liam's demeanour as bundle-of-nerves laid-back. Nerves came out two ways. When she was like that her shoulders went round her ears and she could only squeak like Minnie Mouse, rooted to the spot. Others were all talk and movement, like Liam, who was six feet two of thin, rangy, humming, egg-juggling blarney. They were both ways to stop you flying apart.

Liam smoked for two, which got the usual animadversions in the storeroom breaks. Colette was keen to inform him that cigarettes were bad for him.

'Hey, I never knew that. You're kidding me, aren't you? Why don't they tell you these things? I wonder if there's anything on the packet to – well, damn my eyes, will you look at that? "Tobacco seriously damages health." You learn something every day. You don't mind it, do you?' he pleaded to Laura. 'Please say you don't.'

Laura didn't. Her upbringing had stressed intolerance as the highest virtue, and she had accordingly embraced the other side. She didn't mind anything much except the things that were plainly wrong, like beating people up or setting fire to kindergartens, and this made her a bit of an outsider in what she sometimes thought of as the Culture of Offence. She was secretly pleased to find in Liam a kindred spirit.

'Some people do find that offensive, though,' Colette said one day, when there had been a lot of righteousness over the TV showing of a film about Jesus which suggested that he, or He, didn't look like Robert Powell in a terry robe. 'You just have to respect that.'

'Ah, I don't know, what does that mean? Offended?' Liam said, reducing his foot-long cigarette to ash with a couple of urgent sucks.

'What does offended feel like? I know what it feels like to be pissed off and angry and scared and all that, but – *offended*? Nah.'

'What about Irish jokes, though?' Colette said in her plonkingly complacent manner, reminiscent of a TV weather girl. 'Aren't they offensive to you?' Liam was from Belfast.

'Irish people tell them. You tell them about the southern Irish, or you tell them about the folks from the next county, it just goes on. I mean the Aussies tell Aussie jokes, or they did when I was there. They've maybe gone all tight-arsed now.'

'When were you there?' Laura said.

'Oh, ten years ago. Seemed like a good idea at the time.'

From this and other such jigsaw-pieces – he had cheffed on the North Sea oil rigs and Channel ferries – she had gained a picture of Liam as a wanderer. Suitably; his appearance suggested it. His loose-knit frame looked as if it weighed about six stone, and he dressed it in intractably unmatching clothes, the sort that are picked up along the way. He wasn't solid.

'It was OK. It was too darn hot, though, and there wasn't any work. I was a bit disappointed. I mean I wanted a bit more culture shock. The older people were Australian enough but the young are American, same as everywhere. They are! That's why it's so pointless going on about Europe. Nobody gives a stuff about Europe except these old crocks who flew with the Dambusters. The young here don't even bother about being British let alone European. They just want to be Americans. They want the whole culture, all of it. Everything else is crap to them. Ever see a kid wanting crisps now? They want potato chips. They won't accept any other term. And they'll only eat chips, y'know chips chips, if they're fries. They want to be invaded. They want to be annexed. True, I'm telling you.'

'My little boy still has crisps,' Laura said.

'How old is he?'

'Seven.'

'Ah – but it wouldn't have got him yet. Watch it kick in. Couple of years. I can't talk. I'm the same. When I went through the stage of writing bedsit songs on an out-of-tune guitar I would put "baby" in the words. "But baby, you know I'm lyyy-ing . . ." I've never called anybody baby in my life. Wouldn't dream of it.'

'Well, I don't know. All I know is I'm proud to be British,' said Colette. Sometimes you suspected that Colette had not been born but put together by statisticians at some consumer survey headquarters. She was the ideal droid, the man on the Clapham omnibus for the brainwashed millennium. All clothes fitted her. Her favourite group were at number one. Her favourite TV programmes were the ones that appeared in the top ten viewing figures, in that order. She fancied Brad Pitt and thought that Christmas was a bit too commercialized and should be about families. And people seemed to perceive this – the chattings-up that came her way in the restaurant were desultory, as if the men knew she was twenty-four and seven months and about to get statistically married at any moment to a man two years her senior whom she had met at a social gathering.

Laura herself came in for a few innuendoes, usually from sweaty businessmen when she was on tables; but her only persistent nods and winks came from an unusual source, a man who came in every lunchtime and whom she recognized from his involvement in various benighted street theatre activities and other Langstead embarrassments. He was a bit long in the tooth for it – perhaps, she thought, that was why he singled her out – and his appearance could only have been carried off by a very young and naïve student who didn't mind being repeatedly duffed over. Sometimes when he entered in full regalia – rainbow woollies, spray-painted boots, smock woven from coconut and rice husks, three-way hair divided between peroxide spikes, dreadlocks and duck's arse, square bank-manager specs – Laura felt like telling him: stop now; don't go any further. The effect is complete, the thing is achieved. You simply cannot look any more of a prat than you do now. So to add anything (flippers, beanie with propeller) would simply be a retrograde step, away from utter stupidity. It would be a shame to let ambition spoil perfection.

Though she didn't say any of this, she felt cruel thinking it. But it was the vanity that turned her stomach, rather than the clutching after youth (and it wasn't as if any young person with a full set of marbles would ever choose to look like that anyhow). After all, hers was a generation that had only ever known a youth culture. *Vide* Liam, whose thing was pop music – historically, encyclopedically: part of a new breed of people who were not young (Liam was well in his thirties, lived-in, receding) but who were enthusiastic and reminiscent about pop as oldsters were supposed to be about Glenn Miller and steam trains. Getting to know Liam, she guessed that this was a matter of stability. He had been all over the place and done all sorts of unprescribed things: it was not a life with the conventional markers, as she supposed hers was. Snapshots of her at nineteen, at twenty-five, at thirty, would show a progression: the passing of stages. Pop music, she surmised, located Liam.

'Tell Laura how many records you've got,' Colette teased.

'Ach, no,' he moaned. 'Don't do that to me.'

'Hundreds he's got,' Colette informed her. 'No, thousands.'

'I confess,' Liam said. 'Sad, isn't it? Just like the feller in that Nick Hornby book except no, I mean he owns a record shop and I haven't even got that excuse. When I die all the different carrier bags that Our Price have used will pass before my eyes.'

The radio was always on in the kitchen, and Liam could name any record that came on within seconds. A chord, a single drumbeat was enough.

'I don't just like anything,' he said in reply to another teasing from Colette. 'Not at all. You've got me entirely wrong there. Everyone has a cut-off point. Laura, back me up here. What's the one sound that you don't like?'

'The alarm clock going off in the morning,' Laura said.

'I make the jokes. There must have been a time when you heard something in a record you didn't like the sound of, that showed what was in the wind. With me it was the farty synth on New Order's "Blue Monday". Suddenly I was afraid of the future.'

'I remember getting an Elvis Costello album and the drums sounded really smooth and chunky,' Laura said, surprising herself with the memory. 'Before that they sounded like dustbin lids. And that must have been the time I started to go off him.'

'Well, I like lots of different music, I do. U2, Whitney Houston, George Michael,' said Colette, consulting her statistical databanks.

It was a good hour later, when Laura was down at the service bay unloading rubbish, that Liam came hurtling after in such a way that she thought she must have done something drastically wrong in the kitchen – thoughtlessly opened a jar labelled 'Salmonella' or absently grated glass into the cheese toasties.

'*Trust*,' he cried joyously. 'I've just thought of it.'

'What about trust?'

'*Trust*. I'm speaking in italics here. That was the Elvis Costello album where the drums sounded different.'

'That was it.'

He looked pleased with himself, then crestfallen. 'Or would it be *Punch the Clock*?'

'Well, it would be round about that time. I suppose everybody hears things differently. You know "Forever in Blue Jeans" by Neil Diamond?'

'I wish I didn't.'

'Well, for a long time I thought that song was called "The Reverend Blue Jeans. You listen next time it's on.'

Liam's chuckle was low and undemonstrative. It was the sort of unpressured laugh that people employ with each other when they know they are going to be friends. Later she heard him crooning it in the kitchen. 'The Rever-end Blue Jeans . . .'

In the looking-glass world of TV, friendships didn't begin and ripen. They were just there, perhaps because everybody in that world lived next door to each other – but then again it wasn't the sort of thing that was capable of being shown. It happened in tiny undramatic doses. You didn't gasp and say, 'That's exactly what I've always thought!' It could be a simple matter of the other person saying, 'Well, I feel shit-awful today,' when you did too but hadn't said it because everybody else seemed chipper. It could be a shared grimace after a subtly off-colour pep talk from the catering manager, a mutually sustained effort to change the subject when Colette came out with some spectacularly ill-informed views about the likelihood of catching AIDS from a used fork.

Laura had never really had a male friend before. She had generally believed, as a rule of thumb, that when a man showed a sympathetic interest in a woman who wasn't ninety or hunchbacked, he only had one ultimate aim in view. Maybe he wasn't going straight for it, but it was the potential that inspired him, as the old explorers set sail with the hope that the voyage would lead, somehow somewhere, to a heap of gold.

Making friends with Liam disabused her of this prejudice. If he really was after some sexual El Dorado, then he was going a hell of a long way round. There were none of the usual gambits – hints at himself as a man of sorrows, extra moiety of gentleness and reserve when in the company of other men to show you that he was a better romantic bet than they, nor even emphatic representation of himself as a Friend because men and women could be, couldn't they, just someone to talk to with no strings attached, he'd always believed that (perhaps the commonest gambit nowadays, and more wolfish than any). He was, it seemed, the exception.

Unless she counted Mike Mackman. After all, she was certain he didn't have his eye on the main chance either. But that was different. It was different above all because she felt at ease with Liam, and she did not feel at ease with Mike Mackman. Thankfully she didn't have to spend time with him. She drew a cheque on her first month's pay and sent it to his address in Champaign Park, and hoped that these instalments would be as close as their association got. It seemed a reasonable hope: she had made a habit of looking out for that big silver hatchback of his, but there was no sign of it prowling Shakespeareland. There was only so much, she reasoned, that he could do: other people's lives just weren't that open to interference.

Maybe it was the confidence work gave her that allowed her to come to this optimistic conclusion: maybe Binkie, or some other mark-my-words figure, would have winced at it. But Laura didn't realize it was misplaced until a day in May.

Leaving work she offered Liam a lift, remembering that the pushbike he usually rode had been pilfered from the store car park. He accepted on condition that it wouldn't make her late for Simon. He knew about her son, though not the circumstantial details. She liked their friendship all the more for its being a happy one – no lugubrious invitations to view each other's scars.

'That's OK. He goes to my friend's house after school and I pick him up from there. It's Towler Street, isn't it? That's not far.'

As she drove she told him about the antediluvian headmistress of Simon's school, who when Simon had informed her, 'My mum works in a kitchen,' had trilled in reply, 'Oh, but that's what mums do!'

'My daddy couldn't handle it when I liked cooking,' Liam said. Laura had got used to the Northern Irish 'daddy' by now. It was rather attractive, as when American Southerners used it. 'But I suppose it just about ranks above hairdressing and ballet dancing in the manly stakes. I mean, you can do catering in the army. I think it was that that reassured him . . . Jeez, the traffic's terrible, so it is. I don't know how you do it.'

They were travelling down Bourges Way; and he couldn't know the resonance of that last remark.

'You don't drive, then?' she said.

'Don't because I can't. I dunno, when I was young cars weren't cool. Like suntans and being good-looking and being able to dance. It was cool to be this kind of pale, incapable stick insect. I blame Wham for the change in that.'

'Well, I don't really like driving. I got out of the habit— Whoops, sorry,' she ground the gears, 'there's the proof for you. My husband always used to drive.'

'Amicable separation, or don't ask?'

'Er, he died.'

'My God. Sorry.'

'January.'

'Sounds like you've had it rough.'

'Not so bad. We're on our feet now, anyway.' Did she experience a superstitious shiver then? Or did hindsight supply it later?

'Shit,' Liam said frowning. 'I believe, I do believe I shouted at you on your very first day. Something about the deep fryer. I was in a tizzy. Shit.'

She laughed. 'It doesn't matter. The awful thing is after a while you . . . you don't want to be a bereaved person any more. You know. Special treatment. You don't want that identity. You want to be like everybody else . . . Which makes you sound hard.'

He made a noncommittal noise. Voluble, he didn't fear silence. After a moment he rolled up his sleeve to above the elbow.

'See that?' he said, revealing a tattoo – the usual queasy colours and pre-infantile artwork, a pictorial bruise. 'Oh, I'm not asking you to admire it. I want you to recoil and then commiserate with me. Looks bloody awful, doesn't it?' He rolled his sleeve down, thin face hawkish with disgust. 'I was nineteen, I think. Had an idea it would help me get girls. Probably would, if you liked the sort of girls who look like bulldogs in tights. I've hated it ever since. I mean *from the very next day* I hated it. Because it is not me and it's on my body. Every time I wash I have this identity crisis.'

Laughing, she said, 'It could be worse.'

'On my bum, you mean? Or even worse than that. I remember these photographs on the walls in the tattooist's place. Chamber of horrors. It was like these people really hated themselves, you know. I mean why not just stick a knife through your head and have done with it?'

'I read somewhere that Prince Albert had a ring through his willie. But I think that was meant to stop him, you know, getting excited.'

'Well, that obviously didn't work. All those children Queen Vicky had.' He gave his lazy chuckle.

'It's not that bad, you know, the tattoo. You could make a feature of it. You could be one of those TV chefs, you know, the ones who act like lads and go on about football.'

'I'll tell you something about these new lads,' he said energetically. '*They were all wimps at school.* Ach, these comedians and singers and frigging violinists and what have you, waving their scarves and going on about footy – they were the ones who stood at the side of the field or the touchline or whatever you call it with their hands down their shorts looking cold and miserable while the big boys were booting the ball about. There must be people who were at school with these guys who see them on TV and think: Him? *Football?* Don't make me laugh! I know because I was one of them – the ones with their hands down their shorts. Jeez, it's a world of fibs, so it is . . . Just down here.'

It was an old low-slung neighbourhood of terraces and Indian groceries. With the odd gentrified exception, it had the cosiness of places that have not been dickered about with. Liam's place was a flat, or upper half of a house. 'You have to use headphones after eleven,' he said, 'but that's a small price to pay for not having a garden. I mean what is this crap about gardens? If I wanted to dig holes and arse about with fertilizer I'd have been a farmer. You take care now,' he said, getting out. 'I still wish I hadn't shouted at you that first day.'

They smiled, he waved and went in. Waiting for another car to pull out of a drive in front, Laura had an appreciative look round. Nice part of town and, she suspected, not expensive to buy into because it fell between two stools. People snapped up houses like these if they were in Fulham and cost an arm and a leg, but if they were moving out to Langstead they tended to do so in search of leafiness, as if having a dried-up crab apple tree in your front garden insured your kids against turning into smackheads. Yes, it was worth considering.

She felt peaceful. The bright spring afternoon was a friendly teatime yellow above the rooftops. A little girl in a red school cardigan stood at an open door on one leg, knocking mud from her shoe idly, woolgatheringly. She looked pretty and self-contained in a way that she would lose in adolescence and might regain in adulthood, though not with the same freshness. A cat on the move paused and froze, half-turning, in a driveway, with a cat's comic *Mission: Impossible* urgency. An early ice-cream van jangled and stopped, throbbing, somewhere near at hand. Laura wished to freeze the moment, the lemon light, the little girl, the cat, the ice-cream van, knowing it would not do. Each moment was relentlessly devouring itself.

Pity.

She sighed and drove on to Shakespeareland and Jan's house, where Simon gave her his usual physical welcome – usual, at any rate, since David's death. She liked it while being unsure what to make of it. Probably an understandable and healthy need for reassurance – she was really there and not going to disappear and all the rest of it. (Angie would give her chapter and verse.) And in the new orthodoxy it was good to touch. People in respectable offices, she had heard, were encouraged to hunker down in a group hug. Her only anxiety was that he would end up a clinger; though she had to admit that he had adapted very well to this new setup. He liked going to Jan's house, a blessing which was due to the fact that Simon was a child and lived in a world of occult fascinations. Large areas of experience were null to him, others exerted a mysterious pull – you forgot this almost ritualistic aspect of childhood. Every child had a favourite animal (Simon's was a camel) – why? Simon yawned at sports, but devotedly watched a wordy hospital drama, could not pass a hardware shop without looking in at its resoundingly dull display of washing-up bowls and watering-cans, yearned to own a mouth organ. And in Jan's house, to his eternal delight, there was an aquarium. Neither Jan nor Ross nor their daughters were crazy about it. Like most aquariums, it had seemed like a good idea at the time of acquisition, then had just stayed around because it had cost a bomb and no one cared to tip the fish down the toilet and acknowledge that the thing had been a waste of money. But with Simon they were at last getting a return on their investment. Just seeing it was a big deal for him, and going to Jan's house after school an unending treat. Laura could see a day coming when Simon would sidle into the kitchen, hug the door, and musingly wonder why they hadn't got one, but at least it hadn't come yet.

'Mum,' Simon said as they drove home, 'you know Kate.'

'Yes.' Kate was the eleven-year-old who, being Jan and Ross's child, had not hacked her wrists with a broken cider bottle at having a small boy around but was actually nice to him and even bought him sweets. The elder girl, Sarah, was fourteen and lived in her bedroom; Jan hazily recalled glimpsing her about a year ago.

'She's got a boyfriend.'

'Has she now? How d'you know that?'

'He put a rubber band in her rucksack.'

'Ah.' I'm growing old, she thought.

'She doesn't like him, though. Look, the window cleaner's here.'

He couldn't be, she thought as she turned into the drive of Number 19: their window cleaner went to prison a lot and was, she knew, incarcerated at the moment.

What the hell was going on?

The details presented themselves to her in awful sequence, like the stages of a migraine.

The van, parked at a respectful distance from the house. Not the big silver saloon but a van with that manly logo, 'MIKE MACKMAN BUILDERS', on the side.

On the front path, carefully set out on a white sheet, a large tub of some kind of filler, and trowels and spatulas and other tools she didn't recognize.

Leaning against the front of the house, an aluminium ladder.

At the top of it, Mike Mackman in workshirt and jeans, with a trowel in one hand and on the other arm something that looked like an artist's palette.

Mike Mackman's feet, chunkily, nimbly descending.

Laura got out of the car, followed by Simon, and waited.

Looking flushed, healthy, and prepared, Mike smiled and said, 'Now, don't say it. What you must remember is this really isn't a big job for me. It's my trade. It's like falling off a log. I can do it in my spare time, no sweat.'

While Laura gasped in speechlessness, he turned his attention to Simon. He made a clicking noise, as to a horse, and said, 'Hello there. You must be Simon, yeah? Did you have a good day at school?'

'Yes, thank you,' Simon said, polite as ever.

'Where is it you go? Parkhill?'

Simon nodded.

'Ah, I was useless at school, I was. Never paid attention. I'll bet you do, though, don't you?'

Simon, who had had the school conversation a thousand times, nodded cursorily.

'I don't understand why you're doing this,' Laura said when she found her voice. 'And – God, I seem to have said that before. I really didn't expect to be saying it again.'

Mike, whose eyes had been dwelling on Simon with a remote nostalgic look, snapped to attention and said, 'Now look. In the first place, I did knock, but when there was no one in I thought I might as well get started straight away. And like I say, this is something I can do. I mean this is a different thing from the money, if that's what's bothering you. Entirely different. This is something I really can offer you.'

'What?' she said, in rising, bubbling irritation. She struggled to keep her hands from deploying on her hips. She had seen Colette do that: it didn't look good.

'Well.' He seemed to resign himself, with a little laugh, to stating the obvious. 'I saw the sign.'

For a moment she thought he was speaking in spooky terms – a sign from above or something – and then she followed his pointing finger.

The estate agent's sign, fixed by the front gate.

'And that really was by chance,' he said. 'I mean I genuinely did have to drive down this way.'

Again the little laugh. And Laura, staring at him, found she didn't know whether to believe him or not. That formula usually meant that you didn't believe, deep down; but in this case she genuinely didn't know. He was beyond her.

'So, I thought, here's something I can do. Right up my street. Actually,' he said, casting a serious critical glance up at the house, 'it won't take that much to get it up to scratch. I know it probably looks a lot and that's why it must all seem so impossible for you, but believe me. Your roof's sound, you won't have to worry about that, and once I've finished pointing up the brickwork – I should think you get a touch of damp in that front bedroom, don't you – and done something about that window-frame, which I can get you a replacement for, no trouble, then you'll see that—'

'I don't see anything,' she burst out. 'I don't see what it is you're playing at. For Pete's sake, this is our home.'

'I know.' Suddenly he was a hurt little boy, smarting and plaintive. 'I know, Laura. That's precisely why I'm doing this for you.' Again he flung a stubby cement-flecked arm at the sign. 'That damn thing. Take it down. You shouldn't have to sell your home. I can see what went through your mind – the place is too much for you, it's too big a job to keep in repair. But this is it, you see: I can do that for you. I'll start on the inside too, when you're ready. Honestly, it won't be much work. These places were built solid. Once a few things are fixed up you'll be all right here for years and years, you and Simon, and you won't have to worry about the upkeep – though of course if anything were to, you know, give you a bit of trouble I'm just on the other end of the phone line and can be here in a flash.' He was away now: his eyes got this uplifted look and he talked at rather than to her, talked out of some deep and turbulent springs of self. 'It's such a terrible thing – I tell you, it gutted me when I saw that sign. Having to leave your home – your *family* home – and all because of me. I just thought, no way. No way. And thank God, I really mean this, thank God that I happen to be someone who can actually help you with it.'

There weren't that many complex feelings in life, not much beyond love-hate and shall I-shan't I. That was why dealing with him was so difficult and perplexing; because confronted with Mike Mackman

Laura really was a prey to a complexity of feelings that had her wishing, more fervently than ever before, that you were issued with some kind of operator's manual at birth. What did you do, what did you say, with this? She couldn't help feeling touched, and sorry for him; she felt mystified by him and unnerved by him; there was a bit of admiration for his persistence mixed in there, and there was a bit of self-reproach for being so ungrateful at what was meant to be kindness, and there was a good deal of astonishment at his obtuseness and his sheer dominating presuming brass neck.

And most of all there was anger. Which had a way of pushing to the front of any queue.

'Look,' she said, feeling herself starting to shake, 'that isn't the reason I'm selling. I'm not *having* to do anything. I'm selling because I want to.'

She was trying to control herself for Simon's sake. Kids found angry voices upsetting even if they weren't directed at them. But the look Mike gave her as she spoke – a look of indulgent admiration at her fragile feminine courage – tipped her over the edge.

'I want to move house,' she said stormily, 'and that's why I'm selling. Isn't that anybody's right, to move house if they want to? Haven't you ever come across that?'

'Is it the memories?' he said, as if she hadn't spoken. 'It must be terrible, I can see that – everything continually reminding you of your husband. But sometimes, you know, people do these things in a hurry. They cut themselves off from the past and then they wish they hadn't. In time, I'm sure, it'll be comforting to have the memories round you. You'll be glad you stayed.'

'I want – to move,' she said, labouring the words out like a dim child reading aloud. 'I just want to make a new start. There isn't any need for you to do this. And even if we were staying, you still – you still shouldn't do it. It's just not . . .' What other expression was there? 'It's not your business.'

'Ah, but it is, though. If I hadn't – if I hadn't done what I did in January, then you wouldn't be leaving your home. Now would you? Eh?'

'Maybe not.' Damn that admission. 'But it doesn't matter. We're moving and that's that.'

'Where? I know, you're going to say that's not my business either. But I'm concerned for you. You and the little 'un.' He cast another misty glance at Simon, who was mooching about the front garden with a child's deceptively oblivious look. 'I've got to know that you're all right. I can't rest easy unless I know you're all right. That's all.'

'We are all right,' Laura said, softening a little in spite of herself. 'I – I don't know where we'll be moving to. Somewhere smaller, you know, nearer town—'

'There. I knew it. You see – you're having to go somewhere smaller because you can't manage this place. See, this is exactly it. I was right. Now look, I can *help* you manage. You can't give up your home when there's – there's help available, Laura, all the help you need.'

'Mike. Listen to me. We don't want any help. We don't need it. I'm selling the house because I want to move. Like I've said before, it's a matter of getting on with life. I can't put it any way that doesn't sound horrible – but really, I don't want anything from you. I'm going to pay you back that money as soon as I can, that shouldn't be too long now that I'm working—'

'What?'

'Working.' She tried to ignore the sounds in her head – screeching brakes, klaxons, alarm bells. Damn it, she thought, why shouldn't I be straight with him? I'd tell anybody else. 'I've got a new job. So now I'm earning—'

'Oh my God, you didn't take a job so you could pay me back?' He spoke in a kind of desperate chant. 'Oh no, oh my God, you didn't—'

'*No*. I got a job because . . .' Don't say anything about money: big mistake. 'Because I wanted to be working. Standing on my own two feet, independent, you know.'

'A job.' He was staring at her as if he couldn't decide whether she had gone mad or was making a very bad joke. 'I don't get it. What about Simon?'

Oh yes, he's got a job too, deep-sea diving. 'What about him?'

Flatly, Mike said, 'You can't look after a little lad and do a job.'

Well, that was it. She knew there were plenty of men, women too, who still inhabited these primeval forests of thought, but to be tackled like this in her own front garden . . . 'I've had enough now. I don't have to account for myself to you. Really, that's enough. I think you should go.'

'I'm sorry.' He passed a hand across his eyes. 'That wasn't right, the way I put that. I didn't mean to suggest . . . I mean, you're a wonderful mother. I know that, I can see that. That's the last thing I meant to— But I'm just so concerned for you, all these things you're having to do, surely you're taking on too much, you're having to play the man's part as well, and—'

'Oh, Mike, women work. They do.'

His face showed what he thought of that. But he didn't say it. He sighed and shook his head and said, 'I don't know. It just gets worse . . . I'm not saying you can't do it. I've seen how strong you are, I'll bet you could do anything you set your mind to. It's you *having* to do it that gets me. I mean, it can't be easy. What about when the little lad comes out of school?'

'A friend picks him up and looks after him until I finish.' This was all she could do: it was no good saying it was none of his business, because he would just keep on. Succinct answers, until he ran out of questions. Then perhaps he would go – though she had a lurking fear that nothing would shift him short of a water cannon.

'I don't know.' Still he shook his head, mournfully. 'I don't like it, no good pretending I do. I mean, you must be so tired, for one thing. It just seems so awful, the things you're having to do when there's no need, it – it really cuts me up.'

'I love working. I love the job.'

'Ah, you'd say that, of course you would. This is it – you're having to be so strong all the time, making out everything's all right—'

'Everything is all right,' she said, 'except this. This hassle is the one thing I could do without. So please.' She gestured at the ladder, the neat array of tools. 'Please just go.'

'All right. If that's what you want.'

'It is.'

'That's good enough for me. What I'll do, I'll finish that pointing-up. I might as well now I've started it—'

'No.' She was amazed at how temperate her voice sounded, because inside her there was a scream to shatter glass. 'Leave it. Simon! Come on. Mike, we're going in now. You go home, and let that be the end of it. I know you're trying to be kind, but it isn't kind, what you're doing. It's interfering and it's making life more difficult for everybody.' There was this to be said for the end of your tether – it was a place of lucidity. 'I never asked you to pay that debt, but as you have, I'm going to pay you the money back as soon as I can. And that's all. So now let's say goodbye.'

Simon tucked his hand in hers, and Laura walked up to the front door and took out her key.

Doing this meant turning her back on Mike Mackman. Never an easy thing in any circumstances, turning her back had particularly unpleasant and neck-tingling associations for Laura. So too did the anger of a man against whom she was trying to assert herself . . . and when she cast the inevitable glance backward she found herself terribly afraid.

Mike was standing there motionless – and motionless as human beings really seldom are, unwavering, unblinking. He seemed massively anchored in her front garden, a tree or stone that would endure through gales and blizzards. All the life in his blockish body was concentrated in his eyes, which glared and glared.

And she was afraid (the fear as familiar as yesterday's clothes) that this was the stillness that presaged eruption. She opened her mouth to speak, instinctively summoning the weak rubbish of the soul – sorry, my fault, listen, what I just said, I didn't mean . . .

But then she saw he was smiling. Shaking his head a little, he smiled that fond, indulgent, resigned, whatever-you-say smile, walked over to the tools set out on the sheet, and began gathering them up. He was whistling, softly, something mildly jaunty which she recognized as she went in: 'On the Sunny Side of the Street'.

Once inside she watched him, from the front room window with its shielding nets, as he put the tools away in the van, folded down the ladder, stowed it on the roof rack. He did it all in an unhurried knocking-off-for-the-day way. She couldn't hear him, but she could see from the shape of his lips that he was whistling all the time.

EIGHTEEN

'Good idea, gel, I don't blame you,' Peggy sighed over the phone when Laura told her about the job. 'You want to get out of the house, course you do. Now you're on your own, only natural. I wish I could get out of the house a bit meself.' She said this with a hint of resentment. 'What about when little 'un comes home? Does he have a latchkey?'

'No,' said Laura, who had no idea what this meant. 'He goes to Jan's – you know, the lady you met at the funeral? Just till I pick him up.'

'Nice lady. I remember. Good to have friends, isn't it? I can't get out to see me friends much.' Again there seemed resentment in her pantings. 'Here, what about Whit? The kids are off school then. What are you going to do Whit?'

Translating, Laura realized this meant the Whitsun break. Peggy was full of this alternative vocabulary: windcheater, five-and-twenty past, washing soda, motor-car, counterpane, vase pronounced vayze. In ten years' time her speech would be as incomprehensible as Chaucer.

'Jan's going to help out with that as well,' Laura said. 'She's been very kind.'

'Only I'd have him here, gel, willingly. He could stop with his nan. Only there's Reg's lot, you see. They've sort of got used to coming here, and there isn't a lot of room once they get sat down. And they are local. So they've got to come first really, do you see?'

'Of course, Peggy. It's all right. I've already fixed it with Jan.' Long before assertiveness had been invented, Peggy had learnt the trick of never doing anything she didn't want to do.

Laura had, as she had said, fixed it with Jan – or rather, Jan had insisted – but she wasn't happy about it. It smacked of taking a mile when given an inch. She couldn't go on imposing on people's good nature as if widowhood gave her some sort of *carte blanche*. By the time of the next school holiday, Laura told herself, she must make an arrangement with a childminder.

'Anyway, gel, you give me a ring any time,' Peggy concluded. 'You ever need to talk about anything, any problems come up, you ring me. I'm always here, I am. Never get out.'

So she had Laura pegged as a gadabout. But even if the offer were sincere, Laura didn't see how she could talk to Peggy about her problems, because strictly speaking she didn't have any. Or rather, such as she had were resolving themselves, at last. The solicitor's fees, not unbearably hefty, were the last of her debts. The murk of her life was steadily clearing.

All except for the stubborn dregs at the bottom. Mike Mackman – or at least the thought of him, for a week had passed since she had found him up a ladder in her front garden and there had been no visitations since then. Her anxious expectation, each time she turned into Duncan Road, that she would find him building her a two-car garage or digging a swimming pool had not materialized.

On the other hand, the cheque she had sent him hadn't been cashed. So you could take it either way – either the fever had passed, or else it was merely in remission.

She chose to cleave to the optimistic alternative, chiefly because it seemed to her – again – that there just wasn't anything more he could do. On the same optimistic theme, she looked to the sale of the house to settle this business finally. When the move came, she had no intention of letting him know where she was moving to, and an ex-directory phone number was a not-too-inconvenient possibility if it came to that.

So there was always the move. Alas, that seemed a long way off. The estate agents sent an elderly couple to view the house almost at once, but as they seemed to be looking for a one-bedroomed bungalow in the country, or maybe a converted railway station with a helipad on the roof, or indeed anything but a suburban semi, it was fair to conclude that this was just a propaganda exercise on the estate agents' part. (Probably, Laura thought, they employed the old couple on a full-time basis, dispatching them to every new instruction.) Well, the estate agents told Laura, the market was pretty sticky, there was no denying it. But they were confident of an upturn: sooner or later, they bulled grittily, they would sell her house. They made this sound like some spectacular and heroic undertaking, like throwing a suspension bridge across a vast river, rather than sticking a photograph in their shop window and charging a thousand pounds for doing it.

Angie came into the restaurant one lunchtime when Laura was clearing tables. She gasped when she saw Laura, and was about to go into one of her hugs when she checked herself.

'Better not, I know. The Gestapo. Can we talk?'

'Yes, I'll just keep pretending to do something,' Laura said, wiping a clean table next to Angie's. 'So how are you?'

'I'm great,' Angie said, nodding repeatedly in the American way, assenting to nothing. 'But so are you by the look of it. How long have you been *working* here?'

'A few weeks,' Laura said. 'I'm enjoying it. Something I needed to do, you know. In all ways. It's a bit dull at times, but . . .'

'Hey, no, I think it's great, I mean it's down there on the ground, it's grass roots. You're an independent lady, that's so *good.*'

'Haven't seen you in here before.'

'Oh, I don't come in often. Bit posh for me. I mean I'm happy with beans on toast and rice pud, you know,' Angie said with a shrug. Laura had seen Angie go through agonies in a pub, drinking a glass of plonk wine and pretending not to know the difference. 'Just I'm supposed to be meeting someone here. Richard – did I mention him?'

'The one who's in conservation?'

'Oh God, no. That was ages ago. He was actually gay though he didn't know it. I tried to point him in the right direction, but . . . No, this Richard's in commercial art. I think we're probably only relating on the sex level, you know, but we'll see. Listen, how's Simon, how's everything? I keep meaning to *ring*, but I've just been so hellishly busy.'

'Simon's fine. Toughing it out. We're – you know, we're getting our life together. The money's sorted out, mainly, and I'm looking to move house some time.'

'Seems like you're on a good learning curve. I suppose there are bad days?'

'Only the usual ones. All in all things are – shaping up.'

All except for one thing, which she didn't tell anyone about, not even Jan. It was a conscious choice: to make a big issue of Mike Mackman would be to acknowledge what, according to common sense, really had no right to be there. It would mean being as over-the-top as he was.

It occurred to her, though, that Angie was perhaps the person to mention it to. All human behaviour was equally meaningful to Angie. She might be able to put a name to what Mike Mackman was doing, characterize it as so-and-so syndrome, cite what proportion of the population suffered from it at some time in their lives.

Just then, however, Angie snapped to attention and whispered, 'Here comes Richard,' so Laura said a warm goodbye and skedaddled. Later she sneaked a look at Angie's companion, who was of the usual sort. Inexplicably Angie seemed to favour men who looked just awful. Not plain-but-homely, not no-Adonis-but-kind-eyes, but real shitbags. It was one of the minor mysteries of life that Angie, attractive and no fool, should continually belly up to men whom you would need a shot of morphine and a protective suit even to consider getting into bed with.

But then Laura felt pretty much that way about the prospect of any romantic entanglement. That even included Liam, whom she perceived as attractive, who had all the makings of a person she could fall for: these things existed only as abstract possibilities, and she would have been crestfallen if he had made any overtures. But either he wasn't interested or else he understood, either of which was fine by her. In the meantime she enjoyed a friendship that reminded her curiously and sweetly of schooldays – especially that lunchtime when Liam learnt that Laura had never been to the mystical top floor of Sprignall's, which was closed to the public and to staff except on explicit summons, and where ancient men in frock coats were reputed to run the whole show from panelled offices with wind-up telephones. He dared her, she dared, and they crept up a flight of echoing stairs to emerge in a silent labyrinth where there really were heavy panelled doors with brass plates and a smell like a disused church. One of the doors opened. They pressed themselves breathlessly into an alcove. A suitably weird and elderly secretary in hornrims and twinset clipped by, but the glimpse into the room beyond revealed the glow of VDUs and the standard matt black and chrome of modern office tech. Still, there was a strong feeling of trespassing in the headmaster's study, and Laura's stomach ached with tense giggles by the time they had scurried back to the restaurant.

'Spooky,' Liam told Colette. 'You wouldn't believe what it's like up there.'

'Oh, tell me-ee!'

'You wouldn't believe me if I did.'

Was this right, to feel this chipper and strong and upbeat, Laura wondered as she drove to Jan's after work. Perhaps it was: perhaps even asking herself the question was only a reflex from the guilt-laden past, when pride always came before a fall. A phrase had occurred to her that seemed worth repeating whenever she found herself looking on the dark side: *Ditch the apocalypse, Laura.* Life wasn't like that: it held plenty of unpleasant surprises, sure, but it didn't brood in that *Wuthering Heights* way.

At Jan's she found that rarity, a touch of domestic discord. Sarah, the eldest girl, was having a tantrum in her bedroom whilst Jan camped outside the door asking what was wrong in between being told that her firstborn hated her unto death. 'I think it's because I went in there and tidied up a bit,' Jan whispered to Laura. 'It'll blow over.' Downstairs Kate, prehormonally serene, sat watching TV whilst Simon watched the aquarium. Laura tore him away, leaving an offering of restaurant-surplus mousse in the kitchen.

'What have we got for tea, Mum?'

'Shepherd's pie. Do your seat belt up.'

'We had shepherd's pie for dinner at school today.'

A familiar ruse for changing the menu, but she swallowed it. 'All right, spaghetti then.'

'Yes,' Simon said in triumph. 'Mum, I saw that man today outside school.'

About to pull out, Laura made a hasty brake. The engine cut out.

'What man?'

'The man who was up a ladder in our garden.'

'When – when was this?'

'Hometime. Auntie Jan was a bit late picking us up. We were waiting at the gate and he was there in a car and he called out, "Simon!" and I went up and he said did I need a lift home.'

For several moments deep primitive channels of herself were filled with molten dread.

'He said what?'

'He said, "Remember me?" and I said yes and he said did I need a lift home.'

And then her mind, like a stalled engine catching, asserted: this is the man who fixed your car and paid your debts and who in his off-the-wall way wants to help you. So it isn't that. It can't be that.

'What did you say?'

Her face must have looked thunderous, because Simon said with a little *moue* of misunderstood innocence, 'I said no and then I went back to Kate. I know you should never get in anybody's car like that.'

'No,' she said. 'No, that was – that was good. You're sure it was that man?'

Simon nodded loftily.

'Was that all he said?'

'Yep. Then he stayed there in his car watching till Auntie Jan came.'

'Then what?'

'Don't know. He went away, I think. Mum, what was wrong with Sarah?'

'Nothing. Let's get home.'

It isn't that: it can't be that. No. When someone hung about a school gate and offered a lift to your child, the shrillest of alarm bells went off – but this, at least, was surely different. Telling herself this kept her together for the drive home. And then the anger took control – literally, took control of her: it felt as if it might lift her off her feet like a rocket-propelled backpack.

Because whatever this was about, she didn't like it. Mike Mackman could have been waiting at that school gate with the most benevolent intentions in the world: she didn't care. She hated it.

She kicked aside a slew of estate agents' details on the doormat, told Simon to go and pour himself some juice, and headed for the phone.

'Mum, can I have some biscuits?'

'Yes.' Where was that damn card he had left . . . ?

'There's only three.'

'Well, when they're gone they're gone.' There it was. She punched the work number. And for God's sake, as if the man shouldn't have known better than to offer a child a lift like that . . .

'Mr Mackman's not here today, I'm afraid. Can I take a message?'

Not the sort she intended to leave. She tried the home number.

'Hello, this is Mike Mackman. I'm afraid I'm not in at the moment, but please leave a message after the tone.'

Hearing that gruff, earnest, straight-arrow voice finished her. She could see him so plainly in her mind's eye – that long silver Audi, his big head with its slightly odd 1970s grooming leaning out of the window, the expression of dogged concern . . . the little lad, the little 'un, left waiting . . .

'Stay away from my son!' she barked into the receiver. 'Stay away from him, you creep! You know who this is! I'm just sick of it! Just get out of our lives! I mean it – I'm just sick to the back teeth with you hanging around us and if you come near my son again I'll . . .'

The words ran out. The backpack sputtered. Laura slammed the phone down.

Throughout that evening and the next morning she waited for the guilt to hit her. She had been nasty – and to a person who meant well. For most of her life this would have meant an attack of guilt so sharp and paralysing it was like mental appendicitis.

She must have gone through more changes than she knew just lately, because it didn't happen. When she recalled the unfamiliar harshness of her own voice yelling into Mike Mackman's answering machine and matched it with a memory of him standing in her hall shaking and crimson with intolerable tears, the guilt was there in some ghostly form – but it didn't become solid. Because none of it made her dislike what he was doing one jot less. She didn't care how bad he was feeling: it gave him no right to meddle with her life in this way. Even putting the most charitable construction on that dubious business of hanging around outside Simon's school – that he wanted to make sure Simon was getting home safely – made it unbearably patronizing and interfering. There was some kindness that simply wasn't kindness. She could see that quite plainly even if Mike Mackman couldn't.

She just wished she had someone with whom to share this perception. Someone to – well, yes, to back her up. That was all she wanted: to tell her story, and then at the end hear the other person say, 'Out of order? Of course he is, I should say so!' But there must have been something of the old, wipe-your-feet-on-my-back Laura left, because she entertained a faint fear that the other person would stare dully at her and say, 'Well, you ungrateful cow. That poor man's only trying to help.'

She certainly didn't want to burden Jan with it, anyhow: Jan had already had to take too much of her life on board. But she did wonder, at work that morning, about telling Liam. There seemed the right combination of intimacy and distance in their relationship; also he was notably easy-going, and probably wouldn't flinch at that uncomfortable gift, a confidence (a trouble shared is a trouble doubled, Laura sometimes felt). And she tended to see him as the voice of sanity. Maybe there were all sorts of neuroses flailing away like loose wires under that approachable surface, but she doubted it.

As it turned out, she didn't need to tell him. That lunchtime Mike Mackman came into the restaurant, and Liam, along with the world and his wife, got to see for himself.

Laura was at the counter, and Liam had come out from the kitchen at the insistence of an awkward customer who had a complaint. The complaint concerned today's special, halibut with pepper sauce, but it was not readily identifiable except as a generalized cussedness which one look at the pop-eyed man gesticulating at the counter revealed to be chronic and incurable. He had on one of those spotted bow ties which announces that the wearer venomously hates everything that has taken place in the world since the invention of the gramophone. Liam apologized humbly for the fact that the halibut was not leek and potato soup or a birthday cake with candles or whatever it was that the crazed one didn't like about it, and flannelled him so successfully that at last he went away saying it was delicious.

'It is not the food *per se*,' he explained as a parting shot.

'Don't call me Percy,' Liam said under his breath to Laura.

'God, thanks, you did well there. I just couldn't get through to him.'

'Treating him on a rational level, maybe. What you have to remember is that he wants to screw up somebody's day. If you—'

'Laura!'

She turned back to the counter to find Mike Mackman gazing into her eyes. He even knew where she worked – had probably followed her here one morning, she guessed, to make sure she arrived safely. But now was not the moment to speculate.

'Laura, how could you – how could you think—'

He broke off, swallowing hard. For a moment it looked like embarrassment – not only Liam but Shirley on the till and the diners at the nearest tables were looking his way – but then Laura knew it wasn't that. Mike wasn't seeing anyone but her. And he was in a flagrantly emotional state. His shoulders heaved and there were beads of sweat in his hairline as he stared at her and at last spoke out again, effortfully, almost with a retch.

'All I wanted – all I wanted to do was make sure the little lad was picked up from school all right. I just wanted to be there and – see him safely picked up, that's all it was.'

'Mike, this isn't—'

'How could you think that?' His voice was audible all over the restaurant now. He leant closer to her, head forward, filling her view

– and to do so he placed his hands flat on the steel part of the counter, where the serving wells were. That, Laura knew, was too hot to touch for more than a second. But Mike didn't seem to feel a thing. 'What you said – that message – that was so terrible, all I wanted to do was make sure he was all right. It's because there are people around like that that I did it. That's exactly why I was checking up, and – to think that you thought I was one of those – bastards . . .'

It was the unwonted obscenity that seemed to snap him back to a partial awareness of himself. His head went up and he threw a glance at Liam and then went on in a voice that was a little lower but trembling, almost tearful, 'I'm sorry to come in here like this, Laura, I'm so sorry, but it's just been – I've been going through hell, knowing that you think of me like that—'

'I don't,' Laura said hastily, 'Mike, I don't. I'm sorry too. That's not what I meant. I was just angry that you – you hadn't listened to what I told you.' She was tingling, wretchedly conscious of the many amazed eyes on her: the little scene could hardly have been more public if they had floodlit it. But she had to answer him – it was the only way. And she was forced, too, to answer him in these reassuring terms, because he was so very upset and she hadn't really believed that of him and, yes, the old guilt had got here at last. Damn, damn . . .

'I always listen to you,' he said, with dreadful sincerity. 'That's why when I found that message on the machine . . .'

'Yes, I'm sorry, I didn't mean that.' But she did mean stay away, and now . . . 'Look, Simon's perfectly all right, he gets picked up from school by a very good friend and there's really nothing to worry about.'

'It must have seemed strange,' Mike said, lifting his hands from the counter at last, and shaking his head to himself. 'I should have thought – I should have realized.' Suddenly he rubbed his hands violently over his face and gave a shuddering groan. 'Oh God, I'm such a fool . . . This is my fault, you know,' he said, darting a look at Liam. 'Not this lady's. I know full well I shouldn't bother people at work like this, so the blame's on me. There mustn't be any comeback for this lady.'

Liam gave a smiling shrug, about all he could do in the circumstances.

'I'm sorry,' Mike said throatily to Laura. 'I've messed up again, haven't I? I keep trying to make things better, but—'

'Just leave it, Mike,' she said helplessly. 'Forget it. I've told you – forget it all, leave it. I don't know what else to say.'

'No.' There were tears standing in his eyes. He glanced round at the restaurant with a kind of savage melancholy. 'I hate you having to work here. I hate it all.' And then he saw that there was a customer waiting to be served behind him – an old lady. It galvanized him as, it seemed, not even a loaded gun could have done. 'I do beg your pardon,' he said, moving aside, and gesturing her forward with all his manly *politesse*. 'I'm holding up the traffic here. Good afternoon.'

And then with that quickness which his size belied he was gone.

Except that, as she shakily served the old lady coffee, Laura saw him pause at the entrance to the restaurant and stare in her direction like an anguished totem for several seconds. She didn't know which was worse – that, or the quite plain opinion of the old lady that he was charming.

As soon as she was able, she went over to Shirley and made her apologies. Shirley raised her eyebrows, waved a hand, and was a little frosty. 'Try to keep them at bay in future, will you?'

It was Liam who sought her out when she went on her break at two. Unable to face the storeroom and Colette's inevitable curiosity, she headed out with her sandwiches and sat on one of the iron benches with which Langstead's pedestrianized centre was perhaps over-supplied – some of them pointed invitingly at litter bins and service bays. She had taken five deep breaths, and gained all the visual pleasure there was to be had from the view of Barclays' side wall, when Liam sat down beside her.

'Was Shirley short with you?' he said, crossing his stick-insect legs. In their checked chef's trousers, scarcely reaching the ankle, they gave him a curiously Dickensian look – some needy clerk with a heart of gold and a name like Tom Swizzlepop.

'Not really.'

'We had a girl working there last year who had half the young fellers in town after her. All used to come in at once and buy half a cup of coffee each, just to see her. I think Shirley's been a bit paranoid about these things ever since.'

'Oh God, is that what it looks like?'

'It doesn't look like anything really.'

'Liar.'

'You going to eat those?'

'Suppose I should. Do you want one?' She watched him eagerly snaffle a sandwich. 'You're a chef, you know. You're not supposed to get excited about cheese and pickle sandwiches.'

'Oh, I don't cook for myself much. You know, it's my job. If you were a plumber, you wouldn't go home and start fiddling with the ball-cock. So, is this guy giving you grief? Tell me to mind my own business, by the way.'

'It's everybody's business after that little show,' she said, laughing unhappily. 'It isn't anything to do with – well, you know, what you might expect.' She glanced at him, calmly eating; and then all at once she began to tell it. Well, she thought as she did so, you were wishing you could confide in someone, and here you are. But this was more like an involuntary confession: it just came out of her, with painful relief, like the sickness that wraps up a migraine.

'Whoa,' he said when she had finished; and then, dusting crumbs from his long thin hands, 'Colette was saying what a dish he was.'

'She's welcome to him,' Laura said, at once regretting it. Because she had felt genuinely sorry for Mike when he had come into the restaurant: she had felt herself in the wrong, an unjust accuser, cruelly ungrateful. Reflection modified these feelings, but there was no doubt that they had acted on her at the time, making her weaken, making her back down from the position she knew she ought to stick to.

But on top of this realization came another – that she had been right to hesitate over telling the story to anyone. Colette's remark was revealing. In essence, she couldn't expect much sympathy. 'You lucky thing!' was the likely reaction from at least a good proportion of women, and men were probably even more liable to see her distress as sheer feminine inconsequence.

Liam's next remark, however, showed that for once she had made the right choice.

'Surely it's harassment.'

He looked at her hard, questioningly. At such times you detected the flinty uncompromising element in him. For all the ease of manner, Laura wouldn't have cared to be the person who tried to make him do something he didn't want to do.

'I suppose. I mean, yes, in that it's a nuisance and a pain and all the rest of it. But when you hear about harassment, it's usually some rejected lover or some creepy obsessive who pinches your underwear off the line or whatever. I mean, Mike wants to *help*. He feels responsible and he wants to help.'

'But you don't want his help?'

'No.'

'Well, I thought we'd accepted nowadays that no means no. Except for a few old judges. Little bit of new-man tokenism there. But it does, though, doesn't it? If somebody keeps doing something when you've asked them to stop it, then it's not right.'

It was what she had been longing to hear, which was perhaps why she found herself playing devil's advocate. 'Yes, but this isn't a normal case. The man's obviously suffering inside.'

'Well, who isn't? Shit happens. Where I come from practically everybody's got some nasty tale to tell. It doesn't mean they build their life on it. Mind you, some do, which accounts for a lot – but you see what I'm saying? People can't go on scratching at their psychological scabs for ever. Or if they do they should do it in private. God, I love it when I talk tough, so I do. Listen, do you fancy a drink after work? I don't mean a blaster. Just a quick one to unwind, if you can unwind after that.'

'Well, I would like to.' The idea was appealing, but unthinkable. She had to pick Simon up, and she didn't want to worry him or impose on Jan by being late. But what made it really unthinkable, she realized, was this new business of Mike Mackman checking up on Simon. If it hadn't been for that, she might at least have considered it. But Mike had planted an insinuating seed: with this new lifestyle of hers, was her little lad really being cared for . . . ?

Damn him.

'But you can't,' Liam said with a smile. 'I know. Some time, though?'

'Some time.'

'It might be the feller's last shot, you know,' Liam said, getting to his feet. 'I mean, hanging around your kid's sailing pretty close to the wind.'

'True, but . . . well, he did mean well.' Laura tossed her sandwich bag into a litter bin, got up. She found Liam giving her that penetrating look again.

'I went out with this girl once,' he said, 'when I was living in Belfast. It finished, and I wouldn't accept it, you know, the old story. Anyway she went to visit her mommy in Coleraine one time on the bus. I got to hear they were burning buses that night, and I hitched all the way to Coleraine and knocked on her mommy's door and said was she there. She was. And I told her what I'd heard and that I was worried so I'd come up to make sure she was all right. Ach, she was all touched and confused, and what a bastard I was. I hadn't done it because I was worried about her. Well, I was worried, but basically that wasn't my motivation. I didn't do it to make her feel good, I did it to make her feel bad.'

'Did she go out with you again?'

'No,' he laughed. 'Luckily she wasn't that stupid.'

They walked back to Sprignall's, threading their way through the busy lunchtime crowds.

'He is pushing it, though,' Liam said. 'Legally. He should know that.'

'Is there any law against watching over someone, though?' Laura said, half to herself. Droves of office workers, sober-suited, middle-aged, milled past her and she realized that Mike Mackman could have been amongst them without her noticing it. Her own living, breathing guardian angel. She found the notion every bit as uncomfortable as when her grandmother used to invoke its supernatural counterpart years ago.

And she found she couldn't take comfort, either, from Liam's story. After all, he had known what he was doing; and cynical calculation in men, because you expected it, was relatively easy to deal with. But she was afraid that Mike Mackman didn't know what he was doing. He was sincere and earnest. The very things, indeed, that her two-faced, two-timing, untrustworthy husband hadn't been. So there was a lesson.

She hoped, remembering the burning look Mike had given her across the restaurant, that it would be the last one she would have to learn.

NINETEEN

The young couple were named, with storybook charm, Frans and Elise. Frans was Dutch, looked like a demigod, and spoke the polished, non-Americanized English which is the preserve of the Continent. Elise was English, pretty and pregnant. The estate agents sent them to view Laura's house the week after Mike Mackman's appearance in the restaurant; and though there had been no word from him in that time, Laura still felt badly in need of some hopeful sign to lift her spirits – for example, an offer for the house.

But as she showed Frans and Elise round, she had an increasing feeling that she was not going to get it. If they were enthused, they were doing a good job of hiding it. They just nodded here and there, and didn't say anything. Sometimes there was a sort of blank bemusement about them, as if they couldn't understand why she was pointing these things out to them (new boiler, extractor in kitchen). It occurred to her that maybe, looking for a bed-and-breakfast, they had walked into the estate agents under the impression that it was a tourist information office, and the estate agents had sent them here for a joke.

'Well, that's the guided tour,' she said as they fetched up in the kitchen, where the silent couple exchanged a deadpan look. 'I think, anyway. Unless there are any rooms I've forgotten about.' She gave a doomed laugh.

'Thank you for showing it to us,' said Frans.

'Yes, thank you very much,' said Elise.

'Pleasure.' Maybe she was wrong: maybe this was a new technological development in the property business – robot house-viewers. The software was a bit primitive just yet, but soon they would be programmed to enquire about the neighbours, run a tape measure across the bedroom, probe the window-frames for rot . . .

'I think it's the one,' Frans said, looking at Elise.

'I think so.' She nodded seriously. 'I think it is.'

Laura did a mental double take. 'You're – you're interested, then?'

'Very much so,' Frans said. 'It's easily the best we've seen.'

'It is,' his wife said, placing her hand in his. 'It is.'

Buzzing with sudden, unexpected hope, Laura said, 'Well, that's great, I mean, do you want to have a look round on your own? Feel free, you know, whatever—'

'No need,' Frans said.

'No, no need,' Elise said. 'This is the one.'

'Well, I'm pleased you like it,' Laura said, with vast understatement. 'What's your – I mean, have you got a place to sell?'

'No. We're in rented accommodation,' Frans said. 'That's no problem.'

This must be a dream, Laura thought.

'It's just a question of finance.' A faint frown of emotion touched his sculptured face. 'I'm self-employed, you see. This always makes it more difficult.'

'Oh yes, I see,' Laura said. But she couldn't imagine even the sternest lender finding it much of a problem. Frans looked about as unreliable as a Disney prince.

Later she had a call from her contact at the estate agents, a relentless young woman named Jackie – though those two syllables gave no hint of the songful uplift with which she pronounced her name. 'Hi, Mrs Ritchie, it's *Jack*-eee. Just been talking to Mr and Mrs Dekker and as you may know they're very interested in your property, which is good news. Now as you may also know they are not actually in a position to make an offer at this point in time. It's all dependent on them securing a mortgage deal and they perhaps are aiming a wee bit high for a first-time buy *but*. Our financial adviser here is getting on to that so it's a case of fingers crossed. I can actually tell you that they are actually very keen, which is great, isn't it?'

It was, Laura agreed. And though she knew that a real offer would have been greater, optimism seduced her.

She dragged out the pile of estate agents' details that had been sent to her. While there was no interest in her own house, she had forborne giving these much attention – no point in getting her hopes up. But some subconscious discrimination must have been at work. Right on top of the pile was the one house that had caught her attention above all others, and that she had found herself picturing whenever she had allowed herself to think about the move. And now, as she systematically went through the sheaf of details, that was the one she kept coming back to.

Usually what seemed just right at first glance revealed drawbacks in the small print (no toilet, lighting by gas), but this was right all the way through. It was remarkably affordable. It had none of those whimsies like striplights over the bathroom mirror or built-in TV stands that revealed the dread hand of the DIY man, who in the course of these labours had usually wired the whole place so that you sizzled like a burger when you touched the light switches. It had a back garden that was genuinely enclosed, rather than shared between three neighbours and the local speedway team. It was an end terrace with two bedrooms, central heating and double glazing. And it was in the very part of town where she had dropped off Liam, and where the afternoon tableau of the cat and the little girl and the ice-cream van had given her such a wistful sense of belonging.

Number 51 Maitland Street. She tried the address over in her head. Mrs L. Ritchie, 51 Maitland Street . . . It even sounded right, as if she had lived there for years.

Disregarding an inner voice that croaked about the inadvisability of counting chickens, Laura telephoned the estate agents to arrange a viewing. It was a different firm from the one that was selling her place, but the woman who arranged the appointment sounded just like Jackie, or maybe Jackie's even chirpier twin sister. 'That's six thirty tomorrow then, Mrs Ritchie. Any problems, just give us a bell and ask for Tray-seee.'

Turning the car into Maitland Street the next evening, Laura felt tight with anticipation. *Something* must be wrong with this place. Look at the street – trim and well kept without being monotonous, post office and general store on the corner, ten minutes' walk from town . . . and it was access-only, with bollards and sleeping policemen at each end. No danger from traffic.

'What do you think of it so far?' she said to Simon as she parked.

'Is that town over there?'

'Yep.'

'When can we move?'

The vendors were a retired couple who were looking to buy a bungalow. 'Somewhere with a bit more garden as well,' the old man said, gesturing to one of those miniature horticultural miracles that old men create behind unassuming urban terraces – cascades of clematis, tubs dwarfed by their own weight of bloom. 'I'm a bit cramped here.' This was about as much as she got from him, as he was chiefly occupied with holding down a small black poodle that was straining every sinew to get at the intruders. The dog wasn't kidding. In the end the old man had to wrestle it to the floor with his forearm in its mouth, like Johnny Weissmuller overpowering a lion, and keep it pinned there while his wife showed them round.

And still Laura found nothing wrong and everything right. Even the decoration of the house was fine as it stood. Being elderly, the owners had not been cudgelled into style, and had refrained from covering the place in dadoes or distressing the kitchen units. The second bedroom had a zigzaggy carpet that made Laura a little queasy; but even this was an advantage in the impressed eyes of Simon, who whispered, 'Could this be my room?' in her ear as the old lady led them out.

Above all, the feeling was right. You could either imagine yourself living in a place or you couldn't; and here even the sound of Simon's feet on the stairs had something recognizable about it. It wasn't familiar: it was the promise of familiarity.

'Well, it's lovely. It's really – just the sort of thing I like.' Laura experienced a flash of empathy with the taciturn Dekkers. It was curiously difficult to express your enthusiasm for someone else's house – perhaps because it seemed as if you were all set to boot them out. 'I am hoping to get an offer for my place soon, and then – well, hopefully . . .'

Hopefully hoping. It might be inarticulate and ungrammatical, but it was exactly how she felt as she drove away from 51 Maitland Street. And in that state she spent the next few days, bolstered by Jackie, who told her that the Dekkers were still very much interested and it was just a question of sorting out the finance.

The days became a week, and the finance was still not sorted out. 'As I say, it's quite ambitious for a first-time buy,' Jackie told her with plaintive brightness. 'Our financial adviser wasn't able to help in this particular instance, but I understand the Dekkers have hopes of an independent mortgage broker. I'll let you know as soon as I hear anything.'

Meanwhile Jackie's twin coaxed Laura about 51 Maitland Street. They had actually had some strong interest from another possible buyer for this actual property, she said; and as the vendors did actually have their eye on a bungalow property with vacant possession they were keen to sell as soon as possible. Laura had no way of knowing whether this was bull to push her into a decision, but she certainly felt pressured and dithery. Should she just go ahead and put in an offer for the house? Ross, hearing her mention this, sucked in breath sharply and proceeded to tell her a cautionary tale that ended in debt and homelessness. And, of course, 51 Maitland Street wasn't the only eligible house in the world. It was just that she had set her heart on it.

Moving house, besides, had more than a material significance for her. It was a leap. That it was also a leap away from Mike Mackman made it, of course, doubly desirable: the fact that the Maitland Street house was selling for nearly twenty thousand less than the price of her own, meaning that the deal would enable her to pay off her debt to him at a stroke, undoubtedly added to its attraction. But when the week passed with him still apparently staying out of her life, she didn't know what to think. There was always the possibility that his outburst in the restaurant had given him pause, made him take a long look at himself, and so on. But knowing how thick-skinned he was, she wasn't laying any bets.

On Saturday morning, which was her appointed time for cleaning house – as well as shopping, laundry, ironing, gardening and all the other manifold tasks which, curiously enough, did not tire her as they used to do before she worked – Simon called to her through the noise of the vacuum cleaner.

'Mum! It's that lady again. I'm going round James's.'

'All right. Be careful of the road.'

She picked up the phone in a state of careful inexpectation.

'Mrs Ritchie, hi, it's *Jack*-eee. How are you? Mrs Ritchie, I think we may have some good news for you on the sale of your property.'

'Oh, yes?' said Laura, thinking: yes!

'We actually have a firm offer for the house. Now I know we've been waiting for word from Mr and Mrs Dekker in that department but there are actually no developments on that score, I'm afraid. This is actually an offer from another source, a gentleman who's moving to the area and is looking to acquire a property very quickly.'

'Really?' Nonplussed, Laura couldn't let the delight sink in yet. 'But he hasn't seen it.'

'Well, the gentleman was satisfied with making an offer on the strength of the details, and that will be pending a full survey, of course. He was only in town for the day and we weren't actually able to reach you to make a viewing appointment. Naturally we let him know that there was another interest being expressed in the property, and I think that settled it for him and he put in the offer there and then.'

'My God. I can't believe it. I mean, it's wonderful, but – it seems a shame about the other couple, the Dekkers . . .'

'It is, but as I say they are having difficulty raising the finance, and really it's a question of whether you want to hang around waiting on that. Whereas this is a firm offer. But of course you're under absolutely no obligation to accept it. I can tell you the offer is a thousand under the asking price. It's up to you, if you're interested, whether you want to push it up. Two thousand under the asking price is more usual for the initial offer so really, you know, it isn't bad at all. By the way, the gentleman doesn't have a property to sell, so there's no problem of a chain at that end and there are no difficulties with the financial aspect. Gentleman's name is Mr Goodrick. We have a contact number for him and can give him your reply to his offer whenever you're ready.'

'My God,' said Laura again. 'It's happened so quickly – I can hardly believe it.'

'That's usually the way, we find – often when you've put it out of your mind,' said Jackie, sounding as if she were breaking, Broadway-style, into song. 'But I must stress that it's absolutely your decision. You can take as long as you like to think it over, you can insist on the full asking price, whatever. We won't hassle you and the buyer has to go through us so, you know, the ball's in your court, as it were. I can tell you, between us, that this is rather a good offer, considering your property hasn't been on the market very long.'

'You can say that again.'

'It is rather a good offer, considering,' Jackie said, seeming to take Laura literally. 'You do sometimes strike lucky like this when you get people relocating, especially with your particular type of property.'

'Yes,' Laura said. She wasn't simply agreeing to the last remark. She amplified it. 'Yes, I'll take it. I'll accept the offer.'

Things were moving fast now. In fact she would have to run to catch up with them.

She felt sorry about the Dekkers, but she feared that further delay would mean her losing the Maitland Street house; and it wasn't as if any real offer had been made. It sounded as if they were overstretching themselves trying to buy the house anyhow – and there was a baby on the way. Maybe missing out would be a blessing. She was sure that some of the rot, at least, had set in between her and David when they had devoted themselves to the pursuit of fitted kitchens instead of each other.

After the phone call from Jackie she abandoned the cleaning and instead dug out a tin of filler from the garden shed and darted about the house dabbing it into every little hole and imperfection she came across. (She wondered incidentally where these came from: some were from nails, some from where David had thrown things, but others seemed just to appear.) If the idea behind this was to soothe the eagle eye of the buyer's surveyor and make him not notice, for example, that the bathroom window wouldn't open, it was pretty feeble; but really it was a displacement activity. It worked off her nervous excitement and postponed the moment of her own decision.

Which she made at last in the late afternoon, phoning Jackie's twin just before the estate agents closed and making an offer for 51 Maitland Street.

She would have to wait until Monday for a reply to that. In the meantime there was nothing to do but try not to spend every waking minute thinking about her decision and its consequences. She took Simon to the pictures that evening and to the park on Sunday; she made cakes and played board games and did all sorts of mumsy things. But as Simon was as excited by the news as she was, the effort to put the whole thing out of her mind was pretty well wasted. He kept talking about what he already called their new house; and in the end she gave in and they spent Sunday evening sketching room plans and verbally moving furniture – which in Simon's inventory strangely included an aquarium.

'My God, not 51 Maitland Street?' Liam said at work on Monday, when she happened to mention the impending move within five minutes of arriving. 'The House of Horror?'

'What?'

'Didn't you know? That was where the Axeman of Langstead lived. They say it's haunted by the ghosts of his victims. You know, they've had exorcists in and everything . . .'

She had half-believed him just long enough to warrant clouting him with a spatula. Colette, coming in and seeing it, raised her eyebrows and clucked her tongue. 'You two,' she said.

Tracey was due to ring about five. Having hastily collected Simon, Laura inserted her front door key at four forty and opened the door to find the telephone ringing.

'Hello?' she gasped. She was prepared, entirely prepared, for this to be not what she wanted to hear – even something frustratingly irrelevant like a cold call by a double glazing salesman. She was so prepared that when Tracey informed her that the vendors of 51 Maitland Street had accepted her offer she couldn't take it in. This had the almost sinister fortuitousness of finding a tenner on the floor.

Then she took it in. Simon looked momentarily astonished when she dived at him, but soon joined in the spirit of the thing and whooped it up with her all round the house.

'When will it be, Mum? When can we move?'

'Well. It takes a bit of time. The people who live in that house have to find somewhere. And then there's the survey and there's a solicitor's search, I think—'

'What's that for?'

'Oh, to make sure they're not going to build an airport in the back garden and things like that. There's a lot of legal stuff you have to go through but – well, it's coming. It's going to happen.'

She said this partly to convince herself. It seemed such a short time ago that everything was mountainous – getting her finances straight, getting a job, keeping a job, selling the house, finding somewhere else to live; and yet here she was, on the peaks.

She had done it.

A memory: David, when she had suggested last year that their relationship needed serious surgery. 'Oh, and I suppose if I don't come up to scratch you'll swan off and be this independent woman putting the past behind her? Get real, Laura. You wouldn't last five minutes without me.' It wasn't a bitter memory now, and what she felt wasn't quite triumph or vindication. It was simply a quiet surprised pride. Because she realized that even up to this very moment, part of her had believed that too.

Being human, Laura followed up her euphoria with an acute bout of worry.

The legal business that she had mentioned so breezily to Simon was, after all, quite a palaver; and then there was the survey which might, for all she knew, turn up something horrendous in the structure of 51 Maitland Street (built on plague burial ground and fast sinking into it). But at least she had no doubts about which solicitor to choose. Mr Bussapoon himself did not do conveyancing, but he was happy to point her to someone in the firm who did. How weird, she thought when this was fixed up: I've got a family solicitor, just like someone in an Agatha Christie book. The surveyor she had to take on the estate agent's recommendation, but gradually her anxiety about this part of the procedure diminished. The Maitland Street house was described as fully modernized and looked it: if anything did turn up that needed fixing it would surely be minor, and could be paid for by the profit on the sale. Whenever these creeps came over her during the next week, she repeated her formula to herself: *Ditch the apocalypse, Laura.*

And of course it all took time, as she had told Simon. But after the initial excitement he seemed to accept this – not for the first time, Laura wondered how she had given birth to so much balance and prudence – whereas she was impatient. The sight of letters on the doormat, which had once been a daily groan-inducing punishment, became a nervous thrill. Naturally they got fewer. She began to wonder whether everyone involved had her address wrong. The only tangible indication of the sale was the sign, which now sported a 'Sold subject to contract' sticker. This prompted a cross-examination from Eileen, who caught her one morning as she was setting out for work.

'Looks like you'll be leaving us then,' Eileen said, in tones so confrontational you might have supposed Laura had sworn on her immortal soul never to do so. Eileen was in charge of a rain-hooded twin pushchair the size of an armoured car and had about a dozen bags of shopping variously hung about her, but still she gave the impression that this was not enough for her indomitable energy. Laura faithfully believed that one day she would see Eileen go by with a load balanced on her head like a native porter.

'Yes, we're moving nearer town. I don't know when it'll be.'

'I think it's a shame, you know, that you feel like you have to do it. When I lost my Jimmy I just wanted to stay where I was. It felt like I still had him with me.'

'Well. You know. The house is a bit big for us.'

'It's a good place to bring up kiddies round here. Have you thought of that?'

'Well, so is the place where we're moving. Anyway, I must get going, I've got to get to work.'

'Ah, I have a lot of things to do myself. Haven't seen your gentleman friend lately, by the way.'

'What? Oh.' Of course, she had met Mike Mackman. 'He's not my gentleman friend.'

'Of course it's nature. We're none of us perfect. You have to be careful, though. Some men will take advantage.'

'Bye, Eileen.'

'D'you think David would have wanted you to sell the house? He was always a great homemaker.'

'Bye, Eileen.'

There was one thing, anyway, Laura thought as she drove to work gripping the steering wheel like a strongman bending an iron bar. At least it seemed likely that Mike had discontinued his watchful cruisings and prowlings. If he had been around, Eileen the human spy satellite would surely have spotted him.

That was one thing, and another thing was the letter that arrived the next morning. At last Laura's impatience was rewarded. It was only written confirmation of her own offer on 51 Maitland Street, but it was progress. Then, during her morning's work, it occurred to her that she had nothing in writing confirming the offer for her place. No doubt it was all in train . . . but the thought niggled her, and when her lunch break came she decided there would be no harm in popping into the office of her estate agents, which was in the town centre, and finding out what was happening.

Jackie, whose bleached hair and walnut sunbed tan gave her the look of a photographic negative, was professionally delighted to see her. 'Have a seat, Mrs Ritchie, and I'll go and get the file,' she said, making a hobbling, tight-skirted sortie into the rear of the office, which was as hot as a greenhouse.

At another desk nearby a shirtsleeved youth spoke ingratiatingly on the telephone. 'Yes, I do realize that . . . I can see your point, I really can . . . Eighteen months, yep, sure, but that actually isn't a very long time with the housing market the way it is . . .'

Laura felt smug.

'Here we go.' Jackie was back, lowering herself into her chair with an almost audible straining of seams. 'What I can tell you is there are no problems and confirmation in writing should be on its way to you very soon. Basically you can get a bit of delay when your buyer's coming from another area of the country. But we do actually have a contact address for Mr Goodrick in Langstead, a friend's address, I believe, which is handy.' She leafed through the file as swiftly as her fingernails allowed. 'Yep. Champaign Park.'

The words struck Laura, but only with a light blow – the blow of a harmless coincidence.

'Champaign Park, did you say?'

'That's right,' Jackie trilled. 'Now the thing is, I understand Mr Goodrick did actually come into the office yesterday, but unfortunately I wasn't in yesterday because I was having my wisdom teeth out.'

'Ooh, poor you.'

'I kno-ow,' Jackie said, pulling a little girl's 'ouch' face. 'So I haven't actually been able to . . . Paul!' She accosted the shirtsleeved youth at the next desk, who was off the phone now and working out something, perhaps his pension, on a calculator. 'Was it you who dealt with Mr Goodrick yesterday? Duncan Road. Buyer.'

The youth looked blank. 'Er . . . Goodrick . . .'

'You left me a Post-it. Mr Goodrick. Big gentleman, fair, moustache . . .'

This time the blow was harder; so hard that it completely numbed Laura for several seconds.

'Oh yeah, I know. He said it was just a general enquiry. Said he might pop in again today to see you.'

'Must be staying down here, then,' Jackie said with chirpy discovery. 'Well, Mrs Ritchie, if—'

'You said a big man,' Laura said, finding her voice. The botanical heat of the office seemed to have intensified, and her blood was thumping in her ears. 'A big fair man with a moustache.'

'That's right,' Jackie said, managing to smile and look puzzled at the same time. 'I mean, when I say big, I mean that in a nice way, you know. Tall. Chunky.'

Laura sat back. Her whole head felt as if it were boiling like a kettle. Was this what it was like when you were going to faint?

The telephone on the youth's desk rang, jolting her.

'What's the address?'

'I'm sorry?' Jackie said.

'This Mr . . . Goodrick's contact address. Whereabouts in Champaign Park?' As Jackie hesitated, she snapped, 'You can give me it, can't you?'

'Oh, sure, there's nothing against that, Mrs Ritchie, but the thing is, all the actual liaising can be done through us, so there's no need for you to worry about-'

'I'd like the address. And the telephone number.'

'Sure.' Smoothly surprised, Jackie consulted the file. 'Mr Goodrick, care of 6 Riseland, Champaign Park . . .'

The card Mike Mackman had given her was at home, but she was sure that that was the address. The telephone number sounded horribly familiar too, she could have sworn . . .

But no. She wouldn't swear to it, not yet. The coincidence explanation was looking terribly weak, on its last legs indeed, but she wouldn't give it up for dead, not yet. She pointed to the stack of directories on Jackie's desk.

'Have you got the phone book there? Langstead residential.'

'Certainly.' On polite autopilot, Jackie handed it over.

Laura found it almost at once. Mackman. There was only one subscriber of that surname listed, and it was one of those that appears at the top of the page and so gains an arbitrary prominence. To Laura's rage-misted eyes there seemed a last touch of shamelessness in this accidental fact.

'Would you like me to jot it down for you?' Jackie suggested, pen helpfully poised over a Post-it.

‘No. It’s all right, thanks.’ Laura closed the book. Now that she knew, she had two choices. Run around the town yelling and smashing windows, or go back to work and somehow hold up the tottering pillars of fury and disappointment until clocking-off time.

‘Well, as Paul said, Mr Goodrick may pop in some time today, so if there’s any question you’d like me to raise with him, I’d be happy—’

‘Mackman,’ Laura said, getting to her feet. ‘His name’s not Goodrick. It’s Mackman.’

TWENTY

She got through the afternoon, which wasn't to say she was her normal self. She performed her tasks, but she was helplessly monosyllabic with her workmates, even Liam – especially Liam. To let any of it out was to let all of it out, and then she might end up wailing like a banshee.

And perhaps not even Liam could fully understand. She wanted to sell the house, and if this Mackman fellow wanted to buy it, then why not . . . ?

There were a hundred reasons why not. But they all boiled down to one simple fact: Mike Mackman *didn't* want to buy it, not in any sane reasonable way. She knew that. He was Doing It For Her. She didn't know the rest of the agenda, but that was undoubtedly the heading.

She was past finding it incredible. Even the stupendous extravagance fitted what she knew of him. What she did find incredible was her own optimism in believing that Mike Mackman, after he had packed away his tools and his ladder the other week, had acquiesced in her selling her house. Or rather, the Family Home – for as far as she could tell, all his thought processes were in these thumping, sentimental, eternal-verity capitals.

Well, whatever he had in mind, she couldn't accept that deal. The sale was off. She tried not to think beyond that, to the inevitable consequences, because they were too dispiriting and frustrating to bear. Instead she bleakly wondered whether he had really supposed he could keep his identity secret. In such a legalistic matter as a house sale it would surely have come out sooner or later: did he suppose that by then she would meekly accept this most unconscionable interference?

But that, she realized, was to assume he was thinking rationally, and everything he had done showed that he wasn't. And by the time she finished work and drove away from Sprignall's, Laura wasn't thinking rationally either.

Not that she was out of control. She had the steadiness that a huge ballast of emotion sometimes gives. She was careful, before she left, to give Jan a ring from the phone in the storeroom and ask her whether it was all right if she was a little late picking up Simon. Then she got the office number of Mike Mackman Builders from directory enquiries. A voice she recognized from last time said that Mr

Mackman had just left: was there a message?

There was no message. Laura set out for Champaign Park.

She was so collected that she even asked herself, as she drove, whether she was a horrible person. This man, against whom she was moltenly incensed, who seemed at this moment to cast a darker shadow across her life than any human being ever had, was a generous and conscientious man who had done nothing nasty to her whatsoever. Therefore, in wishing him to go to hell and in intending to tell him to do so, was she not a horrible person?

There was something missing from that equation, though. Namely, the man was a fruitcake and he was buggering up her life and she had really, truly, finally had enough.

To get to Champaign Park, Langstead's new model dream, you had to traverse the Belvoir estate, Langstead's old model nightmare. People used to call it the Belsen until it passed into the hands of a generation to whom the name meant nothing. Other run-down parts of the town could still give the impression that they had been a good idea at the time, but it was hard to see how the Belvoir could ever have been thought a good idea. Mugger-friendly walkways and underpasses honeycombed the place, testimony to a short-lived belief that people didn't like walking down streets. Concrete pubs, damp-stained and weathered as lighthouses, loomed at the main interchanges. Though the boarded-up windows and dense graffiti made them look as if they had been shut down for years, they were the only establishments still open apart from the odd valiant Asian grocers, barred like Alcatraz. The houses had been built with their backs facing on to the road, perhaps because of some notion on the part of the planners that common folk never used their front doors: the result was a burglar's paradise.

And then all at once you crossed a junction expecting more of the same and you were in a strange buffer zone of meadows with little low-slung office developments, like baroque stables, plonked in the middle of them. Developers' signboards vied at the roadside, inviting you to a four-bedroomed executive good life in what was presented as a cross between Sherwood Forest and the Emerald City. This was Champaign Park. You were in it before you knew it, mainly because they had gone overboard with the leafiness, but also because the strange idea that what people hated most about life was streets had persisted here. The roads twisted between pretend copses and sprawled round long pointless curves, revealing abrupt clusters of neo-Georgian redbrick houses, some of which were half-finished and none of which seemed to have street names. Which one of these clusters was Riseland? Laura, helplessly cruising, would have stopped and asked someone if there had been anyone to ask, but no one walked around here: there weren't even any footpaths. She was just thinking she would have to park the car and march up to somebody's front door and ask where the hell she was when she spotted a discreet sign half-smothered in leaves: 'Riseland.'

Number 6 was, unexceptionally, a detached house with a double garage and a wide gravelled drive and a smooth front lawn (which was no bigger than the front gardens on the Belvoir – the plots of Champaign Park were actually quite small and the place was pretty much a rip-off.) What alerted her, and set the throbbing anger within her revving and smoking, was the familiar sight of the silver Audi in the drive.

She parked at what she presumed was the kerb and walked up to the front door. There were carriage lamps on either side of it. About to knock, she found the door flung open and Mike Mackman, in tie and shirtsleeves, gazing at her with a kind of rapt bashfulness tinged with alarm.

'Laura! I saw you from the window, I . . . Are you all right? Is there anything wrong?'

'Can I come in?'

'Of course, of course . . .'

He almost staggered, stepping aside to let her in. For a moment she thought he was drunk. Then she realized he was overwhelmed by something else entirely: having her here. He couldn't welcome her, *usher* her enough. He walked backwards into the hall like a courtier.

'This is a surprise. You could have knocked me down with a feather when I saw you. Come in, have a seat . . .'

'It can't have been that much of a surprise,' she said.

She had followed him into a large square living room with a front bay, but she didn't sit. She stood facing him, her shoes anchored in thick fluffy carpet.

'How do you mean?'

He didn't look shifty – he wasn't made that way – just faintly sheepish and pink.

'You're Mr Goodrick,' she said.

The pink became brick-red. Then he hung his head, laughing a little, nodding.

'Well, you've . . . I've got to hand it to you, you found me out pretty quick. I should have realized – you're a smart lady, you'd soon . . .' He chuckled ruefully, folded his big arms across his chest. 'Goodrick was my mother's maiden name,' he said with a kind of hushed revelation, as if that explained everything.

'I don't care whose name it is. It was you. You were the one who made that offer for my house.'

'Yes,' he said, 'I did. I'm glad you've accepted it. I would have offered the full asking price but, you know, that would have looked a bit odd. Plus there's this money that you still keep trying to pay back to me. What I thought was, I'd offer a thousand under, and then we could call it quits on that money. Then everything would be straight, you wouldn't have to feel you'd got to pay me anything, and you and Simon would still have your home.'

'What?'

Mike looked pleased with himself. 'Your home. That's what it's all about. This was meant to be a surprise later on, but there's no harm in you knowing now. Once the purchase has gone through, I'm going to gift the house back to you. Then you'll have financial security, and you can stay in your home, and you won't have to work . . . Listen,' he said, seeing her abrupt movement – a kind of flex of despair, 'listen, don't you worry about the technicalities of it, because I'll make the gift properly. I'm going to get my solicitor on it so that it's absolutely tight as a drum, the deeds in your name and everything. I'll have no title to it at all. I've worked it all out. It's the perfect solution.'

No longer sheepish, Mike appeared radiant – a visionary in sight of his goal. And Laura found she just couldn't look at him any more, not without screaming. Her eyes roamed round the room, seeing its shop-window furnishings, the buttony leather chesterfields, decanter and crystal glasses, glossy nests of tables, deep-framed hunting prints, festooned curtains, a table lamp in the shape of a spinning-wheel, and she thought randomly: he didn't have money once. The room was an embodied idea of wealth, half-squire, half-glitz, like a set for a porno shoot.

It might have made her feel sad, but she had no room for sadness. She scarcely even had room for amazement at the ultimate craziness of his plan. Buying her house, and giving it back to her.

Whee.

'You know I can't accept this,' she said.

'Maybe you feel that way now,' he said, wagging his head judiciously, 'but once you've thought about it—'

'You *know* I can't,' she said vehemently. 'You knew from the start. Why else did you hide your name? Eh? Why didn't you put in the offer under your own name?'

'Well, because I knew you wouldn't accept it, but—'

'Exactly. And doesn't that say it all? You knew this is something I don't want but you went ahead and did it. Secretly. Hoping you could – foist it on me before I realized. You just can't do this to a person, God damn it—'

'But it was the only way,' he protested. 'Otherwise you'd end up having to leave your home, and I can't stand by and watch that. I'm sorry, I just won't let it happen—'

'It's none of your business.' She took a step towards him across the lush carpet. She was wild, burning up. And yet, a random perception, the wasteful senses still working away even at such times as these: the smell of carpet shampoo and polish. He has a cleaner, she thought.

That always leaves a different smell from your own cleaning. 'Watch my lips. It is none of your business.'

'It is, though.' He looked hurt, misunderstood, but not at all resentful. 'Laura – who's going to look after you if I don't?'

It was then that she felt like flying at him, fists whirling. She actually made a move, but her fury had turned inward, knotted and paralysing, and the movement turned out like a totter. In an instant he was at her side, hovering, fussing.

'Listen, why don't you sit down? Have a drink – or a cup of tea maybe. It's stress, that's what it is. That damned house-selling business, it's too stressful, that's another reason – and then there's that job of yours. I'll be glad when you give that up. It takes too much out of you . . .'

'No, I'm going,' Laura said, pulling away from him. She would have to: she literally couldn't bear to be with him much longer. 'I only came so that I could tell you face to face what I think of this last bloody stunt of yours. And that is—'

'I know, I do know it must look a bit interfering,' he said, seeming to draw complacently on an infinite reserve of patience. 'And the last thing I expect is thanks. I don't expect anything. I'll have the knowledge that you can keep your family home and care properly for Simon and that's all I need. But I'm sure after a while you'll look back and realize it was the right thing—'

'I'm not accepting that offer!' Now she was shouting. It was all the more alarming because of something that had been slowly dawning on her – the silence of this house. No sound of TV or radio or plumbing or clocks ticking, and no sound from outside. The place was like a sealed showroom. She tried to control her voice. 'This is what I'm . . . Don't you see? It's off. I'm not selling the house to you, can't you—'

'But that's the point, Laura. You're not selling it to me because I'm going to give it back to you—'

'Oh God.' She stumbled past him to the door, feeling as if she were choking. Even now there was a part of her that just wanted to run, to hide . . .

But that was no good: not with this man. She drew a deep breath.

'I'll get on to the estate agents straight away. I'll stop the sale. And then that's it.'

He looked bewildered. 'How do you mean?'

'I mean if you don't keep out of my life I'll – I'll go to law.' Absurd phrase – shades of Rumpole of the Bailey. But it was all she had. 'I'll go to law to keep you away. That's all I can say.'

'Laura, you're upset. I swear it's that damn job, you shouldn't—'

'I've told you what I'm going to do. Now it's up to you.'

He opened his mouth to speak – to say, obviously, more of the same; and then his face changed. It darkened – not with anger, but as if an actual light had left it.

Finally, he had taken it in.

Seeing this, Laura didn't soften, simply because it was out of the question. But something did open up within her: she did not so much feel sorry for him as admit that it was possible to do so, in some parallel universe where she was not half-mad with disappointment and frustration.

And then the light came back again.

He gave a gentle, pained smile. It was as if, having taken in what she said, he had somehow erased it.

'You're upset,' he said. 'This must all have been a bit of a shock for you. I can see that now. Of course, I should have thought. One minute you're facing the prospect of having to uproot yourself and lose your home and then suddenly it's all changed and you're – well, I should think you're pretty well groggy with it. Now I tell you what. I own a holiday chalet up on the North Norfolk coast. It's a smashing place, all set amongst these woods overlooking the sea. Picked it up for a song a few years ago. I go there when I get time, you know, which isn't very often.' A chuckle. 'Anyway, I reckon you and Simon need a break. Why don't you take the key and go up there for a week or ten days? A fortnight maybe – there's loads to do. All this house-selling business grinds pretty slow anyway, so it'll be all right. As for your work, just tell them you're sick – in fact, no – tell them to chuck their job. You'll have plenty of money when the sale goes through, and I can tide you over till then. I reckon a good break by the sea is just . . . Laura! Where are you going? Wait . . . !'

But she was already running, getting out of there, knowing now that the end of your tether was further away than you ever dreamt.

TWENTY-ONE

Mike rang her twice that evening. The second time he was tearful and incoherent. Both times she hung up on him.

She fully expected a hammering on the door after that. But when it didn't come, and the phone stayed silent, she wasn't fooled. It was only a matter of time. He would do something else, sooner or later. Unless she did something in the meantime.

There were other tasks, now – miserable, embittering things; but they didn't take long. The bewildered Jackie was instructed that the sale was off. Well-meaningly, she got back to Laura with the news that Mr Goodrick, on being told this, had upped his offer by two thousand. Repressing a scream, Laura made it clear that she would not accept any offer for 19 Duncan Road from that quarter, not now, not ever.

As far as she knew, nothing had been put in writing and nothing was watertight until the exchange of contracts, which had been a long way off: house sales fell through all the time. But equally for all she knew Mike Mackman now had some legal claim against her, if he chose to pursue it. This didn't bother her. If he turned nasty, at least she would know where she stood; in some ways it would be a relief. But there was no sign of any such thing. Turning nasty was the last thing on his agenda. He just wanted to help her.

She had already incurred some legal fees, though. That was one unpleasant consequence. She wasn't surprised. Nor was she surprised when Jackie sighingly informed her that she had been in touch with the Dekkers and found that it was too late. Understanding that Duncan Road was sold, and having secured a mortgage deal, they had made an offer for another property. 'I believe this one is actually more within their means,' Jackie said. Trying to reassure. But knowing full well, as Laura did, that they would have taken Laura's house if it hadn't been for that 'Sold' sticker – which Laura climbed up and ripped off herself, cursing all the curses she knew.

Cursing was no good, though. No good cursing as she withdrew her offer for 51 Maitland Street. Jackie's twin, Tracey, was reassuring too. She did understand, she said, and was sure the vendors would too . . . but without a firm offer on her own place, and with the vendors looking to move quickly, Mrs Ritchie really wasn't in a position . . . Though Tracey promised to keep her posted on Maitland Street, Laura knew there wasn't much hope. That house was a snip. She wouldn't be surprised if someone bought it very soon. She would be surprised if no one did.

So the counted chickens had turned out to be dead ducks. Addressing what had happened – this total collapse of her hopes – in flippant terms didn't mean that she didn't feel it intensely. It was just that the only alternative was howling at the moon.

She hated herself for having built up Simon's hopes, though; and all the more because he took the bad news so well. Perhaps, she thought with a burst of self-pity, he's just accustomed to being let down by me. And all I need now, she thought with a second burst, is to give somebody food-poisoning in the restaurant and get the sack and that'll be the full monte.

What kept her going was that resolution which had sprung to her lips in Mike Mackman's hotel-lobby living room. *I'll go to law.*

She hadn't known exactly what she meant by it at the time. Thinking it over, she still didn't. But plainly the first step was to go to a lawyer.

It would mean more expense that she could ill afford. But also she couldn't afford not to. This wasn't going to stop of its own accord. She knew that now. The knowledge was late in coming, maybe – or maybe she had been running away from it. Not any more.

Mr Bussapoon agreed to see her, though when she gave him a brief outline on the phone of what it was about, he was a little cagey. He wasn't sure he could help her with this particular matter, he said. His speciality within the firm was inheritance and family law. But Laura considered him an ally, and didn't want to talk to a stranger. And when at last her appointment with him came, he listened very attentively to what, despite her rehearsals, came out as a rather incoherent story.

'Essentially, then,' he said, when she had finished, leaning back with his hands behind his head, 'you feel you've been subject to harassment by this man.'

'Well,' she said, a little taken aback by his casualness, and a little prickly in consequence, 'I don't know about *feeling* it. I have been harassed by him.' And a voice, perhaps habitual guilt at its last gasp, said: have you?

'What I mean is, this whole harassment business is a minefield. I'm not being dismissive of your situation when I say that there are men – and women – who have done infinitely worse things in terms of harassment, nuisance, and even downright sinister behaviour, and their victims have got no joy out of the law whatsoever. It's the same if you approach it from the other side and involve the police. They can't do anything until an offence has been committed. Now, understand me, that isn't to say a court wouldn't ultimately find in your favour if you did pursue it. But it's a question of whether you want to.'

'Well . . .' The mention of court was dispiriting. 'I suppose I was hoping that you could do something, you know, legally, without going to those lengths.'

'Any legal process you begin carries the implication that it will end in court. Sometimes the person reacts in such a way that it isn't needed. But in essence you have pressed the start button . . . Look, from what you've told me this man hasn't broken the law in anything he's done – except trespass. There you're on slightly more solid ground. You found him on your property and interfering with it. There you've got trespass and nuisance. So far so good. But you've also got the problem of proving it. Were there any witnesses to that?'

'Well, no . . . unless the neighbours were peering through the nets. I don't know. I suppose it's my word against his.'

'It is, but another factor is whether this man feels he's done anything wrong. From what you've told me, he doesn't, which means he may not dispute facts like these. Then again, if it comes to a question of fighting his corner . . .'

'I don't want to win anything. I just want him to leave us alone.'

'Of course. But you must understand that once the law is involved it does become a matter of winning and losing. If he should feel that you are impugning what are to him the harmless actions of a helpful citizen, it's his right to fight back. He might consider you're defaming him. He might claim he's the good guy. I'm bound to say that others might share this opinion.'

She studied him a moment.

'What do you think?' she said. 'What do you think of it yourself?'

Her dealings with him had always been formal, and she found it hard to imagine him having an ordinary personal life outside this office. At once she felt she shouldn't have asked this.

But to her surprise he smiled and said, 'I'm a very private person. I like to live on my own terms. I would absolutely hate it if something like this happened to me.'

Laura experienced a small inward sigh.

'But,' Mr Bussapoon went on with a delicate wave of his fingers, 'as I've said, this is a notoriously difficult area. It's not just the matter of obtaining a judgment, there's the question of enforcing it. One finds this so often in divorce and separation cases, where the granting of an injunction, say, against the man means he's supposed to stay away. How do you make sure he does?'

An injunction: it had an attractive sound, non-threatening but firm and absolute. Mr Bussapoon read her expression and her mind.

'Injunctions aren't granted willy-nilly, I'm afraid,' he said. 'It is quite a big deal.'

‘It seems as if everything is,’ Laura said with a sudden excess of gloom. She wanted to put a stop to something that was involving her in anxiety, frustration and stress, but it appeared she could only do so with more of the same.

‘Well, it is up to you. You can still stop short of taking action. You might try informing him in writing that you intend to seek legal advice, and see what that does. Possibly the Citizens’ Advice Bureau might help you in composing such a letter. Just the sight of their letterhead sometimes works wonders.’

She shook her head. ‘Just telling him isn’t any good. He’s got this image of me that I’m – too proud to accept his help, things like that; and that just makes him worse.’ She suffered a shudder as she said this, which she tried to cover with a rueful smile and a weak joke. ‘Bet you’ve never had to deal with anything as weird as this before.’

But Mr Bussapoon seemed to feel he had strayed far enough into informality. ‘It takes all sorts,’ he said, which could have meant anything. ‘All right, what I suggest – and that’s all it is, a suggestion – is that I send him a letter in regard to the trespass, which is at least a definite infringement of the law. What we call a letter before action. Or “call my bluff”, if you like. This would be a letter without prejudice, with you offering some sort of concession.’

‘How do you mean, concession?’ Once upon a time Laura would have liked the sound of that word, with all its implications of letting things slide, avoiding confrontation – hiding, in fact. But now she didn’t like the sound of it at all, and recognized the change in herself.

Good: but she hoped the change hadn’t gone too far.

‘Really, it’s just a matter of opening a window for negotiation. If he’s got any sense he won’t pursue the dispute but undertake not to trespass again. I know the trespass is only part of your problem with this man, but the point is you’ve pinned him down to something. Usually that’s enough. You’re not brandishing the law at him like a stick. You’re just saying you’ve got it in your hand.’

‘I see,’ Laura said.

And she did see. Really this was pretty much what she had hoped for when she had approached Mr Bussapoon. She had the law-abiding person’s innocent faith in, and fear of, the Solicitor’s Letter; it had always seemed to her scarcely less intimidating and effective than the Black Spot.

But now with this talk of concessions, of backing down and seeing sense, she wondered whether in this case the weapon were a mere peashooter. So much of it seemed to depend on Mike Mackman meeting them halfway – on a degree of self-awareness that he just hadn’t shown. Mike Mackman seeing sense? If you strapped him down and repeatedly injected him with something he might, but that was about it.

No, it still seemed to her that really putting the frighteners on him was the only sure way – and if that meant taking the deal all the way to court, then so be it. And yet she had to go along with Mr Bussapoon's suggestion. She had to, because he was the solicitor and he knew what he was talking about; but also because in the last analysis she couldn't be easy with the idea of hounding the man down as if he were some sort of sadistic stalker. She didn't need reminding that Mike Mackman could always say in his defence that he was only trying to help – because even now, after all that had happened, a part of her made that excuse for him. How could you bear malice to a man who bore no malice?

So in a way it was a relief that Mr Bussapoon's plan of action was relatively so mild. It stated her case, it was a warning: it left Mike his dignity, but it didn't pre-empt any other action she might need to take; it was great, all round. She just didn't think it would work.

But she told the solicitor to go ahead, and over the next few days lived in dull expectation of a distraught phone call or, worse, visit from Mike, wanting to know why she was doing this to him when all he wanted was to help her . . . Thank God, again, for the job, which kept her from brooding during the day; whilst in the evenings there was distraction from an unexpected source. The TV schedules were filled by an international football championship, and Simon, after a seven-year lifetime's indifference, suddenly contracted football fever. Watching companionably with him, she found a lot more interest than she expected. Even when the football part was dreary, the international part was piquant. Stereotypes were available for testing, and some had plenty of mileage in them. The English team really did look stodgy and podgy and John-Bully; the Italians really did look balletically slick and menacing, like the Sharks in *West Side Story*. The Spanish, enthusiastically chopping at their opponents' legs, seemed to think they were at one of those picturesque fiestas where the high point of the entertainment is knocking the heads off tied-up animals. Then there was the weirdness of the national anthems. The smaller the country, it seemed, the longer the anthem: some were practically symphonies. And Laura noticed that not even the French team could follow 'La Marseillaise' through to the end. It always sounded, after that stirring opening, as if a bar each from ten different songs had been strung together.

Probably she was entertained for the wrong reasons, but she was entertained – which was a different thing from saying she was able to relax. As far as she was concerned, life was on hold. Any nice things that went on were merely like magazines in the waiting room.

The letter arrived on Saturday morning.

Here was another piece of postal lore – letters that came on Saturday tended to look less important. They had been posted on Thursday or

Friday, sure, but they still had a weekend air about them, so that you opened them with a certain casualness. But after the first glance, Laura found she couldn't be casual about this one. She sat down with a cup of strong coffee and made herself read it very carefully. It was important to make sure that she wasn't dreaming, and that the letter wasn't going to turn into a bird and fly round the room which in the meantime had become a supermarket where all the shoppers were staring at her because she'd come out in her nightie . . .

The letter was two letters. One was a cover from Mr Bussapoon, the other a copy of a letter sent to him by Mike Mackman's solicitor.

Laura kept going over the unequivocal phrases, savouring them. She was almost tempted to read them aloud.

> Mr Mackman deeply regrets any inconvenience or distress caused to Mrs Ritchie by his actions. It was his intention to offer assistance to Mrs Ritchie in the aftermath of her bereavement, for which he was unwittingly responsible; but he fully accepts that the efforts he has made in this regard have become intrusive of Mrs Ritchie's privacy and a source of nuisance . . . Mr Mackman freely undertakes to make no future communications with Mrs Ritchie either personally or in writing unless at her express request. He further undertakes not to frequent the area of her home and her place of work except as his legitimate business shall require . . . Mr Mackman also wishes it to be known that he is now undergoing professional counselling for the emotional stress which resulted from the road accident involving the late Mr Ritchie and which he believes to be in some degree responsible for any unacceptable conduct he has shown . . .

Mr Bussapoon, cagey as ever, stressed in his covering letter that this, though satisfying, was a voluntary undertaking: they couldn't hold him to it. But Laura was more optimistic, simply because she knew Mike Mackman as he didn't. Mike was giving his word – and Mike was old-fashioned about such things. And perhaps that was precisely why the solicitor's letter, about which she had had doubts, had hit home. It challenged him to do the right thing, and she knew how punctilious he was about that.

Laura poured a second cup of coffee by way of celebration. She felt a quiet, cautious elation that didn't warrant anything stronger. No counting chickens this time, she told herself. She would just carry on steadily walking towards that distant illumination which *appeared* – she would only say that – to be light at the end of the tunnel.

Angie made a flying visit later that day – appropriately, as Laura had had counselling on her mind since reading the letter. If counselling had been the thing that had finally cooled Mike off, she thought, then she would never scoff at it again; but beneath this surface flippancy she was genuinely glad that he was getting help at last. Memories of that silent, solitary, showroom house of his, filtered though they were through her anger at what he had done, had oddly disturbed her of late. Maybe some sort of counselling had been what he needed all along.

Maybe she had needed it too, as Angie had insisted. But today, at least, Angie did not press telephone numbers on her, so perhaps something of the peace that letter had given her showed.

Angie, in fact, had new plans for her.

'You're looking great. You're looking very solid and together. I'm wondering whether it's time to test out some new waters. This guy I'm seeing, Richard, he's got a really nice friend who's been through a hell of a divorce and still has a lot of healing to do. He's a lot like Richard, in fact I had a bit of a yen for him myself but it wasn't on. Now wait, I *know* it's too soon to even think of anything, you know, heavy. I'm just suggesting company, peeping out of your shell a bit, having a laugh, sharing a meal, being around men. This is such a common misconception about bereavement, that it does away with sexuality. And then when people find it's still there in them, they feel guilty.'

'Well, if it's still there in me, it must be underneath something else,' Laura laughed, 'because I haven't spotted it.'

'Hey, no way. Aren't you masturbating?'

'Angie . . .' Laura cast a nervous glance at Simon, but he was absorbed in the football on TV.

'It's healthy, it's good, it's release,' Angie said in a slightly lower tone. 'I was talking to an eighty-five-year-old woman who does it every night. Better than sherry and sleeping tablets. I want to highlight it in health guidelines for the old. But listen, about this guy. I'm not putting any pressure on you. I'm just asking you to think about it.'

Laura was doing so, with no great enthusiasm. She simply wasn't ready for the singles game, no matter how decorously played. This was leaving aside the fact that the man in question, if he was to Angie's taste, was undoubtedly a bumptious plug-ugly with serious hygiene problems.

'It's kind of you, Angie. Maybe another time. Right now I'm just – well, I'm happy with settling into my routine, you know, the job and being with Simon and paying the bills. That's enough for me at the moment.' And please, she thought, don't press. The long contest with Mike Mackman had left her low on assertiveness.

'Listen, that's fine. I understand. The main thing is, I've planted a little *seed*.' Angie glanced round at the TV as Simon loudly acclaimed a goal. Her expression was split, uncomfortable. Football was liked by the working class, therefore good, but flag-waving and competitive, therefore bad. 'All those *people* . . . We need to foster community events. A woman I know on the council has been pushing to get a carnival for Langstead for ages. But there's so much apathy. And I find it hard to believe that *nobody* can play the steel drums . . . Hey, I forgot, what's happening with the house move?'

Nothing, was Laura's resigned answer. Oddly enough, resigned was what she felt a few days later when, in town on her lunch break, she looked into an estate agents' window and saw a photograph of the Maitland Street house half obliterated by the red-lettered word 'SOLD'.

Well, crying over spilt milk was doubtless as inadvisable as the counting of chickens. She had, at least, some kind of guarantee that these things were not going to happen any more. All being well on the Mike Mackman front, she would only have the standard-issue, reliable, everyday bad luck to contend with.

Telling herself this, she found the cynicism more willed than genuine. Perhaps it was the undeniable presence of summer that woke a cautious Pollyanna in her. She had greeted recent summers with misgivings for the same reason she had welcomed winters: summer was the time you stopped locking yourself away. Now the sunny days seemed full of innocent potential. She could go places with Simon (maybe he could fulfil his generous promise to teach her to swim). But the summer also meant the school holidays, and here was something that needed fixing.

Simon was unusually mutinous about the prospect of a childminder. She wondered, indeed, whether it was too soon for this, six months after the loss of his father. Being away from her at school was one thing: he expected that. But lacking her during the school holidays was new, and different, and he didn't like the sound of it.

'Mine played up at first,' Jan said. 'But they soon got used to it. In fact they seemed to like being at Mo's as much as being at home. I'm sure he'll get along fine. Mo's brilliant. You won't have to worry about a thing.'

Laura was more than willing to accept Jan's recommendation. And the childminder, Mo Greenall, who lived with two children of her own, in Miranda Avenue, the pleasantest part of Shakespeareland, signalled that she was more than willing to take Simon on for the duration of the school holidays. She sounded, from Laura's phone conversation with her, very cheery and down-to-earth and friendly – a fact which Laura tried unsuccessfully to convey to Simon.

'I bet she's horrible,' Simon grumped, hitting the settee in a double-jointed sprawl that to an adult would have been excruciating.

'Well, you don't know that. I realize it's awkward. I mean, everyone's shy meeting new people.'

'I'm not shy.' Simon headbutted a cushion, his face a study in pink stubbornness.

Don't do this to me, Laura thought. You're not due to start hating my guts for another seven years yet.

'What we'll do is just go and see Mrs Greenall,' she said. 'Then you can see for yourself what it's like and we'll take it from there.' Oh God, perhaps this wasn't right. Perhaps she was, after all, a cavalier and neglectful mother and was inflicting lasting scars on her son, so that he would end up with bodies in his basement . . . 'She looked after Auntie Jan's girls when they were younger. Auntie Jan says she's really nice.'

'I'll bet she looks like Bugs Bunny.' Simon delivered this with as much satisfaction as if it were an epigram of unanswerable, Wildean trenchancy. Laura tried not to smile, wondering how children developed this capacity to crack you up just at your sharpest moments of parental dilemma.

They made a reconnaissance visit to the childminder's house the next day after Laura had finished work. Simon's attitude hadn't changed, but all his weapons were, fortunately, psychological rather than physical: he had never been the sort of child to cling mulishly to doorposts or make a heart-attack-inducing run for it when faced with something he didn't like. Pulling up outside the house in Miranda Avenue – a modest and attractive Metroland-style detached, pleasantly free of leaded porch-lamps and fiercely neat hanging baskets – Laura looked at Simon, sitting beside her tight-lipped as a Resistance fighter on his way to interrogation, and told herself: if he really doesn't like it, I'll think of something else.

Mo Greenall, who answered the door, didn't look like Bugs Bunny (it would have been a considerable moral defeat for Laura if she had). She was a fair, plumpish woman whose rosy cheeks, bright eyes and wet-look perm gave her the appearance of having just completed some healthful exercise. So did the jogging bottoms and sweatshirt she wore.

'Excuse the gear,' she said, beckoning them in. 'I've just been having a good thump.' She pointed to an open door that led to the built-in garage, where there was a boxer's punchbag suspended from the ceiling, dispelling the momentary illusion that she bashed her charges. 'It's Laura, isn't it, and Simon? How do, Simon. Come on through. Dan!' she shouted up the stairs, whence music was pounding. 'Down a bit, please. Just a few hundred decibels.'

She led them to a big kitchen-diner, where a washing machine was chuntering and the oven was exuding rich garlicky smells. There were heaps of magazines and newspapers, which had been genuinely heaped rather than arranged in heaps. Painted directly on the wall above the dining table was a large colourful butterfly. On the transoms above the doors, Laura noticed, clever things had been done with dried flowers. Exactly the sort of things you saw in magazines that made you determined to do them yourself, except you never did. A fair stocky girl of about thirteen was seated at the table with a chess computer. She gave them a friendly hello and said, 'Mum, it's your go.'

'Half a minute.' Mo put the kettle on and then leant over and made a move on the computer. 'Check.'

'Bummer.'

'This is Lisette. Dan's my other one, he'll be down in a minute,' Mo said. 'Sit your bums down. That's all there is of us at the moment. My husband's a technician on the oil rigs, so he's away a lot. He tells me that's what he is, anyway. Might have a double life. Goes off with the circus or something.'

'Your go, Mum,' Lisette said.

'Let's see . . . Check. Well, it's nice to meet you at last. Jan mentioned you quite a while ago. Where is it you're working, Sprignall's?'

'That's right,' Laura said. 'Well, the restaurant, anyway. I mean, I don't cook or anything, I just do the, er, you know, dogsbodying.'

Now here was a turn-up. Simon had sat himself down with his usual stoic politeness; and it was Laura who was feeling, intensely, the strangeness of this. Of course, other people's cooking and laundry always smelt curiously different from your own. Their domestic arrangements, in fact, no matter how conventional, always seemed slightly off-centre simply because they weren't yours (how odd, you thought, to put the washing-up liquid bottle just *there*). And it was pretty plain, at once, that this was a nice household that had both life and ease in it. But it was so very much someone else's house that it was Laura who found herself, for the first few minutes, rather crushed by the fact.

'So how are Jan's girls? I haven't seen them lately.'

'They're fine. Kate's quite a friend of Simon's.'

'She's a nice kid. Sarah too, though I should think she's at that age, isn't she?'

'Well, there's the odd bit of tension in the air.'

'Tell me about it . . . Hello, devil, just talking of you,' Mo said, as a boy of about fifteen appeared, loose-jointed as a marionette. He was fair too, though the current plastered-down, caught-in-a-downpour look partly disguised it as far as his hair went. The complexion was unmistakeable, though. Laura wondered whether the father had perfect skin as well, and whether, when they were all out together, they got resentfully pelted by potato-faces.

'What are you saying about me this time?' he said, adding, 'Hi.'

'Saying what a good lad you are to your old mum.' Mo gave him a playful pinch, which didn't get through because of his clothes. These were the height of teen style, meaning they looked to have been randomly put together from the sporting wardrobe of a very fat colour-blind man. 'This is Laura and Simon. We might be having Simon this summer if we're lucky.'

'All right?' Dan said, sitting bonelessly down next to Simon. 'Been watching the football?'

While Simon timidly exchanged opinions on the deficiencies of the England team, Mo got down to business. 'Well, I've been registered since '91. As a childminder, I mean. I was registered as a nutcase years before that. Now I can forward you some references if you'd like—'

'Oh, Jan recommended you. I mean – that's good enough for me.'

'Well, she's told you my rates. For that you get a sort of happy medium between wrapping them in cotton wool and letting them do just what they like. I mean, I don't have to tell you, it's hard, isn't it? Basically I don't expect them to sit up at the table silently playing with an Etch-a-Sketch all day. You ever have one of them? Boring, weren't they?'

'All straight lines.'

'This is it. Hey, I've drawn another square, great. If you want them to stay absolutely put, that's fine. It's also fine for their friends to come calling for them here. The rec actually backs on to the garden, which is handy. I usually go for a kickabout there once a day. Kids mostly put me in goal. Probably because I fill it. Any dietary allergies or preferences, just let me know. Dan's a meaty and Lisette's a veggie, so I'm used to it.'

'Mum, you know Melissa George, she's a vegan now,' Lisette put in.

'Is she? You don't want to be, do you?'

Lisette shook her head. 'Can't have cheese on toast. Couldn't live without that.'

'Well, thank goodness. Not that I'd mind cooking it,' Mo said to Laura. 'It's just having to say, "My daughter's a vegan." Sounds like they're from another planet, you know. Three eyes and a silver suit.'

'Simon's very good about food. Even likes spinach.'

'Like me. I'll eat anything that doesn't move. That's why I'm this shape.'

'You? You're a good shape.'

'Oh, say it again! Dan, switch the tape recorder on. I like her. How come you never put any weight on, Daniel? You're always eating.'

'Burn it all off,' he said, 'because I'm so intense.'

'Oh, is that what it is?' Mo smiled at Laura. 'Never left him anywhere before?'

'Well, he's been going to Jan's house after school, just until I finish work. But – no, it's all a bit new to us both.' Laura glanced over at Simon, and then noticed something in the corner of the room that in her nervousness she had missed.

Simon had spotted it, though. His eyes hardly left it. It was a large and well-stocked aquarium.

'That's a nice one, isn't it, love?' she said to him, getting in return a nod of rapt solemnity – the nod of a connoisseur who has spotted the acquisition of a lifetime in a junk shop window.

'My husband's thing,' Mo said. 'And Dan's. I can never *quite* see the thrill myself.'

'Fish, fish are brilliant, there's a whole world in there,' Dan enthused, beckoning Simon to follow him. 'Come and have a look.'

'You eat fish, Dan,' Lisette told him.

'Only dead ones. You got one of these at home?'

Simon's headshake expressed a universe of regret.

'These guppies are new, they're not accustomed yet. And that one, Dad sent away to London specially for that . . .'

Watching, Laura felt that Simon could do a lot worse than turn out like Dan. Be lanky, image-conscious, music-addicted, but retain the ability to talk in polysyllables.

'You're staying for a cup of tea?' Mo said. 'Even if you don't like the look of us. No obligation. *I* don't like the look of us sometimes.'

'Thanks, that'd be lovely.'

She liked the look of them very much. And any lingering doubts whether Simon felt the same were utterly dispelled when Dan said to him, 'We've got a pond in the garden as well. Want to have a look?'

'Can I, Mum?' Simon asked; and gave her a look as if to say – *see,* I told you it would be all right.

TWENTY-TWO

It was his doctor who had first suggested to Mike Mackman that he should have counselling, when he had gone to the surgery to try to get something for his insomnia. The doc was a good sort. He'd spotted that something was playing on Mike's mind.

'It's that road accident, isn't it?'

'I suppose it must be,' Mike had said.

But it wasn't, not really. Not the accident itself, though it had cut him up at the time. It was the consequences.

'Do you still have nightmares about it?'

'No.' He didn't; and though he wanted something for his sleeplessness, he hated telling lies.

'I know you may feel this is really not your cup of tea,' the doc had said eventually, 'but I'd like to put you in touch with a therapist. I'm not dismissing your problem. I just feel in a case like this that counselling might be a help, rather than me dishing out sleeping tablets.'

The doc was only partly right. It was true that that sort of thing wasn't generally Mike's cup of tea. He was a practical man: as a rule he didn't think there was much that couldn't be sorted out by a bit of hard graft and not feeling sorry for yourself. On the other hand, he had great respect for people who knew their jobs. Always the world had presented itself to Mike Mackman in simple dualistic terms: there were things that were admirable and to which you gave proper respect, and there were things that weren't, which he generally ignored as his time was valuable. The framed qualifications in the doc's office had always elicited his respect. A vague feeling of rightness, almost of vicarious pride, came over him when he looked at them. Here was a man who had done his training and paid his dues. It was solid, it was achievement. Surely, Mike felt, the world couldn't be as bad a place as some people seemed to enjoy saying it was – not when a man could command this sort of expertise, hang its visible form on his walls, build himself so securely on what he knew and believed.

But there were always the knockers and the doers-down, who preferred to pick faults rather than admire. It was an attitude Mike couldn't understand. He certainly hoped he could never be accused of it. So in spite of his doubts he went along to see the psychotherapist the doc recommended. After all, a psychotherapist must surely know his business too. The study of the mind – now there was a remarkable thing. He didn't entirely go along with some of the things he had heard they went into – a lot of emphasis on how your childhood and so on had made you the way you were, whereas he had a straightforward and simple belief that you made your own bed – but still it was clever stuff, and Mike wasn't about to dismiss it out of hand.

The psychotherapist turned out to be not a him, but a her. A middle-aged lady of the tailor-made sort, who had a very refined and educated way of speaking. This surprised him at first, as his own doctor was pretty down-to-earth, but Mike was the last person to be put off by that. In the course of his trade he had sometimes come across people of quality – at Chamber of Commerce functions, occasionally when doing a building job on their houses out in the country – and he had nothing but respect for them. They had class, sheer natural class. Like this lady – you could tell she came from a good family. He knew it wasn't a world he could ever enter. He had made a fair bit of money, but money wasn't the key, which was one of the remarkable things about that world. He could admire it, though, as a pattern, and he did: he had been taking *Country Life* for years.

The fact that the psychotherapist was a woman inclined him, if anything, to be even more co-operative. It was one of his steadfast beliefs – and Mike Mackman's beliefs were all like that, a clutch of inalterable convictions that were more like internal organs than abstract products of the mind, so hard and tight and physical were they – that women should always be afforded a greater degree of politeness and consideration than men. That was just the way it was. And it applied to womankind in general. He knew that some men cynically availed themselves of this convention – womanizers, looking out for the main chance; which he thought disgusting. You were sincere or you weren't. He had heard a lot of that brutal, exploitative talk about women in the course of his work, and though to some extent he accepted it – you couldn't expect men on a building site to be choirboys – he never joined in.

So he gave the psychotherapist the deferential attention he would give to any woman. Though it all seemed to be based on endless talk and he didn't set a high value on talk, he gave it a go.

The trouble was, she kept probing him about the accident, and the guilt of it, which seemed to him pretty pointless. Of course he felt bad about it: he made no bones about that. Nor about the fact that he felt he had a responsibility to the woman whom he had deprived of a husband and provider. But when she pressed him on this, he found he had nothing to say, or nothing that there seemed to him any point in saying. Laura Ritchie and her child were now his responsibility: it was a settled thing within him. It was up to him to be their protector, for always. It was a duty, but not a burdensome one. In fact it was a great good that had come out of bad, because it was a thing he could do, a thing he seemed marvellously and fortunately equipped to do. It certainly wasn't a problem for him, except perhaps in its practical details, so he didn't see any reason to talk about it.

And though he could chat with the best of them, when he didn't want to talk about something he didn't: that was it. Shutting up was easy. He didn't want to be rude to the psychotherapist, but when she got on to this track, he simply couldn't follow her.

And though he did his best, he couldn't follow her when she went off down another track – his past, his marriage, all the rest of it. He really didn't see the point in digging over that old ground. The failure of his marriage was a great pity, and not just personally. It gave him a feeling of vague embracing disquiet, just as the sight of those framed qualifications in the doctor's office gave him a feeling of vague rightness, because of his beliefs. Marriage, he believed, was for life. It was one of those deep, basic, holy things that life was built on. Mike had no time for politics or society or any of those abstractions. His heart and mind were engaged only by those fundamentals: marriage; children; work; home; family. But sadly his marriage hadn't worked, and there had been a divorce, and his wife had remarried and lived in Wales, and the whole thing was a dead letter. He retained a profound regret that there had been no children, because he felt that might have saved it, but beyond that he really didn't think about it.

As for when she began asking about his childhood and upbringing, he couldn't help thinking, with all due respect, that this was a waste of his time and hers. There was nothing to say about his childhood. It had been happy, the way a childhood should be. There had been five kids and sometimes things were tight – his father had been a jobbing builder and a good one but success, steady success, had tended to elude him – and there had been the odd run-in with his parents, as was only natural; but all in all they never went without. They made their own amusement, as kids didn't seem to be able to do nowadays, and the whole family were as close-knit as could be. As families should be.

(That was how he remembered it, anyhow. His brothers and sisters had all moved away from Langstead when they grew up and as a consequence had rather lost touch, which he thought a great pity; and when he had met up with his brother Terry a year or two ago and they had talked about old times, Terry had shocked him by saying they were awful. 'Come on, Mike,' he'd said. 'It was a bloody claustrophobic setup. All living in each other's pockets. Mum knackered herself looking after us all and making ends meet and Dad could be a right overbearing bastard.' That wasn't how Mike saw it at all, and he could only shake his head and presume that Terry, who had moved to London, had picked up some smart sophisticated way of talking that didn't mean anything.)

So he couldn't help wondering, when he came away from the psychotherapist's, why he was bothering with it. But then he had to be honest with himself and admit that he did have an ulterior motive.

Mike hated double-dealing so implacably that even the idea of having an ulterior motive made him prickle with shameful sweat. And he couldn't have lived with this one if it hadn't been for the absolute purity of the aim to which the whole deception was tending. Simply, he had to keep the counselling going because his solicitor had made such a point of it in that letter. It was a shield. It fended off the threat of the law which Laura had so pluckily made. He didn't need it, but pretending he did was useful because it pacified Laura. When he received that letter from her solicitor, Mike had recognized that the time had come, not to back off, but to seem to back off. Otherwise she might make some rash move that would really force him into a position where he couldn't help her any more.

Which would be disastrous. He didn't think any the worse of her for not perceiving this. If anything, he thought the better of her, admired even more her heartbreaking courage. But he couldn't let it happen – he would never forgive himself. That was why he had made that voluntary undertaking. Otherwise the law might indeed have entered the picture, and though he had a deep respect for the law and authority in general, he couldn't expect it to understand a situation like this. It couldn't be expected to understand, for example, that poor Laura, shattered and bereft and trying so gamely to prove she could cope, just didn't know her own mind. Of course she would say she didn't want his help – because it was the strength and support of her husband that she wanted. And of that Mike had deprived her. If she saw it as practically an insult to suppose he could make up for that loss, then he honoured that feeling. It was the feeling of a true wife and mother. But he had to keep trying: by hook or by crook, he must make up for it. Maybe some time she would come to recognize what he had done, but he didn't look for that. He didn't mind if it never happened. All he wanted was to look after her, be strong for her. Be her rock.

But of course the law, if she said he was pestering her, was duty-bound to take her at her word – and quite right too. The law couldn't know that that was her grief and pride talking. So he would have to box clever. His own solicitor, when he had consulted him about this, had been alarmed; and then relieved when Mike had agreed so freely to that undertaking. What Mike didn't tell him was that he had no intention of keeping out of Laura Ritchie's life. He had just come to a realization that, for her sake (and *everything* was for her sake), he would have to do it in a different way.

He was very much alone in this, but he didn't feel any resentment about it. There was no reason why these doctors and solicitors and what-have-you should understand, because they didn't know Laura

Ritchie. They couldn't know her as he did – down on the gut level – the place of love and birth and death, the only stratum of feeling that was worth bothering with. They hadn't seen her as he had seen her, in the waiting room at the hospital where the sight of her noble, stricken, so womanly face had been blasted on to his consciousness. They hadn't seen her cry – not abandoned, indulgent tears, but pure helpless tears that she had tried valiantly to keep at bay. They hadn't seen her with her little boy at her side, a mother through and through even though her heart was breaking. They hadn't seen her going out to work for that little boy's sake, imprisoned in a horrible uniform behind the counter of a café instead of in the pleasant home that she had made and where she fitted in so beautifully. And they hadn't seen her feistiness, her touching display of strength that must cover the most awful fragility, at the prospect of losing that home.

So he understood. He bore no grudges. And with the psychotherapist he could only try to do his best and patiently wait for each session to be over.

As he drove away from today's session, though, he felt a certain impatience mixed with his relief, and wondered how long he would have to keep this up. When, in other words, did these bods pronounce you cured of whatever it was they supposed you had in the first place? Today, for example, she had kept on about his marriage again, which suggested that she really didn't know what to do and was just spinning things out. Something about this feeling of guilt, and wanting to go back and change what had happened, and whether that applied to his marriage too. Did he feel he had been a good husband?

Well, of course he did; but obviously not good enough, because they were divorced. As far as he could tell, he had done everything that a husband should do. Kim had never wanted for anything. If she saw something she liked in a shop window, she got it. The house had been done up just the way she wanted it, which was a bit too feminine for his taste at times – the huge lace canopy over the bed, the silk all round the dressing table, the valances and frills and tie-backs and fluffy white rugs. She had style, though, there was no doubt about that. And he made it clear that that home was her domain, even to the extent of behaving as if he were a fortunate guest there. He remembered how he would tiptoe round that king-sized bed in the mornings so as not to wake her. He was the breadwinner and she shouldn't have to be up when he was – and if she did get up, she should just be in her silk dressing gown, sipping real coffee from the filter machine. (He didn't like that stuff, but then his personal tastes were very simple and even spartan. He liked to have the best that money could buy, especially when it came to cars, but that was just a matter of paying for quality, which was always economical. Indulgence for its own sake didn't interest him. Sometimes Kim would say with a faint frown, as she unwrapped the latest gift he brought home, 'Mike, why don't you get something nice for yourself now and then?' And he would try to explain, but could not, that he wanted her to have things, and that that, for him, was like having things himself.)

A devoted husband. Yes, he would call himself that. But certainly not perfect. Mike had a good deal of confidence and he knew his abilities, but he was not conceited. Obviously, in some ways he had been a disappointment to Kim. She was a social animal as he was not: he had to attend the odd do, even put on a monkey suit now and then, but he tolerated this for the sake of business. Kim couldn't get enough of it. She wanted to go out all the time. This was a difference between them. He went along, but he didn't enjoy all the chit-chat. He found it trivial, and he disliked the current of flippancy that ran through such gatherings. Serious talk was all right, but he couldn't abide all the mickey-taking that went on in the world today. He was often worried for the kids growing up in such a world, with no respect for anybody or anything. There was too much knocking. He had always heartily detested that TV programme with rubber puppets caricaturing famous people, and had been glad when it was taken off at last. His own politics were Conservative, but he hadn't liked seeing the politicians of the other persuasion being mocked like that either. They were doing their job. It was all too easy to knock.

So the socializing had been a bit of a problem between them. Sometimes when they were driving home – he always made sure not to drink, so that he could drive her home safely – she would reproach him. 'You just sat there. You didn't talk. And when you did it was all heavy-going stuff.'

This would surprise him. He was quite happy being quiet, as long as she was happy. He had an immense fund of physical patience.

'I could tell you didn't enjoy it,' she would say; and he would try to tell her that what mattered to him was for *her* to enjoy it. That was all he wanted. But this seemed to make her more frustrated.

Incompatibility, he supposed. Perhaps, too, he had spent too much time at work, but those were the years when his business was really taking off, and inevitably it made great demands on him. The point was, he was doing it for her, and for the children they would have. He would try to impress this on her, but sometimes it would make her strangely angry; and when he kept explaining it, really trying to make it clear to her, she would only get more angry, instead of calming down – a thing he could never understand.

(It was true that it had all been for her – no bull. After the divorce, he kept working and striving, simply because he didn't have anything else. But there was no reason for it. There was no goal, no vision. At least there hadn't been, until now.)

'Do you feel, when things go wrong, that they're usually your fault?'

the psychotherapist had asked him today.

Again, with all due respect, a stupid question. It *was* his fault that Laura was a widow – no two ways about that. But he certainly wasn't helping her out of obligation. It was a thing he wanted to do – a thing that, in a curious way, he was made to do. So that was straightforward. As for the marriage, probably it was six of one and half a dozen of the other . . . though when it came down to it, he believed that the man was always more at fault in these situations, simply because it was the man's job to keep the wife happy. Obviously he had failed in that, because there had been, at last, an affair. And, of course, that was the end. He was strict, in fact absolute, about such things. It didn't matter how much you cared for a woman – she put herself beyond the pale when she behaved like that.

Waiting at a junction, Mike debated whether to call in at the yard or go straight home. (He still thought of the premises of Mike Mackman Builders as 'the yard'. That was all it had been once – a sidestreet builders' yard with an unheated prefab containing a telephone and not much else. Now, having bought the neighbouring filling station when it folded, and expensively converted it, he had an office suite and depot that could hardly be called a yard, but the name stuck. Perhaps it was an internal reminder, to stop himself getting puffed up.) Home, he decided quite quickly. Once it had been quite a pleasure of his to stop by at the yard even during the evenings, to look over plans and accounts and invoices, to feel himself on top of things. But he had got out of the habit lately. He had a very good building manager and an efficient secretary; and he had been on site at Goldcrest Park all day, which was quite enough. He knew that the housing association who had awarded them the contract for the development had been seeking him urgently – something to do with the installation of water meters for the individual properties – but that too could wait. He had other things on his mind.

Not least the things the psychotherapist had said, which kept bugging him. This business about children and did he regret not having them . . . Well, he thought, what man wouldn't? He was a nest-builder, had never pretended to be anything else, ardently wished for his line to continue. Family was important – in fact he couldn't think of anything more important. But more than that, he loved kids. Kids were great. It was dreadful the way the world didn't accommodate itself to kids now. It treated them as a nuisance. There were so few places you could take them. And they had all these terrible temptations put in their way, forcing them to grow up before their time. Chasing a half-deflated football about, climbing trees, going on long bike rides with a few jam sandwiches in a paper bag, swimming in the old gravel pits . . . these were the things he remembered from his own childhood. And for Mike they had a mystical essence of truth about them. They constituted a standard; in fact he could only think of them as classical. You couldn't touch them, rather like classical music, which he didn't really like or understand but which he could never hear without a sort of humble, willing submission.

Of course he had got up to some mischief when he was a boy, but that was natural. It was all innocent stuff, and it was the innocence that was missing in today's world. Any kid could turn out well as long as you protected that innocence and gave them the proper guidance. That was why he had volunteered his services for that Outward Bound school up at the Lakes last summer. He had done a bit of sailing in his time, he was handy with outdoor pursuits, and he loved kids, especially if there was a chance of teaching them a few practical things, as his father had done with him. It gave them confidence. There was nothing worse than growing up cack-handed and unsure of yourself.

It wasn't a happy memory and he had chosen not to tell the psychotherapist about it. They hadn't so much told him to leave as gently suggested that it wasn't working out, but still he was hurt and puzzled. They had said something about demanding too much, that you couldn't expect adult dexterity and strength in a child, but he couldn't understand what the fuss was about. Surely the whole idea was to make them aware of their capacities: you pushed them so that they could discover things about themselves. The boy who had cried and complained had been fourteen, after all, and at that age Mike had been helping his father mix cement. It would have been different if it had been a girl, but boys were meant to be hardy. He was still convinced that if he could have stayed a few more days, he could have sorted the lad out. He would have had the lad putting up the sails all by himself and feeling as pleased as punch and hardly believing that he was the same lad who had cried about the blisters on his hands; and in years to come he would always remember that achievement. Mike just couldn't understand it. It wasn't always kindness to be kind, which he'd thought they'd understand. The lad was going to grow up and find himself a girl eventually, and she wasn't going to be too impressed if he couldn't look after himself and her in the way she had a right to expect.

Later there had been a complaint from the parents too, which the organizers had shielded him from. Good of them, but there had been no need – he had been quite prepared to fight his own corner. Not that he would tell parents how to bring up their own children, but they simply weren't doing the lad any favours mollycoddling him like that. There wouldn't have been that damage to his hands if he'd kept plugging away instead of giving up. They would have hardened: that was the whole point. What hurt Mike was the fact that the Outward Bound school wouldn't have him back. He felt he had such a lot to offer.

At home he shucked off his jacket and ate a cold pasty from the fridge, without a plate, munching noisily. He was hardly aware of eating, and though he stared at the TV, he was hardly aware of what he was watching either. He didn't care for many programmes: the news was depressing, comedies were plain silly, films rarely held his attention. He liked the occasional factual programme that showed you how things worked, and he had enjoyed above all the old American soaps, *Dallas* and *Dynasty*. It was the way of life he admired, the furnishings and the clothes and the cars. The Americans knew how to live. He had promised Kim that they would have a ranch some day.

But tonight he soon turned off the TV and put some music on the hi-fi instead: a tape of country and western songs. (He liked technology, but he hadn't bothered to upgrade to CD, not when there was only him doing the listening.) He loved country music of the mainstream Nashville kind. He liked accessible pop, too, especially if it featured those big thrilling female voices like Cher and Whitney Houston, but it was country that really got to him. Country locked directly into those deep, quintessential elements of Mike's self: it was about first and last things; it was the sound of the heart. He remembered Kim once complaining that it had no wit, but to Mike that was the point: that was what he liked about it.

While he listened he drank Glenfiddich from a chunky tumbler. By no means a big drinker, he enjoyed a good Scotch and sometimes felt the need of it as an aid to reflection. The music was an ingredient of this too; also the many table lamps, which under usual circumstances he didn't trouble to switch on, contenting himself with the overhead light. This evening he had all three ingredients – as he had, in fact, most evenings lately.

And the subject of his thoughts was, as usual, Laura.

Tears pricked his eyes as he thought of her, out there, a precious glow in the dreary dusk of the town. A woman alone, so very vulnerable. Look at the way those brutes from the finance company had homed in on her. Thankfully there wouldn't be any more trouble from them. He had made sure of that, not only clearing the debt but making it plain to them that their visit had been out of order. He was not a violent man but he could look after himself, and he believed they had understood his displeasure.

And yet there were more where they came from. Not necessarily direct threats to her wellbeing like them, but subtler dangers. An unprotected, unsupported woman was liable to every species of exploitation and depredation, especially one made frail by a terrible bereavement. Knowing this, and knowing he had to keep away, just tore him apart.

Soon he had to go to the toilet. A weak bladder was the only flaw in his oxlike constitution. This gave him the chance to check up on the windowsill above the toilet cistern, a thing that was important to him. There were five items on there: a can of hairspray, a bottle of aftershave, a comb, a shaving stick and a little bowl of potpourri. He always kept them there and he liked to see them. Just them: nothing else. At first he would replace the can of hairspray with an identical new one when it was empty, and convinced himself that really this was a perpetuation of the same can. But then it wouldn't do and he stopped using the hairspray, so that what was there was *genuinely* the same can. For the same reason he never used the aftershave or the shaving stick, though he was allowed to use the comb.

Now he studied their layout and, after a small adjustment of the potpourri bowl, was satisfied. Lynne, his cleaning lady, knew the ropes now. She never put these items elsewhere, as she had disastrously on first coming to work for him, and she even made a creditable stab at putting them back exactly as they were after she had wiped the windowsill. She was worth her hire for that alone. With most domestic matters Mike was careless, even messy; that didn't matter when there was only himself to consider. But about these five items on the bathroom windowsill he was particular. He felt that they were lucky, somehow. Also, in an odd way, they were his confidants. With his weak bladder he saw them many times a day, and they seemed to look back at him – even to share in his thoughts.

'I've got to find a way,' he said to them now. 'I've got to. It's so important.'

When he went back to the lounge a new track was just beginning on the country tape. 'Ah,' he said to himself, because this was one of his very favourites. 'From a Distance'. The song got him where he lived – the Americans had the exact phrase for it.

And as he listened and drank another Scotch, he found the song doing more for him.

From a distance.

He was a little bit tipsy, but it wasn't because of that that his eyes were filling with tears again. They were tears of relief – relief that he could see his way clear again. It *could* be done.

It could be done from a distance. With care and forethought, he could still watch over Laura and her little lad with the utmost effectiveness. 'Someone to Watch Over Me' – there was another old song that put it in a nutshell. That was what she must have and would have.

He stopped drinking immediately – he could do that, thank goodness, quite easily, and that was why he was its master and not its servant – because he wanted to be clear-headed in the morning. In fact, the effects of the drink seemed to have disappeared altogether with the dawning of his idea. He even considered the possibility of getting in the car and taking a drive down to Duncan Road now – just to look, to check, to reassure himself. But he soon decided it wasn't worth the risk, not with alcohol in his bloodstream. He of all people ought to stay aware of road safety.

And besides, he had to keep himself safe for her sake.

The next day, after a night of fruitful insomnia, Mike shut his Audi away in the garage and walked to the yard. There he took possession of what he fondly referred to as 'the old van'. It was the van he had used when he was first starting out, back in the days when he had laid the bricks himself. Now there was a fleet of vans bearing his name, but he had kept this one in a garage at the yard, ostensibly for emergency use but chiefly for sentimental reasons. The van was white, and unmarked. When he tried the engine the familiar rugged sound of it gave him a feeling of tender nostalgia.

He waited until ten, when Laura was sure to be at work, and then drove in the van to Duncan Road.

He needed first of all to be assured that the house hadn't been sold. Though he regretted the fact that his plan for the place hadn't come off, he hoped at least it had been a stalling action, putting off other potential buyers. The sign still read 'For Sale', which was good. Moving would be a dreadful mistake which she would only realize when it was too late – as he had tried, without success, to tell her. Not that he minded her stubbornness. The refusal of women to see sense, he thought, was one of the charming things about them. And you had to remember that all her behaviour was distorted by the grief of her bereavement: she literally didn't know what she was saying or doing. Which made it all the more vital that he should stay alert on her behalf.

He knew that by cruising down this road he was breaking the terms of his own agreement. But he felt that at some deeper level he wasn't – because she wasn't aware of it. That was the important thing. It was actually seeing him around that distressed her, and after an initial phase of hurt at this he had come to understand. Having the man who had robbed her of her husband physically before her must be a terrible trial to her nerves.

From a distance, then.

The sleepless night had thrown up all sorts of ideas, some concrete, some vague. It was one of the latter that made him turn the van into Beatrice Road, which ran parallel to Duncan Road and, he was sure, backed on to it on one side.

The houses didn't directly overlook, of course, in a neighbourhood like this. On the other hand, the developers who had run these places up in the thirties hadn't had *that* much leeway with the land. Every rear aspect terminated in the back of another house, even if it was at a respectable distance.

The thought of being in sight of Laura's house, being able to see the little lad playing in the garden, perhaps even to see in at the windows, filled Mike with an exquisite longing that he recognized, reluctantly, as just too exquisite. That was an ideal, not reality; and Mike was a realist, canny and practical. You had to be, to get anywhere in this life. But he believed too in pursuing your dream. You could make your own luck, if you were dedicated enough.

This was how it seemed when he saw the 'For Sale' sign halfway down Beatrice Road. Something to do with luck and something to do with dedication.

Counting the houses, he calculated that this wasn't the one that backed directly on to Laura's – that would have been too much to hope. But, he reckoned, it was the one that adjoined it. There would be a diagonal view – what sort of view he couldn't tell.

He parked outside the house, studying it. The uncurtained windows indicated that it was vacant. Better, better. The vague outlines, the merest thumbnail sketches of a plan that had brought him here were becoming rapidly firmer. This was how it usually was with him. He trusted his instincts. Following your nose was better than any amount of theorizing. He had stayed out of several business deals that had looked superficially promising just by attending to his gut feeling, and had been proved right each time. He wondered if his feeling about this place was right.

An old person's house, he thought. The owner had either gone into a home or died, having scarcely stepped out of the house for the past twenty years, and the estate agents were having a job to shift it because of its condition. The exterior didn't look too bad, apart from the tell-tale crumbling beneath the windowsills, but inside the place would be just as it was in 1930: stone sink, high-level WC, no heating, probably even round-pin sockets. He knew because he had bought up several such places to remodel and sell at a profit, back before the housing market went kaput. Usually from this particular estate agents, Cady's, an old auctioneering outfit that mainly dealt in commercial and development properties. He knew Roy Cady pretty well.

After a last look Mike pulled away and headed for Cady's office in town. He was still guided by instinct: his mind moved in a fashion that was both rough-and-ready and methodical, like a soldier crossing a bridge made of two ropes, suspended in air but intensely purposive.

Cady's office was in an old squeezed sidestreet building, more like a solicitor's than the general run of estate agents. It was dim and cramped in there, with a hatstand and ashtrays and the rattle of an old-fashioned typewriter. Mike admired Roy Cady's refusal to modernize and his insistence on running a hands-on business. It probably wasn't wise in this day and age, but it showed standards.

A young lady started to deal with his enquiry, but then Roy himself came out of his inner office and, seeing Mike, at once took over. There were some people at the Conservative Club who knocked Roy for his rather obvious toupee and for his talkativeness, but Mike had always got along with him.

'Beatrice Road, yes, that's an interesting house,' Roy said, after they had chewed the fat for a while – business, the housing market, the eternal wrong-headed obstructiveness of Langstead's lefty council. 'The old girl who lived there had to go into a nursing home. It's a shame you couldn't see it the way she had it. I mean, it needs a hell of a lot doing to it, but it was individual. She collected pictures – nothing worth a damn, probably, but the way she'd hung them everywhere, it was attractive. Like a gallery, really. They've all been sold, anyhow. Her nephew saw to that. Between you and me I think he's living in hope, do you know what I mean?'

Mike understood. He detested that sort of calculation.

'But as I say, it really needs modernizing. It could be a terrific house, though, once its potential's been realized. You could bring it up to scratch while retaining some of the original features and have something really quite special.' Twitchy, Roy smoked a menthol cigarette, scattering ash on himself. 'So, Mike, you're looking for something in that line?'

'Well, it's a possibility, you know. Now the market's on the upturn I wondered about going back into renovation.'

'What have you got on at the moment? Is it the Goldcrest Park thing?'

'Starter homes, yup. The specs are stingy and the site's on the wrong side of the A road, if you ask me. But that was the housing association – they wouldn't listen. All college boys and girls with housing diplomas and no experience of the real world. The houses are nice little places basically. Then there's that new garden centre development which doesn't look as if it's ever going to get the go-ahead.' Mike fingered the typed details for 22 Beatrice Road. The asking price reflected the state of the property: but it would still be quite an outlay, and Roy's talk of the potential of the place was ninety per cent bull. Not that Mike blamed him for that – it was business, and he would do the same. But it was bull nevertheless, and probably Mike would have to have a conflab with his accountant if it were to be a business purchase. (Now that he thought of it, his accountant had been pressing him for a meeting for some time. But he kept putting it off. He had other things to think of.)

'Listen, I've got a client to see at half-past eleven, but I'm free till then,' Roy said. 'What do you say to going over and taking a look at the place now? I would like you to see it. I really think it's right up your street.'

Mike consulted his watch. He was still edging, groping across the ravine, one step at a time.

But he most certainly wanted to see inside that house.

'All right. Much appreciated, Roy.'

They drove separately, Roy raising his eyebrows when he saw the old van. 'Car's in dock,' Mike explained. 'Thought I'd fall back on Old Reliable here.' This little lie, though it was part of a larger one, somehow made him acutely uncomfortable.

A strong smell of must, sadly blended with old-lady perfume and the sweetish reek of someone who hadn't been able to look after herself, met them when Roy Cady opened the door of the house in Beatrice Road. Roy kicked aside a heap of junk mail. Obviously the place hadn't had many viewers just lately. Mike felt the crunch of loosened quarry tiles under his feet.

'I do wish you could have seen it with the old girl's pictures up,' Roy said, gesturing at the white squares that dotted the yellow-brown walls. 'Had such character. Now this front room actually needs very little doing to it, as you can see. Maybe some work on the bay. These original fireplaces, as you know, are very sought-after nowadays . . .'

Mike nodded absently, making a swift assessment in spite of himself. This room alone needed a great deal doing to it. The chimney breast was damp, the bay was falling apart, and the wiring looked thoroughly untrustworthy. He made the same cursory examination of the dining room, which had a cracked ceiling and a walk-in pantry that no one in this day and age was going to want, and that would be awkward to knock through because of that main joist . . . But his interest was only really aroused when they got to the rear of the house.

'Obviously this kitchen isn't up to modern standards,' Roy said, rapping optimistically at the pipes, 'but your plumbing is basically sound, and really it's just a question of adding modern units.'

'No electric cooker point,' Mike said, going to the window. It overlooked the back garden, but it was so grimy he could hardly see out. He rubbed at the glass with wetted fingers. 'And only a cold water tap.'

'No. Yes. Well, obviously there's scope for improvement, which is why it's priced so realistically. There's a very nice little garden out there, mainly lawn, some very nice mature shrubs. The old girl had a man in for the garden. Now here you've got the cloakroom – phoo – which once again needs, you know . . .'

Mike's heart skipped a beat. Through the little hole he had made in the grime, he could see the fence at the foot of the garden, and beyond that the rear of a semi. Now the one adjoining that, he reckoned . . .

'We'll have a look out there, if you like. There's a good timber shed. An outside tap, too, which is useful. Surprising how many people are looking for that. Gardening and so on, it's . . . Damn. Half a mo.'

Roy's mobile phone was ringing. He spoke irritably into it whilst Mike, feeling quite dreamlike, tried to widen the hole he had made in the greasy murk of the window and see what he was sure, what he *knew* must be the house . . .

'Mike, I'm so sorry about this. That client I was telling you about. Turned up at the office earlier than expected and he can only stick around till twelve, then he's got to get back for an appointment in London. I shall have to . . . Look, do you want to carry on here? You probably want to see upstairs and everything . . .'

'I would like to,' Mike said, watching as Roy fumbled in his pocket. 'Now I'm here.'

'Well, I'll tell you what. There's the front door key. If you could just lock it behind you and pop it back to the office when you're done. How would that be?'

Mike held up his hands. 'Fine, Roy. Appreciate it.'

'I really will have to skip off. Hopefully I'll see you a bit later, but if not, you know, give me a buzz any time if you want to know more about the place. OK?'

'Thanks, Roy.' Mike took the key in his hand. He was relieved to see that the hand did not tremble. 'Take care now. Don't – you know, rush too much on the road.'

He waited until Roy had gone before walking down the hall and climbing the stairs.

Thin narrow stair carpet, worn through almost to the hessian backing. Perilous for an old lady: it was a wonder she'd survived. But you often found this in such places – frail old things blithely living charmed lives in deathtrap houses.

On the landing he glanced about a moment, getting his bearings. Large bedroom at the front. Glimpse of a dismal bathroom, the ancient tub with its slimy green stain looking more like an outdoor tank. And here, another large bedroom which surely looked out to what Roy Cady's trade called the rear aspect.

Mike went in. The feel of the bare floorboards beneath his shoes told him they were rotten, would probably turn to mush when you lifted them. He crossed the room to the large uncurtained sash window, and gave a gasp.

There it was. You could see it from here so clearly, more clearly than he could have dreamt. Probably the adjoining house gave an even better view, but he wasn't complaining about this one. From this window you could see straight into Laura Ritchie's back garden. You could see the back door and the rear windows of her house. There were no nets or blinds in those rear windows either. Even with the naked eye he could see truncated lines of furniture, interior doors, shapes and shadows.

It was, literally, a window on her world. That world he had sworn to protect and keep inviolate. That world of which he longed to be – needed to be – the benign presiding spirit.

Standing there, looking across the neat grid of gardens at Laura Ritchie's home, Mike had a vivid memory. It was of his very first pet, a puppy that had been given him as a boy. He remembered holding it for the first time and feeling its trembling, trusting fragility in his hands. He remembered the contrast between its weak helplessness and his own strength, his responsibility, and how it had given him a bracing sensation. A sensation that was stern and yet uplifting too.

He felt as if he could stand here, looking into Laura's precious world, for ever.

He laid his hand palm flat on the glass. Even now a part of him noted the way the glass gave and observed that the window-frame was rotten: there wasn't much in this place that didn't need attention. But this was mere reflex. Mike wasn't viewing this house in the light of an investment opportunity. It was something else entirely.

It was a watchtower.

Mike squeezed the front door key tenderly in his hand. Then, with an effort, he tore himself away from the window.

He went quickly downstairs, consulting his mental map of Langstead for the nearest key cutters.

TWENTY-THREE

Just before the schools broke up for the summer holidays, Laura received a surprise visit from her mother-in-law.

Peggy and Reg rolled up on Saturday morning in the same venerable Consul, driven by the same silent weirdie named Marj, that had brought them to David's funeral. Lest Laura and Simon be too overcome by this familial attentiveness, Peggy swiftly made it clear that they only happened to be passing through. The three of them were on their way up to Cambridge to attend a concert given by a young Irish crooner whose epidemic popularity with the orthopaedic generation made Laura fearful of her own maturer years. Was she too doomed to adore this inexplicable entertainer, who sang soporific Celtic chestnuts in a self-pitying bray that made Johnny Ray sound positively raunchy, and whose old-young face looked like nothing so much as an Identikit put together from three conflicting witness reports?

'We'd love a cup of tea if you're making one, duck,' said Peggy, who seemed to have grown larger, to the extent that her neck started somewhere below her shoulders. 'We were going to stop at the Little Chef, only they're so dear there.'

'This is a bit steep, gel,' said Reg, freely examining the gas bill that lay on the dining table. 'You want to get on to them about that.'

'Well, I've checked it with the meter, it is right,' Laura said.

'You want to get on to them all the same,' Reg said with his aggrieved look. 'Getting on to' people was his favourite pastime.

'Come and give Nan a kiss, Simon. Dear, ain't you grown?' Peggy said, making this sound like the progress of some lamentable disease.

Undoubtedly Simon had grown physically – either that or his clothes were shrinking – but it just wasn't a thing that was apparent to your eye when you were with him every day. Far more obvious to Laura, though she hoped not to Peggy, was the new reluctance underneath the politeness as Simon approached his grandmother. He was losing his infant imperviousness, and starting to find Peggy a bit off-putting. Laura felt sad about this, then not so sad as Peggy proceeded to cross-question her about the school holidays and then, when she heard about the childminder, to be rather a bag about it.

'Well, you've shook me, gel. I thought you'd pack that job in rather than leave him with a stranger.'

'Mo's a registered childminder. She's very nice.'

'Mo? What sort of name's that?' Peggy quavered.

'Short for Maureen,' Reg said with dark disapproval.

'And I can't give up the job,' Laura said, prohibiting herself from saying more. It was still Peggy's belief that David had 'left her all right' and, bag or not, Laura didn't want to destroy it.

'Well, I suppose it's up to you,' Peggy sighed. 'I can't say I like it myself. I don't know what David would have said.'

'I like it round that lady's, Nan,' Simon put in. Laura realized, with gulp-inducing love, that he would have said the same if he had hated it. 'She's nice and there's an aquarium and a fishpond and there's this boy called Dan, he's dead nice.'

'Bless him!' said Peggy piteously. 'I wish you could come to your nan's for the summer. It's a pity I can't manage it. She's a useless old nan, ain't she?'

Not really, Laura thought. Just a bit self-absorbed, and greedy, and indolent, and obtuse, and thoughtless, and inclined to believe any good of a man and any bad of a woman. Apart from that, she's a doll.

But thankfully she wasn't a fixture, and once they had snaffled their refreshments the three were very soon on their way. Why they had to be on the move so early for an evening concert in Cambridge, thirty miles up the motorway, was a question she didn't care to ask. Maybe the time would be needed to knock out one row of seats and then winch Peggy into position.

Well, Laura told herself, she shouldn't let her mother-in-law's carping get to her. Simon was the important one. She didn't allow herself to be lulled by the fact that he was upbeat about going to Mo's. It was only a prospect as yet. He still might hate it.

As it turned out he didn't. He liked it. He said he did, which was something but not everything, because Laura knew the stoic lengths children would sometimes go to rather than make trouble. She remembered vividly the state of terror to which a pair of school bullies had reduced her, but she remembered even more vividly her determination never to breathe a word of it at home.

But Simon not only said he liked it at Mo's, he showed it. He was happy to go there in the morning. He was quite happy to leave, too, when she picked him up after work, but he didn't aim for the car like a cannonball when she pulled up outside the house. Sometimes he hung about a little to show her something – a piece of Lego architecture, a striking new development in the aquarium or the pond. (These rather baffled her. The fish just swam around.) And away from Mo's, he talked freely and fully of the things he had done there. It sounded fun. She might even have felt a tinge of jealousy if it had not been for his reply when she asked him what he wanted for his birthday, a few weeks away. 'A watch,' he said. 'So I'll know when you're coming to pick me up.'

Most of all he was impressed with Dan, Mo's son, who was either on a retainer from Mo or else had taken a genuine shine to Simon. To hear Simon tell it, Dan knew everything, had an inexhaustible fund of fascinating anecdote, and could conjure an absorbing game out of an old tennis ball and a cardboard box. It was a clear case of elder-brother syndrome, and Laura could only hope that Dan wouldn't get tired of the clinging admiration of his mother's young charge. Laura could also see that Dan did have a lot going for him. He didn't seem to suffer from the hormonal humps, and if he was shooting up smack or trashing cars he was considerate enough to keep these activities private. He really was interesting to talk to, having apparently so far avoided the teenage conclusion that the world was an empty sham, desert of lies, worthless pantomime, and stinking conspiracy to prevent him expressing his innate superiority of soul. He could even laugh at himself.

'Phew, you're dressed for it,' she said, finding him clothed from head to foot in stifling black on the hottest day so far of what looked to be a blazing summer.

'I'm in mourning.'

'Oh dear.'

'He asked Andrea Purviss to go out with him,' Lisette said.

'Is that bad?'

'She's going out with Ian McDowell,' he said gloomily. 'Has been for ages. They're practically engaged. So she told me.'

'Ian McDowell looks like Brad Pitt,' Lisette said.

'He does not. Well, a bit . . . She was really nice about it. Like you would be if this spotty kid suddenly asked to go out with you. You know. Too kind to laugh sort of thing.'

'You're not a spotty kid,' Laura said.

'I am next to Ian McDowell.'

'Andrea Purviss looks like Demi Moore,' said Lisette.

'Oh, well,' Laura said. 'I'm sure she's not worth going into mourning for.'

'Oh, it's not that,' Dan said. 'I'm in mourning for my brain. I must be brain dead to have ever thought Andrea Purviss would go out with me.'

More fool her, Laura thought. But perhaps Dan had too much of the gangling, James Stewart nice guy about him. Her own adolescence wasn't so far away that she couldn't recall what passed for a dreamboat then – usually someone who looked as if he would throw you out of a fast-moving vehicle while solemnly studying his cheekbones in the rearview mirror.

Mo was reassuring about Simon too. 'He's a pleasure to have,' she told Laura. 'You're right to be worried, because some kids don't take to it. It's not that they're clingers, usually, they're just loners. I don't think it's fair to try and change them if they're like that. Adults are allowed to be loners, aren't they? My Phil's a bit that way.'

'Is he?' Looking around at Mo's noisy, vital household, Laura couldn't quite imagine it.

'I know it sounds strange. He can be with us, but he'll shut himself off. It's a mind thing. I did know it when I married him, but it seemed fair enough. I just accepted that I wouldn't quite have all of him.'

Laura thought of Vikki Trayford in her kitteny flat. She realized that this thought, which had once been a wearyingly regular visitor to her mind, hadn't popped up for a long time.

'Perhaps you never do,' she said.

'With men? Course you don't. That's why it's best to make a deal with yourself from the start. Cuts both ways, anyway. Like with my Phil – when we started out he wanted to know, like they do, how many men there'd been before him. So I cut the figure by half and told him that. It was just easier. I don't know, they're funny about that, aren't they? They want you to be a spotless virgin but they expect you to leap about like some porno star as well.'

'That's right,' Laura said, but she felt a fraud, timidly monogamous as she was.

And as she intended to stay for now, in spite of another exhortation from Angie to make up a foursome with her slab-faced beaux. The intention was chiefly based on an appreciation of what she had now. Because the summer brought smooth sailing to Laura, perhaps the smoothest sailing she had known, and she didn't want any waves to disturb it. The job was going well, her finances had become a sustainable resource instead of shrinking like a rainforest, and Simon was happy. And she was able to enjoy these things simply because the one obstacle to her enjoyment of them was removed. The Rumpole-of-the-Bailey business had done the trick, and Mike Mackman was staying out of her life.

When people casually used the phrase 'a weight off my mind', they perhaps didn't know how physically exact it could be. The sensation of a weight lifting from her as the summer went on was so palpable that sometimes she felt literally buoyant, about to lift off the ground like a moonwalking astronaut.

Occasionally she felt a little bit mean about this very fact. It was terrible to think that you could feel this good about not seeing someone. She didn't wish him any harm; indeed she wished him all the best. But a very little reflection showed her that she could only wish this when he was off her back.

Liam, whom she let in on the good news, was more robust. 'Ah, screw him. He was making your life a misery. That's what the law's supposed to be for – to stop people doing that. For once, it did what it's meant to do.'

'Well, I hope he's all right, anyway.'

Liam shook his head. 'You people amaze me. I can't say you women because that's sexist, but you people of the other gender. Here's yer man, he's messed you about, made you half-mad with worry about what he's going to do next, stitched up your house sale and generally acted like a prize pain until you have to get a solicitor to make him back off. And now you hope he's all right.'

'Well . . . yes.' She shrugged. 'That's what I've always wanted. I bet you'd feel the same.'

'I don't know. Men are control freaks, that's what you've got to remember. When a guy wants to take care of a woman he's really saying he wants to control her. They're all bachelors, even the married ones. Everything in its place. I've got it too, I know. If someone puts one of my records back the wrong way I hate it. I'm flapping round going, "Spine outwards, spine outwards!"'

Laughing, Laura was afflicted again with a feeling of innocence. 'Men' to her just meant David: she had no range of comparison. Perhaps because of this, she spoke out worldly-wise.

'No,' she said. 'I don't swallow this thing about half the human race having one set of characteristics. There are plenty of men who aren't control freaks, you see them—'

'Ah, they are around women.'

'Well, what about gay men?'

'God, that's the worst of all. A relationship between two men is a head-on collision of control freaks. It's an all-out battle, so it is. A demolition derby.'

'Oh, you can't know that.'

'Can't I now? Ah, it's not everything you know about me, Mrs Ritchie.'

'Really?' She was aware of her own eyebrows going up in a very cartoony way. And yet side by side with the surprise was a quite contrary feeling: if there was such a thing as unsurprise, she felt it.

'Ah, sod it, it's no big deal,' he said, after a moment in which he seemed not so much to regret what he had said as to wonder why he had said it. 'It makes me sound like some big swinger which isn't the way it was at all. Maybe it was the fashion thing again. It was briefly trendy to be bi back then, or pretend you were. Round about the time of the Buzzcocks' third album. But it did feel right when it happened. Afterwards I thought, nah, that was one hell of a mistake, what was wrong with me, must have been the junk. I used to do a lot of dope then – fashion again. Now this was rubbish. I think it's just one of those things that's in you. Except now you're not supposed to think that. It's gone back to everybody's either one thing or the other and if they're not, they're kidding themselves. Which makes me either a gay guy who's repressed it for the last fifteen years, or else a straight guy who irresponsibly played at it. This pisses me off a bit.'

They were in the storeroom, and as he spoke Laura gently closed the door to with her hip: Colette was in the kitchen nearby, and she was definitely not the sort of person to take sentiments like these in her stride. He saw what she was doing, and gave a grin of collusion that had gratitude in it too. For her part Laura felt obscurely flattered; also very curious.

'Do you think everybody's a mixture like that?'

'No. There are one hundred percenters too. There's one not a million miles away from here, in fact. Footballers, they're always one hundred percenters. Guys who are really into cars, they are, though not motorbikes. People who work with computers. Publicans, though not barmen or waiters. Women who collect dolls and teddies. Men who wear pullovers with the, you know, damn stupid little insignia on the breast . . .'

'You're making it up now . . .' Laura laughed.

'It's true it is, I'll show you. We'll do an experiment when we go the pub Friday week, I'll point them out—'

'Friday week?'

'Shirley hasn't told you yet? She will. It's my birthday. I was fool enough to let it slip and now Shirley's arranging this thing for us all to go down the Market Inn for a drink in the evening. That's the part I know about, anyway. I've a suspicion there'll be something more. Please God not a kissogram. Actually I was hoping you'd be the mole for me, let me know beforehand . . . What's up?'

'Friday week . . . The thing is, that's Simon's birthday as well.'

'Hey, snap! How old is he?'

'He'll be eight . . . and I promised that day after work we'd go to McDonald's, and . . . he's been with a childminder while I've been at work, you know, now school's finished, and so I really want to spend time with him that weekend because . . . oh, damn.'

She felt desolated in a way she could hardly comprehend. She would rather have had teeth pulled than let Simon down, but that didn't alter this strange feeling. Gone was the weightless buoyancy. Gravity pinned her right back down.

'Hey, no worries,' Liam said. 'It's only a wee booze-up. Just the staff. No big deal at all.'

'It's your birthday, though.'

Liam laughed. 'It's my thirty-seventh. They get less exciting.' Then he seemed to see that she was not able to take this lightly. There was a silence that contained a shift. 'Laura, I do honestly understand,' he said. 'Don't think I'm just saying it. One thing, though.' He gave her a sort of serious smile. 'I really would like to meet Simon some time.'

I think I made a bit of a prat of myself there, Laura thought afterwards. But telling herself this, and telling herself that it didn't matter anyway because Liam was so understanding and easy-going, didn't lift her. Continuing to feel down, she decided when she clocked off work to follow that classic women's magazine prescription for the blues: treat yourself.

The usual recommendation was a facial or a hairdo, but Laura had something else in mind, something that had repeatedly caught her eye since she had started at Sprignall's. On the floor below the restaurant was a whole department selling artists' materials. The presence of an art college in Langstead sustained it. She had often seen the students, pale earnest fashion-survivors, knowledgeably mooching there. She had only seen them in glimpses, though. The place had represented temptation and so she had tried to shun it.

Today, however, she went right in. For a while she just wandered about fiddling and touching and surrendering to the sensations, long forgotten but heartbreakingly familiar. She rediscovered the texture of toothed watercolour paper, the lovely dusty finger-stain of conté-crayon, the promising devil-may-care blackness of a 9B pencil and the reliable flexibility of that prince of pencils, the 6B. She squeezed the fat tubes of oil paint with a lover's lubriciousness. She cradled an A5 block against her wrist, feeling how companionably it fitted there; she wrestled joyfully with unwieldy A1, with its brash invitation: *Come on! There's loads of me! Draw on me right from the shoulder, big and bold!*

Everything was expensive, but in that too lay part of its allure. When they made this stuff, the prices said, they were taking you seriously. They didn't expect you to copy Snoopys with it. They expected you to mean business.

She returned the compliment and bought three Rowney blocks, a fistful of pencils, some compressed charcoal and a basic set of pastels. Then she ran out full of guilt and triumph.

She put the stuff away that evening until Simon had gone to bed. Then, feeling oddly furtive as if she were preparing to watch a blue video, she got out her A2 block and the pencils and sat for some time staring into the whiteness.

When the hand holding the pencil began to move across the paper, it was as if someone else had joined her in the living room and was guiding her arm. The old Laura – the Laura who had faded, been buried, then transformed during the disappointing years? Or was it someone else – a new Laura, who was going to do different things, who was not a finished creation of the past but a cluster of possibilities, who dared to begin again?

TWENTY-FOUR

Mike had found something – a pleasure – that reminded him of cigarettes.

It was satisfying and yet by its nature unsatisfying. It was his nightly vigil at his watchtower, which he impatiently looked forward to all day, which afforded him moments of exalted, almost transcendental joy, which he knew very well was a great piece of luck in the scope it offered him for watching over her and which he knew also was about as much as he could hope for with things as they were.

It was all of these, and yet it wasn't enough.

(That was the funny thing about the cigarettes. He had been a thirty-a-day man for years. Then, about the time he and Kim were trying for a baby, he gave it up, deciding it wasn't doing his body any good. As he didn't want to smoke any more, he just didn't, and thought no more about it. It was easy. But for some reason Kim couldn't understand this. She seemed to think he was pretending when he said he felt OK. 'No cravings?' 'No.' 'Don't miss a ciggy in the morning, even?' 'No, why should I?' She had looked long and hard at him. 'God, you're weird.' He had laughed, but he really didn't see anything weird about it; and he didn't understand why Kim grew ratty with him at times like these. Once on holiday in Cornwall they had got caught in a downpour walking back across the cliffs to their hotel. Kim had a coat, and an umbrella, which she kept pressing him to share. He wouldn't hear of it: she was the one who mustn't catch cold. 'But you're drenched,' she kept saying. Which he supposed he was: he only had on a sweater. But it didn't matter, the sweater soaked it all up anyway, as he told her. 'This soaks it up – see? The wool soaks the wet up.' He showed her. He remembered the rain pouring from his eyebrows, and remembered not minding a bit. 'I'm all right,' he kept saying. And in the end she had stamped her foot and cried, 'Oh, you're bloody inhuman sometimes!' It was odd. Sometimes it seemed that the more considerate he tried to be, the more impatient she got with him. He put this down to her not having children. For women, children were a natural outlet: they weren't quite right without them.)

The watchtower wasn't enough, in as much as it was passive. What he longed for was to take a more active role in safeguarding those precious lives that he saw progressing, in charming miniature like a doll's house, from his dark vantage. Thinking of things he might do helped fill the dull times, when the curtains were closed or when they were in bed, though the effort was frustrating too. Because of her pride, he had to be so careful. The one thing that taxed him above all was to stop her selling that house. He understood her motives – no doubt she saw her poor dead husband in every inch of it – but she was going to regret it so deeply later, when the memories lost their pain and turned to gold. His initial plan hadn't worked and he couldn't think of another. He had toyed with the idea of getting a friend to make the purchase on his behalf . . . but he didn't really have that sort of friends. He had always been rather self-sufficient, and such friends as he had had belonged to the time before his marriage. Once you were married, he believed, you should be all in all to each other. Another thing that Kim didn't seem to understand.

'Why don't you go down the pub or something?' she would say sometimes. 'You could meet Doug. You don't have to hang around here.' She would frown as if in pain.

'No, I'd rather stay here. Obviously you're not feeling too hot.'

'I'm perfectly all right. I'm just *saying*.'

'No. I'll stay with you.' Because of course she wasn't all right, to be talking in that way. The last thing he was going to do was go off and leave her at a time like that.

So he couldn't do it via friends. Nor could he see any way of stopping the sale, if someone did offer to buy the house. His hope was that if someone came to view it, he would surely see them doing so from the watchtower: after all, with Laura working full time (awful thought!) the viewing would have to be in the evenings or at weekends – which was when he was watching. He had a clear view into the dining room and a reasonable view into the kitchen, with some occasional shadowy glimpses through the upstairs nets, and then there was the garden. With this visual information at his disposal, he would surely spot someone being shown round. And then, and then . . . well, he had a hazy idea of leaving the watchtower, going round to Duncan Road, following the prospective buyers when they left, finding out where they lived, and then somehow persuading them not to buy . . . The idea grew hazier as it continued, but that didn't trouble him too much. He was pretty good at thinking on his feet. And he was sure that if those circumstances did arise, he would know what to do when the time came.

(The same applied to the question of what would happen if someone else came to view his watchtower – the empty house in Beatrice Road. When he had returned the key to Roy Cady after having a copy made, he had come out with some flannel about being very impressed and needing to talk with his building manager – but of course that wouldn't stop Roy showing the house to anyone else who was interested. The best he could do was hope; and, when he was in there, slide the bolt on the front door. If Roy or one of his staff found they couldn't open it, they might conclude they had brought the wrong key or that the old lock was stuck. It would give him warning, at any rate.)

All this did not mean to say that Mike was unhappy with his watchtower. He was happier than he had been for years.

He got there as early as his work allowed (sometimes earlier – he was leaving a lot of things to his manager that he would have supervised himself before he had found this task.) He equipped himself with some basic necessities in that back bedroom with its near-perfect view: a camping stool, a pair of binoculars, picnic box and flask of coffee – more to keep himself awake than because he felt the need for refreshment. Just watching was enough for him. He forgot about everything when he saw them in their home. He had a torch, too; though the power was on, he didn't think it wise to switch on lights. As it happened, he scarcely needed it, the nights were so light now. Warm too, so he didn't need any heat in there. And he had a sleeping bag, into which, when all the lights in her house were out, he sometimes crawled for a few hours' sleep. The sleeping bag was a later development. For the first week or so he went home once Laura had gone to bed, but sometimes this could be as late as one in the morning, and leaving the house at that time seemed to him likely to attract the neighbours' attention. Staying overnight also enabled him to watch over her in the morning too, before she set off for work.

And it was a blessed, almost miraculous stroke of luck that he *had* decided to do this, as he very soon discovered.

Lucky too that the sleep was only in the form of light catnaps, with a lot of wakeful thinking in between. Often he would think, very simply, of what he had seen that evening. Ordinary things: domestic things; ordinary, domestic, and sacred. Laura making dinner in the kitchen, her movements casual, loose, at-home, with here and there a sudden dart that he interpreted, with fond amusement, as a pan boiling over or a burning slice of toast. (He even felt he could smell those cosy kitchen smells at such times.) Laura suddenly disappearing and reappearing wearing a comfy jumper instead of that horrible striped blouse that she had to wear to work. Laura and Simon at the dining table: Simon getting up, moving out of sight (switching on a TV, Mike guessed), and Laura's gesture for him to sit down, kind and motherly but firm – with the binoculars he could almost tell what she was saying. The desolating vacancy when they were gone into the invisible front of the house, where the living room was; but then, the heartlifting moment when the kitchen light came on and one or other of them came back into his view. Usually Laura, but he had noticed that sometimes Simon came in and filled the kettle and prepared the cups. He never poured the boiling water, though: she came to do that.

Careful, and quite right. She was a damn good mother. The feeling of pleasure, innocent, protective, tender, was almost oppressive in its clutch at his heart when he saw this. And often tears would spring to his eyes when he saw the lights finally go out in the house. There was an American TV series that always concluded with a shot like that: the lights going out and the family settling down to sleep. *The Waltons*, that was it. He had always liked it. It was a bit sentimental but at least it was wholesome. Once again, though, people knocked. Like his brother, sneering about their family background. 'All sat round that bloody table like the Waltons. Except the Waltons' dad was all wise and ours was a pillock who talked out of his arse.' It shocked Mike to hear this. His memories of that kitchen table, with the family all gathered tightly round it and his mum moving sturdily about the stove, were warm, nostalgic, almost mystical.

In fact he sometimes dwelt on those too, when he lay in his watchtower. He wasn't usually one for looking back. Probably it was the influence of his psychotherapist, who still kept on at him to dig into the past. He tried to oblige, but he found the whole thing boring, especially her insistence on getting at the truth about his marriage. Who did he feel was to *blame*? – she kept hammering at that. And he had told her: a bit of both, no doubt, but mainly him because he obviously hadn't kept his wife happy. End of story. But then she wanted to know if he had put his wife on a pedestal – really, with all due respect, a stupid question. What man, he wondered, *didn't* put the woman he loved on a pedestal? There was no point in being a married man if you didn't. (Sometimes the thought of those words, *married man*, made his eyes water. They were so significant. He had heard somewhere that Churchill got like that later in life: certain words would set him off because they were so meaningful. Mike thought it right, absolutely right, that certain things should retain this sanctity, even in the modern world with all its progress, a lot of which he approved of – the material side. Without being at all conventionally religious, he believed that some things were holy. Like marriage. He hated to see people doing marriage down nowadays.)

So yes, he had put Kim on a pedestal. He didn't see anything wrong with that. When the psychotherapist said, in her gentle probing way, that it was 'hard to live up to an ideal', he just grunted and didn't pursue the matter. He didn't think it was hard, and had personally never found it so. Anyhow, it was all in the past. You wouldn't get anywhere fooling around with a lot of old memories. Especially when they weren't wholly reliable. He had great faith in his memories of childhood, for example; but from what his brothers said it seemed they didn't tell the whole story. That wasn't so bad: people's opinions always differed, and witnesses to a crime, for example, never seemed to see the same things. More problematical was the memory of the way his marriage ended. The psychotherapist was intent on getting at that, but Mike wasn't having any. On the one hand, his innate gallantry balked at what seemed like telling tales against his wife; on the other, he was hazy about the details.

There was that day he had come home from work in the mid-afternoon – something he hardly ever did. But he was suffering from one of his occasional migraines, and while he usually took a prescribed tablet for this and then just carried on working, today he had left the tablets at home. Unusual circumstances, then. Also if he ever did have occasion to go home during the day, he phoned Kim first to let her know; but this time he didn't, for some reason. Unusual, and precise.

But from then on the details became sketchy. Lying in the sleeping bag in his darkened watchtower, in musty silence, Mike investigated them. He had parked the car in the drive (had he? or had he left it in the road?) and gone in and called Kim's name the way he always did (had he? or had he made no sound to let her know he was there?) and had looked around the lounge and seen a gin bottle and glasses and then gone upstairs.

Mike's eyes blinked in the darkness, sought the grey square of the watchtower's window – comfort and consolation.

He had gone upstairs, definitely. There was no other way that he could have seen Kim and the man in the bedroom. Also there was a very precise visual image of the man, naked, struggling to get to his clothes and being unable to do so because his foot was caught in the folds of the bedsheet: he struggled and thrashed exactly like a man caught in shackles. The man's face was quite clear in his memory too: red with exertion and perhaps something else, rather unshaven (and was it then or now that some semidetached part of Mike registered a proud distaste at the fellow's going to a woman unshaven, a thing he himself would never dream of?), youngish, small-eyed. But then the memory became a simple précis. He had thrown the man out and there had been an angry exchange with Kim and then she had gone too. And then his marriage ended and there was a divorce – this over a period of time, of course, but as far as he was concerned it followed directly on.

He wasn't aware of any blanks. When his solicitor had mentioned a possible assault charge being brought against him by the small-eyed man, Mike had been amazed. All right, yes, he'd thrown the man out of his house, but he wouldn't exactly call that assault. After all, the man was playing around with his wife (Mike wouldn't use any stronger term).

Apparently, Mike remembered his solicitor saying, *apparently you picked him up and held him over the banisters. And then you broke his arm.*

Mike remembered scoffing at the time. Lying flat in the sleeping bag, his shoulder blades and elbows sharp against the floorboards in a way that most people would have found excruciatingly uncomfortable, he felt like scoffing now. But he wasn't sure.

His arm is certainly broken, Mike.

Well, that doesn't prove anything. How does he reckon I broke it, then?

You . . . apparently you got hold of it and . . . you held him still and you broke his arm.

Oh, but it was ridiculous. Mike thought it then and he thought it now. No doubt there had been a certain amount of roughhousing in getting the man out, but to actually do something like that, something that brutal . . .

He had said as much, and stuck to it. In spite of a faint memory of gripping and twisting. In spite of the echo of a scream that didn't sound like Kim's. In spite of the fact that Kim left the house that same day, with hardly any possessions. Because he knew he just wasn't capable of something like that, even in a situation where one might fairly say that the man deserved it. To do him credit, the man (Mike heard his name, but didn't bother with it: it wasn't the man Kim later married) must have realized this, because he didn't press charges in the end. Wisely, Mike thought, because he would just be showing himself up. Any court would agree that he had done just about the worst thing it was possible to do – destroy someone's domestic harmony – and that he had got off lightly.

All I can say, Mike, is that you don't know your own strength.

His solicitor had said that with a regretful shake of his head, and Mike's memory was certainly clear on that point. Because that was the absurdest part. It implied that he wasn't in control of himself in some way – like a child. And it was as a child that he had last heard those words. In primary school, where in an outburst of temper he had – he freely admitted this – held another boy's head down inside a desk and slammed the lid down on it. This was wrong and he had taken his due punishment for it. Probably at that time he didn't know his own strength, being big for his age. (The other boy had called him Mucky Mackman, which angered him not on his own behalf but on his mother's, because she always worked so hard to make sure they were well turned out. And that was one memory he would swear by, in spite of those hints later on from his brothers, who seemed to suggest that their mother was some sort of hapless slut.)

But when you were a grown man it was different. He could only conclude that his solicitor was being, as ever, cagey and cautious. As far as Mike was concerned he had come home that day, there had been a . . . discovery, and then his marriage had been over. He certainly wasn't going to say any more than that to the psychotherapist, no matter how much she fished. She told him, with a touch of impatience, that he was fighting her. It wasn't that. He just wasn't interested.

Besides, he was able to think far more clearly and constructively when he was lying in his watchtower than when he was in that arid consulting room. Here he was close to the heart of things. The presence of Laura near at hand, the sight of her little domestic world, enabled him to make sense of things, put his life in perspective. He could see now that, for all the hard work he had put in and all the material success he had enjoyed since the divorce, he had been a man without a purpose. So in that strictly limited sense alone, what had happened on Bourges Way in January had proved a blessing.

He could never think of it as such in relation to Laura and Simon, though: not at all. Everything he was doing was only making up, feebly, for the loss they had sustained. What he had done to them was pretty much what that small-eyed man

(had he gripped his arm and stared into those eyes and then with a sharp jerk brought it down and— Had he?)

had done to his own household.

But he had a lifetime in which to do the making up. And one night as he lay in the watchtower, wakeful, though it was after three, he had just thought of another idea when he heard the noise.

The idea was for Simon. He could start a bank account in Simon's name. That was something, he was sure, you could do without needing a person's consent. He could keep adding to it; then when Simon was ready to leave school it would be there to help him on whatever path he chose to take in life. He might want to go to college: Mike was no scholar himself, but he had plenty of respect for people who had the brains for it, and . . .

Just reaching up to tuck his hands behind his head, Mike froze. His breath stopped.

The noise was indistinct, irregular, a faint scratching on the surface of his hearing. For several moments he couldn't locate it. Perhaps it was coming from next door: unusual if so. They were a quiet middle-aged couple who kept themselves to themselves. Once or twice they had plainly seen him coming into the watchtower, and he had made a habit of carrying a few building and decorating tools with him for cover. The only sound he was used to hearing from that direction was the heavy clunk of their back door being locked at night, and this . . .

The tentative noises had stopped.

Mike sat up, ears straining, eyes turning in the darkness.

A sudden, neat smash made him start to his feet. That wasn't next door. That was downstairs – at the back of the house, by the sound of it. He recalled that the back door had a glass panel.

He stood still for a minute, breathing deeply, listening to further sounds below – quick, purposeful rattlings. He was collecting himself. His first start had, indeed, had fear in it, but the fear was to do with the fact that strictly he shouldn't be here.

But now he knew this was a different matter, and he was not afraid at all.

Picking up his torch, he walked softly in stockinged feet to the bedroom door and slipped on to the landing. There he paused and listened again. A swift scranch told him that the person was in the house.

He switched on the torch, but kept the beam directed down to his feet. With infinite care – he knew how they creaked – he began to tread down the stairs. (He could be very quiet when he wanted to be. It was another of the things that had seemed to fill Kim with an inexplicable impatience. 'You don't have to creep around me like that,' she would burst out, apparently not understanding that he was trying to be considerate.)

More noises from below – the kitchen. Hasty rummagings, like an animal searching for food. He had no need to ask himself who would break into a vacant property. He knew that they were a prime target. Whenever his company finished a development you could expect at least half of the properties to be broken into before they were occupied. People would take taps, light fittings, even whole kitchen units; and they made a beeline for any builders' materials. They would take anything nowadays. Nothing was safe.

Nobody was safe.

The hairs rose at the back of his neck as he thought of that. The enormity of it . . .

Halfway down the stairs now, Mike abandoned the attempt to be silent. He just walked steadily down, and along the hall, and into the kitchen, where he lifted the torch and shone it right in the face of the young man who had just sprung away from the cutlery drawer and was staring at him as if he were a ghost.

Young, thin, ferrety. His denim jacket was too small for him and there was a pathetic wisp of moustache on his upper lip. Even as he experienced a wild surge of hate, Mike was discriminating: he hated the young man not for who he was but what he represented.

There were several seconds in which the young man seemed not so much to threaten as to consider threatening, like a dog that stands braced and foursquare, sniffing, gathering all the sensory information. Meanwhile Mike simply looked back at him, with no overt expression that he was aware of, even lowering the torch a little so that they could see each other better.

Then the young man breathed, 'Jesus,' and was on his second step to the door when Mike seized the collar of his jacket.

The young man did some swearing and thrashing, but very soon Mike had him tight by the scruff like a rabbit and pushed him up against the wall. Then he pushed him, literally, up, until his feet weren't touching the floor.

And though Mike was in a rage it was, again, a discriminating rage, concentrated and purposeful. There was a glowing indignation in it too. Because if the boy could do this in Beatrice Road, then . . .

Finding his captive struggling furtively to get a hand to his jacket pocket, Mike slapped him hard, enough to set him whimpering, and then reached in there himself.

A knife – some sort of barbarous hunting thing. He dropped it to the floor.

'Now if I killed you here,' Mike said reasonably, 'I don't suppose anybody would care. In fact I don't reckon anybody would even know about it.'

The young man's head wriggled and jerked as he moaned terrified swearwords. He seemed unable to believe what was happening to him. The same might be said, Mike thought severely, for the innocent householders waking up to find themselves facing an intruder with a knife. The thought made him bunch his forearm muscles and with a quick jerk clout the boy's head smartly against the wall. He doubted it would hurt him, not a good-for-nothing clown like this.

'Aaugh!'

The cry seemed to Mike theatrical, even cartoony. He gave the young man another shake and then dropped him. Moaning, the young man fell into a crouch, his hands tremblingly cradled over his skull.

'Jesus . . . oh, Jesus . . .'

'You were lucky this time,' Mike said. He looked down with disapproval at the crooning, monkey-like figure. He decided against a kick because the lesson was learnt and that was the main thing. But the young man must have feared the kick anyhow, because with a last foul-mouthed groan he made a pained scuttle for the back door and hooked it.

Mike inspected the damage to the door. Being so old it hadn't needed much forcing, and it would be a simple matter for him to repair it tomorrow. It must have been one hell of a shock for that yobbo, he thought, breaking into what looked like an empty house and then being confronted like that. Perhaps he really did think he'd met a ghost.

But Mike couldn't laugh about it. It was deadly serious. As he climbed the stairs again his own words hit him a delayed blow.

You were lucky this time.

Mike went into the dingy bathroom and slurped fusty-tasting water from the tap, splashing some on his face. A dreadful reaction had set in now, and he was shaking.

He stood in the doorway of the back bedroom, looking at his sleeping bag.

Suppose he hadn't been awake and alert; suppose he'd been sleeping right there. It just showed that you had to be always on your guard.

It wasn't fear for his own safety that was making him shake and sweat, though. At least, not his own safety for his own sake.

He stepped over to the window, knelt by the sill and trained his binoculars on Laura's house. A darkened house in the dead of night could easily look sinister, but this one never did. It looked both enchanted and awfully vulnerable.

A half-moon was shining, making the lawn at the back of the house look like a patch of soft silvery fur. He imagined a black silhouette stealing across it, darting, looming suddenly at the rear windows, reaching up, testing . . .

And that was supposing he saw it happen. And if he did, how much time would he have?

Several houses further along Duncan Road he could see a garden and patio brilliantly revealed by a security light. God, if she only had one of those it would be something. She was just too vulnerable there.

Perhaps in a way that yobbo breaking in had been another blessing (though it was hard to think of it as such at the moment, sick and tremulous as he felt). After all, it had confirmed that she did face very real danger. In gaining access to this house Mike had, indeed, been seeking a place to watch over her at night – to reassure himself that all was well with her world. But he hadn't seriously entertained the possibility of physical perils like this.

Too optimistic, of course. What was it she had said to him the day those loan sharks had been pestering her? Something about an Englishwoman's house being her castle. Precisely what it was meant to be, and precisely what it wasn't in this shocking world. You only had to open a newspaper. Crime was everywhere: there was no respect or honesty any more, and the law-abiding person was continually at risk from elements like that rascal he had just sent packing. Even the fact that he was carrying a knife was pretty mild by today's standards.

Mike lay down. He felt bad. He felt he had failed Laura, had allowed his watchtower to become a pretext for sentimental woolgathering rather than employing it as a genuine means of protection.

Well, he thought, not any more.

He didn't mean to sleep; but some time around dawn he must have drifted off, because presently he was gasping up from a nightmare in which the yobbo was back, but transformed and powerful as Mike was powerless. He was laughing and showing Mike something – something that looked like a bloodied wig. Mike didn't want to look, but the yobbo gripped his head and thrust the thing in his face, while somewhere a child was screaming out . . .

Feeling terrible, Mike lingered in his watchtower long enough to see the curtains open in her house and to catch a reassuring glimpse of both of them moving about the kitchen. Then he hurried home to wash, and to change his clothes. The sight of the five items – shaving stick, comb, hairspray, aftershave, bowl – on his bathroom windowsill soothed him a little. He wondered what sort of night they had had.

Lynne, his cleaner, arrived just before he left for work. She was a cheerful young woman with a peroxided topknot like a comical pineapple. Mike felt she was probably no better than she should be, as his mother used to say, but she was honest and worked hard.

'You all right, Mr Mackman?' she asked when she saw him.

'Yes, duck. Why shouldn't I be?'

'You look a bit peaky. Bit tired.'

'Must have a summer cold, I think,' he said. He hated lying, and even a fib as small as this left him feeling uncomfortable.

'There's messages on your answerphone, by the way.'

'Right.'

He listened to them, not without an initial deep breath and an inward steadying of himself when he pressed the play button. It was always like this ever since Laura had left him that message. It wasn't that he feared her bawling him out again – she had been right, absolutely right, to do that – it was just the thought of suddenly hearing her voice, here in his own home. He had to prepare himself, so powerfully did it affect him. When she had visited him here he had been in a state for hours afterwards.

But the messages were only to do with work. His building manager, saying they really needed to sort out this matter of the water metering with the housing association. His accountant with some gripe from the Inland Revenue, saying he plainly hadn't grasped the new tax rules governing sub-contracting. Some time-waster with a quibble about a quote for a barn conversion. Mike ignored them and set out for Goldcrest Park.

This was a worthwhile contract, but as he drew up at the site he felt glad he wouldn't have to live here. The housing association had squeezed in too many plots, and the specifications were very basic even for starter homes. Worst of all in his view, the surroundings were open-plan, and adjoined a wasteland of allotments. A burglar's paradise, in other words. At that thought Mike felt the sweat tickling in his hairline again.

Construction was on schedule, at any rate, which was fortunate: he hadn't been able to give the project the hands-on attention that was usual with him. He realized this when he stopped himself, just in time, from expostulating with the site foreman on the absence of protective headgear. Of course, it wasn't a hard-hat site any more: they had almost finished the interior rendering.

Brian, at any rate, was the person he wanted to see. Mike stumped about the site with him for a very short time, asking questions without heeding the replies, before coming to the point: stalling and flannelling just weren't in his nature.

'Brian, I wanted to ask you. Still do some shooting?'

Brian was a stolid lump of a man whose curly hair and perpetually innocent expression made him look younger than his years. Mike thought him just a little bit of a sycophant, though he knew his job.

'Yeah,' Brian said eagerly, 'when I get time. Yeah, I'm always up for it.'

Mike nodded, gazing over at the allotments. Toolsheds, lean-tos, odds and ends of corrugated and timber fencing, overgrown patches choked with bramble. Imagine this place at night. Anybody could lurk about here, watching.

'Mm,' Mike said. 'Only I was thinking of going up to Norfolk this weekend – you know, the chalet. I was wondering if I could borrow a gun again. Miles of woods up there. I thought I might try my hand.'

Brian looked surprised and gratified. 'Yeah! Course you can. Have to be a bit careful, of course,' He threw a stagy glance over his shoulder. 'You know how it is.'

'Oh, sure, sure. This is it. I'd like to get hold of one of my own, but these things are tricky.' Brian, he knew, had a collection of at least half a dozen firearms – unregistered, of course. They were his passion. Mike had been shooting with him once, a year or so ago, at Brian's slightly unctuous urging. They had gone to some lonely woodland over Dunmow way. Mike hadn't disliked it – as a boy he had been taken shooting by his father a few times, and he had a pretty good eye – but he always felt there was something dissatisfying about such all-male amusements, just as he had never much wanted to go to the pub when he was married to Kim. But he knew that Brian was perseveringly keen to get someone else interested. Some of the other men on site, Mike had heard, kidded him about it less than kindly and referred to him as Rambo.

'Yeah, yeah, no sweat,' Brian said. 'Actually I've got myself another piece now. There's a lot of people wanting to get rid of them, you know. If you want one for yourself some time, I can fix that up.'

'Might do,' Mike said, nodding. 'Might well do. Once I get the feel of it again. Been thinking about it a lot lately, actually. It's good exercise, isn't it? And I reckon I need that. Bit of a tum.' Again he felt slightly soiled talking like this, because he hadn't been thinking anything of the kind. But what he had to remember, in all such dealings, was that they were steps towards a vital goal and that the end really did justify the means.

'It is, you know. It's the best exercise there is. And it's natural, because man is a hunter, you know? You can't get away from that. So, what you thinking of – shotgun, yeah?' Brian did a mime of drawing a bead on a bird in flight.

'That's right,' Mike said. 'Shotgun.'

'No problem. Now I haven't got a whole load of ammo at the moment, but . . .'

'That's all right, a few rounds, whatever you can manage. It's just to get my hand in.'

'That's on the north coast, isn't it, your chalet? Sheringham way?'

'That's right.'

'Yeah. Took the kids up there once. Just for a few days, you know. Couldn't afford to stop long. Yeah, beautiful round there, cliffs, woods, I mean it's really unspoilt, isn't it?'

'Oh, it's a picture.' Plainly, with thoughts of a good turn returned, Brian was angling for an invitation to use the chalet some time. Mike let him go on. He wasn't thrilled by the idea of letting Brian and his crew stay there – they were a troublesome bunch from what he had heard – but there were worse bargaining counters, and he could swallow it if it came to that.

'Yeah, you can't beat the good old British holiday as far as I'm concerned . . .' Brian seemed to feel he had laid a clear enough trail of hints. 'So, how do you want to do it? You want me to drop it round yours?'

'I'll pick it up from you, if that's all right. How about this evening?'

'Nice one. Make it after seven, eh? Tina'll be down the bingo by then. She's not too keen on the shooting business, for some reason. Save any trouble, you know what I mean?'

Mike nodded, trying to conceal his distaste. He didn't think much of a marriage based on such bad faith and subterfuge. Some of these men talked about their wives as if they fairly despised them.

He stayed on the site till eleven, but then his patience ran out. There was somewhere he needed to be and something he needed to check on. Memories of last night, and thoughts of that naked silver stretch of garden, made it absolutely imperative.

This, he knew as he parked the van in Duncan Road a hundred yards down from Laura's house, was simply not on as far as his undertaking went: if she were to catch him at it there would be hell to pay. But it was a weekday and she should be at work, and if there was a risk of tattling from her neighbours he would just have to run it. He needed to know what sort of security she had in that house. He kept thinking of the way the door in his watchtower had yielded, so easily and terribly.

He paused at the gate of number 19. No car. All right then. He opened the gate, walked up to the front door, and lifted his hand to knock. But he only made a faint tapping. He just wanted to assess this door . . . He felt relieved: the door was quite new, the glass in the top looked to be reinforced, and there was a deadbolt lock as well as a Yale. She could do a lot worse, he thought. He made another pretend knock and then, after a glance back at the empty street, shuffled over to the front bay window. He pressed his face to the glass and tried to peer down at the inner frame. And that, unless he was mistaken, was a good Carr window-lock. Strong stuff. But of course it was the rear of the house that was the most vulnerable.

Access to the back was via a timber gate by the drive. He wondered if she kept it bolted: he could probably climb over it if so, but he was so very exposed here in the daylight, anyone might see . . . But then, to set his mind at rest . . .

He had just laid his hand on the latch of the gate when a voice spoke behind him.

'You'll not find anyone in, love. She's at work.'

He turned, with enough presence of mind not to do it hastily, and saw the Irish neighbour he had met here before. She had paused on the pavement outside the front gate, her hands resting on the handle of a shaded pram.

'Oh, hello,' he said. 'I did wonder whether . . . just thought I'd try in case. Never mind.'

'Works every weekday,' the Irish lady said, and clucked her tongue. 'It's not what her husband would have wanted to see, but there. I suppose it can't be helped.'

But it can, it can, thought Mike with a kind of surge at his heart.

'Oh well, never mind,' he said; and with a smile for the baby lolling its bonneted head curiously round the hood of the pram, 'That's a bonny one you've got there.'

'My youngest daughter's youngest,' the Irish lady said with pride. 'Was it anything urgent? I'll mebbe be seeing Laura later. I could tell her you came round if you like.'

Mike was pretty sure he didn't show it, but he was alarmed. 'Oh no, that's all right, it doesn't matter.'

'No trouble.'

'Well, actually, I'm not pushed for time, I might as well pop into Sprignall's and see her now.'

'OK then.' She seemed satisfied; but of course there was nothing to stop her, when she saw Laura, saying, 'Did your friend get to see you . . . ?'

'I dare say there are worse jobs,' she went on, 'but it seems a shame. With the little lad and all. Of course, we all need money, don't we?'

'Can't do without it.'

'There's the clothes and shoes and everything. They grow out of them so quick. And of course the little lad's got a birthday coming up, and they want such presents nowadays.'

'That's right,' Mike said after a fractional hesitation. Simon's birthday. There ought, he thought mistily, to be a tremendous celebration. If it was up to him . . . Then the mists cleared as a diamond-sharp thought came to him. Smiling into the Irish lady's spectacles,

Mike decided to follow his instinct about her. He believed she was trustworthy, salt of the earth in fact: his sort. 'Actually . . . between you and me I was rather hoping that Laura would be out. The fact is I wanted a look at the garden – just the rough dimensions. It's a bit of a surprise for both of them, for Simon's birthday. I had an idea to hire out one of those bouncy castles, you know? Have it sent over on the day. So if you wouldn't mind not saying anything—'

'Oh, that's a nice idea,' she said, nodding vigorously. Her eyes were faintly speculative. Mike didn't mind her thinking what she was plainly thinking – it would probably encourage her to be secret – but she couldn't have been more wrong. 'Oh, that's a smashing idea. Don't you worry about me, love. I won't breathe a word.' She nodded at the side gate. 'I think she keeps that locked, though. If it was the back garden you wanted to see. I'm sure she keeps it locked while she's out.'

'Very wise,' Mike said. What now? Well, all he could do was carry it through. 'Well, all I need is a rough idea. I wonder if I could climb over.'

'I should think so. Big strapping feller like yourself. Go on, love. I'll stay here. I'll vouch for you if a copper comes by.' She laughed, and Mike laughed too.

In a moment he had scrambled over the gate, and hurried round to the back. He made a hasty assessment of the patio doors, and was not reassured by what he found: as was often the case, they were pretty frail. Nor did the kitchen window please him. There was a small ventilation pane at the top, the sort that people mistakenly thought no one would get through and that criminals look on as a gift from the gods. No, it wasn't secure at the back here. Its only advantage was . . . well, he turned to look at it. His watchtower. The window looked surprisingly far off from here: also dark, empty, and faintly sinister. For a moment an inexplicable depression lowered over him. Then he remembered the Irish lady and hastened back to the gate.

'Any good?' she said, when he scrambled over.

Mike sucked in breath and winced. If he said yes and the bouncy castle was a no-show on the birthday, she might well say something about it to Laura. 'I don't know. I'm not too sure for the one I had in mind. I'll check up: if not, I'll think of something else. So keep it under your hat, eh?' He winked.

'Ah, don't you worry about me.'

'And how about you? You'll keep it under your hat, won't you?' he added to the baby.

'Well, at least his birthday falls on a Friday,' the Irish lady said, 'so his mum'll mebbe be able to get home from work a bit early.'

'Oh, yes. Ah, it's horrible when you have to go to school on your birthday, I remember that myself.'

'Oh, but the kids are off now. They broke up the other week.'

Mike found himself staring for a moment – he simply hadn't thought of this, he had lost track of things . . . 'Oh yes, of course. Summer holidays, of course they are.'

'This is where the problem comes in when you're working and you've a kiddie,' she said. 'I wouldn't be easy with it myself. I'm sure these childminders do a good job, but it's not the same. I always had mine at home in the summer. But I suppose Laura's got no choice.'

'Yes,' Mike said absently, with a feeling as if the sun had gone in, 'yes, of course. Not the same . . .' Becoming aware of her scrutiny, he gathered himself and smiled. 'Well! I'd better be off, anyway. It was nice talking to you. You take care now.'

He got away – a little too hastily, perhaps, he felt: but there was such a beating in his brain, and he needed to think. He drove the van as far as the local shopping parade, then pulled up in the car park and sat with his arms across the steering wheel, chin on his hands.

A childminder! It was a shock. The word had such a dismal sound to him – a horrible modern sound, suggestive of all the family-destroying attitudes that he found so discouraging nowadays. Childminders, and crèches, and single parents, and care, and maternity leave . . . these things afflicted him in his very bones with a sense of abiding wrongness.

Of course, he should have realized it was the school holidays; he should have known that the poor little lad would end up in this position. Not that he blamed Laura. He had no doubt she had done her best, and as long as she stubbornly believed that she had to work something like this was inevitable. But childminders . . . weren't they just paid strangers? No matter how efficient and dedicated they were, it simply wasn't the same. They weren't family.

Mike felt angry, chiefly with himself. The acquisition of the watchtower had made him complacent. All the time this had been going on, and he hadn't known. He should have: it was his business to know.

Well, it wasn't too late to find out. He really needed to be put in the picture, because the more he thought about this the less he liked it. It gave him a bad feeling. All right, if something happened to Simon while he was out of Laura's care that would surely convince her that this whole course she was following was a big mistake, but that was no way to learn. Better if she realized it before any harm was done. The newspapers, or at least the newspaper he took, were always full of stories of what happened to children when they were with these so-called professionals. The fact that they charged a fee for their services made it even worse in Mike's eyes: any woman who took money for looking after children was, as far as he was concerned, simply unnatural.

Mike scrabbled sightlessly around the dashboard, located a chocolate bar, and began feeding himself with it. He had to keep remembering to eat lately.

The thing he had to do next was not an action he greatly relished, not least because it involved a risk to the terms of his undertaking; but there was no help for it. He had, at any rate, the unmarked van.

Four o'clock saw him waiting in the van outside the entrance to Sprignall's car park. People coming in impatiently pipped their hooters at him and once an old jobsworth came out from his wooden hut to ask if he could help him, meaning send him off with a flea in his ear. But Mike stuck it out, and at last was rewarded by the sight of Laura crossing the car park.

He glanced at his watch, and saw with displeasure that it was four fifteen. Surely four was her clocking-off time: what did these damned slave-drivers think they were playing at? Exploiting her, of course, because she was a widow with a kiddie and needed the job. Or believed she did. With infinite concern he watched her go over to her car, dressed in that damn uniform. She looked weary. He hoped that car wouldn't play up again. Garage mechanics would take advantage. God, he thought, his fingers tightening on the steering wheel, she was at the world's mercy.

Mike lifted his head as he saw a man hurrying across the car park towards her. He was calling something, though she hadn't heard him yet, was opening the driver's door and about to get in. What . . . ?

Then she turned and saw the man, and in the same instant Mike recognized him. The chef fellow he had seen when he had gone into the restaurant. Mike watched, motionless, as the two spoke briefly; then the chef got into the passenger seat. He was laughing.

This was unexpected – wholly unexpected. Mike felt blank. There was such blankness that when her car turned out of the gate of the car park and pulled away he was staring and immobile for several seconds and very nearly lost sight of her before revving the engine and slipping after her.

Well, here was another blessing, because this was obviously something else he needed to know about. Keeping her car in sight but maintaining a careful distance, he followed her out of the town centre and on to the ring road. As he drove he searched among the debris on the dashboard for the pack of indigestion tablets he was sure was there. He had always been a little susceptible to this complaint, probably because of his habit of eating and running, and now it was at its worst. It felt as if a hard hot pebble were lodged somewhere in his lower chest. But somehow this feeling was also part of the tight, clenched bafflement with which he viewed this latest development.

His respect for her was so great as to be impregnable: it was a huge protective wall and wasn't about to be broached by any such piffling suspicion as this situation might arouse. That was why there was such perplexity in him. He was like a man who would have to reconcile some newly revealed scientific anomaly with a faithfully held religion.

He followed her into the old terraced streets on the north side of the town centre, registering his usual distaste. Awful old places. All right enough if you were poor but what possessed people to live here when they didn't need to was beyond him. Hardly any drives or garages, and the front doors were practically on the pavement. Kim had been brought up in a place like this and it had been one of the joys of his life to be able to take her out of it into a world of space and en suite and thick carpeting.

Suddenly, surprising him, the brake lights of her car came on. He managed to swing the van into the side of the road and shut off the engine unobtrusively.

He watched. And then, understanding, he almost wanted to laugh with relief, and with amazement that he could even have supposed his faith would be tested.

The chef got out of the car, waved casually, and taking out a key went up a path and into one of the poky houses. Laura pipped her horn and began to pull out.

For the moment Mike was so overcome with sheer realization that he had no time for the minor disapproval that followed on from it. As he pulled the van out and set out after her, however, he allowed the disapproval to register. So she gave the chef a lift home: all right, people did that with their work colleagues. But the man ought to understand that she had a child to pick up and that it was thoughtless of him, to say the least, to take advantage like that. Where was *his* car? With that job he could surely afford to run one. In dock, maybe: that was all he could think. Mike could not imagine any grown-up man who was not actually penniless not having a car.

A child to pick up. Mike stiffened and concentrated, dismissing the chef from his mind. That was what this was all about: the child. Mike needed to find out about the childminder who looked after Simon, and he had no doubt that Laura picked him up from there after work. She must, he thought with pain, be so desperate to see him by that time. She was missing out on so much; and children grew so fast. In a sense he had not only robbed her of her husband, he had defrauded her of her own son's childhood too, because for a good deal of it she simply wouldn't be around.

Awful, he thought, just bloody awful, this whole situation. He was simply going to have to change it. If it was the last thing he ever did, he was going to put this right somehow.

Laura seemed to be heading for the Shakespeare estate. Going straight home? Surely not – unless she wanted to change out of that wretched uniform before seeing Simon. But no, that wasn't her style.

Anyhow, now she had taken quite a different turning. Miranda

Avenue: these were the best properties in the district. He had toyed with the idea of moving here himself when he was married; but he liked things new. Not new-fangled – neo-Georgian was the only style he approved – but new-made. He was baffled when people filled their places with second-hand stuff. Kim had occasionally tried to introduce the odd second-hand piece to their home, but he could never abide it.

There was very little traffic around here, and he had to be careful about keeping his distance. When Laura drew up outside a detached house fifty yards ahead, he pulled in to the kerb at once. There was a road map on the dashboard, and he unfolded it and held it partly in front of him while he watched.

Simon came running out of the house almost before Laura was out of the car. Poor mite. It was enough to break your heart, seeing the way he hugged her.

A woman had come out of the house too, and was talking to Laura. Well, there was certainly such a thing as love at first sight, and at the first sight of this woman Mike didn't like her. He thought there was something cocky and bossy and unfeminine about the way she stood out there, in some kind of boiler-suit outfit, throwing back her head and laughing. Her hair was a mess too. Of course one couldn't judge, but to Mike she just gave off an air of modern slovenliness that he didn't care for one bit.

However, he was prepared to make allowances. He trusted Laura's judgement, for one thing: she wouldn't leave her child with just anybody and maybe this woman was about as good as you got.

Well, he would simply have to find out.

Mike waited patiently until Laura and Simon had said their goodbyes and driven away and the jumpsuited woman had gone back indoors. Then he started the engine and drove slowly past her house, making a note of the number.

That night in the watchtower Mike didn't sleep at all. For some of the time he was occupied with cleaning up the shotgun that Brian had lent him. Brian's house had been a fearful mess when he had gone there in the evening – of course Tina, his wife, worked too, an arrangement Mike thoroughly disapproved of when he paid Brian a perfectly good wage – and he hadn't hung about, though Brian had pressed him to stay for a beer. (God forbid that the childminder's house should look like that.) Once he had the shotgun well cleaned and oiled he leant it against the windowsill and took a good scan of the area through his binoculars and found, to his pleasure and relief, that the anxiety caused by last night's events was considerably relaxed. He wasn't complacent, but he was prepared.

Still, he didn't seek sleep. His mind was fixed on number 71 Miranda Avenue. At times he felt a bubble of stymied impatience rise within him, like the indigestion it aggravated. He needed to know about that place and his inability to find out seemed both frustrating and unjust, simply because it was so crucially his business: it was rather as if his bank had refused him access to his own money. By the morning he felt deeply depressed, and even the sight of Laura and Simon in the kitchen of their home, larking about as she ran a hasty comb through his hair and then put a clip in it and showed him his laughing reflection in a mirror, only slightly lifted his spirits.

And then, when he went home, help came from an unexpected quarter. On impulse he said to Lynne, who was sorting his washing in the laundry room, 'You know anything about childminders, Lynne?'

'Depends what you mean,' she said. 'You needing one, are you? Got a little secret you never told me about?'

'Friend was asking me,' he mumbled through the lump of stale cake with which he was improvising breakfast. 'Looking out for one.'

'Well, my friend Maddy, her mum used to do it. She packed it in, though, couple of years ago. Got arthritis in her hands. Quite young as well, comparatively, you know. Shame.'

'So anybody can do it?'

'Well, I don't know about that. If you're a proper childminder you're supposed to be registered. You see the adverts sometimes in newsagents and that. "Registered childminder." You know.'

'Registered with who?'

'Authorities. Social Services, I suppose. They'd have to be, when you think about it. Because they're responsible for the kids in their care, you know, legally.'

'Mm. Yes, of course.'

He went upstairs to shave. Social Services. It got worse. Social Services, Social Security – to him it was all one shadowy dubious world that he made sure he never had to enter. The thought of Laura and Simon entering it, even peripherally, made him feel sick. He studied the five items on the bathroom windowsill as he shaved. A dot of foam got on to the can of hairspray and he wiped it off fastidiously, making sure not to move the can from its position.

Hello. I'm looking for a proper registered childminder. I wondered if there were any in the area of the Shakespeare estate . . . He rehearsed it in his mind. There was a dual distaste in this: not merely at the lying, but at having to enter that dubious world himself, talk on the phone to its inhabitants. But he would have to do it somehow. If he was going to go round there, he would need the woman's name.

'Mrs Greenall?'

It was the only name he had been given, and so he found himself stupidly saying it when he called at the house in Miranda Avenue early that evening even though the door was answered by a teenage boy.

'Mum!'

'Who is it?' The voice came from the rear of the house, along with, Mike noticed, a smell of garlic.

'Don't know.' The boy raised his eyebrows, pleasantly enough, at Mike.

'It's ab – about the childminding,' he got out. He felt nervous, like a spy behind enemy lines.

The boiler-suited woman appeared, wiping her hands on a towel. 'Hello,' she said. 'Did you want me?'

Overweight for that gear, Mike thought randomly: something too old and bold about her face. He found himself making a rapid comparison with Laura, even wondering what would have happened if it had been this woman he had robbed of a husband. Different, though: entirely different. He felt that this woman wouldn't have been that bothered.

'Mrs Greenall? It's about the childminding,' he said. 'I was looking for someone. Er, proper, you know. Registered with Social S—Services.' He nearly said Security. 'You were recommended.'

'Oh, that's nice to know,' she said smiling. 'They must have me wrong. No, come in, would you? I've just got something on the boil.'

He followed her down the hallway into a big kitchen-diner, feeling stiff and breathless. His eyes darted, seizing details. Untidy, though the décor and the furniture suggested there was no actual lack of money. He noticed various ethnic-type twiddles and knick-knacks, the sort that never looked clean. The boy had preceded both of them, and was in the kitchen attending to some raw beef set out on a chopping board. Mike expected the woman to tell him to leave it, and was surprised when he said, 'So right, I've chopped it up, diced it I mean, now the flour, yeah?'

'That's it,' the woman said. 'Season it first. That's add salt and pepper to it.'

'Duh, didn't know that,' the boy mocked.

'Domesticate them early, that's my motto,' the woman said, inviting Mike to a seat at the dining table. 'I'm Mo, by the way. Egon Ronay over there's Dan.'

The boy did a cheerful mime of tipping a hat.

'My name's Clifton.' It was Brian's surname, the first thing that came to him. 'I've got a little lad, you see. His mother's . . . we're divorced. And I'm working so I need, you know, somebody . . .'

He was interrupted by the noisy entrance of a young girl, who galumphed in and wailed to the woman, holding out her right hand as if it were dreadfully wounded, 'Mum, it's broken, *look*, it's gone and broke right off . . .'

'Oh dear, tragedy and disaster,' the woman said, taking the girl's hand and examining it. The source of distress, Mike saw, was a broken fingernail, grown longer than he thought suitable for a child of her age. 'Yup, it's broke all right.'

'It took me *ages* to grow them . . .'

'I know, duck. It's a shame. You'll just have to file it straight. Worse things happen at sea, Lisette love. Sorry about that,' she said to Mike, as the girl stomped gloomily off. 'Minor catastrophe. You were saying about your little boy. How old is he?'

'Seven,' Mike said. 'Nearly eight. I'm – I'm working, you see. So I need someone . . .'

'When was it you were thinking of? Only I'm afraid I'm booked up until the end of the school holidays. I've got one little boy, just the same age as yours actually, and then another little girl starting next week. She's been abroad with her parents. That's as many as I can take, I'm afraid. I've got my own two as well, you see. Good as gold – most of the time,' she said with an ironical wink at the boy, 'but I don't go over that limit. Especially with my husband not here.'

'Your husband . . . ?'

'He's working away. Oil rig. Should be seeing him in September, if I can remember what he looks like.' Laughing broadly, she shucked a heap of papers off a chair and sat down.

For a moment Mike couldn't speak. At the very least he'd thought there'd be a husband around. But this woman was actually alone. And bringing up two children of her own – rather oddly, in his opinion. The whole setup gave him that feeling of wrongness, down in his gut where feelings were always to be trusted.

'Is that any good to you?' she said. 'I'd guess by your look it isn't.'

'No,' he said. 'It's, um – well, I needed someone straight away. Never mind.'

'I am sorry about that,' she said as he got to his feet. 'School holidays are the busiest time, as you can imagine. Have you had far to come? Can I offer you a cup of tea?'

He shook his head. 'Thank you.' He could have been anyone – absolutely anyone – and here she was inviting him to stay for tea.

'Mum,' the boy said from the kitchen, 'the washer's stopped. Shall I move it on?'

'Yes, switch it on to thirteen, could you, love?'

'Here, is my kit in there? Only I'm going to need it tomorrow.'

'Why, what happens tomorrow?'

'Oh, Mum, I *told* you. We're playing at the Woodwiston Centre. There's a team coming down from Cambridge.'

'Footballer, are you?' Mike said: he felt he was being awkward and should say something.

'Baseball,' the boy said. 'There's not many teams around. That's why it's really important,' he added with an anguished look at his mother.

'Well, I dare say it'll be ready,' she said. 'When's the match?'

'Game. Three o'clock. But I'll have to set out about two, it'll take me an hour to get there.'

'Not an hour,' his mother said. 'Three-quarters at the most. I've told you a billion times, don't exaggerate.'

The boy groaned. 'Old one.'

'It'll be ready. When did your old mum ever let you down?' She shrugged at Mike. 'It's a pity I can't oblige you. But I'll tell you what, I know one or two others who do childminding. You might have better luck there. I could give you some numbers—'

'No, it's all right,' he said, making a move for the door. 'I'm sorry to have troubled you.'

'Are you sure? I can easily—'

'I'll get on to Social Security, Services, I mean.' He had seen all he wanted to see: he needed to get out.

'Well, if you're sure . . .'

Blundering into the hall, he nearly bumped into the girl.

'Sorry,' she said unconcernedly, then held up a small peaked cap. 'Mum, Simon's left this behind.'

Mike, staring at it, felt his breath catch in his throat.

'All right, love,' the woman said. 'I'll give Laura a ring in a while, but they'll probably leave it. He'll be here tomorrow. Well,' she said to Mike, 'sorry about that. Hope you have a bit more luck.'

'Yes,' he said. 'Thank you for your time.'

He got out of there.

His mind was so full that for several moments he looked dully and uncomprehendingly up and down the tree-lined avenue for his car. It just wasn't there: all he could think, as he stood gazing about in the warm soft-scented dusk, was that it had been stolen. In his preoccupied and anxious state he even found himself connecting the theft with the people in that house, and the back of his neck began to burn as he felt himself being made a fool of and laughed at.

Then he remembered the van. Of course. It was parked across the road, practically in front of him.

Cracking up, he thought ruefully.

He drove home with careful concentration. In the kitchen he found Lynne had left him a home-made lasagne, with detailed instructions on how to heat it up. She sometimes did this, though it wasn't part of her job. A good soul.

He turned the oven up high and bunged the lasagne straight in, taking it out after what he supposed was about fifteen minutes. It tasted cold in the middle, but he didn't much care, shovelling it in anyhow. The food was only a necessary ballast for the whisky, which he needed to get to. Because he needed to think.

Think.

He put the country tape on the hi-fi. He didn't sit but roamed about the lamplit lounge with glass in hand. He had a window partly open in the warmth of the evening and from time to time came a faint waft of meaty smoke: someone in the close having a barbecue.

'From a Distance'. When the song came on he listened for half a minute and then abruptly turned it off. It seemed to mock him tonight.

Well, he had seen – certainly seen enough. He was in the picture. And it wasn't a picture he liked at all. You could try to put the best construction possible on it and still it made no difference: that childminder business was definitely not on.

Simon's left this . . . I'll give Laura a ring . . .

The second whisky briefly opened a questioning door in his mind: was he feeling himself supplanted? Was that what it was all about?

But no: he slammed the door shut. That was the sort of question that damned psychotherapist would ask him.

(And he had, by the by, certain suspicions about her. During the session last week he had spotted a framed photograph on her desk and had said, conversationally, 'Sister?' 'No,' had come the reply, 'friend.' He hadn't taken much notice at the time, but afterwards it had struck him as odd in a not very nice way. He hoped he wasn't prejudiced, but there were some things that were natural and some weren't; and it certainly made you wonder about *her* suitability to be investigating the health of your mind.)

No, no, it wasn't a question of jealousy or anything like that. After all, he wasn't about to let such personal silliness get in the way of what was a very serious responsibility. What was troubling him was something far more basic and important. Something profoundly *wrong* that it was his burden and privilege to have spotted, almost at once.

He found he had drunk three generous glasses of whisky rather quickly. His bladder was already protesting. He went upstairs to pee. On the landing he paused, arrested by a sudden speculation. Now wasn't it just about here that that man – whatever his name was – had claimed Mike had assaulted him? Got him against the wall in a straight-arm lock and then . . .

Crack.

But there wasn't room, surely, for anything like that, here between the banister and the wall. The landing simply wasn't broad enough. Supposing Mike had got him on the way out of the bedroom, and pushed him like this . . .

Crack.

He seemed to see a pair of small terrified eyes begging into his and feel hot male breath on his face . . .

But of course it was rubbish, he was simply picturing it because that was the tale he had heard, and anyhow it didn't matter because he had far more important things on his mind and he must think of them, must give them the attention they deserved.

The things on the bathroom windowsill would help him. As he went in they seemed to greet him like a gathering of friends, sympathetic and reliable, the salt of the earth.

'Not right,' he muttered as he peed. 'It's not right.' Just saying the words made him feel better, less tight and perplexed. Also more certain. Nothing was right about it: that woman, no husband, trying to look after someone else's kids for money when she could hardly look after her own . . . 'You see,' Mike murmured, washing his hands, 'all the – all the angles of it. This is what you've got to think of. Maybe she does her best, but . . . but look at it in there. She's got two kids of her own. They're always going to come first.' He glanced at himself in the mirror above the sink. As he had no personal vanity, and regarded appearance as irrelevant in males, the haggard reflection didn't mean much to him.

'Not right,' he muttered again, and gave the five items a mental farewell before turning out the light. The woman's own kids were always going to come first. Laura must see that.

Perhaps with so much on her plate at the moment, she didn't see it. In fact he knew that must be it, because she was a wonderful mother and would never knowingly put her child at risk. She just didn't see it.

She must, though. She must see it.

TWENTY-FIVE

Friday was usually the best day of the working week. Probably this was because it was the last day of the working week – at any rate, it was for Laura and the rest of the restaurant dogsbodies, who on Saturdays were replaced by teenagers who could be paid in glass beads. Shirley and Liam rarely got a Saturday off. So it was lucky, as Colette remarked with her usual tact, that they didn't have partners. Colette was seeing someone seriously now. He was hunky and had a good sense of humour. They had their own song and everything.

But usually the Friday spirit infected Shirley and Liam too and gave the day a cheerful atmosphere. That it turned out differently this Friday was due to a number of things. Shirley was niggly. PMT, she confided to Laura with an abrupt apology after getting at her for being wasteful with the margarine; but when Laura sympathized, she was curt and contrary. 'It's no big deal. I shall be glad to get rid of this. Shouldn't be too long now before I hit the sexual scrapheap.'

Then Liam had a run-in with a customer who complained that his gammon wasn't cooked. He was a youngish, bullish eighties character, coloured a sunbed orange except for a broad patch of red at the back of his neck where the gold chain hung, or rather dug in. 'It's pink inside,' he barked, 'look at it, it's facking pink inside.' No, he didn't want another one. He wanted to shout about and say 'fack' and prove that he'd eaten in better places than this. Probably he was undergoing a crisis involving the disappointing realization that his house wasn't worth what he had paid for it, that the novelty of a mobile phone wore off, that his kids would grow up to be tree-huggers, and that he had generally been conned. But Laura could see that this would be hard to bear in mind when you were being shouted at as Liam was.

'Irish ponce,' the throwback concluded, stalking out.

This was pretty tame compared with some of the stuff he had been saying. But it must have got to Liam; because later, when Laura was loading the dishwasher, he came ambling over and said in the tones of someone refreshed by reflection: 'D'you know, I've been thinking about my alleged Irish poncehood and whether, you know, the cap fits. So. Irish, OK, can't deny it. Ponce, well, I assume yer man there means not a straight-ahead kind of guy, with a certain hint at the rarefied namby-pambiness of my occupation. OK, I am a chef, with everything that entails. But I've also been thinking about the alternative, you know. Because your average working-class English male is, let's be honest, a *Sun*-reading beer-bellied thick-headed racist, obsessed with sport and cars, blessed with all the style and wit of a concrete toilet, fixated with sex despite the fact that he hates all women including the poor cow he bamboozled into sharing his bed and washing his socks for him, slavishly patriotic in spite of the fact that he knows bugger-all about the country that was unlucky enough to spawn him, and conceited as hell despite the fact that he dresses like a tosser and even in a good light looks as ugly as a pitbull straining to take a crap. So. All in all I'm pretty happy with my Irish poncehood. What do you think?'

He smiled, but he was breathing hard and fast.

'Do you feel better now?' Laura said.

'I do,' he said, walking away with his head up.

But if he did, he plainly felt worse again later, when in the course of a fifteen-minute break in the storeroom Colette managed to say an impressive number of irritatingly foolish things. Laura wouldn't have called it a record number, and she remembered, besides, the tendency of romance to turn you into a dumb cluck; but Liam clearly wasn't in the mood to make allowances, and at last he flipped with surprising thoroughness.

'Her whole family. All four of them. Cancer.' Colette was retelling a true story from a women's magazine. As well as the ones that were all careers and fellatio, she enjoyed the ones that were full of people's loved ones dying of horrific diseases. 'Isn't that terrible? She's ever so strong, though. She feels they're still with her. She can still feel their love, you know, and their memories are all around.'

'In fact it hardly matters that they're dead at all,' Liam said.

'You can scoff. She's got a lot of faith.'

'Faith in what? In the God who snuffed her family? Great.'

'Well, we all have to die some time. Anyway, there's a purpose behind everything. You've got these terrible diseases but then you've got these marvellous doctors and people like Mother Teresa and you wouldn't have one without the other, would you?' Colette smiled sweetly.

'Now I've heard everything.'

'Ah, it's easy to knock. Anyway, they'll probably find a cure for cancer soon.'

'That's hardly going to bring back the people who've died of it.'

'They might not want to come back. It's probably nicer on the other side.'

'My God,' Liam cried, 'you really do think this is the best of all possible worlds, don't you?'

'It's a good life if you don't weaken, I believe that.' Laura remembered

Eileen saying just this. Clearly it was a platitude that united the generations.

'Never watch the news?'

'Oh, I think they deliberately show more bad news than there really is.'

'And why would they do that?'

Liam's tone of deadly enquiry made Laura feel that the time had come to break it up – but short of turning the fire extinguisher on the pair of them she couldn't think how.

'To make us give more to charities,' Colette answered calmly.

'So let me get this straight.' Liam stabbed out his cigarette. 'Nothing bad ever happens, but if it does, it's a good thing anyway because it makes people do good things.'

'Oh, Liam, I don't expect you to understand,' Colette chuckled. 'You and your records and whatnot. You never take anything seriously anyway.'

Liam's look was black. Laura dearly wished Colette hadn't said that.

'It's you I can't take seriously, Colette,' he said. 'The day I do, I shall be deeply worried about myself.'

As it happened Liam seemed more troubled by this outburst than Colette. She only remarked to Laura, 'I think Liam needs a girlfriend. He's tense,' whilst Liam spent the rest of the morning behaving with the gingerly, frowning politeness of someone who feels ashamed of himself.

Leaving aside the manner of its expression, Laura found herself inclining more to Liam's pessimistic viewpoint. She was surprised to find this in herself, as there was nothing that she was feeling particularly pessimistic about at the moment – rather the reverse. It was just a matter of temperament: her mind moved on the downbeat. She found an illustration of this when clearing tables in the restaurant that morning. A grievously handicapped young woman in a wheelchair was with her family at one table: gaunt, speechless, twisted, she lay in the wheelchair as if being pinned there by some merciless force. An elderly man who obviously knew them well stopped by to chat. With the woman in the wheelchair he adopted a direct and bawdy facetiousness: 'Hello, gorgeous. How's my favourite girl, then? How's my dream girl? You going out tonight? Eh? You going out tonight, sexy? I wish it was me. I'd take you out. I'd be in there like a shot.' Probably this was meant as a special sort of kindness, but seen in another light it also looked like unthinkable cruelty. It all depended.

Unthinkable cruelty was how Liam seemed to see his behaviour to Colette.

'I ought to apologize,' he said to Laura when they went out on their lunch break which, the restaurant being a restaurant, was well after lunchtime. 'But then I have to ask myself, would I be apologizing for Colette's sake or just to make myself feel better, in which case I'm not being sincere.'

'You've lost me,' Laura said. 'Anyhow, it wasn't that bad. All you did was get ratty with her. It happens.'

'What, just because she didn't agree with me? Great. So I'm going to have a go at everybody whose opinions are different from mine.'

'Well . . .' She gave him a sidelong look. 'There was more to it than that, wasn't there?'

He shrugged, then nodded. 'I suppose . . . Are we going to the chippie?'

They walked to Mr Chips, an all-day grease spot owned by a Greek Cypriot who mined an endless vein of innuendo from the jumbo sausages he served.

'It was the stuff about cancer and death and everything,' Liam said as they waited for chips. 'I got funny about it basically because I can't handle it.'

'You not having a jumbo sausage today?' Mr Chips asked Laura, waving one about. 'It's too big for you?'

'Not today, thanks.'

'It doesn't usually bother me. I mean I feel OK about it now,' Liam said, though he was as strung-out and twitchy as Norman Bates. 'What it was, I went out with this girl when I was about twenty, she was eighteen, she got leukaemia, she died. Nah, listen, you do get over it. I mean you actually forget about it. We were boyfriend and girlfriend, that's all, I mean how much can anything strike deep when you're that age? You do, I'm afraid, actually genuinely *forget* about it. And then you get caught on a bad day with something like – well, like what Colette was saying. And you turn funny just because you realize that you had forgotten. You think, shit, that happened and I've just left it behind. And so, snap.'

'My God.'

'I suppose I shouldn't be telling you, I should be telling Colette, but . . .'

'Well, no. I'm glad.' This morning she had been, perhaps rather smugly, removed from it all: standing by while they got messily on with it. But she recognized now that she was very much at the centre of things where Liam was concerned. He had chosen to tell her; and just as important, she understood. Not in the wishy-washy, yes-all-right sense that people usually meant when they said 'I understand'. She really did understand. Again it was a matter of temperament.

It was perhaps as a result of this recognition that she said to him, there in the steamy and greasy and less than hygienic ambience of Mr Chips, 'You know you said you'd like to meet Simon some time?'

'I would,' he said, seeming to come out of some dark reverie.

'Well, how about this evening? I could cook us something. Or . . .' She was suddenly abashed at the thought of cooking a meal for Liam, who was, after all, a chef. Then again, he was going to eat these chips.

But Liam was prompt. 'Tonight, yeah, that'd be great, I'd love to.' He smiled. 'Thank you very much.'

'That's all right.'

'What time?'

'Say about half-seven?'

'Half-seven, fine.'

They laughed a little. It was odd how taking an organically grown friendship a step further involved a revival of artificial formalities.

Then they laughed more as Liam pointed out an advertising poster behind the counter. 'PIES,' it read, 'for that delicious, tasty flavour.'

'My Lord, it must have took the advertising men a long time to think that one up,' Liam said. '"Delicious, tasty flavour . . ."'

They ate their chips on the hoof, as Mr Chips' eat-in accommodation was uninviting. The sun was fierce today, and in Langstead town centre pink English skin was being exposed to it by the square yard in a way that would have horrified any sane inhabitant of Jeddah or Rio. Some male office workers had opted for an outfit combining jacket and tie with Empire-building shorts below, this ensemble giving the effect of the third act of a very traditional farce.

'You must have gone through a lot of guilt,' she said.

'Well, no. I didn't kill her. Whoever invented the leukaemia did. Ha! Try that one back home. They all hate each other but they hate atheists even more. No, I know what you mean. I'm still alive and enjoying myself while she's dead sort of thing.'

'That sort of thing.'

'Well, I don't suppose there's anything I can tell you about that,' he said, looking at her.

It was the first time they had done any more than skirt the subject of David; but it felt right, just as inviting Liam over had felt right.

'It's true you forget,' she said. 'Even within quite a short time, you find you can go a whole day without remembering, consciously. You don't really forget though, because it's in you. You're not necessarily thinking about it, but it's there in the person you are.'

'I can even remember feeling glad that it had happened when I was young,' Liam said. 'Thinking, thank God it didn't happen when we'd been together years, that would be so much harder to get over. How's that for selfishness?'

'Average human standard, I think,' she said.

'It's really nice of you to ask me over. I feel chuffed. You're sure I won't be putting you out?'

'Yes, it's a damn nuisance, I was going to do a lot of other things.'

She bumped him off the pavement with her shoulder: he budged her back and they fooled pleasantly on their way back to work.

Very sixth-form, this – chips from the paper and playful shoulder-charges in your lunch hour. Laura knew, though, that their relationship, wherever it was going, was not staying there. She had pushed it forward: whether across a line, or just towards it, she had no way of knowing, because she was operating blind.

Knowing what she wanted would have helped. From embarrassing experience Laura knew that saying *I don't know what I want* was a good way of disclaiming responsibility after you had got it. But at the moment she just wanted to have Liam round to meet Simon, eat a meal, and spend some time with her that wasn't at work. Beyond that, blank. And she was damned if she was going to exhaust herself going into it. You could take this self-analysis business too far.

She hoped, and had hopes, that Simon would be all right about it. Hanging out with Mo Greenall and her family had done wonders for his confidence, and his habitual good manners had always stood him in good stead with new people. Still, having someone enter his home was a little different. Maybe a little bribery was in order: she could get his favourite dessert (tiramisu – he had a child's instinct for fashion) when she picked up some shopping on the way home. The interior struggle this produced in her was quickly over: it was a remnant of the old combative days with David, who would tick her off for childcare malpractice. 'You shouldn't *bribe* him like that,' he would intone sternly. 'Life isn't going to be that way.' Then he would go on talking about bonuses and tax incentives.

And what *was* she going to cook this evening? She wondered, as she drove away from work at four, whether to ask Mo for some ideas. There was always an appetizing smell in her vivacious kitchen.

She drew up outside the Greenalls' house in Miranda Avenue and gave a little pip on the horn. When Simon didn't come hurtling immediately out she felt half sorry and half pleased. It was good that he no longer felt the need to run to his mother's skirts the moment she reappeared on the scene. But still . . . Ruefully she recognized the first of a series of milestones that would lead to her on the telephone, old and querulous: 'No, I'm not ringing for anything particular, dear. Just haven't heard from you lately . . .'

Laura knocked and waited. Often the frantic tattoo of Dan's music could be heard from outside, but today there was nothing.

She knocked again, feeling hot and sticky and ready not only to take off her work clothes but to throw them a long way from her. Maybe, she thought, they were all in the garden – or perhaps they'd hopped over to the playing field at the bottom . . .

'Are you Laura?'

It was a very old tiny lady, peeping out into the sunlight from the porch of the house next door with as much fragile caution as if a blizzard were howling down.

'That's me, hello.'

'They're not there. They had to go a little while ago. She tried to ring you at work but she couldn't get through.'

'Oh . . . Where did they go?'

'Mo asked me to look out for you. I said I didn't mind. I can't do a lot as a rule. But I said I didn't mind.' The old lady nodded, congratulating herself. 'She said to tell you when you came. They had to go to the hospital. It was the boy.'

Laura felt as if a cudgel had come down on the back of her neck. 'What – what boy?'

'The young one. What's his name . . . He got hurt. The hospital rang her so they had to go straight away and see him. That's why I had to look out for you.'

'What boy?' She managed not to scream it.

'Mo's boy. Dan, that's it.'

Dan . . . How awful – and how awful of her to feel even this momentary surge of relief.

'What was it, do you know? How did he get hurt?'

'I don't know. An accident, perhaps. The hospital rang, you see. So they all had to go down there. I said I'd look out for you and tell you. I didn't mind.'

'Thank you . . .' Laura was running to her car.

Dan. Not Simon. After the relief and the guilt came a renewed anxiety. The hospital . . . At once her mind sketched a scenario like the one she had gone through in January. God, no, not Dan . . . Her mind skipped on to Simon, who looked on Dan with something like hero-worship. It would tear Simon up . . . Of course, Mo would have to take Simon along to the hospital: he was in her charge, there was nothing else for it. And God, poor Mo, what she must be going through . . . ?

Ten minutes brought her to the hospital, where she impatiently spent another five minutes patrolling the car park for a space. Weirdness of life: the last time she had come here she had been the dismal star of the occasion, summoned to that little warm room with the window looking out, in. Now she was very much in the position of Jan back then, a supporting player, helpless on the periphery.

The difficulty in finding a parking space added to her sense of being caught in a nightmare; the tight rows of cars suggested some eager demand for something here, a sale or a show, crowds flocking. Even her footsteps were dreamlike, the hot tarmac sticking to the soles of her shoes and making her progress up to the accident and emergency doors horribly laborious.

Accident and emergency. She presumed this was the place – here where her two lives, before and after, had met. It looked different. There was a television, high up on the wall in the lobby, showing children's TV: two teenage girls were gossiping and squirming on a low-slung banquette. Perhaps this was all a mistake – perhaps the old lady had got the wrong end of the stick and they had actually gone on an outing or something . . .

She approached the reception desk.

'Excuse me . . .' the English excuse-me, said to people who were there to answer your questions. 'I believe there was a – an admission, a Daniel Greenall, about fourteen . . .'

'Are you a relative?'

'No. What it is, his mother's looking after my son, she's a childminder, and so she had to bring him, I think. Apparently the hospital phoned her . . .'

The receptionist looked tart and flicked through a yellow pad on her desk and for a further dreamlike moment Laura thought that that was it, that she was being ignored, dismissed . . . But then she was being given detailed directions, just as solicitously as if she were a relative, and in a moment she was riding in a lift and the lift doors were opening on to a corridor and there at the end of it she could see Simon, sitting beside Lisette on a pair of plastic chairs, just inside a doorway.

A different room entirely, she told herself as she hurried towards them. Not that awful resuscitation room where she had last seen David, swathed and turbaned . . .

Simon, turning his head, had spotted her. His expression – eager relief cutting across wretched apprehension – penetrated her heart.

'Mum!' He was on his feet, and coming up to meet her. 'Dan got beaten up.'

'Oh no, how terrible,' she said, holding Simon's hand. It was terrible – but with the idea of a car accident still fresh in her mind, it didn't seem quite so terrible. She remembered the baseball match Dan had been due to play in today. Had it turned nasty, ended in fighting . . . ? You expected that with football or rugby, maybe, but . . .

'They've just finished doing him,' Simon said, leading her in.

It was not a room but the end of a small ward. From the corner of her eye Laura saw a boy with a raised leg hugely encased in plaster, a spectrally thin teenage girl who sat bolt upright in bed and stared at the opposite wall . . . Meanwhile her attention was fixed with horror and puzzlement on the bed in front of her, where Mo was sitting and holding someone's hand. Horror, because the figure in the bed was hurt badly enough to make you moan aloud. Puzzlement, because he didn't look like Dan at all.

Lisette, still sitting with folded hands on the plastic chair, looked up at Laura.

'He didn't cry,' she said.

Mo turned and saw Laura, who put her arms round her and hugged her. The look on Mo's face was so recognizable – the look of being utterly unable to help a person whom you would have ripped out your own heart to help.

'You got the message, then,' Mo said. 'I wasn't sure about asking old Kitty, she's not exactly on the ball, but I didn't know what else to do, I tried to ring your work, and of course I couldn't leave Simon at home, you know, I had to bring him with me, it's not very nice for him I know but . . .'

'Ssh, it's all right,' Laura said. 'What on earth happened?'

The figure lying in the bed turned its head drowsily towards Laura.

'Hello, Mrs Ritchie.'

'Oh, Dan . . .' The voice, certainly, was Dan's; and having heard it she was able to discern Dan's features amongst the puffy mass of flesh on the pillow. 'Oh you poor thing, how on earth . . . ?'

'Got mugged,' he slurred through swollen lips. 'Mum – Mum always said be careful when you go to London. Never thought it'd happen here.'

'They reckon all this'll go down,' Mo said, attempting a clenched smile. 'So it won't . . . spoil his beauty for long. He's got a cracked rib and all along his side is bruised black and looks – well, pretty nasty.'

'You don't want to see it,' Dan said to Laura.

'And,' Mo said, her voice fluting but not quite cracking, 'that arm's broken, I'm afraid. He's got to go for some more X-rays soon.'

'It's funny,' Dan said, reaching over with his right to touch the slinged and webbed and horribly akimbo left arm, 'that doesn't hurt so much.'

'Broad daylight,' Mo said, biting her lip. 'Young lad walking along. This happens. Still, we've got wonderful computers nowadays.'

'My God,' Laura said, 'I can't believe it. Have you seen the police?'

'Yes, they've been and gone away,' Mo said. 'Dan, are you sure you can't think of anything else? Whoever did this, I want him, I want him myself . . .'

''Slike I said.' Dan's eyes, tiny and uncommunicative beneath plum-like swellings, turned away. 'He jumped me. I couldn't really get a look. I was just coming through the underpass to Woodwiston and he – he jumped me. He was big.' A tear welled, blinding him. His mother squeezed his hand. 'He was just big and he laid into me.'

'A man?' Laura said.

'Man with light hair,' Dan murmured.

'A young man?' Mo said.

'No, more . . . older type, in a suit – like the one who came to see you about the childminding. That's all I . . . I was just so scared.'

'God, what sort of man could do a thing like this?' Laura said.

'Point me to him,' Mo muttered. 'Just point me to him.'

'Did he take anything from you?' Laura said.

Dan's head moved in a faint negative.

'You're sure you didn't know this man?' his mother said.

Dan's head moved again, the negative fainter. His trapped eyes looked away.

'They're keeping him in tonight,' Mo said. 'Then they're going to see how it goes. Probably in a few days' time he'll be home, they said, but we'll have to see.' Mo needed, Laura saw, to scream, cry or hit somebody.

'Would have to happen in the school holidays,' Dan said.

'Sorry,' Mo said to Laura. 'Not very nice for you – coming out of work to this.'

'Don't be daft,' Laura said.

Or thought she said. Because she couldn't be sure: a vast roaring had suddenly filled her ears. It was the surge of her own blood as a feeling came over her – a notion, a suspicion, an apprehension, you could call it what you liked because it had no definition, it was just a kind of physical attack from within.

A big fair man in a suit. Like the one who came, apparently, to see Mo about childminding . . .

No, it couldn't be. This feeling or whatever it was would fade, it was like the paroxysm of panic that came over you when you were convinced you had left the gas on and pictured the house in flames and then you remembered, you accessed a visual memory of turning the gas off and then it was all right and you laughed with relief . . .

No. He wouldn't do anything like this. This was just too crazy, it didn't make any sense, and anyhow he had stayed away, he didn't know what was going on in her life . . .

'Dan,' she found herself saying, 'would you recognize him again?'

His frightful badger eyes met hers for a moment.

'No,' he said, with a chill, hollow emphasis. 'I wouldn't recognize him.'

The blood surged again and Laura felt the roots of her hair prickle. Then the feeling receded and left her holding, not a certainty, but a hard sharp question, like some fearful weapon she was going to have to use.

She was on her feet and touching Mo's shoulder.

'I'd better get Simon home,' she said. 'Will you be all right? Will you ring me if there's anything I can do, anything you need?'

Mo nodded: looked over with a little smile at Simon, who was wiggling on his chair, lamp-eyed, ashamed of his impatience to get out. 'Poor little beggar, he's been really good,' she said. 'Not very nice for him. You must be wondering whether you made the right decision. Leaving him with me.'

The words and the tone were so unlike Mo that they could only be put down to the exhaustion of distress.

But their effect on Laura was to bring that roaring to her ears again and to make her grasp, more firmly, the deadly question before setting out to find its answer.

TWENTY-SIX

Being shunted again from pillar to post was probably the last thing Simon needed. But when Laura dropped him off at Jan's after leaving the hospital she had good reason. She didn't want him going where she was going. And she didn't intend being long about it.

If this crazy suspicion were true, she didn't know how she would set about proving it to anybody but herself. Nor, if confirmation came, did she know where to go next. For now she needed to have the question answered simply for her own sake. Because if it were so, then she was responsible for Dan's lying in that hospital bed just as much as if she had attacked him herself.

She used the callbox on the corner near Jan's house.

'I need to know where he is.' She kept repeating it to the secretary who answered and who squeakily informed her that Mr Mackman wasn't in. 'I've tried his home number. I need to know where he is.'

At last the technique paid off. On site at Goldcrest Park. 'But visitors to the site aren't—' Laura cut her off, was on her way.

The suspicion might be wholly unfounded. That would still leave one hell of an ugly problem, namely why a big man in a suit should choose to set on a fourteen-year-old boy and put him in hospital. But a problem of a different kind. In this case, it was the logical explanation that was the terrifying one.

At the building site in Goldcrest Park she left her car on a mud verge that had been grass and then picked her way across heat-rutted earth towards a Portakabin that must, she presumed, be the site office. Two shirtless men loading a skip outside one of the toy-like houses whistled perfunctorily, as if jaded by dutiful lechery.

Dan . . . Broken arm, cracked rib, poor pounded face – and worst of all, somehow, that fear in his eyes and in his voice when he had spoken of his assailant. She had told herself to put such images out of her mind while she was here – their weight was too imbalancing; but she thought of them as she mounted the steps of the Portakabin. And as she did she was struck with simple disbelief, like an intrusive discord in music.

Mike? *Mike?*

'Laura!'

He was behind her, and grasping her arm, and it was all she could do not to yell.

'I'm sorry, I'm sorry, I didn't mean to startle you.'

He was gazing at her, crushed and wondering and, as ever, as if she might grant him the gift of some ineffable, eternal revelation.

He was wearing a suit.

She felt sick.

'I need to speak to you,' she said, shrugging off his hand.

'All right,' he said. He looked apologetically down at the hand, as if caught in some revolting act. And then he said, with tremendous poignancy, 'How are you?'

'Can we go in here?'

He nodded humbly. 'After you.'

Suit. Boy-blue eyes, thick tousled hair. Smell of cologne and outdoors. Voice perpetually light and husky with that peculiar schmaltzy sincerity.

Again the rasping note of disbelief. Mike? *Mike?*

It sounded loudly enough for Laura, going in, to find herself at a loss how to begin. She stared about, seeing a desk, a filing cabinet, sheets of Roneoed schematics, and Mike hovering with a chair, flicking at it with a handkerchief, his face contorted with fastidious apology . . .

'You must be wondering,' she said, clearing her throat, 'why I've come.'

His eyes, pinned by hers, were pale and still.

Then he chuckled and shook his head and moved quickly over to the window, pulling it shut with an over-hearty gesture. 'Good Lord, you don't need a reason, I should hope,' he said. 'You could come every day as far as I'm . . . Well. Sorry. You know.'

'Well, I don't really.' She didn't sit. 'I mean, I was given to understand that you'd stopped all this. I had a letter to that effect.'

Mike spread his hands, struggling for words. 'I . . . I still care. I still worry. No use pretending.'

She didn't say anything: just stared at him.

'But that's not to say I . . . I mean, I've made an undertaking and I've stuck to it. I can say that for myself, at least. I'm a man of my word.'

Still Laura said nothing: just fixed him, gripped him with her eyes.

'So . . .' His face had begun delicately, almost girlishly, to colour. 'How's young Simon?'

'He's not too good.'

About to move, Mike stood in visible suspension. 'Eh? In what way?'

'He's had a bit of an upset.'

'Poor lad. What's the matter?'

'Somebody hurt a friend of his.'

'That's terrible.' Mike looked down, frowning. 'That's a terrible thing. How do you – how do you mean?'

'His friend got attacked.'

Mike shook his head. 'My God . . . Is he all right?'

'Who, Simon? Or his friend?'

'Well, Simon, of course – and his friend, is he—'

'Who said it was a he?'

For a moment Mike's mouth hung open redly. Then he shut it with a snap. His eyes seemed to bulge a little, as if he had swallowed something down. He shrugged.

'Well, I just assumed, you know, a boy usually has other boys for friends. Look, Laura—'

'His name's Dan. Dan Greenall. His mum's the childminder who's looking after Simon while I'm at work. I had to get a childminder, you see. With it being the school holidays. Not an ideal arrangement, as you can imagine.'

'No. No, I can see that.'

'Poor Simon. Because he was in Mo's care, he had to traipse down to the hospital with her, he had to hang around in this horrible ward full of awful sights wondering when or if I'd come and take him away from it.' Now the blood was thumping in her ears again, so hard that she could scarcely hear her own words. It didn't matter: the words were just stepping stones, taking her to the truth. And it didn't matter if it was a truth he would admit to or that could ever be proved. She believed it in her blood. 'You see, when I placed him with a childminder I never thought of anything like this happening. I never dreamed—'

'Oh, Laura, it's a terrible shame, but this *is* what happens, this is the risk you run when . . . Look, this is what you've got to remember. No matter how well these people look after your kid, it's always going to be their family that comes first. It's natural, isn't it? The childminding's a money thing. With their own, it's just more important. That's what's so wrong about this whole business. Kids should be with their mothers.'

'Yes,' Laura said, watching him, his flushed cheeks and the dogmatic strokes of his big forefinger wagging in the air. 'I suppose you're right.'

'Of course I am. It's terrible you should have to see it through something like this, but really . . . you know, it's maybe a blessing in disguise. Poor little lad, having to be dragged about like that. I mean it's not right, Laura, it's really not right . . .'

'No. Of course it's not.'

The flush on his face had become a glow now, a glow of boyish vindication. 'Well, now look, I don't know what you think's best to do. I mean – is that why you've come to see me? Do you . . .' He swallowed before pronouncing the holy words. 'Do you need my help?'

'Oh no, Mike,' she said. 'I think you've done enough.'

'Look, forget about all that before. This is important, isn't it? This is really getting down to it – your little lad's welfare. That undertaking I made, we can still stick to that if you like, but we'll just sort something out so that Simon doesn't have to be left with these people who—'

'It hasn't stopped, has it?' From somewhere on the site there came the whine of a drill. As it rose in pitch it created strange aural illusions, the meow of a cat, the skirl of bagpipes, a child crying out. 'You haven't let it go at all. You're still checking up on me.'

'Well, really, Laura,' he said with a little stating-the-obvious laugh, 'it looks like I need to. This latest thing . . .'

'Yes, it's really shown me, hasn't it? It's really been an eye-opener. You could almost think someone had deliberately done it. To show me.' She took a step towards him. The give in the Portakabin floor evoked a tactile memory in her: the floors of mobile classrooms back in primary school, hollow and spongy beneath your plimsolls. 'To show me the error of my ways.'

For a moment Mike looked faintly afraid of her. But she didn't take any notice of that.

'How do you mean?' he said, addressing the question with serious innocence.

'What do you think?'

'I think you're upset and you're not thinking straight. I wish you'd sit down. There's a kettle in here. I can make you a cup of tea and—'

'How did you know? About the childminder, about Dan . . . You must have been spying.'

'Look, Laura love, I don't know what you're talking about. This childminder business, well, you've just told me about it and that's all I . . .' He gave the little laugh again. 'You can't seriously think I'd have anything to do with it.'

No: not in any normal sane world; and even now she found it hard to believe that the world Mike inhabited was so different from that. She found it hard – but she did believe it. In a way that was the straightforward part. Get over that, and you were still left with Mike's transparent eyes and big clean hands and clumsy pained decency. You were still left with the fact that you could never prove a thing and that he wouldn't admit it under torture because he had the fanatic's belief in the rightness of what he did.

Whoever had done this to Dan had left him scared enough to want to forget the whole thing. Laura was willing to bet that he would walk past an identity parade and shake his head, even supposing there was a way to take things that far. So in that sense it had worked. And even though she had no intention of taking Simon away from the Greenalls, giving up her job and letting Mike Mackman be her eternal Father Christmas, it had worked all ways. Because she just couldn't be secure any more.

The thought of Dan in that hospital bed, and the sight of this big ox pantomiming his perplexed concern, was enough to make her cat-wild. The feeling went beyond anger, into echoing spaces of rage and hate where consequences ceased to have meaning. But another feeling intervened. And that was fear.

If Mike could do a thing like this, then it was time to be deeply afraid. If her gut feeling was right, then this was an obsession without limits. And it was impregnable. The threat of the law, which she had been assuming, all this time, to have done the job, hadn't even dented it.

Rage, and fear. OK. But what really gave her the feeling, as she stood gazing into that hurt innocence, of being sucked down into a whirlpool, was bafflement.

How was she ever going to make it stop?

'Look,' Mike said, stuffing his hands into his pockets. 'I'll be honest. I've been trying to get help – like it said in that letter. It's some trick-cyclist malarkey and I can't pretend I go along with a lot of it. But it's maybe done something – helped me sort my feelings out. I know that you need a bit of . . . space. I can see that if I'm forever hanging around, that reminds you of your husband and what you've lost and so – ' he made the dogmatic gesture with his forefinger – 'that was wrong. That was wrong of me. And that's why I've tried to back off. Keep my distance. But I've done a lot of thinking too and you can't shake me on one thing. I took your husband. I did that, Laura. Nothing can change it. And if you take something in this world you have to put it back . . . Not now!'

His voice rose to a sudden bark as someone knocked on the door of the Portakabin. It made Laura jump – flinch.

And as she heard sheepish footsteps go away and felt her racing heart judder back to something like its normal rate, Laura experienced a moment of grim understanding. There had been no rebuilding, after all: no new Laura, confident, capable, in control of her own destiny, had risen from the waste and wreckage of the recent past. Because here she was again, frightened, trying to assert herself against a man who would deny her will and call it care. Here she was again being told what was good for her and wondering why it felt bad for her. Here she was again: living with fear.

And with that realization she felt herself struggling up from the whirlpool, resisting its pull, powering up to the light and air and saying to Mike with a laugh, a real belly-laugh that felt good inside: 'Mike. Oh, Mike, you don't know anything about my husband.'

She had plainly cut across his chain of thought, and he frowned slightly before saying, with a respectful dip of his head, 'No, I don't. I . . . I feel that as a great shame. I wish I could have known him. There's the terrible thing, you see, because—'

'Because instead, you accidentally killed him. But let me tell you something, Mike – may I? Before you start in on the maudlin stuff again. When you did that, *you did me a favour.* That sounds terrible, doesn't it? I know. I went through hell thinking it and trying not to think it. But unfortunately it's true.'

Frozen, open-mouthed, Mike stared at her. Somewhere that moaning chameleon creature, the drill, had fallen abruptly silent, as if it too were listening.

'You see, you didn't rob me of anything,' she went on. 'David was a bastard. A double-dyed, two-timing, fist-swinging bastard who would have had us either in casualty or queuing up at the soup kitchen if you hadn't been lucky enough to run him down. So when you try and fill the gap, Mike, you're on the wrong track altogether. Like the house – why would I want to live there any more? I was bloody miserable there – with him. Me and Simon, we're well rid.' Exultation: finding the right words, oh they were so right even if they were wrong. 'So I have got a lot to thank you for, after all. But not the things you supposed. Which is funny, isn't it?'

'You're upset. That's all. You're upset.' He spoke dully and mechanically: but the glance he threw around the stifling room was the roll-eyed febrile look of a horse about to bolt. 'Laura . . .'

'I'm not upset. I stopped being upset a long while ago. I started living again. You let me do that. So all the rest really doesn't matter.'

'Laura!' His clenched hands came out of his pockets as he lurched towards her; but she didn't flinch, not now. 'Don't you see – don't you realize what you're saying . . . ?'

'Yes. That's really what I came here to say, Mike. Do what you like. It doesn't matter. It's just pissing in the wind. There never was a tragedy, Mike. Just a farce.'

It wasn't what she had come to say: what she had said had come to her. But she couldn't regret it, any more than you could regret life or death. Regret depended on choice, and there was no choice about truth.

She left him. Picking her way across the site to her car, she expected at each step to hear him calling after her.

But this time, at last, Mike didn't follow.

TWENTY-SEVEN

Mike didn't know how long he had sat at the desk in the Portakabin, staring at the door where Laura had left. Or where someone had left, at any rate: it was hard (impossible?) to think of that person as the Laura to whom he had devoted himself. He must have been sitting there a long time, however, because when Brian came in, he looked startled and said, 'I thought you'd gone home.'

Mike stirred. 'What's up?'

'Well – we're packing in. I was just coming to lock up.'

'What . . . ?' Mike looked at his watch. Past six. 'Oh, right. Well, leave it. I'll do it.'

'All right.' Giving him a speculative look, Brian went to the door; then said, with an ingratiating smile and a nod, 'Nice-looking.'

Mike stared at him.

'Anyway.' Brian coughed. 'See you. Oh, by the way, they sent the wrong stuff again. That tiling, it's still not a match.'

Mike shrugged.

'Right.' Brian coughed again, seemed to consider adding something, then left.

Mike sat on, looking out across the allotments, and at the pearly colour of the summer sky.

'Bye,' he said.

At length he took out his keys. He sorted through the bunch and found the key to the van. It was a funny thing about the keys. Always before, the clinking weight of the great bunch, palpable token of property and security and a stake in the world, had given him that deep-down sense of rightness. And now, it didn't. Just that.

He supposed this was a feeling he would have to get used to.

This feeling of everything being blighted and soured. It was inevitable. After what he had just learnt, nothing could be the same.

Some people might say this was extreme. A titanic disillusionment such as he had suffered shouldn't, after all, invalidate *everything*. But one thing Mike knew about himself was that he was a whole-hearted man. An all-or-nothing man. He couldn't be cynical or worldly-wise to save his life. In essence, what Laura had just told him had destroyed his ideal, and destroyed him.

For a while he was even able to feel a kind of gloomy apocalyptic drama about this. Staring out at the beautiful summer evening, he seemed to see himself as some battered and beleaguered figure, perched on a crag above a dirty ravening world, full of suffering integrity. Well, this was what you got for trying to behave well in this life: this was what you got for believing, for having a dream . . . But he couldn't sustain that comforting fantasy for long. He couldn't be detached – even now, when such a grating raspberry had been blown in the face of all that he had considered sacrosanct, he couldn't cease to care.

He began weeping. He didn't know what he was weeping for – the death of innocence, perhaps; the knowledge that all his holiest and purest feelings had been, as she had said, a farce. It wasn't that he had thought Laura to be perfect – good God, he wasn't such a fool – but you could consider something precious and admirable without calling it perfect. Indeed it was her beautiful feminine typicality that had so moved him. She was simply what a woman should be. Contemplating her had given him that feeling of rightness, like seeing a baby gurgling in a pram, lighted windows in a nice house, church steeples and white weddings and Christmas trees.

Woman, wife, mother; by terrible accident, widow; and all of it now, explosively, desolatingly, a sham. She had hated her husband and was glad to be rid of him.

Mike howled, his face buried in his hands. Yes, that was what he was crying for: mockery and ruin. But other images came to him as he wept. Some were hallucinatory – Laura as a pretty butterfly escaping from his cupped hands. Others had the precision of recent memory – not a butterfly in his hands but an arm, a young arm stiff with terror and suddenly *crack* not stiff any more, not braced in that way but terribly yielding and a boy's cries in his ears echoing round the shady-cool underpass . . .

No, that couldn't be right, wasn't he mixing that up with a time before, another time when his illusions had been blasted away, the time he had come home to find Kim with another man in the home he had created for her, in their fairy-tale wedding-cake bed, and he had got the man on the landing and looked into his small eyes, small and foxy, not wide and heartbreaking like the eyes of the boy . . .

Mike slammed his hands on to the desk, knuckle downwards so that pain jarred through them, lurched to his feet. No, that wasn't right either, because . . . because it couldn't be, he was a nice guy and he had always, always *done his best* and it wasn't fair . . . it simply wasn't fair . . .

He couldn't think about it any more. Sitting here, thinking the unthinkable, was going to send him mad. He stumbled down the steps of the Portakabin and hurried to the van. (Not his car: he'd put away the car: done for her, again done for her sake, everything everywhere he looked bore that impress.) He took his handkerchief out (what was that blood?), wiped his eyes, then keyed the ignition and bucketed away from the site.

All destroyed. Here was evidence of it – because he had never before voluntarily gone to a pub to drink alone. But there was nothing to stop him: only his beliefs, which lay all about him like so much broken glass, glinting and dangerous.

TWENTY-EIGHT

It was only after Laura had picked Simon up from Jan's, arrived home, kicked off her shoes, murmured a prayer of thanks that Simon accepted the TV as a temporary substitute for the attention she owed him, and poured herself a glass of wine suspiciously approaching a tumbler in size, that she remembered Liam was coming this evening.

She groaned and thought about putting him off, but neither of these was actually a true reflection of her feelings, as she quickly realized. For a start it would be giving in again to the disruption of her life. She didn't doubt that Liam would understand if she cancelled, but she didn't want to be that sort of person – forever having problems, perpetually having allowances made for her. And besides, she did feel the need of some thoroughly adult, sceptical, unsentimental, drink-quaffing company such as Liam's. She still had the sickly innocence of those boy-blue eyes in her head and she needed to rinse it out.

In the kitchen she investigated the fridge and cupboards, looking for something she could throw together, telling herself unconvincingly that such meals often turned out better than menus that had been elaborately planned. Simon noiselessly appeared and slipped his arm round her waist.

'Hello, lovey. How are you doing? That was a bit horrible today, wasn't it?'

'Can we go and see Dan again?'

'Of course. We'll go tomorrow. Take him a present. But they think he'll be able to go home soon anyway.'

'Steven Evans' dad got mugged. In London. They pulled his watch off him and it was like burn marks on his hand.'

'Ooh, ouch. Well, it does happen, I'm afraid. Not very often. You should always be careful, but that doesn't mean you should go around being frightened.' She stroked his hair. 'I'm sorry you had to go to the hospital today, love. It wasn't very nice for you.'

He seemed to address this seriously, then shook his head. 'Wasn't very nice for Dan. Mum, he said when he has plaster on his arm I can write on it. Can I?'

'I should think so. Don't press down too hard,' she said, wanting to laugh and cry her heart out at the same time. 'Listen, love, you know Liam, the chef where I work? He's very nice. His birthday's the same day as yours, I forgot to tell you. Anyway he's coming round tonight.'

'For tea?'

'Well, yes. I've got to think of something to cook.'

'We could have squigglies,' Simon said, peering in the cupboard. 'Squigglies' was Simon's generic name, and a very good one, for the numerous coy shapes of dried pasta you could get now (sea-horses, Mickey Mouse's ears, DNA helix), and as the evening was sultry and she didn't have much time a pasta salad seemed as good an idea as any.

'Squigglies it is,' she said.

She put the pasta on to boil and then on the off-chance rang Mo's. She found Mo in: Dan had insisted they go back home and eat, as well as feed the fish. They'd go back to the hospital later. 'The X-rays are good. Radial fracture. It'll probably be completely mended in time for him to go back to school, poor bugger. And they've given him something to take down the swellings. And we left him talking to this girl who seems to have taken a shine to him in spite of the Quasimodo look.' Mo gave a windy, stressed chuckle. 'Which just leaves the question of who'd do that to a young lad and what I'll do to him if I catch him.'

After the phone call Laura hit the wine again. No answer, of course, but what was? She had a suspicion that was within spitting distance of a dead certainty about who was responsible: she had been speaking to the man a little while ago.

And what she had said to him, out of sheer spontaneous wits'-end fury, had been a more effective blow to him than any physical blows that she or Mo or a whole rugby team armed with blackjacks could have rained on him: of that she was pretty sure. Somehow, finally, she had fixed Mike Mackman's clock. But she had only found the wherewithal to do it after an innocent person had suffered terribly, which didn't say much for her. All she could cite in her defence was sanity, her own and the world's. You acted according to that: even faced with compelling evidence that someone close to you was a complete flake, you went on behaving as if they were playing by the same rules as you were.

That had been her mistake, then: failing to recognize just how murky and tainted were the waters through which Mike Mackman moved, how little there had been of rationality in his actions. Now she had stymied him by getting down on his level. But she couldn't be sure that was enough.

Enough, maybe, to put the lid on his fixation. He had had her pegged as a saintly widow scarcely more consolable than Queen Victoria: she was more like Judy freed from Punch and had told him so, incidentally completing her own process of self-revelation. He couldn't survive that intact. But as she mixed the salad and resisted the temptation to chug more wine, Laura wondered whether she ought not to pick up the phone and report him to the police anyhow.

Maybe, indeed probably, they wouldn't be able to pin it on him. Also she would have to give reasons for her suspicions, the whole thing would get back to Mo, and Mo might understandably wish to punch her out for putting her family at risk. On the other hand, it would be nice to know that some sort of official justice was being meted out to Mike, even if it was only a questioning by the constabulary.

And against that there was, of course, that tiny grain of possibility that she was wrong. Everything about him during that exchange in the Portakabin suggested she was right. But perhaps, while that grain of possibility remained, it was best to stick with her own brand of rough justice. After all, she had – God help her – more influence over him than the law.

She just hoped she could find a way of looking poor Dan in the face.

'Mum! Someone at the door!'

Her hands were greasy. 'Could you answer it, Simon?'

She heard his footsteps go down the hall. And for a moment she entertained the horrible thought of hearing Mike Mackman's voice on the opening of the door, that awful dripping macho sincerity: *It's me, I just had to see you. Oh God, Laura, this has really cut me up . . .*

'Hello there.' Liam's voice. 'Er, I'm Liam. You're Simon, right?'

The horrible thought vanished – twinge of an enduring injury finally on the mend.

TWENTY-NINE

The pub was called The Volunteer. The woman was called Gillian.

Mike had bought her a drink, initially, because he had found himself standing at the bar next to her for the second time when he was getting his own second, because of the nod they gave each other in recognition of this fact, and because he believed women shouldn't buy their own drinks.

And because it didn't matter. Same with the pub. He had driven into town, parked the van, and gone into the first pub that didn't look packed. He wasn't sure how you'd characterize this place. Not a young pub anyhow: there was a jukebox but it was playing quietly, the décor was plush and restful, and they were serving bar meals. It would do.

As for the woman, Gillian, he supposed he could characterize her pretty well. She was alone, and she was in a pub, and she was past thirty, and she was dressed up. He had too much gallantry to label her a tart: she was just not the sort of person he would have paid much attention to. His values were different.

Before, at any rate. But things had changed. From today, everything had changed. And so it didn't matter.

He didn't sit with her or talk to her, after buying that drink. He wasn't even consciously looking at her. He was thinking, with his gaze vaguely in her direction. He was thinking about the way he had been conned, though there was more sorrow than anger in his thoughts. The vision had been beautiful, after all, even if false, and it was hard to relinquish.

After a while his eyes began to take in certain points about the woman's appearance. She was rather nicely dressed, he thought, with that silvery wide-shouldered top that was glamorous without being trampy, and nice feminine hands. Also he noticed the way she politely but firmly dismissed a boozy man who made a clumsy attempt to chat to her. That was good, he thought: ladylike. After his experience today, finding muck and filth where he had thought there was gold, it was like a small gift to see something like that.

He had no consciousness of decision, of getting to his feet and going over to her: he just found himself doing it.

'Excuse me, I wondered, are you waiting for anybody?'

'Well, I was,' she said with likeable frankness, after a moment's hesitation, and gave a humorous look at her watch. 'But it looks like I'll be waiting for ever.'

That brought out Mike's chivalrous instinct. It wasn't on, keeping a lady waiting, even in this sort of situation.

Which wasn't his sort of situation: he was a marriage and family type. But of course, now it didn't matter. And she did seem rather nice.

'Would you allow me to get you another drink anyway? While you're waiting?'

He sat with her, aware of her perfume – delicate, not one of those cheap reeks. He had beer, she white wine.

'I feel a bit of a fool really. I'm supposed to be meeting someone on a . . . well, it's one of those dating things. Through an agency. He hasn't turned up, which makes me feel a bit . . . Unless you're him, by any chance?'

'Oh, no, not me.' After a moment he added a laugh, remembering how Kim used to tell him to lighten up. 'No, afraid not.'

'Well, that's a shame. I didn't think you could be, because he said he'd be carrying a newspaper. All very cloak-and-dagger. He must have got cold feet.'

'Could have let you know, though,' he said seriously. He wasn't being conventional: he thought this was bad. 'Letting you sit here on your own like this. I think you're well rid, if you don't mind me saying so.'

'Oh well, I'm not on my own now,' she said, tasting her drink and looking at him over the top of the glass. 'I can't really blame him. It's very nerve-racking, this business. Don't know why I started it really.'

'Why did you?' Mike said. Perhaps a little brusque, but he wanted to know.

'Oh, you know. Tired of being on my own. Thought I'd give it a whirl.'

'However did you come to be on your own?' He meant this question quite seriously too, though the look she gave him in reply was arch.

'What about you?' she said, tasting her drink again. Delicate – not swigging: he liked that. 'Aren't you on your own?'

'Divorced.'

'Well, there you are. That makes two of us.'

'Life's bloody well not what you think it's going to be, is it?' he said with sudden fierceness.

'No,' she said with a pretty, resigned look. Her fairness, he thought, was probably bleached, but it was tastefully done. She was so slenderly made, too: like a bird. 'Still, perhaps we've got it all to come, eh? That's the only way to look at it.'

'I suppose.' Taking a pull at his beer – almost drinking the whole pint down, in fact – he became lost in dark mazy thoughts, and when he came to himself he was ashamed and apologetic. 'Had a hell of a day. I'm sorry. Can't shake it off.'

'Oh, don't worry, I know how that feels.' A very easy, understanding person, he thought; the absent date was a fool. 'Was it work?'

'Work, no. Nothing as simple as that. I had a hell of a let-down today and it's left me . . . well, it doesn't matter.'

'Dear.' How soothing she was. 'Would it help, you know, to tell somebody about it?'

Tell . . . ? He couldn't tell it: it would rip and tear him coming out, like a hook being drawn from a fish's mouth.

'Probably just bore the pants off you,' he said. For a moment he felt he had been guilty of innuendo, and felt his whole face flush.

But she simply smiled and said, 'I'm a good listener.' She crossed her legs, and he noticed in spite of himself the curved shape of her calves.

'No, no. You tell me about yourself.'

This was his habitual courtesy, but also something else: his mind, even while it was with her, still kept straying into the shadowy maze of his disappointment, and it was easier if she was talking. She told, and he gave her a reasonable attention. There was a job in an office, and a marriage, and a divorce, and a flat near town. There were spots in her talk that caused in him a flex of disapproval – some anti stuff about her boss, a joke about her hangovers . . . but then, of course, it didn't matter now.

They had several more drinks, swiftly. Mike felt them, and Gillian seemed to be feeling them too: she leant confidingly across the table and her gestures became urgent and expansive. For his part, Mike felt the drink making him up, patching him together. He had come here in such bitterness of soul that oblivion had seemed the best he could expect. But this was better: this was surprising. He found that his mind was inclusive, that he could roam those dark thickets of disillusion at the same time as he paid a close, even intimate attention to Gillian and what she was saying.

'. . . I wonder how Nettie is. I hope she's a bit better.' She had several times mentioned Nettie, her cat, who was poorly with conjunctivitis and had to have regular eye-drops. 'I think the drops are working. I must remember to give her another one when I get home. Three times a day it is.'

'Beg pardon?' He hadn't caught that last bit – a crowd of sporty young men had come in and were making a devil of a noise at the bar.

'I said three times a day.' She giggled. 'That should be enough for anybody.'

Mike gave an obliging chuckle, though he didn't greatly care for that sort of talk; then glanced in irritation at the youths yawping round the bar.

'You've got a sort of sad look sometimes,' she said. 'Give us your hand. I can read palms a bit. I can tell you if you've had a disappointment.'

'Can you?' he said. He surrendered his hand. Her fingers on his palm were tremendously soft and ticklish. He felt breathless, and he seemed to flicker internally from the dark to the light and back again.

'Oh yes, see – there's something here that came to a stop. See?' He couldn't see anything. 'But that – that's a line of opportunity. Definitely.' She seemed to grow abruptly bored with this, and turned his hand over, playing with the fingers.

'I . . .' He found it enormously difficult to speak, and not just because of the noise. 'I dare say you're worried about – your cat.'

'Yes. I keep thinking about her. But it's a shame, you know, I don't really want the evening to end.' Her head swayed as she smiled up at him.

'It's got very loud in here, hasn't it?' he said.

She nodded, smiling.

'Well, I could give you a lift home, if you'd like.' His sober driving resolution fleetingly crossed his mind, but he was beyond caring.

'OK. You can see Nettie. See how she is. And I've got some wine, I think.'

She was a little unsteady as she stood up. Mike could feel the drink in his head, but his body was deft. He helped her on with her jacket, and was inexpressibly touched by her look of surprise.

'You really are a gentleman, aren't you?' she said.

He felt that he couldn't with truth return the compliment and say she was a lady . . . but of course, it didn't matter now.

THIRTY

'No, Mum, that's a disadvantage card,' Simon said. 'You can only trade that in when you're on a black square.'

'I am on a black square, aren't I?'

'No, that's your base,' Simon explained, with the kind patience of an extremely dedicated teacher in a remedial class. 'Your go,' he added, more hopefully, to Liam, for whom thank goodness. Simon had a love of the kind of fiddly impenetrable board games that had a whole bound book of instructions and that men, for some reason, seemed able to get their heads round. At least with Liam here Simon was getting some sort of a game: she always lost with shameful speed.

The meal had gone very well, at any rate: Liam hadn't looked in sad cheffy disdain at her pasta salad and Simon hadn't been tongue-tied at the presence of a stranger. Now they were sitting with the patio doors open to the warm evening and Laura had put off making coffee for the second time: Liam had brought more wine and it was going down very nicely. Liam too didn't seem noticeably averse to drinking it.

'Now wait a minute. I can't be in the tower again, so I can't, I've already been in there,' Liam said in dismay.

'You didn't use your advantage card! Now you have to wait till the door opens again.' Simon seemed tickled, and not just at being ahead. He seemed to find something irresistibly droll and winning in Liam's speech.

Which there was, Laura thought. The wine and the company had brought her to a tolerable state of contentment. She wasn't at peace with the world – a mental image of Dan's bruised eyes and then of Mike Mackman's blustering disingenuousness put paid to that – but she was, at least, at peace with this part of it.

Perhaps this incompleteness showed; because when a little later she came down from seeing Simon to bed, Liam remarked as he put the board game intricately back into its partitioned box, 'Was that an off-licence I saw down the road here? Only I thought, they might still be open, if you feel like getting quietly blasted.'

'Well, I do. But I don't know if I already am.' She flapped away a mouse-sized moth that had come in through the patio doors, briefly considered getting a duster and catching it, then decided to live with the terror instead. 'You must be a mind-reader.'

'Well, you didn't actually say "What a day" when I came in, but you sort of looked it.'

She sat down in the wicker armchair opposite him, picked up her glass. 'I'll say it now,' she said. 'What a day.'

He regarded her amiably, neutrally, and didn't press. 'I apologized to Colette, by the way. Just after you left. Got my courage up. I don't know if she was really listening because her feller was waiting for her in the car park . . . What time does that shop shut?'

'Josie's? Oh, about midnight. Sometimes not even then.'

'I'll go in a minute.' He settled his endless legs more comfortably. 'This is nice here. This is really very nice. Simon's a nice kid.'

'Yes, he is.'

'This booze is very nice too.'

They laughed. In the distance a last fanatical lawnmower puttered into silence.

'So, you ever get any more grief from the builder feller?'

'You really are a mind-reader,' she said, nearly spilling her wine.

'Shit. Wish I wasn't. Is he back?'

She told. Not urgently or desperately: just letting it float out in the summer air. There was no feeling of confessional, because somehow she had known she would tell Liam at some time anyhow: it was part of the new ground they found themselves on.

'Well,' he said at length. He leant across from where he sat, long-reached as a limber mantis, and refilled her glass. 'Oh boy. He needs nailing.'

'Can't prove anything.'

'No. Well, maybe. You could always tell the cops what you think and leave it to them. They've got their ways. He might crack.'

'Maybe.'

'If you're right, the guy is dangerous. And he wants locking up.'

'I know. But that's just it. I hate it being my responsibility. This is where I get really whingey but honestly, Liam, I don't want that responsibility. Doesn't that sound awful?'

'No,' he said promptly. 'It sounds totally reasonable.'

'I just don't want to be his – his keeper.' The word didn't quite convey what she meant, but it would have to do.

'You think he'll lay off now? After what you told him?'

She nodded. 'I don't see how he can't.'

'About your husband. Were you laying it on thick – the stuff you told him?'

'No . . . I just told the truth.'

'Jesus.' Liam thought. 'So you had that. And now you have this.'

'Whoa,' she said, sitting up. 'That makes me sound like a victim. I don't want to be like that. Moaning my woes.'

'Ah, you wouldn't be like that.'
'I am now. Sorry, Liam. It was nice just to get it off my chest.'
'No worries.' He smiled. 'So you want to forget it for a while?'
'Yes please,' she said from her heart.
'OK, what say I go and get another bottle?'

THIRTY-ONE

This wasn't meant to happen, Mike thought while Gillian kissed him. It didn't matter, of course: there were no standards to maintain, no ideal to live up to any more. But still, it wasn't meant to happen.

Oh, but of course it was, a voice told him, as the woman did exciting and damnable things with her hands. *Of course it was, man. What else did you think all this was about? Where do you suppose the whole thing was leading, if not to this?*

The flat was, he thought, rather a ratty place, crowded with knick-knacks that would make it impossible to clean, and full of throwovers and hangings that made him think of things shabby and not-quite-right, covered up and disguised. It was noisy too, with ancient clanking radiators and a constant rumble from the traffic on the main road outside.

But she had slickly made the best of this, reducing the lighting to a single low-wattage table lamp and putting some music on the mini hi-fi. He liked the music – it was some sort of violin thing, very classy – and he liked her, in a way. She was very feminine. Even her fuss over her cat, which only had a runny eye and was now crouching in its basket watching them sourly, struck him as rather charming.

It was just that this wasn't . . . It must seem as if he had come out looking for something like this, and he hadn't at all . . .

She had produced some sort of sweet fizzy wine from the fridge, but they had hardly drunk any before she came to him with a sort of drowsy sidle. And now there was this, which was never meant to happen even though he found he wanted it very much.

(Indeed if he wanted it, then what was wrong? Perhaps it was having it demonstrated to him that he wanted it. It was as if she had divined some secret about him that even he hadn't known. And he didn't like that.)

But the kissing, and those abominably thrilling things she was doing with her hands, were taking him right out of that dark maze of thought – and that was good, wasn't it?

Also he found himself feeling flattered, empowered, when he began kissing and touching her on his own account. She moaned and sighed and smiled in a way that startled and then gratified him. This was, plainly, him doing the right thing.

And so when she stood up and took his hand he did not so much follow her as go with her into the bedroom.

He saw from the corner of his eye that it was even messier than the living room. But there was time only for a glimpse. She started pulling him down on to the bed and pulling off his shirt at the same time, in a groping, all-over-the-shop way. Her eyes looked bleary, even drugged. She pawed at his groin and then with an impatient noise began dragging off her knickers. He was shocked and greatly aroused. His mind seemed to hurtle through dark and light spaces, heading towards some awesome new horizon. He uncovered himself and she smiled and again it was as if she knew him better than himself.

Kneeling on the bed, the room rocking around him, Mike reached down with his right hand and touched her. Her hips arched up to meet him. She made a whining grumbling noise in her throat and then hooked her arms round his neck and fairly clawed him to her. She kept pecking and nibbling restlessly at his face. Feeling the damp contact down below, he grunted, in momentary fear that he was going to finish before it started. He smelt her perfume and her body as her dopey eyes sought his.

'Oh, darling . . .' she murmured to him. 'Oh, my angel . . .'

And all at once Mike felt his mind rushing backwards, careering wildly through dark and light and showing him many things, a million flashing images just the way it was supposed to happen when you drowned and revealing, at the last, a brilliant burst of truth. And he pushed himself out of her grasp, thrust himself upwards with a great gasp of breath exactly like a man saved from drowning – he saw it all now! – and struggled backwards on the bed, covering himself up.

Squirming after him, she murmured, 'Angel, what's wrong? What's . . . ?'

And he simply couldn't help it: his disgust, his outrage and indignation at what she had done and what she was still trying to do, was so overwhelming. Dear God, the evil cow – taking him away from the woman who needed him! Just like some cunning witch in a story, snaring him, leading him away from the right path . . . Oh, it all fitted. His terrible misjudgement of poor Laura lacerated him and made him cry as he pounded down with his fists. Just think of Laura, caught in an unhappy marriage, but recognizing that marriage was for *life* and *binding* and sticking with it, a true good woman . . . Not like this filthy tart who had no respect for such things, just took what she fancied . . . had homebreaker written all over her . . . Dear God, he had been a fool not to see it – poor Laura, pouring it out to him today and he had judged her so harshly instead of falling down and worshipping the damn ground she walked on as she deserved . . .

Gillian's screams were muffled by now, liquid and bubbling. Mike, panting over her, experienced a moment's regret; and then something turned the regret into a last flourish of fury. It was the sight of his red-flecked wristwatch. The time. It was late – getting on for midnight; and all this time he had been away, away from the one place on earth he should be, and *anything* might have happened to her . . .

The last overarmed blow made the mattress bounce like a trampoline, and there were no more screams.

Mike finished his dressing quickly. He felt quite sober now, which was good as he had to drive. His old resolve, like his sanity, was restored. And he had to keep himself safe, because he was needed.

He was seen only by the cat, crouching, weeping, as he set out for his watchtower.

The extra bottle of wine that Liam fetched from Josie's store tasted, as the extra bottle always tends to, no more alcoholic than shandy. Likewise, it seemed after they had drunk it to have been as strong as meths. Laura looked foggily up at Liam – they had been going through her record collection, with much glutinous recollection and dogmatic insistence that kids today were unaware they were born – and said, 'Is that you swaying about, or is it me?'

'It's the room,' he said. 'No, the house. I think you've got insecure foundations.'

'That's the nicest thing anyone's ever said to me.' She laughed, and then the laughing seemed not such a good idea. It had adverse effects on the balance. 'Coffee,' she said, getting complicatedly to her feet.

'Strong and black,' he said, following suit. 'The only thing.'

The kitchen looked as bright as a sound stage. Wincing, she made coffee whilst Liam washed the glasses with ponderous delicacy.

'I was thinking,' he said, steadying himself against the sink. 'It's the funfair on Lang Heath next week. Maybe it would be nice to go. You and Simon. With me.'

'Oh, that'd be lovely.'

'You think Simon'd like it? With me there, I mean?'

'I think so.'

'*I'd* like it. It's . . . I don't know, it's better. I mean I'm thirty-seven. Fifteen years ago all the places you want to go are the places they don't have kids. Then you change. You like the places they do have kids. I've this friend, Andy, he's my age and he's got this ponytail and he goes to clubs and stands there leaning against the bar with a Grolsch bottle trying to look like Jack Nicholson and, oh God he's a nice bloke but you know . . . ? King Canute holding back the tide. Thanks.' He accepted the mug of coffee. 'Anyway, I've had a really great time and I'd like to again.'

'Well then, we will.' She smiled. 'Maybe not with so much wine.'

'Oh God, fools. Masochists.'

'Let's go back,' she said, ushering him to the dining room. 'The air'll help.'

They sat again by the patio doors, holding their faces to the night breeze.

'There,' she said. 'That makes you feel better . . . In a feel-even-worse sort of way.'

He laughed, and then said studying her, '*Do* you feel better? You know. I piped down about it and I can again if you like. I just wondered . . .'

'No, it's all right.' She sipped the strong coffee. Her mind felt quite clear, now she came to examine it, and she didn't think it was that bogus clarity of booze which leads you to believe you've solved the mystery of the pyramids with one stroke of intuition. 'I have been thinking about it . . . unconsciously, if you know what I mean. It's been there at the back of my mind. Probably that's the only way you can think about something like this. And I know I can't just hide from it. If that man did – if he was responsible for what happened today, then it's . . . it's monstrous. I saw that at the time but not the way I should have, not in my bones, maybe because I'd . . . sort of got used to him. But now – if a man can do that to a boy just to prove a point, just to get at me and make me give in . . . I don't *know* that he did but if I've even got a suspicion that he did then . . . then I've got to go the police, haven't I?'

Liam made a sort of bow. 'Only question is when.'

'Tomorrow.' She finished her coffee. 'I'll do it tomorrow.'

'Would you like me to come with you?'

'You don't have to do that.'

He shrugged. 'I'm at your disposal, if you can wait till I finish work. And speaking of which, I don't know whether you ought to sleep on your own tonight. I know you're not on your own, but – you know.'

'Well, I . . .' She felt how a stammerer must feel. 'I was wondering whether you wanted to stagger home or stay here overnight, because it would be easier . . . only . . . don't take this wrong, because if I say not yet that might sound like not ever and that isn't what I—'

'Christ,' he said laughing, 'on this much wine it'd be a miracle. No, really, Laura – I'm saying just what you're saying. That wasn't meant to be a cheesy line – about not being on your own tonight. I just mean on your own in the house. I love being with you, whatever. And anyway, what's the secret of a good sauce?'

'Time.'

'Exactly.'

'And stirring it so it doesn't stick to the bottom.' Looking at him laughing, she felt an absurd mixture of pleasure, disappointment and anticipation, with a bit of trepidation thrown in. She had done the right thing: it was true that she wasn't ready; but another truth loomed in the offing, and she felt it to be very close upon her when she looked at him like this. Oo-er, she thought, laughing too.

'Well, the spare room's next to the bathroom,' she said.

'That'll be handy. No, actually, I feel a hell of a lot better now, do you?'

'I do. When do you have to be in tomorrow?'

'Not till ten, thank the Lord.' Liam picked up his filled ashtray and looked at it with mingled shame and scorn. 'Look at that, will you?' he said. 'There's my life ebbing away. Is your bin out here?'

'It's all right, leave them.'

'I will not. Being a smoker gives you a healthy dose of pyrophobia. I know they're killing me slowly, but I don't want them to do it overnight.' He went out with the ashtray to the side passage, briefly swallowed up by darkness: she was curiously relieved when he reappeared. 'Nice night,' he said. 'Starry.'

'Do you know the names of the stars?'

'Me, no, haven't the foggiest.'

'Good,' she said getting up. 'I don't know, I always think there's something creepy and anal about men who know the names of the stars.'

'How about men who know the names of all the Buzzcocks' B-sides?'

'No. Strange, maybe. Not creepy.' She suffered a moment of anxiety which she realized was referrable to David: saying something like that and then finding he had gone silent and dark and having him turn on her much later, hissing, *Strange? What was that supposed to mean . . . ?*

'Strange,' Liam chuckled. 'Strange I can handle. You know, at school I used to sit next to a boy called Tony Strange. He was really brainy, really good at science. Wouldn't it be great if he's grown up to be Dr Strange?'

She locked the doors and turned out the lights, and they tiptoed upstairs. The spare bed, she was afraid, was a bit musty, but the way Liam threw back the quilt and blinked eagerly at the inviting softness suggested that he wasn't likely to notice. She whispered that she would wake him at eight and then mouthed an awkward good night and went to her bedroom, pausing to peep in on Simon. He was asleep in typical posture – neck at an impossible angle, seat sticking up; but he would leap up in the morning without a twinge.

The sight made her think again of Dan; and she briefly touched and flinched at the cactus-like thought of any harm coming to Simon. Police, tomorrow; it was settled.

Climbing into bed, she expected sleep to roll over her like a tank. But the strangeness of having Liam in the house kept her awake and blinking. She lay on her back listening to the creak of the spare bed as he settled down. Eventually she turned on her side, knowing she tended to snore if she slept on her back – not that sleep seemed anywhere at hand. The next thing she knew she was opening her eyes to the full light of morning.

It could have been noon for all she knew, and it was a relief when she groggily deciphered the numerals on the clock-radio: seven thirty. Dressing-gowned, she went downstairs and found Simon already in the living room and glued to Saturday morning TV, his weekly marathon of pleasure: the cartoons started up at dawn and went on forever.

'All right, love? Liam stayed in the spare last night, did you know?'

Simon nodded, rapt. 'I heard him snoring when I got up.'

'I'd better wake him in a minute, he's got to go to work. Would you like some breakfast?'

'Is there any Coco Pops?'

'I think there's a few left. There's loads of that other cereal.'

Simon made an expressive face. He had chosen that cereal, but it transpired that he had chosen it chiefly, if not exclusively, for the plastic gift that came with it. Fell for it again, she thought, making his breakfast.

She took Liam up a cup of tea. His spiky head moved in pained acknowledgement in the depths of the pillows. Laura's pubescent embarrassment at the sight of his bare shoulders quite took her by surprise. Yielding to a selfish impulse, she took quick possession of the shower. She knew this was unhostessy of her: it was just that in the unwashed morning she looked and felt like one of those preserved Neolithic bodies they pulled out of peat bogs.

As she hurriedly washed, though, she took stock and found feelings that were good and unexpected. There was hardly any hangover to speak of; and the simple fact of getting up in the morning with Liam around filled her with a ludicrous joy. It was something to do with not being alone, which suggested that she had been lonely, which in turn was surprising – she hadn't been aware of it. Whatever it was about, the sound of him moving around next door – the sense of him in her life – made her buoyant in a way that, if she had known it before, she had certainly forgotten.

Looking only moderately seedy, Liam was emerging as she came out of the bathroom.

'Morning,' she said with the smugness of someone who is ready first. 'How you feeling?'

'Agh. What did you do last night, cosh me? Actually, truthfully, not too bad. I do not want to go to work, mind you, but I suppose that's not unusual.'

'Well, bathroom's free – there's a clean towel there. Do you fancy some breakfast?'

He winced. 'Nicotine and caffeine only.' He smiled. 'Damn it, you look good.'

'Oh . . .' she said, or a burble to that effect, and went downstairs, just succeeding in not falling down them.

By the time the coffee was made Liam was downstairs, dressed and relatively bright-eyed if not bushy-tailed: one of those men, Laura noted enviously, who could look all right with just a cat-lick.

'Never shave at weekends,' Liam said, passing a dismissive hand over his chin. 'You can get away with it in my job anyway. Makes you look a leetle bit Franch. Like one of those sentimental frog chefs who've got a life-long obsession with their mother's cooking. Sorry, shouldn't say frogs, should you? It's just that they *are* their own stereotype.' He stood at the open patio doors and breathed in the summer air appreciatively. 'You just know they were brought up in this bee-yootiferl farmhouse in Provence or somewhere with this irritating *Maman* doling out classic cuisine all day. I mean, my mommy couldn't cook anything much beyond fish fingers, but she's still nice, you know? Ah, God bless you . . .'

He came over to the table as she poured him coffee.

'You not an eater in the mornings?' he said.

'Not as a rule. The only time I was keen on breakfast was when I was pregnant with Simon. Always get things the wrong way round.'

Pulling out one of the dining chairs, he accidentally clipped her ankle, which was in the way.

'Oops, sorry – just take your leg off . . .'

'No, that was me.'

Laughing awkwardly, they met each other's eyes and then to her intense surprise Laura found herself leaning forward across the table and kissing Liam on the lips. He put his arms round her. They stayed like that for a minute, inclining to a clinch at a strange angle, like ice skaters. It was quite chaste and measured and yet not so, not at all. When they drew apart she cleared her throat loudly, as an alternative to moaning low, and that made them laugh again.

'Told you I get things the wrong way round,' she said. 'You're supposed to be amorous the night before and then not be able to look at each other in the morning.'

'I'm finding it quite easy to look at you,' he said. 'Come here.'

They inclined together in another skaters' kiss. The bristles on his face were surprisingly soft and ticklish. When he muttered, 'Damn, I wish I didn't have to go to work,' it was as if her own mind had taken on a voice.

'Suppose you've got to.'

'Uh-huh.'

They made sad faces at each other over this tragedy, then laughed.

'You'd better drink your coffee.'

'All right.' He sat down, smiling at her, and then he bounced backwards, his arms flying up in the air and a smoky bloody hole blossoming suddenly in his midriff.

Laura was screaming, not hearing her own screams because the noise of the shot had left her ears whining in momentary deafness. Liam lay on the floor, his chin pointing upward, gagging and trembling.

She turned round and saw Mike Mackman standing at the open patio doors. He had a shotgun in his hands, but there was an expression of appalled misery on his face as if he had just witnessed this event and was shocked by it.

Her hearing adjusted and through her screams she heard what Mike was saying. In a high desolated voice he was demanding of her, 'Why, Laura? Why?'

Then he lifted the gun again and, shaking his head, pointed it at Liam, who was making a feeble crawling motion with his elbows.

Open-mouthed, her throat flaming, Laura made a stumbling lurch at Mike, not really able to move like a human being, just impelling her body towards him. She collided with him and the gun dipped as it fired. Her right leg seemed to disappear and be instantly replaced by a furious orgy of pain and her face hit the bloody carpet just before Mike, sobbing tenderly, could catch her.

THIRTY-TWO

Sobbing tenderly, Mike lifted Laura's half-conscious form into a wicker chair.

For a moment he was convinced he had killed her, and was ready to turn the gun on himself. But now he saw it was only her leg. Her poor leg. The wound pulsed through the mangled rent in the knee of her jeans.

Still much to cry for, though. A death – the death of innocence, truth, faith. Throughout his long sleepless night in the watchtower, from the time she and the man had turned out the lights and disappeared to their so dreadful reappearance together in the morning, Mike had prayed. He had really prayed for innocence to prevail.

No. And so things had taken their course.

God, had it *all* been for nothing? Even after that last meeting, when she had so dented his belief, he had managed to recover his faith in her . . . And then to go and spend a night with a man . . .

The gun had expressed his anguish, though it could not speak it eloquently or strongly enough.

Mike lifted heavy eyes at the sight of Simon standing rigid in the dining-room doorway, wailing. Poor little lad: no fun for him. He went over and got hold of Simon's arm, began explaining that this had to be done, but the wail went up like a buzz saw and was too much for him, so he clouted Simon over with his open hand and made him quiet.

But in that ensuing quiet – punctuated by slamming doors and agitated voices somewhere around – Mike found something.

Call it a last resort or last resource. At any rate it was a last thing: a truth beyond truths, a moment of ultimate vision that produced an assertion of ultimate faith.

Mike believed in Laura. And, wiping the tears from his face, he believed in himself.

He darted upstairs, grabbed a quilt, brought it down and gently wrapped it around her.

It was going to be all right. Because, in spite of everything, it wasn't really her fault. She just needed protecting.

That was the essence of it. She needed protecting from men like that scum on the floor there.

Most of all – bless her heart – she needed protecting from *herself.*

Swaddling her like a babe, he picked her up and put her over his shoulder and carried her to the front door. He had left his van in the drive, after hurtling round here from the watchtower. He could pop her in, Simon too, and they would be off.

Who better, after all, to protect her? What she needed was to spend some time away from the world, and with someone who really did have her best interests at heart. She simply couldn't trust anyone else, as last night proved. She just ended up being taken advantage of. Poor Laura.

He opened the front door and carried Laura out. One-handed, he flung open the back doors of the van. He saw faces goggling at him. He recognized the Irishwoman, the neighbour.

'It's all right,' he shouted. 'I got him. I'm going to get them to safety. It'll be all right.'

He laid Laura gently down on the floor of the van. She was stirring, her eyelids fluttering. He hurried back and scooped up Simon under his arm, ignoring the man – twitching, dealt with. He picked up the shotgun too, which was just as well because when he got back outside the Irishwoman had approached the van and was looking in at Laura, crooning something.

'Get out of it,' Mike said, waving the shotgun cursorily at her. She scuttled backwards, nearly falling. He didn't want trouble, just no more interference. There had been too much interference between him and Laura. 'We're in a hurry. No time to waste.' He put Simon in beside her: the little lad gave a brief roused struggle, his eyes blobbed and searching, before Mike slammed the van doors and locked them. People were standing outside houses all along the road. He heard a man shouting at him: it sounded, from the tone, like a precursor to trying something. Mike felt a flicker of respect for that. But he wasn't hanging around. He had to get his charges away. He jumped into the driver's seat and was powering the van away at speed even before the door had closed.

He felt very nervous and worked up, and he had to restrain himself from honking at the traffic. Saturday morning, of course, shopping day – only to be expected. He would feel better when he got out of Langstead. The quickest way to the Norfolk coast was by the A road to Norwich, but he thought it wise not to use that today. Anyhow, he knew plenty of rat-runs.

Once they got there, things would be better. He could take care of them properly. He was sure he had some tins in the cupboard at the chalet, and a first-aid kit too. And the little shop down at the foot of the woods would be open. Anyhow, it was a beautiful day, even here in the dingy town. Imagine it there, by the sea! It would do her a power of good. It was a shame this hadn't happened before, really.

But he had no regrets. She and her little boy were depending on him now, and he wouldn't fail them.

THIRTY-THREE

Laura thought she was in bed. The quilt, gathered round her throat, was quite familiar. She was lying down. She was in bed and Simon was waking her.

'Mum, Mum . . .'

His face was terror, pity, passionate anguish.

She lurched up to a sitting position, remembering all, knowing all.

'Simon . . . are you all right, what did he do . . . ?'

'He knocked – me – down.' He was racked with shivers, could hardly talk for them. She tried to hug him. But she felt so weak. Then she realized that the weakness was pain. A great part of her self was taken over, occupied by pain, leaving a feeble remnant that couldn't do much. She found she couldn't even sit up, and sank back.

'Mum, Mum . . . !'

'Ssh . . . it's all right . . . come here . . .' She got her arms round him, had him lie panicky and spasmodic beside her. 'Do you hurt anywhere? You bleeding at all, anything feel broken?'

Simon shook his head violently, pointed downwards. 'Mum, look, look at you . . .'

Down where her right leg was, or had been – there was only fire and rage there now – the quilt was soaked through: sodden, sordid with blood.

'I know,' she said, and her mind seemed about to float away like a balloon, quickly to be gathered back by the fragile string. 'It's all right . . . it'll stop . . . it's not that bad, you know, it will stop . . .' She tried to look around, turning her head slowly. They were in the back of a moving van. It smelt of turps and paint. There were a few oily rags about, a plastic drum on its side rolling backwards and forwards, a length of hosepipe hanging on the side panel, nothing else. She could just see the head and shoulders of a man in the driving-seat, and the very tip of the handle of a shotgun on the passenger seat. She knew the man was Mike Mackman, and she knew what he had done, and she wanted to kill him. But she had been shot in the leg and was half-dead from it and her little boy was hurt and frantic with terror and there was nothing she could do. She could throw a rag at him, maybe. Or she could rail at him.

'Mike! You bastard! I'll kill you, I'll kill you . . .' That was as much as she could manage. Her voice tailed off, ran out. She could hear how pathetic she had sounded. She sobbed.

'Mum . . .'

'It's all right, love. It's OK.' Simon, Simon only, could fetch her back from those chill reaches, the place of pain and despair where she was seduced by surrender. She got a hand up to her face and scrubbed at her eyes, scrubbing too at a memory of Liam bouncing backwards, an astonished puppet sown with a firework.

'Where are we going?'

'I don't know, love. It'll be all right. The police'll come and find us.'

Simon clutched at her, fierce and terrified, considering this. She fought against what felt like physical waves, rising up her body to the level of her eyes and threatening to engulf her. She didn't know where they were going; and she didn't know if it was a place where the police would find them.

And wherever it was, she had a strong, sane, reasonable belief that they were going to find her dead, because that blood wasn't stopping at all. It felt like what it was, thirty-three years of life simply flowing out of her.

It was not Eileen, who was hysterical, but Laura's other neighbours the Stimsons who were the first to enter the house after the van had screeched away and who crouched arthritically to comfort the shot man gasping on the floor of the dining room until the police and the ambulance arrived.

'All right, mate. All right now. You'll be all right,' one of the ambulancemen kept saying as he lifted Liam's shoulders to the stretcher. He had seen people survive worse wounds, and he usually had a feeling for death that he didn't get here, but the surgeons were going to have to go some.

The police couldn't get much out of Eileen either. 'I know the man,' she kept braying. 'I've met him. He's a lovely man. He's a lovely man.' Fortunately most of the street had come out at the sound of the shots, and eventually the police had a full description and the licence number of the van.

Not soon, though: the police had come prepared for a siege, then had to readjust, and everyone kept talking at once. The APB went out thirty-five minutes after the van had left Langstead.

THIRTY-FOUR

Mike didn't stop the van until he reached the chalet, eighty miles away up on the Norfolk coast where wooded cliffs encircled a bay of equal remoteness and beauty.

He was tempted many times, not for his own sake – he could have driven twice that distance without a twinge – but for the sake of his charges. It was hot in the back of the van and obviously not very comfortable, and he would have liked to have given them a drink and some reassurance – told them, for example, that they were going to be taken care of properly at last, that they were going to the coast to rest and recuperate and that everything would be all right there.

But he couldn't risk stopping the van, even though the route he took was through the back roads of Suffolk and Norfolk amongst innocent-looking market towns and villages. It just wasn't worth it: he couldn't let anything else interfere with his task of, at long last, giving them the care and protection they needed and deserved.

So all he could do was call out an encouraging word now and then and concentrate on getting there quickly and safely.

The chalet: just get to the chalet. That was the sole beacon to his mind, which felt, now, wonderfully concentrated and purposeful, stripped of the superfluous. The chalet had always had an almost magical significance for him. He had first purchased it as a gift for Kim; but though she had quite liked going there at first, after a while she pronounced it dull. Still it never lost its appeal for him, even after the divorce when he used it infrequently because he didn't like being alone. He never ceased to value it: it was just waiting for the right time. It had to be laid at someone's feet.

And now was the time. He felt almost unbearably moved when at last he took the turning past the little fishing town and the van began to climb the steep road through the green woods to the chalet park, with the calm sea glittering through the trees on his left.

'Nearly there,' he called out. 'We're nearly there now, folks.' He glanced back over his shoulder, and frowned. Poor Laura looked dreadful. Her face was paper-white, the lips were dry and flaky-looking, the eyes shadowy and half-closed; and the little lad was curled up against her side whimpering like a lost pup.

But never mind: she would be better when she got to the chalet.

Rest and sea air, that would set her up. She had been through a hell of a lot. No more stress, that was the prescription. And you couldn't choose a better place. This chalet park was very select: each chalet was set in its own individual clearing and you weren't overlooked at all – not like some places further down the coast where they crammed them in like damned caravans.

'You'll like it here,' he called cheerfully, as he negotiated the narrow twisting road, glimpsing through the trees signs of occupancy in most of the chalets, parked cars, sun loungers: of course, it was the height of the season. 'I guarantee that. I can guarantee you'll like it here. I should think you love the seaside, don't you, Simon? Yeah. Always used to go to Clacton when I was a lad. The whole family. Buckets and spades. Us kids used to be so excited. And sometimes Dad used to let us bury his feet in the sand.' He chuckled. 'We'd have windmills, and rock. And fish and chips every night. Real chips in those days, fat as your finger. Yep. Real family holidays . . . Here we are.' With a lump in his throat, he pulled the van up on the hardstanding outside his chalet.

He had, though he said it himself, got the best one. Right at the crest of the cliff, and completely ringed by fir trees – except for the gap that opened up in front of the living-room picture window, where you could look right down to the bay. It was just perfect.

Mike got down from the van and stretched luxuriously, sniffing the salty, piny air, feeling the sun on the skin of his face like a blessing.

They would be all right here, the three of them. Really, there was no reason why they shouldn't stay here for ever.

He went round the back of the van to open the doors.

The doors opened and the light streamed in on Laura, but she didn't stir, unsure whether this was one of the dreams in and out of which she had been drifting as she lay on the floor of the van and fought in a confused three-way battle – her will, her pain, her weakness. It had gone on, it seemed, for ever, and she had no expectation of it ending.

But the van had really stopped, and the doors were really open, and Mike Mackman was really reaching in.

'Ssh,' she said, as Simon, who had been for some time in a kind of clenched trance, began squirming and crying out. 'It's all right . . . Simon, love . . .' Her lips moved only with difficulty, as if talking were a complex manoeuvre. All the time she had been trying to murmur words of reassurance to him, but they had grown more croaky and clotted as her mouth and throat dried to a point where they seemed not flesh but some hard dead material, wood, stone.

She tried to sit up. Simon, wriggling at her side, glared up at the man in the van doorway and then she saw his eyes flick to the side, to the dazzling spaces around him, the possibilities. She couldn't urge: but she prayed.

But to run, even if he were capable of it, was to leave her. And Mike had seen the flicker of his eyes too, and shaking his head he made a grab.

'Come on, young 'un. You first.'

He carried Simon away, under his arm, leaving Laura lying on the floor of the van and looking with dazzled eyes into a perspective of sun-dappled woods with sea beyond. He left her there – but of course, she wasn't going anywhere. Pretty, she thought. Pretty place to die. The balloon of her mind sailed upward, and she scrabbled at the string.

'Now then.' Mike was back. He smiled down at her. 'I'm sorry it was so long. But I think you'll find it's worth it now you're here.'

'Mike . . .' Her mouth was a cracked desert floor, the surface of the moon. 'Mike, I . . .'

'I know,' he said. A frown wrinkled his forehead, briefly. 'It'll be all right, though, Laura. You'll be all right now. I'm here to look after you.'

'Doc-tor,' she said, effortfully as a baby getting out a brand-new word.

'No,' he said, gathering her up into his arms. 'What's that thing? My mum used to say it. "Three doctors who do more than any can, Dr Diet, Dr Quiet and Dr Merriman." You'll be all right, Laura. You're quite safe now.'

He carried her round the side of the van. She saw a single-storeyed building like a bungalow, faced with timber and topped with a flat felt roof. By the door there was a wooden plaque painted with the word 'Kimmike'. Her balloon mind, off on another flight, wondered what it could mean.

A room with a broad net-curtained window looking down through those woods. Simon standing in the middle of the room, weeping silently, his knuckles crammed into his mouth. A warm musty closed-up smell. A corner-unit seat, red and leathery and gold-buttoned. He was laying her down on it.

Laura located a spring of energy within herself, or thought she did. She pushed herself up from the clammy leather, tried to swing her feet to the floor, swearing. This was meant to be the preliminary to some firm, decisive resistance – perhaps hopping over to Mike, knocking him out, hopping in search of a phone, getting help, generally bringing this nightmare to a sensible and just conclusion.

But with the agony of her weight on the injured leg, all she did was crash moaning to the floor, and the alien thing that had been her right leg clumped down after her with such new starbursts, such infinitely regenerating galaxies of pain that she could only shrink to a tortured knot of consciousness, a tiny ball of self held in the palm of agony.

Time had no meaning. After some unguessable portion of it, she had enough of herself back to open her eyes, and find she had been placed again on the leather seat, her legs up. Simon was fastened to her arm, kneeling head lowered and trancelike again, as if trying to work a spell on her. Mike was standing looking down at them, his big hands on his hips. He had shed his jacket and there were stains under the arms of his white shirt.

'Now perhaps that'll teach you to take things easy,' he said, with mock sternness. 'Honestly. The only way to get you to rest is to *make* you. I know because I'm the same. Really, though, Laura, that's what you're here for.'

Looking up at him, she found her lips moving convulsively, though even she didn't know what she meant to say. She sought curses, perhaps, the true curses that would have come to the lips of her primeval ancestors, dwellers in woods.

'I'm sorry?' He bent to listen, then slapped his leg. 'God, I know. You must be parched. I'm so sorry. I'll get you a drink of water.'

He disappeared into the next room. Hugging Simon with what strength she had, Laura set her dimming eyes roaming about, looking for something, anything. Door to the outside . . . small dining table and two tubular chairs . . . framed prints of sailing ships . . . the big window . . . woods beyond, and sea, empty, remote, unpeopled . . .

'Mum!' Simon's voice was tiny, scalded with crying. 'Mum, you're white, you're all white . . . !'

'All wight!' Mike said cheerfully, coming back. He carried two plastic beakers of water. One he put in Simon's hand. 'Can you manage that, matey?' The other he held tenderly to Laura's lips.

She drank. Her huge unwieldy tongue stirred and wriggled, trying to reaccustom itself to the strange substance.

'There . . . gently now. Don't choke. How's that?' He sat back on his haunches, studying her with concern. 'You do look peaky. It'll take a while, I know. But you'll soon be set up. I always feel better after spending some time here. You know how you get. A bit stale.'

Physically, perhaps, she could speak now, but her mind wouldn't let her. Instead she put out a hand and clawed back the quilt in which she was still wrapped, so that her right leg showed. It was an abomination. She showed, told, spoke with her eyes.

And Mike looked down at the leg, and saw. But he didn't see, really. He looked up at her and smiled, and Laura knew despair.

'I'll tell you what,' he said. 'You need something a bit nicer than water. Now obviously I haven't got anything in – only a few tins. But there's a little shop just down at the bottom of the park. Nice old couple who run it – they work ever so hard, seventy if they're a day, remarkable, isn't it? What I'll do, I'll just pop down there and get a few things. Now, while I'm gone I want you to really take it easy. And I mean easy. Do you promise?'

Mechanically, Laura nodded her head.

'All right then.' Mike went to the window, picked up a small key from the sill. He turned it in the lock on the window-catch and pocketed it. 'I'll only be a few minutes.'

As soon as he was gone, locking the door behind him, Simon began to wail, great sirens of terrified release. Laura could only hold him by the shoulders and huskily beg him. She hadn't got the strength to shake him, even though this tiny time of hope was diminishing so rapidly.

And then all at once he stopped and, shivering, sat up and faced her.

'Simon. Try and find a way out. Yes? Try and find a way out quick – and if you do – run. Yes – yes – run straight away, as fast as you can, keep going, till you find somebody . . .'

He was good. He darted into the next room – must be kitchen – and she heard a door rattle.

'It's locked, Mum . . .' His footsteps sounded agitatedly again. 'Can't open the window . . .'

'Come back in here, Simon . . .'

He was back. His desperate obedience would have broken her heart, if she had been in a position to feel its breaking.

'Love . . . you've got to try and smash that window. Throw something at it . . .' The wave of nothingness rose up to the level of her chin again as she lifted her head to point. 'Chair . . .'

Hope was strong enough to supply an instant image of the chair crashing cinematically through the window, breeze whipping in, a neat escape-sized hole forming. But Simon wasn't strong enough, and the tube-framed chair was light, and the window was double-glazed. It gave a great boom and rattle, and withstood.

Simon bent down and with a grunt, and the wide-eyed hapless perseverance of a child, threw the chair at the window again. It hit him as it bounced harmlessly back again, and he yelped.

And he lost it. He was conscious of it, and his face was creased with shame; but he could only sit down on the floor, like a much younger child, a tot losing its balance, and cry that he couldn't do it.

'Oh, come here . . . come here . . .'

She was losing it too: losing life. She was bleeding to death, and she wanted her son with her.

She was cuddling him when, a couple of minutes later, Mike came bursting in fresh and whistling. She noticed the tune: 'On the Sunny Side of the Street'. She noticed too the legend 'Happy Shopper' written on the plastic carrier bag he was holding. She supposed this was how it would be. Random, useless noticings, while the tide crept up to extinguish her.

'Right then,' Mike said briskly. He saw the chair on the floor, frowned, but picked it up and set it right without comment; then came over and, standing over them, delved into the carrier bag with a teasing, guess-what look.

'Mike . . .'

'In a minute, love, in a minute. Now – here's some goodies to keep you going.' Into Laura's lap he poured half a dozen assorted chocolate bars. 'Didn't know which ones you liked best so I got a selection. But don't go and pig out all at once, because I'm going to make us a spot of lunch and it'll spoil your appetite. And this . . .' he took out a can of cola, popped it, and put it into her hand, 'to whet your whistle. Now, I hope we all like beefburgers. They don't have a lot of choice at that shop, really. I mean you can't expect them to. Frozen stuff mainly.' He waggled the box of frozen burgers, winked. 'I should think you like burgers, don't you, Simon?'

Simon's head was buried in Laura's chest: he wasn't going to look at the man any more.

'Shy,' Mike said. 'He'll perk up when he smells these, I bet. Now I'll just go and turn the gas on and pop them under the grill. Won't be a minute.' He gave Laura a kind, understanding look. 'You'll feel better when you eat. You'll see. You just need a bit of pampering.'

He went into the kitchen. Laura listened to the noises, pop of the gas, rustle of Cellophane, rattle of the grill. Random noticings. All she was fit for. She was sitting in blood. She was very weak. She was made of air. She could only hope Simon would be all right. The police would no doubt come, eventually, but she would be dead by then, and so the only place for hope was Simon and what would become of him.

'Oh!' Mike exclaimed in the kitchen, with more rustlings. He came running through. He held something out to her. She tried to focus on it.

'Help pass the time,' he said. 'Nothing too taxing, you know, because you're here to rest up, don't forget.'

It was a puzzle book. There was a model in a swimsuit on the cover, holding an outsized pencil.

'These are good, just for fun, you know,' he was saying. He looked like an enormous child, standing by, anxiously awaiting approval. 'They have these find-the-word squares. See – they can be upright or down or, you know, diagonal . . .'

'Mike . . .' She was managing, somehow, to shake her head: the tide must be temporarily low.

'What? Oh! Of course, you need a pencil. Must be one somewhere—'

The tide must be low: she succeeded in reaching out and holding his arm just as he was about to set jauntily off on a pencil search.

'Mike . . . You've got to give it up.' Her voice came out slow and ethereal and spooky. Clear, though. 'You must see. Give – up. You shot Liam.' The memory in all its detail was mercifully beyond her: her body, stern defender, couldn't take it. 'Get help. Give it up.'

He looked down at her, perplexed, watching her lips, as if she were speaking a foreign language of which he had only a shaky grasp.

'Tell – the police.'

'Oh, Laura.' He tucked his fists on his hips, businesslike. The smell of cooking beef wafted in the air. 'Look, you don't have to worry any more. This is what I'm trying to tell you. I'm here to look after you. That's – that's my *job*. I keep trying to get it through to you. But what do you do? Carry on worrying. Now I want you to stop it.'

Gone, she thought. The boy-blue eyes that dwelt on her weren't inhuman. They were very human. But he was gone: he had shifted on to a new mental ground, had happily set up camp in a place of his own with its own topsy-turvy rules.

'Mike . . . I'm losing so much blood . . . I'm dying . . .'

Like a large lively dog he gave a heavy snorting breath through his nose that she felt on her face.

'Now that's just the sort of talk I won't have. You've been through a rough time. Things look black sometimes, I know that; and you can end up doing daft things. But that's why I've brought you here. To make you better.'

'I'm dying, Mike . . .'

'Look.' He struggled to maintain his patience. 'You're not feeling good. You need a lot of care. I'm not disputing that for a minute, Laura. But who can take care of you better than me? Eh? No one, that's who. I see it now. I didn't, for a bit, when you told me about your husband. But then I got my head round it and – well, all the more reason. There's all the more for me to make up for. I can give you all the care and protection that he never did.' He shook his head. 'You're just so vulnerable. That's the pity of it. When I saw you'd spent the night with that – that man, I just . . . Well, never mind. That's finished with now. We've just got to concentrate on getting you better. That's all I'm concerned with. It's all I ever want to be concerned with. I thought I could do it from a distance, but I see now I had the wrong idea entirely. This is better. This is the right way to . . .'

He stopped, sniffed. The cooking smell had turned acrid. Laura saw smoke curling above her head and then heard an abrupt, airy *pop* from the kitchen.

'Jesus, the burgers . . .'

He ran into the kitchen, and she heard him yell in surprise. There were panicked clattering noises. Then he was running back through the living room, holding out at arm's length a grill pan, charred and flaming and spitting fat.

'Bloody hell – bloody hell . . .' He kept muttering in distracted dismay while he fished the doorkey from his pocket and, ducking down, inserted it in the lock of the front door.

Startled into himself, Simon had his head up and was staring.

Holding down the tide, Laura whispered in his ear. 'Run, Simon – when he opens the door run and run and run . . .'

Mike flung open the door and thrust the grill pan forward. The rush of breeze blew the flames back at him and he flinched and cursed and dropped the grill pan on the doormat. He dropped to his knees, flapped at himself, tried to pick up the pan and burnt his fingers, at last succeeded in getting it outside, shuffling on his knees.

'. . . run run *run* . . .'

Laura screamed it, summoned strength to launch Simon forward.

Simon, her son, a small god she adored with her ebbing lifeblood, ran straight and true and fast out of the open door and into the woods.

'Hoy!'

Mike, prompt but clumsy, gave a rambling cry and staggered to his feet. Laura saw him go pounding after her son. And now no random noticings. No weakness. If weakness, then deny. She floundered down on the floor and, taking her weight on her arms and good leg, dragging her injury like a ball and chain, she crawled across the carpet. Mind painfully stitching a pattern together. Simon would run and run and Mike would run after him and probably, yes probably at last catch him, and in the meantime . . .

Her crawling limp punctuated with surges of pain, she followed the hot throaty smell and roar. In the kitchen, the grill of the gas cooker was full on. Beneath it greasy drops sizzled, doing their best. Help them. With one hand she grabbed at a hanging tea towel, missed it, won it. She raked it through the gas flame, whirled it around – where? There was a pile of old magazines – yes. She flung it on. There was a black smoulder. The edges of the pages caught, reluctantly. Not much. Oh, something else. Oh, Simon, run. She pulled out one of the magazines, blew and blew on it to make it burn like a torch as she humped and lurched caterpillar-like or snail-like, her slimy trail blood-coloured, to a cupboard beside the sink. Oily rags, maybe, cleaning materials, oily burny. She flung the cupboard open. No oily rags.

Just barbecue equipment. Just stuff like that.

Just a can of paraffin oil.

'Ah-hah ah-hah ah-hah . . .' She heard herself gasping out these frenzied gloating syllables. But now her test. Oh, Simon, Simon. Torch in one hand, can of paraffin in other hand. And thus burdened, get to the door.

Desperation overriding agony, she swung the mad leg round, got on her behind, began inching and rowing herself backwards with her sound limb, out of the kitchen. A memory that must at *once* be jettisoned – Liam on the floor of her dining room, blasted, trying to pull himself thus – go, go . . . Oh Liam, oh Simon . . . Right hand upending and trickling the paraffin across the carpet as she wriggled, left hand gripping the torch aloft, skewwhiff, away, and please God no burning flakes drifting across her body because then she would lie here and burn, oh Simon . . .

Laura reached the open front door. And here was Mike with Simon tucked under his arm, frowning down at her – *no*, that was a vision of despair, and she had done with despair for now because the doorway was empty and she was going to do it.

She tipped the last of the paraffin on the doormat, scrambled and flopped on to the concrete outside, and then tossed the torch in.

It lit blue and sudden and with a deep booming note like a drum. She saw a livid snake of flame ripple purposefully across the living room towards the kitchen and then she was labouring like a wounded seal across the hardstanding, oh towards the blessed trees, let him not come now oh Simon Simon . . .

Yards, feet, inches: aeons of time passing. He was going to come, too soon. She could smell the piny resin, beautiful. He was going to come, though, too soon. Off the concrete now and on to spiky grass. Ferns and heather. Up above her head. She squirmed in, in. She lay still and turned her head, and at that moment, perhaps five feet from her, Mike came running, pounding past.

He had Simon gripped under his arm, but he was running at full tilt. He was yelling.

'Laura . . . !'

Seen.

No, not seen. It was the chalet he had seen, smoking, blazing, its windows red eyes. He was running straight at it. Legs pumping. For dear life.

'Lau-raaa!'

He let Simon go, dropping him like a bundle, and her son rolled in the grass a little way away from Laura.

Twined ferns crushed and odorous in her clenched fingers, Laura lay panting in the wood like a snared animal and watched as Mike threw his arms up over his head and ran straight into the burning chalet. He was shouting her name as he did so. She could hear him shouting it still, for a time, once he was inside. But soon the roaring and the crashing and the wild rumpus of fire was all that could be heard.

She kept watching the door.

Mike Mackman didn't come out.

Trying to save her, he had saved her.

Simon, looking around, saw her through the ferns. He crept over to her. He was silent and breathing fast. They held each other, rocking, looking at the fire, for some time.

Then a hand touched Laura's shoulder and she screamed.

* * *

'And you are the gentleman who found Mrs Ritchie and the little boy?' the police sergeant said, leaning against the bonnet of his cruiser, which was parked outside the burnt-out chalet.

'That's right,' the old man said, impatiently brushing smuts off his spectacles. 'Mine's the next chalet along – over there. I saw smoke through the trees and so I just came over to see what was up. And I found them curled up there. Terrible state the poor woman was in. Will she be all right?'

'She'll recover. She lost a lot of blood, I understand. But she's in hospital and she'll be fine.'

'Well, I really mean mentally. She was . . . well . . .' The old man shook his head. 'I'm quite shaken.'

'All right, sir. Sit down here a minute. It was a hell of an ordeal for her. We've just been in touch with the constabulary at Langstead, which is where she's from. The shooting incident took place there. Her boyfriend was shot too, by the same chap who died in the fire. But we've got word that the boyfriend's had an operation and he's pulling through. So like I say, she should be all right. No need for you to worry.'

The old man shook his head again. 'Well, if you say so. But you didn't see her when I found her. I just put my hand on her shoulder and, you know, offered to help her. And she absolutely screamed. Wouldn't let me help. "Don't help me," she kept crying out. "Don't help me, whatever you do don't help me . . ."'